Lucy E,
Road To Victory

Cassie Horner

A novel
By Cassie Horner

MAD DOG INK.LLC

WOODSTOCK, VT

To my husband, Tim Sink;

my mother, Doodie Horner;

and my cousin, Diane Hutchinson

Lucy E.

Road To Victory

November 1895

MAYBE IT WAS THE RAIN THAT REMINDED HER, THE RAIN THAT MIGHT HAVE CHANGED EVERYTHING IF IT HAD COME THAT LONG-AGO DAY. Maybe the rain would have stopped him, cooled the heat in his head, the fire that ate at his heart. She could play the "what if" game forever. What if the rain had come? What if David had not been injured in the war? What if Samuel had not been so foolhardy? What if she did not have that quality that had misled them? What if there had been no war? What if her first husband, Hiram, had not been struck down by cancer in 1865? What if she, Lucy E., had not had two children still needing her? What if David had not been so embittered by the loss of a wife, and then two of his sons? You see how the game is played. It changes nothing, of course, leading the mind so engaged to taunt the heart with promises.

So Lucy sat – a tiny woman, not even five feet tall, thin almost to the point of death with her own cancer – in the north room of what was now her daughter's house. It was a cold room and never filled with much light, but the two windows faced the mountains. Always she could look out, her straight-backed chair in just the right place, and see not just the rolling range of mountains across the horizon, but the top peak – Mount Washington. She thought that if she could but stay within reach, even with her eyes, of the mountains, she could get through anything.

It was night, and the rain had woken her from a fitful sleep, so broken with bad and odd dreams that she could not decide if it was better to be awake with her pain or asleep with it nudging at her unconscious.

When you see her, the inclination is to fall back on the cliché "bird-like" to describe her fine features, hawk-like nose, and determined eyes, but go beyond that and you will see the roughly painted figure on the prow of a large ship, the face determinedly set toward the interminable waves. Lucy E. is tough – hard times and age long ago turned whatever plain beauty she had to gristle.

To say where things go wrong, she avoids. But the rain spattering on the bare, hard ground outside her windows leads her fancy to that one night she blames for everything: how she, so full of hope and renewal, saw it all go, worse than before.

The fact was her husband, yes, her husband, David Beede, burned down Samuel Hannux's house.

g

PART ONE

Horse Trader

Chapter One

MARCH 1871

T HE FIRE CHANGED MY LIFE. Up until then it had been ordinary. I knew as soon as I heard about the early-morning blaze that destroyed Samuel Hannux's house that my husband David, my David, had done it. He had a look of barely contained intensity. He had a smell on him that later I thought was from the fire – the stench of smoke – but perhaps that was my imagination, because he had not waited around to watch the house erupt in flames. He did not stay to see if the man and the two children got out. What pierced me was he did not even care about the children. He wanted his enemy destroyed, and like a man back at war, he set fire to the back of the shed.

The night was a dark one, March 27, 1871, near North Street and the hill road in Lancaster, New Hampshire, and cold, so cold that the fire in Samuel's woodstove burned hot. The occupants, in bed up the narrow stairs, were saved because he was wakeful, mindful of the need to go down and stoke the stove. He started awake, hearing a crackling like water down rocks in a stream, and rushed into action, screaming for the two children he had taken in after their father died. The boy and girl ran out from their bedrooms, little Cornelia Kimball clutching the gray tiger cat. They made it out with the clothes on their backs and the cat, to stand and stare in shock as the two-story, plain-frame house was turned into a fiery torch.

And so Samuel's precipitous move to Lancaster that very month was a disaster. He was left with a stinking ruin on a piece of farm. Four days later, he signed the deed for another property almost in sight of the first one. What if, if only, he had hired a wagon and horse and gone back across the bridge over the Connecticut whence he had come, back to Guildhall, Vermont where he should have stayed in the first place.

❦

Chapter Two

AUGUST 1865

I FIRST LAID EYES ON DAVID AS I WAS CLIMBING THE WIDE FRONT STEPS OF THE NEAT WHITE TOWN HALL ON THE VILLAGE GREEN IN LUNEN-BURG, VERMONT. I was with my neighbors, the Phelps, Mary and her husband, Augustus. We lived close to an hour's drive from the village, on a farm up in the northeastern corner of town on the road to Victory over Mount Tug. It was early August, and the boys were home from the war – most of them, anyway, who had lived – and the supper was to celebrate their return and the end of the fighting. I had almost not made it. My husband, Hiram, had a crisis just before I was set to leave with the Phelps. He was dying, clearly, by then. The cancer had spread before our eyes, eating even into his cheek below his left eye. I rarely left him, but Mary had convinced me to go.

"You need to get out. Just this once," she said. "He will be alright. Fanny can stay home."

Fanny was my daughter, named for my mother. She was eleven, small like me, with dark hair and dark eyes like no one else in the family. And she was slow moving, not like me, more like her father with his heavy calmness I had known since I was a girl.

"She is too young," I said.

Mary looked at me with astonishment, "Fanny? Oh, Emeline (for that is what I was called then), you know Fanny will be alright caring for her father for a few hours."

"I will go then," I gave in, thinking, yes, my daughter would be capable of keeping him peaceful for a little while. That is what she had been doing for the nearly two years of his illness.

Neither of us mentioned her brothers. The eldest, Charles, a veteran of the war, was twenty-two, and already deep into his life, with one marriage to his cousin, Malinda, behind him, and another coming I could see by the light in his eyes when he looked at another of his cousins. The younger, Abiather, named for my father, and called Biathy, was simple – not in possession of his faculties. The census taker used the word idiotic. He was twelve and drifted around the farm when he was not working. He could work, if he was kept close to hand and directed. He could milk the cows, his dark head buried in their side, crooning to himself and them. It pained me to see him, though I should have been used to it. Mostly I was, but sometimes it all came over me – the waste of him. He was handsome, and could fool a stranger until he spoke in a jumble of words and sounds.

I was glad to be leaving behind the sickness and worries of the farm that was barely a farm ever, and less so with Hiram ill.

The Phelps' wagon was in the dooryard when Hiram had a spell.

"Mama!" Fanny said in a sharp whisper to me, standing in the doorway of the bedroom she and I shared. "You have to come."

I was just adjusting my bonnet in the uneven glass of the mirror. I had moved it there when Hiram got so ill I couldn't sleep in the bed with him, and had moved my clothing and combs and hairpins in with Fanny. One or the other of us was always with him or within calling distance.

I ran behind her to the room where he was laid up. He was sitting bolt upright, sweat pouring off his red, damaged face. His eyes were frantic, and he was panting like a dog spent from running coons. She had been trying to cool him with a wet cloth, but he had flung her hand away, unable to stand any touch at all. I tried to soothe him with my voice, but it seemed to agitate him so I stopped. Mary appeared, too, by the bed. All we could do was watch as he struggled, moving so far away from us we feared him gone. But as quickly as it started, the spell passed and he submitted to my and Mary's removing his nightshirt, and giving him a bath with the cloth to take away the sweat. I had sent Fanny away to wash her face, streaked with tears I don't think she knew she was crying. Once he was into a new nightshirt, and the sheets had been changed under him, Mary and I were sweaty and tired down to our bones. I went in search of Fanny. She was sitting on the steps of the porch with Mr. Phelps, who occupied the old rocker. I smoothed her hair back from her face and pulled the hair loose from its braids and re-plaited them smooth.

"He's alright now," I said.

"I know," she answered. "Go to the party."

"Of course not," I said, startled at the notion.

"Really. I will be good with him," she insisted. "It has happened before. Now he will sleep. Biathy is here. He will stay with me."

"Look at what a mess I am," I said, willing to be coaxed.

"Go and clean up. You can shake out your dress."

Mary and I did our best to clean up, scrubbing our faces and taking off our dresses to shake them out, letting down our hair and smoothing it back into buns.

"What a mess we are," I said to her shakily. "Augustus is patient."

We were late to the celebration. Augustus urged the horse to good speed down the long hill into the village. He left Mary and me off by the town hall and went away to settle the horse and wagon on the green. I had the basket with my blackberry pie over my arm, and was climbing the steps. They were wide steps and I have a small frame, so I concentrated on getting up them with the heavy basket without tripping. Near the top I looked up and there he was – unfolding from his lean frame propped up against the window as if to come to me. But I was up before his gesture could be carried out. I saw him first from below so he looked huge, even bigger than he was which was big. He was six feet, one inch, with glossy black hair like the feathers of a crow and dark brown eyes. He was lean from the war years, but his build showed signs of filling out. Like many of the veterans, he wore part of a uniform, in his case the cap and jacket – the buttons dull from wear. He made as if to take my basket, but such was my confusion of emotion at seeing him, I ignored him and pushed past him into the hall.

There were dozens of people there, many I knew from Lunenburg, but many I did not since the men who had enlisted in Lunenburg from other towns were there, too. The noise of all of the voices was high, and after the eating from the long string of tables set about in what seemed like every inch of space, there were speeches. My sister's child, Myalina, and her husband, George Gage, were there, making the long trip from the next-door town of Guildhall where they lived with his parents. She kissed me dutifully and asked for Hiram. We had been at her wedding when she was a girl of sixteen. Now she was a woman of twenty and looked every bit of that and more, with one baby at home and one more dead. Her husband was quiet, pulled into himself like a turtle startled by a horse and wagon. I knew she did not have an easy time with that one, not since his three years of war.

George's brother, Horace, was there, too. A veteran like George, he had enlisted in the Third regiment much earlier, at the very start of the war, and though he came home earlier, something had happened to him and his health was ruined. He drank too much and stood on the fringes of the party, his black eyes too big for his sunken cheeks and high pale forehead. He had been handsome once. I knew this from Myalina. And he had been married before the war to a beautiful girl by the name of Myra Ann from over Benton way across the river. She died while he was away, and was buried in her family's plot near her many siblings who had died young.

George and Horace's mother, Betsey, was not from the common stock. She was a Rowell. Her father, Aaron, owned river land, at first south a few towns in Bradford, and then north of here in Maidstone with his high-born son-in-law, James Follansbee. It could have given his daughter airs, to have come from a well-to-do farmer, but she was not like that. She had not married well, and that could have made her bitter, but it did not. Harmon Gage ate through money like a woodchuck eats through the garden, always getting to the just-ripe tomatoes before you do. Some comfort it must have been to her that two of her daughters, Jane and Lauraette, married well into the Fiske family – brothers, though those girls would not live long lives, either of them. Betsey soldiered on, brave face to the world anyway, though Myalina said it seemed to go deeper than that. She was practical, and had drawn around herself her niece by marriage, Martha, as well as her daughter-in-law, Myalina. It was true her sons, Horace and George, had come back from the war, but she had lost another son, Charles, to consumption toward the end of the war. It had been his frailty that kept him home with her, and then killed him.

This may sound like cheap gossip, but you might as well understand the details of the people where I lived. Martha was a daughter-in-law of Betsey's sister, Sally, who married Clifton. This girl was a Gray, and married Robert Hutchins who died in Washington of pneumonia during the war. Not that he was alone in that, as men died by the thousands of sickness. But she felt it hard herself. She had no children and soon married Hosea Aldrich, another man of the war, who had served with my son,

Charles, and been taken prisoner in the same skirmish that had caused the injury to my son. Betsey had drawn those two into her household, finding a place for them to live at a neighbor's, and they ran herd on Horace, especially Hosea who even at the party stayed near him like a second skin. Betsey was determined to keep the farm. Those Rowell sisters were clannish, and all lived with their husbands in western Guildhall in the hills – one sister married to Aaron Wheeler, another to the Carr man, and another to a man whose name I can't remember. But Betsey had made a move to Lunenburg to a place she thought was better land to keep her sick son protected.

None of these were happy thoughts as I stared from face to face, their stories flying through my mind. But I was determined to laugh and be merry, and talk to as many people as I could, storing up stories to take home to Fanny and Hiram. Charles was there, too, scanning the room in search of who knew what. He was a small, compact man with dark hair and blue eyes the color of cobalt marbles. He and Myalina nodded with a cool civility to one another, as if she were acting for her sister, Malinda, who he had first married. Like I said, he was a veteran of the War of the Rebellion. He had seen battle and been shot in the shoulder while on guard duty in Louisiana when the enemy ambushed the train. He had been paralyzed in his right arm, and was disabled, though he was learning to compensate, and was some help to me on the farm. That injury had not got him home immediately, but he survived and made it back from a place I could hardly credit the distance of on the map in the schoolhouse I had sought out when we got the letter from him in the hospital.

All the while I talked to Betsey and Myalina and kept an eye on Charles, I knew the black-haired, dark-eyed stranger was in the room. I knew he kept track of me even as I did of him, but I did not let him see me looking.

It was when I was leaving that he made his move. Suddenly, he was at my elbow, his hand pulling lightly at the base. I jerked my head up to him, and that is the first time we made eye contact. It was like the time lightening struck the maple tree in the north pasture and split it down the middle. Melodrama, you may say, but that is how it went.

"Let me drive you home," he said.

"I live at home with my husband and my children," I said coldly, trying to pull my elbow away.

He held on. "I know," he said. "I have found out all about you."

This made me mad, because he had found out about me and I had not been able to ask about him. And because no woman likes to be found out about so quickly.

I yanked my elbow back and Mary, who had missed nothing, wedged between him and me, and pushed me outdoors between herself and Augustus. That was that and we were in the wagon and on the way up the road to Victory and home.

℘

Chapter Three

SEPTEMBER 1865

H IRAM DIED IN THE FALL, WHEN THE FIELDS HAD GONE THE COLOR OF A CATAMOUNT'S FUR, AND THE LEAVES WERE IN FULL COLOR. He died peacefully enough – worn out by his long suffering. I think of him often now, sick as I am. Mine is quieter than his or maybe he fought differently, like an animal trying to get free of a trap, whereas I struggle like an itch where scratching only draws a wound deeper and deeper into the blood. Fanny was on one side of him and I was on the other. It was just before four in the morning, the dawn not far off, the high and long stillness of the night not yet broken by the cows in the barn blatting for Biathy to come and milk them. In fact, he appeared in the doorway just as his father passed, and then disappeared like a spirit himself and I heard the kitchen door bang shut, the sound echoing in my nerves as it shuddered the windows.

Hiram had gone quietly, his breathing slower and slower, the pauses longer and longer until he stopped. We each held one of his hands, to comfort ourselves, too. His spirit had gone the night before, when he had stared at the two of us, looking right into our eyes, first Fanny and then me. And he had gone. But his body had taken longer, letting us get used to the idea of his absence.

We sang to him, a hymn, Pleading the Promises. "Behold thy waiting servant, Lord/ Devoted to thy fear/Remember and confirm thy word/For all our hopes are here."

Biathy had not gone to milk the cows but to fetch Mary.

"Emeline," she said. "Emeline." She held me, and Fanny put her arms around me, too, so I was like the filling in a sandwich and warmed by it.

Fanny and I were not close. She was her father's daughter. We were too alike and too different. His death did not change much except it took away the reason we had for unity. He was buried in the far pasture, two days after his death, September 27, 1865. He was forty-seven years, nine months old. Fanny was eleven and old for her age. She had not gone to school, even though it was just down the road. She had not gone to school and I did not make her. Later, I would know she blamed me for this even though she had not wanted to go. She had followed Hiram everywhere on the farms where we lived. She had not seen the poor times, though, like Charles had and that made them different.

"What am I going to do?" I asked Mary, my hands husking ear after ear of corn in the late afternoon sunlight in the doorway of the barn. She was helping. Fanny had gone to the house to start supper. It had been too long that I had been asking this question of myself.

Hiram's illness had come on slowly. At first it seemed it was the hard work. He was older than me by almost eight years. Mornings he seemed to have more and more difficulty getting out of bed. His skin had a gray cast. I put him to bed for a few days. He seemed better after that.

"You're working too hard," I told him.

He shrugged. "What am I to do? Biathy and I can only do so much. There are no men to be had to help out even if I could afford to pay them."

It was spring, and there were fields to plant with corn and some wheat. There was the big garden Fanny and I tended – at least we could do that, along with minding the house – the days of doing laundry, ironing, baking, cleaning, cooking, and mending clothes. We had two cows, an ox, and the horse. Later, there would be hay to cut and rake and bring into the barn. There would be corn to cut and store. There would be vegetables to put by for winter.

"Augustus will come over and he is getting some of the neighbors to help," Mary told me that fall.

"We are grateful," I said. "He is not better. You know."

She nodded.

By then he was in our bedroom most of the time. On the day of the corn harvest he dressed and came to the porch, but no further.

"It is cancer, I am afraid," the doctor said. "He is swollen. He is in some pain. His color is not good. There is nothing…." he trailed off, looking sorry.

Almost two years later, he was dead. I could not be sorry for him, that his suffering was done.

"Why does it keep going on?" he had started to ask me in those last months of his pain.

Mary and I sat in the doorway of the barn, she on a milking stool and me on a pile of hay, husking the corn, a week after Hiram had died. It was quiet, soothing work, but I was not feeling quiet or able to be soothed.

"What am I going to do?" I asked. "We can't manage like this much longer. Not with just me and Fanny who is just a girl and Biathy."

I had managed when Hiram was still alive, thinking somehow as long as he was alive he might not die, there might be a miracle and everything would go back the way it had been. Our neighbors had been so kind, and Biathy was a strong, strong boy, but all of this could not go on forever. I had paid the mortgage month after month, scrimped on whatever I could, taken what amounted to charity – something I had said I would never do again after the year when we hit rock bottom in 1850 and were on the paupers' list in Lyman. It was the goodness of neighbors this time, and of Mary and her husband, Augustus. But it could not go on forever. Now I was a widow, with a young daughter and a son who was a child, on a hill farm. And winter was coming.

"What am I going to do?" I asked my friend.

"You will have to marry," she told me.

To his credit, David Beede did not come around right away. He banked his impetuosity and held from coming for three months. He waited until just before Christmas, near the turn of the year, when the cold was at its worst in late December and we were burning wood at a rate I calculated with a lump of fear in my stomach. I was by then more scared and lonely every day, sitting in the only warm room of the house, knitting, darning a sock, trying to converse in a normal way with Fanny, while Biathy sat waiting for his meals and for the rounds of the barn.

I cannot say I did not think of him. I cannot say I did not wait and wish for him to come, though I never thought it would be possible.

g

Chapter Four

VERMONT-BORN
1794 ONWARD

WHEN I SAID I KNEW HIRAM FROM THE TIME I WAS A CHILD, I WAS BEING LITERAL. He was older by eight years, a vast difference at that age, and never paid much mind to me, but I knew him as one of my older, revered cousins. My family was living away from northern New Hampshire, in the central Vermont mountains, when I was born in 1826. I even started school in that distant place. I first met Hiram when I must have been four, almost five. I had had my first year of school in Vermont, and then we moved to Lyman, New Hampshire so I was worried about where I would go in the new place that was really an old place to my father and my mother. That was my worry when we had just come back from the one place I thought of as home to the new, old place where my father's kin lived and where he and my mother and my older sister and brother had lived. We moved to New Hampshire in the spring of 1831, when the roads were dry of spring mud and there was still time to do the spring planting on the new land my father bought. It was early in that summer I saw Hiram for the first time. He came to help my father get the new farm going. His father, my uncle, brought him from across the river in Vermont to Lyman where we now lived. It was home to my uncle, too, and it was worth his day of travel to get shot of a mouth to feed when he had ten others at home.

At twelve, Hiram was big as a tree to me. He had a lot of hair at first when he came, that tended to be unruly in the hot weather, until my mother, exasperated with looking at him, sat him down and cut it. He was my brother Elisha's age and they might have been friends, but Elisha was sickly by then. That was why my father needed help. He was friends with my other brother, Abiather, named for my father.

I took to following Hiram around at any chore that didn't involve the field and the horse where I was not allowed.

"Scat!" he told me. "Go and play with your doll. You're like a deerfly buzzing at me."

He had enormous hands that he would have to grow into, and a tireless capacity for work. Unlike most of us in the family, he had blue eyes, a blue lightened by gray. He was not handsome by some standards, but he was good to look at with even features and skin that turned brown as an acorn in the sun. He did not like having a four-year-old girl on his tail, popping up from behind the hay in the barn or waiting for him on the porch when he came in from the pasture. That only made him more appealing.

"You always had something to say, all kinds of explanations and questions," he told me much later, when he had really noticed me. I was fifteen and he had come back for a visit.

My father and his father, Samuel, were brothers. They had other brothers, too, Elisha and Elijah. They were the four who had been old enough to come first with their father, Elisha, from Massachusetts south of Boston to Lyman, which was then a wilderness in 1799. My grandfather had first bought land in 1794 in Keene, New Hampshire, from a man he knew in Taunton, Massachusetts. Keene was a hundred miles north of Taunton, where all of them were born. It was a hundred miles south of Lyman, to where they traveled by boat on the river and on foot behind a wagon, setting off from the river to the hills where the farm would be.

"It was opportunity," my father often said. "Opportunity for better living for all of us." He lived by that, and while his three brothers stayed in more or less the geographic region where their father had planted them, my father kept moving. He kept buying land and half-improving it and then selling it and buying more. He did not have a lot of money so he had to choose what he bought carefully, or rather he should have. He could not afford the best land, and he liked the hills, he liked the mountains. The land was cheaper in those places, and rock-ridden. He would clear a few acres and then sell to someone else, sometimes back to the larger landowner he had bought from. My older sister, Fanny, told me the places he lived after he left Massachusetts as a boy. In New Hampshire, he lived in Keene, in Lyman where she and my brothers were born, in Bath where he bought his first land, and in Westmoreland near Keene where his mother's family lived. In Vermont, he lived in Plymouth near more of his mother's relations, in Mount Holly where I was born, and in Shrewsbury where I went to school. Then he was back in New Hampshire: going to Lisbon, Bath and Lyman, and, at the end, returning to Lisbon where he died, not much over fifty years of age.

All of that exertion for prosperity on my father's part, and yet, in 1850, Hiram and me and Charles, and my brother, Abiather, and his wife, Lovisa, and their children, were on the pauper's list. My sisters, Fanny, the eldest, and Wealthy, the youngest, had escaped. For Fanny, escape from this poverty was because of her marriage to a man who farmed with persistence. For Wealthy, it was because she had married a man from away who had some small means from his father, though he also had my father's inclination to move. Her prosperity was stunted by this and by the fact that, in 1850, she and her husband were started on a cycle that was almost like a clock ticking – having children about every two years that would eventually add up to thirteen.

Telling this, I shake my head to clear it of the buzz of too many relations like bees flooding a field of clover blossoms. The bees have, at least, the purpose of honey.

That last statement is cryptic but I think you can figure out what I am saying.

My Uncle Samuel, Hiram's father, who became my father-in-law, was like all of those Presbrey men. He was small of bone, compact of build, with a pointed chin and deep-set eyes. He wore a small beard mostly on his chin. My father did not wear a beard, but otherwise, the two were very similar. Hiram's mother, Eunice, was a Wilbore, and so related distantly to both her husband, Samuel, and to my grandmother, Wealthy Wilbore. All of that generation of my parents seemed to know one another generations back to when some long-dead Presbrey or Wilbore had come from England to Massachusetts.

As I have said, whereas my father, Abiather, had never stopped anywhere more than a few years, his three brothers were more settled, or so it seemed to me by the time I was old enough to know. Samuel had settled across the river in Lunenburg, with Eunice, and a family that grew to eleven children. He farmed there, and he and Eunice died within days of each other in 1856, not of old age, but of spotted fever. They are buried in the cemetery near the village green.

His brother, Elisha, named for their father, also went to Lunenburg where it is safe to say he prospered, leaving one of the finest farms along the river when he died in 1853. He was, we all felt, rich. He married Hannah, the sister of his brother's wife, Eunice. She died just at the end of the War of the Rebellion, in the summer of 1865, not long before the party at the town hall celebrating the return of the men. Elisha and Hannah, too, are buried in the village cemetery. His one son died at the age of two, and his daughter married a man named Smith who would play a big role in helping me out of hard times.

Elijah, the fourth brother, and the eldest, never left the county.

There is a famous saying I learned in school, but I will change it to say "all roads lead to Lunenburg."

That is where I buried my husband, Hiram, and that is where I met the man who would alter the course of who I was, like a sandbar in the river changing the way the water goes. It was nothing I ever intended. I did not understand soon enough who he was. Another what if: what if who he was had come out sooner? – like a piece of pine sap in the fire that takes time to heat up until it shoots sparks onto the hearth.

§

Chapter Five

NOVEMBER 1865

I WAS SITTING IN THE KITCHEN MENDING A SHIRT FOR MY BOY, CHARLES. Charles was built about like his father and did not use his clothes hard, but the cuffs on the blue cambric work shirt were worn so I was turning them. It was a cost-saving practice to extend out the life of our clothing. It involved a painstaking picking out of the stitches that attached cuff to sleeve, and reattaching it wrong side out with the less-worn fabric on the outside. It made a shirt good for even hard use for another year or two, and kept the man from looking raggedy.

I did not mind this work. It kept my hands busy and my thoughts focused on making neat, even stitches. By some lights, his beau, Amanda, could have been doing this. Whether she would not or could not, I did not understand. I knew he was not always kind to her and she was very young, and childish, I felt. It puzzled me that he had turned out so difficult and demanding, and so unlike his father and sister Fanny.

"Why do you bother her so?" I asked him the day he had brought me the shirt, complaining of her lack of care for his clothes. "It is a work shirt, that's all."

He gazed at me with amusement. "I am just like you, can't you see that?"

"Alright, I'll do the shirt," I said, not choosing to answer him.

Instead I gazed back at him, shaking my head. He had my beaky nose, and dark hair though his, for now, was thicker. His eyes were blue, and they were trader's eyes, watchful for bargains and for business.

"You should be easier on her," I said. "She is young, and not used to that work."

This time he chose not to answer.

"I have to look good," he said.

"What are you down here for?" I asked. "You didn't come all this way for me to mend a shirt."

He looked at me slyly. "I am thinking of buying land."

"With what?" I said. "Did you stumble on a money bush in one of those fields of yours?"

Then he was angry. "You do not know all my business."

"Maybe not, but I know you do not have the money for land."

"A man can look, though," he said sharply. "A man can plan for a different time."

I softened, "Yes, that is good. That is a good thing for you to do."

I sewed in silence for a few minutes.

"I have my own decisions to make," I said.

He gave me a hooded glance, one of those he was so good at with his deep-set eyes. They were set deep enough that in some light they gave no reflection at all. He did not want to put anything into words. But I did.

"I have to marry."

This time he was silent, appearing to watch my stitches, tiny tracks of stitches recreating a shirt of his into one a man with a future could wear in his own fields and barn.

"Who?" he asked. "You have someone in mind."

It was my turn to look cagey.

"You do," he persisted. "I can tell by your voice."

"Perhaps," I said. "Perhaps."

He smiled a little. "Alright, I will wait to be surprised."

"Mary knows," I said, aloud, surprising myself.

"Of course she does," he said.

"Oh, take your shirt and go back to work."

"I am thinking of buying land from Augustus," he said.

"Up here?" I was surprised again, this time at him. "The land is hard. You know it is full of rocks and some of it is just worked out."

"It is a place to start," he said. "If he will sell some of the woods I can clear enough for a field and a pasture. I know enough to make a farm from scratch."

I nodded.

"I can do what your father did. I can make the land pay me back. I am determined to do this. I won't keep working land other people own. There is nothing in that."

"But you don't have the money," I stated, not as a challenge, but a fact that would have to be worked on.

"Not yet."

He took his mended shirt from my hands, and bent to kiss my cheek. He left me with a gift of things to think on, positive things, instead of missing Hiram and the worry over what to do next. For once, I sat with my hands still, folded on my apron. By the time I got up to put on water for tea and peel potatoes for supper, I had a plan.

Chapter Six

NOVEMBER 1865

"YOU NEED TO FIND A WAY TO GET THAT MAN UP HERE," I TOLD MY DEAR FRIEND, MARY PHELPS, THE NEXT MORNING.

She had formed the habit of coming over to my kitchen every morning, after her early kitchen work was done. It was a walk of a mile. Even in the cold, she liked the exercise. She was tall for a woman and had wide shoulders and big hands and feet, much to her dismay. She did not run to fat, though, and her strong body transported her to my house with ease. Often, she brought a basket, with just-baked bread or a pie. These victuals helped and from her, I did not mind.

"I am your charity case," I told her once. "Your good work."

"Hah," she replied. "It is like helping a temporarily injured fox to eggs."

We had that sometimes sharp, good-natured relationship.

"You are the toughest woman I know," she added.

When Mary and I put our heads together, anything seemed possible. And we laughed, oh, how we would laugh – at a kitten staggering with new legs, or a story she heard at the store in the village, or even, on occasion, at Fanny's solemnity – as if we were silly girls and she the scolding woman. "Come and be silly with us," Mary would say, drawing Fanny into the crook of an arm until Fanny started to giggle, too.

She reminded me of the close times I had had with my sister, Wealthy, who I did not see now since she lived so far away.

Hiram and I bought our farm from Augustus Phelps. It was not a bad place, with a barn in pretty good shape and the house, though very small, had room enough and comfort.

"I will miss you when you move," she said wistfully that morning after Charles had come.

"Perhaps I will still be your neighbor," I said.

She started. "What are you plotting?"

"You have to get that man up here," I said.

"We don't even know his name," she said.

"But you can find out," I told her.

"You don't even know anything about him except he is tall and a looker," she protested.

"Then that is where I will have to start," I answered.

"How can I possibly find out without drawing the notice of every wag in town?" she protested more.

"We will make up a list of all of the men who came back from the war and even those who did not. Tell them in the village you are thinking that we should have another party. Tell them we should get all of the names of the men who were at the last one so we won't leave out anyone."

"It will not be easy," she said. "You do have a plot."

"Perhaps," I said.

And at that, she shouted with laughter, a deep-throated guffaw that woke the dog, who was used to her, for a moment from his sleep.

The first and only time I had met the man I would learn was David Beede, future husband, he had been dressed like many of the veterans, in parts of his uniform. In his case, he wore the gray cap with its faded visor and the jacket, its buttons tarnished from wear. That is how I knew he was a soldier. I knew he was single because he had offered me a ride home, his forwardness even then a factor in how we got on together.

Mary, to her credit, quickly went about her task of finding out who he was. If she fooled anyone, I cannot say.

"You come with me," she said, the next morning. She had come early, too excited to wait, and Fanny and I were still clearing up from breakfast. She had left her household chores to her domestic – not a luxury, she always said, but a necessity for her with all of those boys. It was mid-week, a school day, and they had packed off early, after helping their father, to the schoolhouse that was a fifteen-minute walk from their house.

"That would never do," I laughed. "People would see through it in a minute. Why would a poor countrywoman like me have any business planning a party for men come back from the war?"

She sighed, resigned to her own solo part in this adventure.

"What are you about?" Fanny asked suddenly, her awareness of mystery sharp.

Mary and I exchanged looks.

"I will tell you later," I told my daughter.

She looked crumpled, in the way she had since her father died. She cried all of the time, at the least provocation. She cried when a sheet got tangled in the wind. We hung the laundry out year-round and it froze into ice creatures this time of year. We brought it in in stages – a pillowcase held like a slab of wood, sliced thin; a shirt carried by the outstretched sleeves – to dry them by the fire. They kept the sweetness of the outdoors, even with the wood smoke that wafted through the kitchen. She would carry in the laundry, and cry as she hung it across lines strung from wall to wall. She cried when her skirt tripped her going up the stairs, and when the muffins burned – "Just on the bottom," I reassured her. "We can scrape off the burnt part."

How could I tell her I had to do what I was going to do?

She looked stricken, standing in the middle of the room, her hands dripping soapy water. Soon, she would go to tend the hens, collecting the few winter eggs, and chattering to them as she scattered the grain and spread fresh hay. Being with the chickens was one thing that soothed her in the cold, dark days.

"Now," she insisted. "You have to tell me now."

"Come and sit then," I told her.

She did as I asked and, smoothing her skirt, waited for me to talk.

"You know how it is," I started, wishing she would just know without my saying. Maybe she did, but she did not help me in this; she made me say it all.

"You know, don't you, how, well, your father…" I stopped.

She did not look like crying now. Her face was set, her butternut shell brown eyes on me.

I took a breath. "He was the farmer," I said. "We have done the best we could while, well, when he was ill. We had to help him, you see. That was what we did was help him. He told us how to keep this going. And you know, Biathy," I stopped again.

She said nothing. That is an old trick she had learned young, that silence would keep another person talking.

"I don't think, you see, you have to see. We can't stay here like this.

We won't make it, not another winter. I don't want you to cry. But, it is plain to see, I have to get married again."

Her shoulders sagged and her chin dropped to her chest. She was very small sitting on the edge of the chair. I forgot how little she was, sometimes, still a girl. Then she lifted her head.

"Who?" she asked.

"I don't..." I started.

"You know," she said flatly.

"Maybe," I admitted.

"Tell me," she pursued.

"I don't know his name," I said. "He was someone at the party in the fall. He is from the war, a veteran. He doesn't look injured or ill. He noticed me, so I think he must be unmarried. He asked to drive me home because he did not know about your father since I came alone. Mary is going to try and find out about him."

There it was, stated as boldly as I could manage, with none of the tittery excitement when Mary and I considered it.

"Alright," Fanny said. "That is what I need to know." She got up primly, and went to the peg rack by the back door for her coat. Mary and I watched without a word while she put on her coat, wrapped the rough knitted scarf around her head and neck, pulled on her boots and then her mittens and went out the door, and into the shed on the way to her chickens.

"Amen," Mary said. It seemed an appropriate word to say in the wake of the quiet composure of my daughter.

We hardly had the appetite to talk any more that morning about the man from the war who had noticed me. She drank her tea, hotted with fresh water so she would be warm inside for the walk home.

"She'll be alright, I think," Mary said, chewing the edge of her lip.

"Yes," I agreed, sighing and wishing that Hiram was still, at least, in the back bedroom, not daring to wish for the way he had been when he brought his calmness and deliberation I had always got from him since I was a girl.

"I'll come back tomorrow," Mary said. "I shouldn't have come so early."

"Another day won't make a difference," I told her.

When she left, I sat thinking of Fanny, and that led to other thoughts. Fanny was pretty, so pretty with her glossy dark hair in curls above her forehead, and her neat person always decorated by a simple thing like a ribbon in her hair or the pin her father brought her back one day when he had come from selling corn in the village and had done extra well. Her smile would build slowly, a slight motion of her lips until she radiated good will and her prettiness grew into beauty. She would soon be twelve. Would she marry at fifteen like my sister, at sixteen like me? I supposed she would, going in just three or four years from the child she was to the quick growing up that love for a man and marriage would bring.

I have never been close to pretty. My nose is too sharp and too short, my eyes are close together. I wonder what it was that made Hiram ask me to marry him. And I wondered in that moment what would make this man from the war ask me. But I am being disingenuous. I do know. I had land.

g

Chapter Seven

MY FATHER

M Y FATHER, ABIATHER, WAS A FARMER, A YEOMAN. This is important to me. Nine out of ten people we knew were farmers, but it was important because it was his identity and because of that, mine, too. Not only that, but he was a farmer, born in Taunton, Massachusetts, who farmed in Shrewsbury, Vermont. That is the first town of my recall, and therefore of particular notice in my life. These facts were so important that Patrick Gleason, the young man who would become my fifth and last husband, the man whose surname I would die with, knew the story well enough to tell it to the town clerk in Jefferson, New Hampshire where we were married in November 1882. "My wife's father, Abiatha, was born in Taunton, Massachusetts," he said slowly enough for the clerk to write it out in the record book of marriages. "She was born in Shrewsbury, Vermont where he was a farmer." That survives even today. It is wrong: I was born in Mount Holly, the neighboring town where my father settled us first in 1822. It was my sister, Wealthy, who was born in Shrewsbury.

But it was Shrewsbury that stayed in my imagination because I was just four when I started school there. We lived way up in the hills, and everywhere you went, it seemed you were going either up or down. Thus it was when I walked to school down from the hill where we lived, on the road about one-half mile from the store at the crossroads where the roads came in from distant Rutland, a big town where my father sometimes went on business, and from two other parts of Shrewsbury.

We lived in Northam, on the border with Plymouth, and the one-room schoolhouse was only a few years old. I walked with my brothers, Elisha and Abiather, and my sister, Fanny. We went on all but the coldest days of winter, my mother and Fanny bundling me in so many layers I could hardly walk, and we went through the muddy season when I delighted in walking the ridges of the great ruts in the road. I loved school, the smell and feel of chalk on my fingers, and the rough desks and benches where I sat straight to learn all I could from the teacher, Miss Elvira Sparks. She was not only pretty, with blonde curls and blue eyes, and pretty dresses always looking new and clean, but tough enough to handle the older boys who dared give her no guff because of the way her eyes could go from light blue to steely gray when she was angry.

How my father struggled with that farm, clearing land of trees and brush, and planting crops in rocky fields that were mostly not flat. It was the climate that beat him, though, with frosts coming some years as early as the first days of September and the ground not thawing or drying enough to plant until way into May or early June.

But I have only good memories of that town – the way the hills felt like a soft, protective comforter. Our little house, like every house I ever lived in, was a small cape, unpainted, and I remember the warm kitchen with the big cook stove, and the fresh smell of spring when the sun was warming up the grassy patches in the yard and under the few apple trees on the hillside above the house.

It is important, though, to relieve any preconceived notions you may have that a farmer, by his nature, is landed. Of course, he needs land, but like many of our neighbors in every town where we lived, my father did not stay put. He was bitten early by the itch to keep moving geographically.

It started with my grandfather, Elisha Presbrey, who I knew well enough from stories my father told. He lived until a moderate old age of sixty-nine, dead the year before I was born. He and my father had some land dealings in New Hampshire. I think my father was the most like him of any of the brothers, and by accounts of my brother, Abiather, they fought. Each of them was convinced he knew the best way to wheel and deal, and come out ahead in the land game.

Maybe my father should have listened more to his father. I cannot really judge the rights of that. Family legend casts Elisha, my grandfather, as the Presbrey adventurer. While his relatives sat content in Taunton where the original William Presbrey had come off a ship from London that anchored in Boston Harbor in 1711, Elisha's spirit larked back to his English forebear, William Presbrey. London-born in 1690, William had been sailing since he was ten years old. That summer day in Boston in 1711, he took a notion to see the city and went with some of his mates ashore. His companions returned dutifully aboard, but he had seen the strawberry fields of Massachusetts and determined to stay. The story goes that he hid out for a few weeks with a kind-minded farmer in exchange for labor. Out of his rash decision that could have landed him in the stocks or brigs or some such place of punishment, rose up a big family, all of whom seemed wedded to the place where he had arrived. All except my grandfather, or so my family legend goes.

Maybe Elisha was influenced by his wife's family, the Wilbores. That is another story – of their ancestor Shadrach's history of rebellion against the established religion, and his flight with others cast out, to help found the colony of Rhode Island. He recanted, though, and made his return to the area of Boston. Anyway, one of these Wilbores (it was once Wildbore, my mother always said, throwing up pictures of ancient men hunting the wild boar in the forests of England) moved out of crowded Massachusetts to Westmoreland, New Hampshire. Wealthy Wilbore Presbrey, my grandmother, died in Westmoreland in 1813, having come down from Lyman and Lisbon to be near her kin. That was the year of the spotted fever epidemic.

My father, down there with her, did not get sick. He stayed after his mother died, working for his uncle on a farm that was large and near the Connecticut River – very different from the mountain land he always owned. A few months after his mother died, he went across the river to Westminster, Vermont where he married my mother, Fanny Snow, on April 25, 1813. If she had any notion of staying near the open land of the river, it did not stick because Abiather waited only a few years working on his father's farm (a long time for him) before he moved her north to Bath, a town abutting the southern end of Lyman, where he had bought land. That was, to the best of what I know, his first purchase. He bought land at the same time as his brother, Elijah, from a man named Smith. It was land that had a sawmill, what my father bought, on the west side of Gardner's Mountain, on the other side of which was the big river. Milling was the trade this uncle of mine prospered at, but it was too restrictive for my father, who chafed soon after settling anywhere.

I know Bath well. I have travelled across the long, wide covered bridge over the Ammonoosuc, the planks clattering under the weight of the horse and wagon or carriage. The settlement of Bath prospered for a time, in its position at the crook of the river. There was a big brick store, with rooms for let above, and a big white church, a big meetinghouse, and an even larger brick church. There were well-built brick homes just north of the village, where a rich merchant, the village doctor, a lawyer and a gentleman who owned hundred of acres settled together to look back and forth across the road at one another's good fortune. Everything was big in Bath, it always seemed to me.

My father's land was, of course, not in or near the village. You crossed the big, wide covered bridge and the road immediately began to climb toward Lyman. My father's restlessness was only matched by his practicality.

"I had money for a certain amount and kind of land," he told me many times. "I knew what I could afford and that is what I looked to buy. Look at what we have. Don't we have enough? There is enough land cleared for the cows and the ox and some crops. There is a house and land cleared for a garden."

I liked to listen to his stories. I was a ready ear for them.

When he died, I was thirteen, and had stored up enough of them, heard over and over, to know enough to be like him if I ever needed to be.

He must have thought to add sawmilling to his farming, but it did not stick, as I have said before – the poor land, the work of sawmilling ("I'm a farmer," he always told me.) or Bath. He sold it a short two years after he took on the mortgage that involved $450, and the next thing he knew he had settled in with his Wilbore relations, this time in Plymouth, Vermont, a base from which he considered farms in the hills of neighboring Mount Holly and Shrewsbury. It was a long, hard journey from Bath, in the early part of the 1820s, being over one hundred miles.

I don't remember Mount Holly, not being born early enough. I would ask my father about that time before I was born and before my memory started.

"It was Wilbore kin," he said. "They had decided to farm in Plymouth. Lydia Snow – kin of your mother and mine, too. Double kin for your mother since she was a Snow by marriage and a Wilbore by birth, and Lucy Snow, likewise, who you were named for partly. I travelled two or three days to get there. They lived way up from the village in what was called the Blueberry Ledges. I helped the men work while I kept looking for the right place to buy. It took me a couple of years; by then your mother and Fanny and Abiather and Elisha had come. We ended up about ten miles from the Snows in Mount Holly. It was good land, abutting right up against Tiny Pond. We were up high, higher than the Snows in Plymouth. The growing season was short, though, shorter than Lyman. But I went for an even shorter growing season in Shrewsbury, to try my mettle as a farmer, I guess." This last he said dryly.

He was only about fifty when he died. I do not know what exactly was the cause – a stroke, I think. He took to bed for a week in that spring of 1839. Fanny and my mother nursed him. I didn't see him fall against the chair in the kitchen when he came in for lunch that day. He was already in bed and the doctor come and gone when I got home from school. I would sit with him. He was unspeaking – the strangest thing since he had always talked and talked to me.

When we moved back to Lyman from Shrewsbury, I was four years old. It was 1830. The trip took days. We had the horse, the ox to pull the wagon, and two cows hitched behind. We came down from the hills of Shrewsbury through the river valley of the Otta-quechee River, through Woodstock, where my sister, Fanny, would later marry a Shrewsbury man, and Quechee, where my sister, Wealthy, and her family would end up forty years later. We travelled the dirt roads, some rough and some smooth, up the Vermont side of the Connecticut River, through Hartford, Norwich, Thetford, Fairlee, Bradford, Newbury, to Wells River where there was a crossing and my father paid for us to be loaded in three trips across the river. We climbed into the hills to Bath and up into Lyman where we stayed with my Uncle Elijah. There were me and my father, my mother, my sisters, Fanny and Wealthy, and my brothers, Abiather and Elisha. The next day we went down to Lisbon where my father had bought land for us.

It was the men who did the business. The men owned the land, and made the determinations of where to go and how long to stay. It was my father who went to the men who had the land, who borrowed the money, who signed the papers in front of witnesses at the office of the town clerk. He would dress up in his good jacket and a string tie neatly bowed at the collar of his good shirt. Once, I went with him, when he had business of a disputatious nature. It was a day in late May and the apple blossoms were out, and the bees humming in them so loudly you heard the sound if you stopped the wagon, but we rode right past, my father keeping the horse to a quick walk. It was early, nine in the morning, and there was still dew on the tall grass along the sides of the road. We were in the wagon and I sat up stiff in my version of a grown lady beside him on the plank seat. I had on my good brown dress and my boots polished as shiny as worn leather could be. They had been Fanny's till she outgrew them. But the dress had been new, the cloth bought in the store in Lisbon and my mother had taught me the steps of laying out a pattern and constructing a dress.

That day, I was twelve, and my father took me to town.

"I have business with the clerk," he said. "So you will have to sit and be very quiet."

"This is my daughter, Emeline Lucy," he told the clerk, a bent-over elderly man, with rheumatism-curled fingers. He nodded at me, and I nodded back in what I thought was a graceful way.

My father showed me into a corner of the room where I knew I was to sit until his business was done.

There was a great deal of talk. It was like the village store in Lisbon where the men gathered and laughed and then argued. I recognized our neighbor, Mr. Dodge, an old, old man, and his son, who wheezed through his nose. It concerned a disagreement over a boundary. My father claimed one thing and Mr. Dodge another. It was a matter of importance because of where the stream in that corner of the property was going. It had oxbowed (a word I was proud to know from school, which meant a stream twisting back on itself). Some land was lost into the flow of water and both men wanted that land back. At least that was how it seemed to me, on my hard chair in the corner where I had been forgotten.

"You'll end up in court," shouted Mr. Dodge.

"Only if you put us there," bellowed my father in the voice he used to call the cows.

"Enough!" the clerk insisted, raising his tones to the utmost of their level – a hoarse whisper.

At that moment, all three men became silent. It was a silence so purposeful and unexpected, I looked around to see what had caused it.

There, just inside the doorway, was a woman.

"Gentlemen," she said.

"Miz Wendell."

"Miz Wendell."

"Miz Wendell."

The three men greeted her and there was a pause with the only sound the wheezing of young Mr. Dodge.

Mrs. Wendell was a woman no longer in youth, but not old, either. She was about the height of my mother, a little over five feet, but with her brown hair the color of our chestnut mare, Belle, piled up on her head, she seemed taller. She had on the most beautiful dress I had ever seen – a dark green so glossy I thought it must be like a gemstone. There was lace on it, just the right amount, I thought, though I had never seen a dress with so much of it.

I knew who she was though I had never seen her before. She was the legendary Dorothy Wendell, known for all of the land she owned and for her reputation for toughness – a quality supposed to be reserved for men. She was wealthy and rarely came to the place where all of her land was, living in a bigger town a long way away.

There was then a mumbling as my father and the two Dodges bowed their way quickly out of the room, as quickly as water drained from a big hole in a bucket. My father had no presence of mind to collect me, so I stayed where I was, frozen in my seat, really forgotten.

Later, my father would admit he had forgotten me and by the time he remembered "did not think it appropriate" to come right back into the so recently vacated room just for me. But really, I knew, he was too much in awe (if awe means fear) of Mrs. Dorothy Wendell. That was a surprise to me about him. I knew he was in awe of his father, but otherwise I knew he took a strong stand with everyone.

When Mrs. Wendell was obsequiously seated by the clerk, and her glossy deep green skirt arranged around her, she said, "I have a great deal to accomplish today. I will only be here this morning. You have everything ready for me. Where are the witnesses?"

At this last, the clerk's eyes bugged. Even from his bent position, they showed. He had clearly forgotten about witnesses for Mrs. Wendell's business.

He got an unexpected and maybe undeserved moment of grace, as the lady's eye caught mine.

"Who on earth are you?" she said. "Is this my witness?"

"She… she…" the clerk was stuttering and sputtering.

"Who are you?" she said again. "Tell me your name, girl."

"Emeline Lucy Presbrey," I whispered.

"Louder, louder," she said impatiently. "And stand up when you are addressed by your elders."

I shot up from the chair, and stood rigidly at attention the way I was taught to recite in school.

"Emeline Lucy Presbrey," I said clearly, proud to have gotten it out a second time.

"Much better. And why are you sitting there in the corner like a mouse?"

Before I could answer, the clerk mastered himself.

"Her father is to be a witness," he told the lady.

"Well, then, get him in here," she said.

In seconds, the usually slow-moving clerk was at the door where he shoved my father, huddled by the door, along with the older Mr. Dodge, into the room.

"Here are the witnesses," the clerk said. "Mrs. Wendell. Mr. Dodge. Mr. Presbrey."

I stood and watched as my father's name was put on document after document, first Mrs. Wendell's, and then Mr. Dodge's and then his – the clerk's continued scratching filling the papers with the elegant handwriting for which he was known.

The clerks never let you sign your own name. You were asked if you could sign and if you could, stated your full name. If you could not, the clerk signed your name anyway, but with a small, rough-looking "x" and, under it, the words, "his mark" or "her mark." My first transaction, many years from that day, was as Lucy E. Presbrey, not as I would have signed it, but full of lavish flourishes, the "L" and the "E" and the "P." My name lent itself to that. Later, I would be Lucy E. Ingerson and Lucy E. Robinson and even later, Lucy E. Gleason. If you want to see my signature, you will have to look at an affidavit I filed with the government for David's war pension. It is not fancy like the clerk's rendition, but plain and easy to read for all who want to study it.

§

Chapter Eight

December 1865

I<small>T WAS ABOUT THE TIME WHEN</small> M<small>ARY AND</small> I <small>WERE FACING THE REALITY</small> <small>OF MY SITUATION AND SHE WAS PREPARING TO GO TO TOWN TO FIND</small> <small>OUT ABOUT THE STRANGER WHO NOTICED ME, THAT MY SISTER'S GIRL,</small> M<small>YALINA, CAME TO SEE ME A FEW DAYS BEFORE</small> C<small>HRISTMAS.</small>

Christmas back then was not much to take notice of, except for maybe an extra cake or pudding for the Christmas meal. Everything else went on as usual – Biathy had the two cows to milk and tend, Fanny the hens, the ox had to be foddered, and the stalls cleaned. The beds still had to be made, and three meals, and the dishes washed and dried and put back on the shelves. The woodstove had to be kept going, and Biathy had to fill the wood box.

In this way, nothing had changed since I was a girl growing up on any one of my father's farms in the hills.

I heard the horse neighing and the echoing of hooves on the road, but when I looked out the window out of habit – not many conveyances passed by on the road to Victory – I expected to see Mr. Phelps who had gone past much earlier. It was Mr. Phelps, but there was someone with him, a woman, and I peered out wishing I could see better as the sleigh pulled by the bay horse moved closer. Mary would be having a visitor, I thought, puzzled as to what woman would be out on a winter's day for a visit so far into the country. Imagine my surprise when it was for me. But I did not figure that out until I had opened the door and could see my niece's face under the shadow cast by her scarves wrapped in layers like a hood.

Myalina was tall for a woman and for a Presbrey, taking the height from her father, Lucius Larrabee, though not, thank heavens, his square face and stocky build – nor his sour expression. Where her beauty had come from, I did not know. All three of my sister Wealthy's daughters were attractive, with long, dark waves of hair and even features. Myalina, the eldest, was the most striking, I always thought. Malinda had a certain lack of richness in her face, pleasing as it was with pink cheeks and a quiet, almost demure cast. And she had the kind of concave inclination to her chest that brought her neck and head slightly forward in an unpleasing way – I should know because I have that quality and so do my sisters, Wealthy and Fanny. It is what we inherited from our mother. My youngest niece, Ella, was still a small child when I had seen her in 1861 when Myalina and George married. She was only nine years old now. But even at four she had an eager, joyous temperament that made her rosy cheeks and bright black eyes appealing.

But Myalina, at sixteen when she married, at eighteen when baby Simon was born, was classically beautiful. She had her sisters' dark hair and dark eyes, but an added depth of expression, a waiting quiet as if she knew as much as the dark water in the curve of the river and would tell you, soon, soon, if you waited.

That day on my porch, beginning even as she waited for the door to open to unwind her scarves, I saw that her beauty had gone from her.

"Myalina, dear. What a surprise! What has brought you?" I drew her into the living room out of the chill, waving an arm in thanks at Augustus Phelps.

"I'll be back in the morning," he shouted, his breath puffing white in the air of the sunny, blue-sky day.

Myalina and I hugged, her arms wrapping around me from so many inches higher than I was that my head rested on her bosom.

"I hope it is alright, Aunt," she said. "I didn't have time to write. George was coming to Lunenburg today and I determined I would come with him and see you. I'll take the stage home tomorrow if I can stay the night with you. Kind Mr. Phelps offered to take me back to town in the morning."

"Of course you can stay," I said. "I can hardly believe my eyes to see you!"

We hustled through the cold parlor into the warmth of the kitchen.

"Fanny, dear heart," Myalina said to my daughter who stood shyly looking at her older cousin. "Come." And she opened her arms so Fanny could walk into them.

Then there was the interruption of getting her layers of warm clothing off of her and setting tea and a piece of fresh-baked bread with butter on a plate near her elbow.

In the light, her garments removed, I could see the pallor of her cheeks, and the lankness of her hair. She wore a plain dress with cinnamon-brown checks, and it hung on her shoulders that sagged under it.

"How is Simon? How are your mother and father? I am starved for news," I said.

"Oh, the baby is fine, I left him with George's mother. And my mother, she is just the same as ever. She is busy." Of course, she was busy with baby Flinty, and Horace just barely four, and probably another on the way, not to mention the boys at home and Ella still a girl. "You know how it is this time of year with everyone indoors, even my father, and the older boys working out with neighbors, but coming back and forth all of the time, tramping snow and frozen mud into my mother's house."

"And you?" I asked. "That is why you have come."

She reddened a little, but gave me a direct regard.

"You can see," she said, "How I am."

"You have been sick. You were sick in the fall and it has not gotten better."

"I thought it was a cold, but I just can't seem to feel any better."

"How is George?" I asked.

She was quiet.

"It is hard?" I pushed.

"It is hard," she said. "He cannot get settled to anything. He can't stay with his mind on any one thing. And he seems not really back, you see? He has lost something and he can't find it. I just had to get away. I had to not think of what he is doing or not. You know, Horace, his brother is ill, and hardly works, and seems to be drinking. That is why his mother got that couple to come and live nearby. We would not – George, I mean, would not – look after him. It was everything they went through, you know. Horace came back to find his wife was dead. He knew of course from a letter after it happened, but that was three years ago so when he came home he expected her to be waiting. I saw it in his face, scanning all of us in the yard when his father brought him home. At last, he was home, but Myra Ann is dead, Aunt, and he wasn't expecting it even though he knew. You would think he and George would be close, but George doesn't like to be in the same room unless there are other people so he doesn't have to talk to his brother one on one. That is what it has come to. And his cousin's wife, Martha, you know her husband died in Washington in a hospital of pneumonia. He was Robert Hutchins, George's cousin. That was three years ago, too. But how is it she has so much life in her and she married Hosea Aldrich right off? He was in the war, too, and was taken prisoner in the same ambush where Charles was injured, and he talks about it. He is as unconcerned as if he had been on some lark in the country with his pals."

Fanny listened, her eyes big. For once, I didn't know what to say.

"What is George doing in the village?" I finally asked.

"Visiting some man he got to know when he was away," she said. "He is always visiting this one and that one. But enough of me. What of you? How are you bearing up? I am selfish to talk like this when you and Fanny have suffered such a loss. I am very sorry about Uncle Hiram. He was a good man."

"We miss him," I said. "We miss him every day." I considered what else to tell her.

"Mother has to marry again," Fanny burst out, then turned the color of a hot coal in the stove.

Myalina studied me.

"Of course," she said. "That would be so."

We were all silent a moment as she considered this news.

"You will need someone to help you here with the farming," she said reflectively.

"Do you know many of the men who returned?" I asked. "Do you remember a tall, good-looking man who was at the party at the church in the fall? He was very tall, with dark hair. He stood out in the crowd. He was older than most of the other men, about my age."

Myalina laughed, a small laugh that took only a small amount of air.

"David Beede, Aunt Emeline. That was surely David Beede."

"Just like that you know. Are you sure? How are you sure?"

She really laughed then, and looked almost sixteen again. "You weren't the only woman casting admiring glances at him," she giggled. "Of course, not me," she added demurely. "I was with George. And that other man is old. Apologies to you, Aunt." She giggled again at this sally toward the old.

"Why, Alma," I protested, half laughing myself, and using her pet name. "Do you think just because I was there without my husband who was ill at home that I had my eye on every handsome man in the room?"

Fanny simply goggled at the two of us. Me, her mother, she could view with haughty regard, but not her beautiful young cousin who she admired.

"The question is," I said, more soberly. "Was he casting glances back at all of them?"

Myalina considered me a moment. "He was looking," she said. "He was looking at you."

"Really?" I asked, feeling a little giddy. "You're making that up."

"No, I'm not. I noticed once and then I started watching to see if it happened again. And it did. So then I made a study of it."

"What do you know about him?" I asked.

She shrugged. "I did ask around, after I saw his interest in you. I was worried about you. He's a stranger. All I could find out was his name, and that he was not with the Vermont army but New Hampshire's. He and his three sons all were. But only he and one of them came back. Be careful, Aunt."

"Nothing has even happened, dear." All of these details gave me pause.

"There must be a solid farmer around Lunenburg or Guildhall," she said. "A widower with some children. At least consider that."

"I wonder why he came to Lunenburg."

"He's working as a laborer on a farm along the river. He has a son with him, a younger boy named George, too young to work. They've got a room in town."

Now my doubts increased. This sounded like a poor man, his family mostly gone, and one young boy to raise.

"There will be someone," I said.

Two days later, David Beede made me a visit.

It was a Sunday, the one afternoon he would not have to work. He looked just as he had that evening in the fall – very tall, head and shoulders above me, with dark hair and dark eyes, and a strongly made face full of strong angles of cheek and jaw. He arrived unannounced in a wagon at two o'clock in the afternoon. He wore a heavy wool coat, and I could see the tips of his polished boots below his neat pants. His face was in the shadow of a wide-brimmed leather hat. It was just before Christmas 1865. He brought me a small wooden box filled with butternuts, the box made of butternut wood and polished to a high sheen. He brought his son, George, a shy, gawky boy of thirteen, who had his father's eyes and hair and a height that indicated he would eventually be as tall.

My heart was hammering as I opened the door to his knock – a soft tapping that I might not have heard in the kitchen if I had not already seen him drive into the yard. I had wanted both to rush to the mirror to smooth my hair and to watch him spring down easily from the wagon and walk steadily, his long legs covering the snowy path quickly, to me. When he knocked, I took a quick look in the tiny mirror in the hall, re-gretting my plain dress as I pulled off my apron, and pinching my cheeks to get some color into them.

I opened up the heavy door in the small hallway. I stood in the door-way, not even thinking to shiver as I would naturally do in that cold air. I stared up at him, and he took off his hat so his whole face, his whole beautiful face, was there for me to see. He was solemn.

"My name is David Beede. I hope you will forgive my intrusion." He offered me the box of butternuts. "This is for you."

"Thank you," I said. "Would you like to come in? You and the boy?"

He waved a hand at his son, and followed me into the hallway and through the parlor into the kitchen.

"We are tracking snow," he apologized.

"It is clean. It will come up easily," I said, hardly able to get the words out I was so short of breath.

When we stood in the kitchen, it seemed smaller with him in the room. He eased George out from behind him. "This is my son, George," he said. "This is Mrs. Presbrey."

"Hello, George," I said.

Fanny had risen from where she was by the stove, her face wooden as she mastered whatever she was feeling.

"This is my daughter, Fanny," I said. "Fanny, this is Mr. Beede and his son, George."

She gave a little curtsey, and a soft hello, minding her manners prettily. I was proud of her.

"That is Biathy," I gestured to the other side of the stove where my son still sat in a straight-backed chair, rocking it slightly back with his legs.

"This is unexpected," David said to me, his eyes seeking mine, making me lift my chin up to really see him. "My coming like this, I mean."

"No," I answered. "No."

He smiled then, a wide, suggestive smile, and I could not look away.

⚘

Chapter Nine

MARCH 1871

THE SHERIFF FIRST RULED THE FIRE WAS CAUSED BY THE STOVEPIPE CATCHING FIRE IN THE KITCHEN. The stove was against the back wall of the kitchen that was also the wall of the shed, so that explained to him why the fire had moved from the back into the front of the house. The *Lancaster Gazette* reported the story: it was a sad event but at least the man Samuel Hannux and his family (the cat was not mentioned) escaped. It reported a simple cause: the pipe was believed to have caught the wood frame of the house on fire. Fires were commonplace in those days, and still are. A fire that destroyed a house or a business or part of a town was news, but not big news unless it destroyed part of a town's business district or involved a person of note, like much later the house fire that killed my fifth husband, Patrick Gleason, would be news – a front-page story.

The fire that burned down Samuel Hannux' house seemed forgotten. David Beede laughed again. But I had not forgotten.

There are reasons why I did not rest easy.

The night of the fire I had been in bed early, as had the children, Fanny and George. It was a cold night, as I said before, and the warmth of the bed with its feather bed below me, a stack of quilts and a goose down comforter above me, and a hot brick from the stove wrapped in cloth at my feet, was hard to resist. Unlike the freezing bedroom of the house Hiram and I had shared in Lunenburg, this room had a hole in the floor lined with a metal tube that David had made to conduct some heat from the kitchen. It did not make the bedroom warm, exactly, but it did give a suggestion of heat so, if there had been a basin of water on the stand, it would not have frozen. That was progress, and a luxury to me.

He had gone out. This was not uncommon. There were taverns in Lancaster – it was the hub of the region and a big town in my eyes – where men gathered, those from the village who could walk and some even from outlying farms who drove a team in for a few hours. The hotel had stables in the back. There were also men staying at the hotel, travelers on business of some kind or another. He liked the conversation, the stories, the news of the country. And he drank, and gambled, too, if the opportunity presented itself, though he had been abstaining, I thought, since I had taken him in again after the terrible events that had taken place between us and between him and Charles in the fall of 1868.

I would not say David was restless exactly, but he had been to so many places during the war that our small town in New Hampshire did not look the same to him as it would have before. The men he met at night in town brought news from many other towns, some as far as Boston and even New York. In this way, he felt connected to those three years away when so much had happened to him.

He would come in afterwards in a different mood from when he went out. He would come up the stairs in his stocking feet, his boots neatly set by the back door, and I would awake sometimes to his sock-clad feet shuffling up the steps or sometimes to his muted movements undressing, a belt buckle ringing on the chair or his watch with its light thump as he placed it on the bureau. Other times, though, I would not awake at all until he slid in beside me under the bulk of the covers and I would feel his cold cheek against my neck and the coolness of his night garments as he wrapped around me to sleep or invite something else.

That night I heard even the door open and close when he came home. I listened for the sound of his adding logs to the fire and the metallic catch of the stove door. I heard his stocking feet come up the stairs, with the creak on the third and fifth treads, and the bedroom door open and shut with his efforts to be quiet. I heard every sound he made from my spot deep in the cocoon of bed, his muffled breathing, and his pants dropping to the floor before he picked them up and shook them with a sharp snap before putting them over the back of a chair.

When he was in beside me, I was ready for him and rolled over into his chest. That is when I thought I smelled the smoke, but I was drowsy and pleased to see him, and showed it. His body felt as tightly strung as a fiddle, but after awhile he slept. I had been listening half-consciously for him that night because I was attuned to his moods. He had been like that – strung tight – for weeks, ever since he learned that Samuel Hannux had moved into the village of Lancaster from Guildhall.

I did not know right away about Samuel's coming. I was home more than David, and we lived in the southern part of Jefferson in a hamlet called Cherry Mountain, near the border of Carroll. I did not often get to the village of Lancaster where the business of the county took place. There were neighbors to visit, including my sister, Wealthy, and the work of the house with the children. It was David who went out, to work as a laborer on a neighboring farm. If there were errands in the shire town, he would go except for an occasional trip when we would all go. That was more often a warm-weather event, though.

I was happy to be in New Hampshire, in a house I owned with good land. I had become Lucy E. by then, embracing my new identity and leaving Emeline Presbrey across the river with the memory of my long-loved husband, Hiram.

We had moved, in truth, because of a certain matter involving David, Charles and me, but I had made up my mind to make a new start here where I fancied we were not known so well.

Three years ago, we had moved, just Fanny and Biathy and me. David had gone off, jumping his bail in Vermont and I was determined to start again. Fanny, who had been a girl then, was now a young woman of seventeen. But he had come back in the spring of 1870 and I, against my judgment and to the horror of my daughter, had taken him and his son into my house.

George was now eighteen. The land took work, but David and his son were equal to it. David still did some work for a neighbor, to bring us extra money, but it was not fulltime. Biathy had left the household the year before and was working and living on a farm back in Lunenburg. It was better that way; David found his silence and occasional garbled speech and the sounds he made disconcerting, and Biathy had a habit of staring long and hard at David, as if always puzzling out who he was. What he understood I was never sure.

I had made a good decision when I bought the property, I thought. While I still coveted land along the Israel River, this would do for now until some other piece of property came up. Mr. Knight, the man who sold me this farm, kept me abreast of who bought and sold what. We had weathered the matter in Vermont, and I had pulled us out of the gossip to a new start. I was beginning to feel optimistic.

That was before I learned that Samuel Hannux had moved into the village in Lancaster.

Why it took me so long to know I can't say. My excuse is I was home and a long way from town. The news came to me from my sister, Wealthy, and Myalina. When they both paid me a visit, together, in January, I knew something was afoot. For one thing, Myalina was nursing a boy. This was no small thing. Baby Simon was now a boy of almost seven, and he had no siblings until Andrew was born the previous summer. Life had not been kind to Myalina in this way. She did not get with child easily; after the birth of Simon, she had miscarried one baby, and then could not conceive. When Andrew was born, it was as if she got her life back, and she filled out, and though her youthful beauty did not return, her cheeks were plump and pink and her dark eyes glittered again with happiness.

Wealthy looked the same as ever, though more tired. She was a rugged woman with a fierce will. Unlike Myalina or me, with my small family of three, she was Biblically prolific. She had borne a child almost every two years since Myalina in 1845. By 1871, she was the mother of 13 children, all living except for her poor boy, Thomas, who she had left behind in the cemetery in Guildhall – a tiny boy of two when he was taken by illness. Besides Simon and Andrew, she was the grandmother of Mary, who was the child of her next eldest daughter, Malinda. Malinda and Mary were living with George and Myalina in Lancaster, taking the name Gage, though in fact the child was, I knew, Luther Hartwell's handiwork. He had come to work a summer and fall before going back to Vermont. We expected he would come back to marry Malinda and claim the child, but in the meantime, they had become Gages, though that fooled no one.

The likelihood of Myalina and Wealthy appearing together, with no children in tow, was so remote that I would have burst into laughter when I saw them had I not been so worried about why they had come.

Wealthy and Myalina had a relationship based on the particulars of her being the eldest child in a huge family. She had, early as a girl, been not only expected, but needed to help with babies. Married young at sixteen to a man her senior by thirteen years, she had started bearing children when her mother was still having her last children: Flinty, Horace, Willie, Johnny, and Frederic.

Mother and daughter did not so much look alike, but they stood straight as poles in the same way. Myalina had not inherited her mother's drooping eyelid, and she was taller and handsome in a way her mother never was, but they gazed out at the world with the same power of expression and character.

Myalina was driving her mother's wagon. The two sat close together on the seat. I shook my head at the sight of them, anticipating what they had come to tell me. I wrapped a shawl around my head and shoulders and went out on the front step to greet them.

"Go holler for George to put the horse in the barn," I told Myalina after she helped her mother, with her short legs, off the high lip of the wagon.

Wealthy rushed forward.

"It is freezing," she exclaimed, pushing past me into the house.

"What has brought you out all this way?" I said, not wasting time on the weather. It was winter; what did she expect but cold?

"Plenty," she said bluntly. "I need hot tea. Where's Fanny?" she looked around the kitchen.

"She stayed the night with Mrs. Carson who has been suffering with gout and can't get out of bed," I told her.

"I can't imagine why Myalina would come all this way," I fussed, agitated that she was not telling me. I set a cup of steaming tea and a pitcher of milk and bowl of sugar on the table.

"What do you have I can eat?" she asked. "I hardly ate breakfast."

"What was the rush?"

"You'll find out soon enough."

"There's yesterday's bread and blackberry jam. Will that do?"

She nodded vigorously.

I cut a big plate of bread and put down the jar of jam, some butter and a spreading knife.

By then, Myalina had come into the room, and shed her winter garments. She came and kissed my cheek and we hugged.

"That was fast," she said to her mother.

"Help yourself," I told my niece. "I'll get you tea."

"I don't know if there is enough bread for two," Wealthy complained.

"There's enough bread for six," I muttered, cutting a few more slices and pouring cups of tea for Myalina and me.

Wealthy ate with the steady concentration of a mother who was so used to interruptions that she had learned to take advantage of any opportunity to eat her fill.

"There's no use trying to stop that," Myalina laughed.

"How are the boys?" I asked.

"Simon is gone to school today and I have left the baby with Ella." Ella was Wealthy's youngest daughter – a girl of fourteen and well used to caring for babies. She would have her hands full with her brother, Willie, and nephew, Andrew, both under two years.

"I want to show you the afghan I am making," I said, and went to get a pile of bright-colored squares I had crocheted, the building blocks of a cover for the bed.

Myalina admired my handiwork and told me about a project of her own, knitting mittens for her boys.

"Are you done?" I asked my sister, who had sat back and was daintily wiping jam from the corner of her mouth. "There is more on the other side. Not there, higher. Oh, give me the napkin!" I dipped the napkin in a bit of tea at the bottom of my cup and scrubbed vigorously at my sister's mouth.

"Enough!" she snapped when she could get her breath.

"Now tell me why you have come," I answered, tossing the cloth on the table and sitting down hard in my seat.

Myalina looked at her mother, and nodded.

"The news you need to know is that Samuel Hannux has moved into Lancaster village," Wealthy told me.

I felt the room reel around me, and my fingers got icy cold, and heat rushed across my cheeks.

Myalina came to stand behind me, her hands warm and solid on my shoulders.

"How do you know?" I croaked.

"Lucius brought home the news," Wealthy said. "He was in Lancaster to get sugar and tea. He takes any excuse to go, you know. The little store in Jefferson is not enough for him. He sat in the store warming up to go back home – that is why he goes anyway – and that was how he heard. You know how the gossip flies there, among men. It was said in passing that a man by the name of Samuel Hannux had bought a house from Horace Sheldon and his wife. It's up in the northern part of the village. And he has two children with him, a boy and a girl with the last name Kimball. Their father died, and then the mother, so he took them in. His mother is dead, Polly Hannux."

"But why would he move here?" I asked. "Why?"

Wealthy shook her head.

"We have talked and talked about why," Myalina added, her voice trailing off.

She and her mother looked uncomfortable.

"What? Tell me," I said.

"Nothing," Myalina said.

"You do know why," I said.

"No, really, Aunt, we don't know. We would tell you if we did."

I stared at them, my mind racing through possibilities, my fingers getting colder and colder.

"You think," I said slowly, "You think that it is because of me."

Their heartbeat of silence said everything, and Wealthy had pinched her lips together tightly.

"That is what we think," Myalina finally put their thoughts into words.

"He thinks he can provoke David," I burst out.

Wealthy sighed deeply.

I started to cry then. I cried in the tight, soundless, tearless way of someone who never cries. Myalina knelt by my chair and leaned her head against my knees. I cried and restlessly stroked her hair, tucking the already smooth, tight strands into the bun over and over.

"What are you going to do?" Wealthy finally asked me, when I was wiping my eyes.

"Wash your face, Aunt," Myalina said, giving me a towel she had dampened with warm water from the tea kettle. "It will feel better."

I dutifully cleaned my face, and she was right, it did feel good to clean away the distress of my crying. I handed her back the cloth, and she turned to put it on the edge of the sink.

"Maybe David will not find out," Wealthy suggested.

I stared at her in astonishment.

"Do you think he knows already?" Myalina said.

"No," I said quickly. "I am sure he doesn't know," though as soon as I said it I knew I was not sure. I began running my mind over his face at supper last night, at breakfast this morning, at the sound of his washing his face in the bowl on the nightstand, and scrubbing his hands after coming in from work each day this week. Did he know? I could not say for certain yes or no.

Wealthy eased up out of her chair. "We have to go," she said regretfully. "We have to get back."

"I wish we didn't have to leave you with this, Aunt," Myalina said. "But it will take me time to get back home and I can't miss the return stage."

"We wanted to tell you ourselves. We were afraid you would find out the wrong way," my sister said.

Myalina went out to shout for George to bring the horse around front. They struggled into coats and scarves and mittens, and hugged me in turn. Myalina took the pile of blankets warming by the stove for the return trip, and I walked out with them to see Wealthy into the wagon, and Myalina up beside her, their knees and laps tucked into the mound of blankets.

I stood outside, wrapped in my workaday shawl that was the color of the light brownish green grass in the fall, waving them on their way. I watched as they drove out of sight, and stayed a few minutes longer, staring into the empty distance before turning with resignation back to the house.

g

Chapter Ten

1861-1862

ONCE THE WAR HAD STARTED, BACK IN THE SUMMER OF 1861, IT TOOK OVER. Even though we were hundreds of miles from any fighting, and most of us had no idea of where those places were we heard about in the news or from the lips of a poor father or mother whose son had died or was injured, the war was everywhere around. Wealthy had no sons old enough. Her eldest, Lucius, named for his father, was just twelve when all of the talk turned to something real and hostilities were called and President Lincoln called for volunteers to fight. It would end quickly, that was the one certainty. If anyone thought differently, they were smart enough to keep their mouths shut. My elder sister, Fanny, who would by rights have had sons old enough, had no children by her first husband who she had married when she was sixteen. She had remarried when she was close to thirty, so her two boys were very young. Of the three of us sisters, I alone had a son of the age to volunteer for service. He did not sign up during that first push when the most zealous sprang forward, but when the three months of their service did not make a whit of difference – it was a war in name only then – Charles enlisted in the early winter of 1862, in January when he was nineteen.

"How will your father manage?" I asked him tightly that last morning at the breakfast table. Maybe I should have been proud, but I was sick with anxiety.

"How are all of the other fathers of soldiers managing?" he put to me. "This is more important than the farm or any other thing."

I could not see it. I simply did not want him to go.

It was just the two of us left at the table, scattered still with the remains of the usual big breakfast served after the barn chores were done – oatmeal, doughnuts, salt pork and milk gravy, and milk and coffee. Fanny had gone outside with her father, holding his hand, her small mitten enveloped in his big double one.

"It's done anyway," he said, referring to the fact of his enlistment almost a month ago. Now it was February and he was leaving soon. Hiram had gone to get the wagon hitched up.

Charles and I had been over it again and again until there was nothing new to add – hadn't been for weeks. I had been so sure I had convinced him to stay put, but he had come home that day in January with a jaunty confidence I had not seen since the war had started and he had seen his friends, his cousin Hollis, even one of his father's brothers, and Horace Gage all sign up in a steady rush. It was not just me holding him back but, since October 1861, his cousin, Malinda Larrabee, who had become his wife that month. She was in her first blush of beauty at fourteen, and since he had seen her the summer before, when he was helping her father hay, he had been smitten.

That was not a source of pleasure to me, even if it kept him back from volunteering.

"She is too young and you are too young. And she is your cousin," I had told him before he married. I had witnessed the moment when he saw her, coming back from the fields at dusk, and she was walking out of the barn with her mother. She was pretty, there was no getting around that. The soft light made her pale face glow. She was small and trim and newly in the curves of womanhood. He was closer in age to Myalina, but those two had always scrapped like brother and sister, and she was being courted that year by George Gage. Charles had never really paid any attention to Malinda who had seemed like a child to him.

"Why is she too young?" he protested. "You were young when you married dad and you two are cousins."

"That is exactly the point," I said. "Don't you know how we struggled? How poor we were? And he was older than you are."

"Who's said anything about marrying anyway?" he said.

I sighed with exasperation. "You should see yourself, all moonstruck by her. You don't even know her."

"Of course, I know her. She's my cousin. I have known her all my life. She's just gotten pretty, that's all."

"Have it your way," I fumed.

"What do you have against her? She's your sister's child."

"I don't have anything against her. I never said that."

51

"Well, alright then," he said, satisfied, and walked off to help his father.

Months later, in the pale February sun coming in the window, I wished I had not protested his courting Malinda. Maybe he would be a father by now and feel an obligation to stay, instead of a soldier packed and dressed to go off from me.

"You've got to get ready, Ma," he said to me. "I'll help you clear. There's no time to wash up now."

I stood up slowly, taking off my apron. "Leave it," I said. "It will all be here when I get home. It will give me something to do. I'll not have you clearing table like a woman. I am proud of you, Charles."

He wrapped his arms around me and rested his chin on the top of my head.

We all rode down in the wagon to the village where the men were gathered to leave in their ranks. He was in Company K, a private, in the 8th Vermont Volunteer Infantry. I saw them all go in a wave of motion, the crowd roaring so loud that when the men were out of sight, the silence was a terrible thing.

But Charles would make it back so I was a fortunate mother. He came back whole, other than an injury to his shoulder in Louisiana on September 4, 1862. He was allowed home, because of the partial paralysis of his right arm. His shoulder always pained him, though, when the weather was wet or the cold bit on a January day, and he never fully recovered the use of his arm where the nerves were permanently damaged. I was so grateful he had come back, so grateful. What mother would not be?

8

Chapter Eleven

HOW WE GOT THE FARM
1860

HIRAM AND I GOT OUR OWN PLACE BECAUSE OF MY DOING SOME HORSE-TRADING WITH HIS FINE BLACK HORSE. I give myself credit because it was my idea, and because I took the lead on this deal and did the paperwork since I could read and write and Hiram could not. I scoured every word of that deed agreement more than once to be sure the trade we made would stick in a way favorable to our interests. The idea may have been mine, but the reason for the trade was all Hiram.

My husband had a way with horses, and a reputation all over town for his mastery of the animals. He had always worked with his father's horses and as a young man was hired out and took the same pains with whatever beasts were under his care and some that were not. Certainly, his talent would have showed itself if we had been prosperous and he had the best bloodlines under his hand. But we were poor and he had the problem animals, the broken down, the untrainable, the abused. He would seek out these types because they would come cheap, sometimes even be given away.

In this way, he acquired the black horse. Nahum Ward was a proud man, a little haughty it seemed or maybe it was just the squint he had and the way he walked that could have been his predilection for fancy boots that might have been too tight. He never gave me nor Hiram the time of day. All that changed when the black mare he had bought at a price worthy of her lines proved too much for him. The story of his close brush with death in the stall took legs, starting with his handyman, John Somers, who brought the tale to the village store.

What happened was this: there was no doubt the mare was fine, but she was nervous and high strung and a better horse than Nahum had ever had. She was too good a horse for him. He was a small, scrunched up sort of man who thought he could never be beat by anything. The sensitive horse did not take to him, his gravelly little voice and his too-quick motions. There had been signs, a bad nip on his shoulder, rough nudging with her ears pinned back, but he claimed in his own visits to the gossip circle at the store that he would best her. He was not a mean man and did not try to hurt her, but she was just too much for him. He could not admit it. He had paid good money for her, and she was a beauty, with a fancy lineage. She was not a workhorse fit for the plow and he would hitch her to his carriage and take Mrs. Ward to church.

The dread day came. He had gone into her stall in the early Saturday morning, determined to make the trip to the village the next day in the style his missus had been expecting. Maybe he was too determined, too jumpy in his approach, but the black horse pinned him solidly against the side of the stall, pushing more and more steadily against him until he was sure he would be crushed. Luckily, John, the hired man, had come into the barn, and heard his employer's rasping breath. He provided an unwitting distraction and the horse turned from Nahum who wasted no time in clambering up the side of the stall where he tipped over into a pile of hay.

John Somers beat him to the store, but not by much and everyone in there saw Nahum storm in around midday, and announce that anyone who wanted that damn black horse of his could have it. He meant it, too, that's how bad he had been scared. He told the story, casting that animal as a work of the devil. He ranted and he raged, and when he was done, he proclaimed again, "If anyone wants her, take her."

Hiram, by some good fortune, was at the store that day. He wanted to cheer me up and took in his head to buy me a little bit of ribbon and a bag of candy – like we were courting again. It would come on me hard, still, some days, that I had lost our son two summers ago. He had been stillborn – all whole and beautiful, but not living. Mostly, I forgot, but not that morning, something about the light over the field in the morning hit me and I was crying.

Anyway, Hiram had done his purchases and was turning to go when he saw Nahum stomp up the steps.

"I decided I had better wait to see what he had to say," Hiram told me later, grinning.

When the second challenge was made, someone scoffed, "Ah, Nahum, you don't mean that. You won't be giving up that horse any time soon, not after what you paid."

Nahum turned his squinty eyes on the speaker, "I do mean it," he repeated. "But none of you will take her, will you?" He extended his chest like a rooster strutting across the yard in the midst of a flock of hens.

"You take her, Hiram," someone offered.

"Yeah," said David Kimball, Nahum's son-in-law. "You're the man to do it. You can fix up that horse."

Hiram at first laughed, thinking the whole affair was a joke. What man would pay good money for a fine horse and then give it away? Like most everyone in Lunenburg, he had seen that black mare – her height, her conformation, her expressive eyes, and her spirit. If Nahum had not been such a proud man, he would have gone to Hiram for advice on how to handle her, how to train her for pulling and the easy ride to church.

"See, even the horse expert of Lunenburg knows better than to take on my mare," Nahum boasted.

This was too much for my husband. He had an even temper, and was never prone to get excited, but that comment made with so much surety, goaded him.

"Alright," he said. And had the satisfaction of the room going still. "Alright. If your offer is sound, if you mean it, I will take the black horse and she will be mine."

"Ah-ha!" Nahum chortled. "A taker at last. Come and get her and she is yours."

"But if I do, she is mine," Hiram said. "Do I have your word?"

"My word, my word, if that is what you want, you can have it. Hear me, everyone," Nahum said to the cluster of eight or nine men, and Mrs. Dodge who was buying fabric for a dress. "This man wants my word and he has it. The black horse is his if he comes and gets her."

Hiram did not waste any time. He stowed the candy and ribbon deep in an inside pocket of his coat, and he and Nahum Ward marched publicly, single file, with Nahum in the lead, to the steady chestnut horse pulling Nahum's wagon and rode with him to his farm. Hiram told me how he walked without hesitation into the barn and went to the stall, and gentled that fine black horse, explaining to her the situation and how he would borrow this halter and lead rope and they would walk all of the way, all of the four miles, to another farm where she would be happy.

When Hiram appeared – hours after the cows had been milked by Charles, and long after supper had dried in its dishes and been covered and put away by me, grumbling all the while – he was calmly leading the fine black horse. My eyes were likely to pop out of my head, I thought.

After he told me the story, much to my delight, with Fanny and Charles and Biathy gathered round, all agog, and even remembered to give me the candy and bit of ribbon, I was cheered up, to say the least.

"So what will you do with the horse?" I asked.

"Are we going to keep it, Pa?" Fanny queried.

"I am going to do with it just as Nahum Ward intended," Hiram said. "He wanted a carriage horse and that is what she is going to be."

I furrowed my brow. "We don't have a carriage," I said tentatively.

He grinned. "No, we don't. But I intend to get a broken-down one from someone I know who has one and will sell it cheap and I can fix it up."

"It will cost money to keep this horse," I said.

"I don't intend on keeping her," he told me. "I'm going to train her and then I'm going to sell her. People in the whole town will be keeping an eye on this horse and what I do with her. I want people interested, and I want people guessing, so you kids stay close-mouthed about her. She'll be sold, alright, for a good price, too, maybe twenty-five dollars, maybe thirty."

That was a good deal of money for us; even taking into account the feed and the broken down carriage, we would come out ahead.

Hiram did just as he said he would do. He bought the soured carriage from Mr. Pratt – the man and his wife had met misfortune on the road coming from Concord one Sunday afternoon when the left-hand wheel hit a rock that had rolled down a clay bank into the road. It bounced up and hit the horse's front leg, scaring the animal so badly that it reared up. This action threw off the vehicle so suddenly that Mr. Pratt, who was not a young man, lost his grip on the reins as he tumbled against his wife. The horse had been on a fast course down the incline and, free of control, rushed ahead, missed the corner and went into the woods, trying to navigate a stonewall. The Pratts toppled out like cordwood from a cart, and the carriage cracked up. Mrs. Pratt suffered a broken leg, and he dislocated his shoulder. He was glad to get rid of the carriage with its bad memories for a few dollars I had stored up for some emergency. I reckoned this was an investment that would reward us.

I noticed that men started stopping by the barn to see Hiram. We did not live on the road to Victory back then, but on a rented farm on the Guildhall border. It was a stretch to say we lived on the way to Guildhall, because we were nearly a mile off that road, on a side hill road, but the men who stopped often made the claim of being on the way to or from Guildhall. Men came from Guildhall, too, claiming to be on the way to or from Lunenburg. It was early spring, just after the mud had dried on the roads, time for preparing the fields and thinking of planting, though it was too early for that, so the farmers had work at home, but that did not stop them from visiting Hiram. He did not have to go to the store to be quizzed about the progress with the black horse.

Men came from miles around every afternoon when the weather was fine to watch Hiram work in the distant field with the black horse. They were not allowed close to avoid spooking the animal, but far away within sight was better than not seeing this exercise with what was once Nahum Ward's property. He was conspicuously absent, of course.

"Oh, he's mad," Hiram told me, his eyes showing his amusement. "He hardly comes to the village and when he does, he has nothing to say to anyone except, 'I need a box of tea,' at the shop, or 'I've come for my letters,' to the postmaster. He hardly says, 'How do,' anymore."

Hiram did the exercises in the field for show. The real work he did very early in the morning in the yard by the barn, and late in the day at dusk when there was no crowd of spectators. For weeks, he gentled that horse, easing her into the workings of the carriage.

"She's coming good," he announced to me daily. I watched him the first time with my breath held as he eased the carriage and the fine black horse out onto the road by our house. Each day they went a little further. Our neighbor, Mr. Symons, knew what went on, and he took the word to the village with witness accounts of the early morning and dusk proceedings.

After the reported successful trip in the carriage up the road past Mr. Symons' place, a man by the name of Rose, a merchant in Guildhall, came the next day to see Hiram. He wanted that black horse, he said. He would pay $50 for her.

Hiram was cautious, "I don't know if I aim to sell."

Mr. Rose pressed him, and promised to call again. "Promise me you won't sell the horse without giving me a chance," he said.

That much Hiram was willing to say.

Mr. Rose beat Nahum Ward by one day. Mr. Ward arrived at the door when I was cleaning spinach for supper. I always looked forward to the time from early into late summer when the spinach burst all green against the dark loam, and I would go out with my shears and cut us a mess of leaves. I steamed them and served them with butter and vinegar.

I was concentrating on getting all of the grit out of the leaves when Mr. Ward knocked on the front door. There is nothing worse than grit in cooked greens, so every mouthful has an unpleasant gravelly crunch. To avoid this I submerged them in a big pot of water and swished them around like laundry. Then I dumped the dirty water and cleaned out the pot, and refilled it. I did this over and over until there was no sand in the bottom of the pot.

When the interruption came, I grumbled.

"Go and open the door, Fanny."

Fanny was almost six years old, precise and helpful already, and she hurried importantly to open the door.

Mr. Ward looked down at the small girl.

"I am looking for your father," he said in his gravelly voice.

"Good day, sir," I heard Fanny pipe. "My mother is in the kitchen."

"I don't," he started to say, but he had no choice but to follow her determined form as it had quickly turned and was leading the guest to me.

I sighed, wiping my wet hands on my apron as I went from the sink to greet whoever it was had come.

I did not let the surprise and elation show when I saw it was Nahum Ward.

"Good day, Mr. Ward," I said. "I expect you are looking for my husband."

He nodded brusquely to me, his hat in his hands like the collection plate at church in the hands of the usher.

"He is out with the black horse," I said.

"Then I'll be off to the barn. I can find him myself."

"He is not in the barn. He is out for a carriage ride on the road," I said grandly, aware of the impression my words would create.

He goggled at me, his squint deepening.

"You are welcome to wait in the parlor," I offered. "I will bring you a cup of tea."

"I would rather wait outside," he said.

"He will be awhile," I said. "They go for quite a ride, you see, he and the black horse and carriage. You will get sunstroke."

His squint grew worse and he harrumphed, clearing his throat and pulling out his large white handkerchief and loudly blowing his nose.

When he was done, he had mastered himself. He was not foolish enough to risk his health sitting outside in the heat of the day.

I led him from the kitchen into what I called the parlor, a room we almost never used and just kept dusted and polished and scrubbed for an occasion such as this. I directed him, kindly, I thought, to a chair with a view out the window so he could see the arrival of the black horse hitched to the carriage. He was not disappointed at the sight, and I certainly was not, refilling his tea cup in my best hostess manner while I watched his face go crimson watching his once-problematical horse gracefully sweeping down the road from the direction of Mr. Symons.

He retained enough possession of himself to thank me for the tea and then he went out to talk to Hiram.

I stayed inside, not because I wanted to, but because I thought it better to let events transpire without me. I knew Hiram would give me a full report once Nahum was safely on the road back to the village.

"He marched out across that yard from the house like he owned the place," Hiram told me. "I knew he was coming because I know his chestnut horse, and there it was tied to the post in our driveway. I waited for him, to be truthful, at the head of my horse, for him to arrive. He was leaning forward, walking so fast as if going into a gale," he chuckled.

"I want that horse," Nahum told my husband, without so much as a hello or good day.

Hiram had this quality, that made him good with animals, of remaining silent until things settled down.

"That is my horse. I never meant to give it up," Nahum said. "I was forced into it by you and those men in Cutting's store. You should have known it was too good a horse to be free. Now you see what a good horse it is, you should buy it from me. That horse is worth more than one hundred dollars. If you don't have it and I don't guess you do, give it back to me. I will sue you to get that horse."

Hiram still did not utter a word and he kept his face down so his hat brim concealed his features. Nahum did not know if Hiram's lips twitched or his jaw tightened or his eyes flashed.

"Do you hear me?" he finally roared, straining his rough voice.

"Oh, I can hear you," Hiram said.

"Well, then?" Nahum said.

"Well, what?" Hiram said.

"Do you intend to hand over that horse to me or do I get my lawyer or the sheriff to come here?"

"You could pay me for the horse," Hiram suggested. "Since it is my horse now fair and square as every man in that store will testify, you could pay me for her. She's worth more now than when you gave her to me. I have already had an offer of fifty dollars."

Nahum looked to explode. His watery blue eyes expanded out of their squint and his cheeks were the red of an overripe cherry.

"That is my horse, my horse," he panted. "If you sell that horse, I'll make you sorry. You're a rascal. That's what you are."

When he stopped, Hiram waited and waited and waited.

Finally, Nahum choked out the words, "I will pay you sixty dollars for that horse, and not a penny more."

Hiram considered this. "I will let you know. I gave the other fellow the right of refusal if I get other offers and now I have yours."

Nahum, defeated and outmatched, fairly ran to his horse and wagon, shouting at the horse, and waving his whip in the air as he sped from our yard onto the road to the village.

All of this set me to thinking. Hiram had already had two offers for this horse that was now fit for the carriage.

"What do you intend to do?" I asked him.

"I think I'll just bide my time. I think you and I might take a ride into the village some afternoon, tomorrow if the day is fair."

I was aquiver with excitement at the notion of my riding into the center of town in a carriage pulled by the fine black horse. I woke earlier than usual, about 4:30 am, just before the daylight, when only a bird or two peeped. Hiram was already up, out to the barn. I washed my face and combed my hair out of its braids into a bun, and dressed, and went to the kitchen to start the fire in the range for breakfast. It was a beautiful morning, sign of a beautiful day. The sun had topped the trees on the far side of the ridge, and the sky was a light blue promising a spell of good weather. I set to making a pan of muffins, getting down the bowl that was a wedding present. It was heavy mustard yellow pottery, with a handsome raised rim and a perfect glaze. I used it for the dough for my bread, the batter for muffins, cakes, doughnuts and biscuits. It was in a safe place and no one ever used it but me. We did not have many things; this was one of the best and I prized it.

Charles appeared, banging the shed door as usual. I winced, as usual. It was no use always telling him to not slam the door because he listened attentively and promised to do better, but something about that shed door led him to always give it a solid thud so wood hit wood like a shotgun blast.

His hair stood up on end, and his white shirt was buttoned wrong so one side of the collar stood up higher than the other. He was so big, so grown up – almost a man.

"Can I go, too?" he asked.

"You shirt is buttoned wrong."

"I was hoping I could go. You can't leave Fanny and Biathy alone so does that mean we all go?"

"Button your shirt right," I said.

"So can I?" he asked, his voice muffled as he concentrated on undoing and redoing his shirtfront.

"Your Pa and I haven't even decided yet if we're going."

"Oh, he said you were, since the day is fine."

"We'll see," I told him.

"Oh, Ma."

"The point of the ride is to help us sell the horse for as much as we can," I told him. "It's not for larking about town."

His face fell. "I could help sell the horse," he said in a small voice.

I never could resist Charles for long.

"If Mrs. Symons' girls will watch Fanny and Biathy, you can go," I said.

"Good!" he exclaimed, his eyes brightening again.

This set Fanny to crying. "I want to go, too! Why should I stay home if he can go?"

"I'm the eldest. You're…" Charles began to taunt.

I cut Charles off before he could add fat to the fire by calling his sister a baby.

"Enough!" I said in my stern voice. "You be quiet," I told Charles. "And you stop crying," I told Fanny. "Your Pa and I will have to decide what is best. Charles, you stay here with your brother and sister, and start dishing up oatmeal."

I went out through the shed, closing the door carefully behind me as my usual example of the way it could be done for Charles to hear, though I doubted he was listening, judging by the ringing of the ladle as he clanged it against the edge of the pot of cereal.

I found Hiram in the barn, finishing forking some hay to the horse.

"It's a good day," he said.

"I see. How do we want to do this? Charles wants to go, and now Fanny does. But if the point is to help sell the horse, maybe they should stay. Or Mrs. Symons might watch the younger ones. Charles really wants to go and he has been helping a lot around here since you're been working with Blackie."

Hiram had refused to let me name the horse. I wanted a grand name like Ebony or Dark Fire. Nahum had called her Naomi – a puzzle to me. Hiram did not give her a name nor did he call her Naomi, a foolish handle, he clearly thought. I called her Blackie, reasoning it was not really a name since it was just her color.

"I think we should all go," he said. "I have been studying the matter. If the family rides to the town in the carriage it will add value since that means I trust her with my children and with you."

I nodded, "We will dress nice, not Sunday best, but go-to-the-village-on-a-weekday nice. Come in for breakfast now."

Once breakfast was eaten, I cleared the table and washed the dishes, with Fanny drying. Then I went to work getting everyone ready for the trip to the village. Hiram got Fanny and Biathy settled in the back, with Charles in the middle to keep an eye on them. I sat up front with Hiram, and we were off on the mile trip to the road that led into the town. We were a family at leisure on a slow ride and not one pair of female eyes that saw us did not report it to those who had not. And not one set of male eyes did not covet that fine, black horse so easily and gracefully pulling the carriage of the Presbrey family.

g

Chapter Twelve

OUR OWN PLACE
1860

THERE ARE CERTAIN KEYS WHEN I LOOK BACK AT MY LIFE. The fire was one, and so was the black horse. While the first was an instrument I had no control over, the second became a tool like a chisel that carves a rock out of the side of the mountain or the mill saw that splits the felled tree into boards. Out of those things comes a foundation, a shelter. So it was with Hiram's horse. He saw the potential in a short-term way – some extra dollars that would make the winter easier with cash for foodstuff we did not raise and for items we considered a wish not a need – some cloth for a new dress for Fanny or me, and shirts for the boys and Hiram, or a new pair of boots. I saw the potential in the long term, as clear to me as the reflection in Neal's Pond in early evening when the water goes still and smooth as a glass so the trees on the far shore are duplicated exactly, though in reverse. With the offer of $60 before us from the man who had so foolishly boasted her away, a plan began to percolate in my mind.

One of the men who saw us the day we rode into town was Ira Douglass. He lived in Guildhall, and was on his way back from Lunenburg the morning we were going there. We met on the smooth stretch of road just out of view of the Connecticut River. Upon seeing us, he slowed his horse – a chestnut with good lines and a jaunty step – as Hiram slowed Blackie. We passed one another carefully, the man tipping his hat to me.

"Good day," he saluted us, drawing up on the reins so his horse stopped.

"Good day," Hiram replied, and I nodded with a smile.

We were then carriage to carriage, each going a different way, but able to converse.

"That is a beautiful animal," Mr. Douglass said.

Hiram acknowledged the remark.

"I have heard about your training," the man said.

"News travels far," Hiram observed.

"Where are you headed?"

"To the village," I told him.

"I have been admiring her gaits."

"She is a pleasure to drive," Hiram said.

"Do you ever drive her, m'am?" he asked me.

"I have not yet," I told him honestly, "but I am sure I could. Hiram does the driving, in our family."

"You have a good-looking family," he nodded, peering as he spoke into the darker reaches of the back of the carriage.

"Thank you," I said. "It is my son Charles, and Fanny and little Biathy."

The thoughts of Mr. Douglass were as transparent as the path of a light summer cloud across the sky. He was interested in the horse, he had noted the characteristics she possessed, and seen our whole family relaxed in the carriage.

My thoughts were not transparent. I kept my smile light and pleasant, the smile of a woman on a rare outing on a warm day with the breeze coming across the meadows where some sheep grazed. In my mind, though, I was doing sums and calculating returns. Ira Douglass owned land in Lunenburg, not far from where we rented. I knew this because it had once belonged to Hiram's younger brother, Leroy, who had died not long after he bought it, and I knew the property had been sold to this man from Guildhall.

Mr. Douglass was a polite man, small and dapper, with a trim suit and a perfectly knotted tie. He had small, clean hands, very pale, and they held the reins loosely.

"If you intend to sell the horse and carriage, I will pay you seventy-five dollars cash," he said.

I was afraid he would hear my heart pounding to hear this amount of money presented, but I kept my mouth shut. I had a scheme formulating.

"We do aim to sell," Hiram said, "Once I feel she is ready."

"You let me know, will you, when the time is come, and keep my offer in mind," Mr. Douglass countered. "Good day to you all," he said in farewell, and we all passed on to our respective destinations.

Coming into town about a half-hour later, Blackie was in good form still, taking us at an easy walk, negotiating the road and calmly passing other vehicles – a wagon loaded with bark, and a horse and carriage driven by the doctor. We crested the long hill into the village about ten o'clock, the back seat almost trembling with the suppressed excitement of Charles and Fanny from the ride, their sense of being the actors in a play, and the proximity to the bustle of the town.

Lunenburg village was built cleverly on a geographically challenging bit of ground. It is at a place where four roads converge. To the east and west, the roads dip down to a noticeable degree, and also to the south. But to the north, the road to Victory, past Neal's Pond, the road goes steeply uphill, with some level stretches, but climbs and climbs to Mount Tug, way up where there are views of the mountains.

The terrain in the village is so challenging that there is only one level surface, on the road between Guildhall and Concord, and so the green is on a hill. The big, grassy square starts on the low side and rises on the slope. When you are on the main road, you look up to the Congregational Church – an awe-inspiring sight even if you are not a Congregationalist as I am not, because it is a large, white clapboard structure with two front doors spaced for beauty and a high steeple and stained glass windows. It would be big even if it were not at the head of a long, grassy incline. Next to it is the town hall, a simply made workaday building with the front facing the green and the long hall to the back. Like the church, it is on a foundation of enormous granite blocks and the many windows are far above eye level, even for a tall man. It was built in 1849, with an imposing series of stone steps, brought in by oxen, that lead onto the porch. As if done that way deliberately, the simple town hall for the business of men contrasts sharply with the grand church for the business of God.

On the far left of the church, within view of the steps, is the cemetery where my uncle and aunt, Elisha and Hannah Presbrey, are buried – the prosperous members of the family. He owned a sawmill and rich farmland along the river. Of their meager family of two children, the boy had died young, leaving only a daughter.

Hiram and I had been poor. We had ended up that way, and he had worked us mostly out of it, with my help, but we were still renters of farms. We could not ever seem to accumulate enough money to buy our own. Hiram and I had married when I was very young, just sixteen. Although he was well into manhood at twenty-four, he had been working as a laborer for farmers. The little amount of money he earned in addition to the room and board never seemed to be something he could hold onto. His father had no resources to offer him help to get started. There were too many children in that family, too many boys.

We were married in Lyman in the summer of 1842 and Charles was born in October of 1843. One baby died, a miscarriage in my fourth month. It was not easy for us to live on what he made as a laborer. We rented a small house on a poor piece of land, where I kept a garden and some hens and we managed to get a cow.

My father had died in 1839, leaving my sister, Wealthy, and me to the care of our brother Abiather. My mother remarried, but she did not take us with her and we did not want to go anyway. We felt we would soon be old enough to fend for ourselves, with the husbands we would have soon enough.

Wealthy married a few years after me, but she did not stay near where we had been living in Lyman and Lisbon. When she was fourteen, my older sister, Fanny, had gone to work in Lowell, Massachusetts, an unimaginable city, in the textile mills. There were distant cousins in that place, some of the Presbreys who never left Massachusetts. She left before our father died, and she returned north only to marry a man in 1837 by the name of Asa Harradon. He was from a family she had known when we lived in Shrewsbury. She wrote us of her marriage that took place in the village of Woodstock, Vermont, a day's journey from Shrewsbury. He had come to meet her there, and took her home.

By the time of my marriage, I was accustomed to not having Fanny nearby and besides, she was enough older that I was always a baby to her and we were not close. But Wealthy and I were close. Even though I was a year older, I depended on her as much as she did me. We were like mirrors of one another, wanting the same things and feeling things in the same way. She would come and stay with Hiram and me, looking after baby Charles, and helping me in the times of my pregnancies that did not produce a living child.

When she married in 1844, she left with her husband on a journey of several days that took them to his birthplace in northern Vermont, near the Canadian line, in Derby and Salem.

That left me to manage the best I could with a young child, and continuing poor health and a sickness in my mind that came from never carrying a child to life in this world. My brother, Abiather, was not having an easy time of it, either. He worked, like Hiram, for other farmers, and had a wife and child to support. For a time, we all lived in the house Abiather had taken on when our father died, trying to pool our resources to get ahead. But we never could.

It was a puzzle to me why we could not since my father had always owned land. There had never been a time when he was poor and without his own farm. I had thought about this a great deal and decided my father had kept turning over the property he owned for, I thought, a profit, even if small, and so he never kept land that was worked out, but bought what needed to be improved. Yet my prosperous relatives had found a farm and stayed put, and that had been the source of what seemed like great wealth to me. Of course, they had been able to afford river land, which could not be compared to the rock-strewn, rough-cleared land of the hills that even my father had been restricted to purchase by his financial state.

In 1850, when I was twenty-four and Hiram was thirty-two, we hit rock bottom. He caught his foot in the loose harness of a horse pulling a mower, trying to control the animal after it broke open a nest of ground wasps. He was dragged a distance, and tore muscles in his thigh so badly he could not work. It took our cash reserve to pay a doctor and then to pay other bills since no money was coming in. My brother had bought his own farm in Lyman by then, but could not earn enough for all of us, and we ended up in the horrible shame of the poor who are in such straits they go onto the paupers' list. You cannot imagine it if you have not experienced it, but maybe you can try. I felt such shame that I could not even go beyond the ragged patch of grass that met the road. Abiather lost the farm, and Hiram and I ended up in the shabbiest house we had ever known, little better than a shed.

"We have to move," I told Hiram, after a few months.

He looked at me in astonishment.

"We have to go across the river into Vermont," I said.

༒

Chapter Thirteen

1852

CROSSING THE BIG RIVER

I F THE FIRE AND THE HORSE ARE TWO KEYS IN MY LIFE, THEN GEOGRA-
PHY IS A THIRD. To live anywhere along the boundaries of the Connecticut River was to experience a freedom of imagination lacking in the
land-locked towns. I was accustomed to the hill country chosen by my
father and so also chosen by Hiram and me. The river is wide and deep,
carving a long trail from northern New Hampshire through to the seaway
south in Connecticut. It slices the land in two, with that which belongs to
Vermont on the west and to New Hampshire on the east. All of the towns
that nudge its banks take on a dual life because of the ability to see across
the waters to another state. Lyman and Lisbon and Bath in New Hampshire and Shrewsbury and Mount Holly in Vermont – the places my father made a home for us – were not like that. You could, in spots of high
ground where the trees were cleared, see across a valley to the smoke of
a distant farm's chimney, and you could often see the far-off mountains,
but that is a different kind of imagination since unless you are a bird you
cannot fly there. I was used to mountains and back-country farms, but
I had an inkling of the power of the river from travelling along its banks
as a girl coming from Vermont with my family. I was only four years old,
but that trip's imprint is indelible, unless I should lose my mind, which I
don't plan on doing. I had never seen such a vastness. It was spring when
we came, so the water was high, swelling up over the banks in low-lying
fields to cover them with a shimmering sea. We had crossed the covered
bridge at Wells River, passing over to Haverhill and then north to Lisbon.
"Almost home," my father said when we waited our turn at the Vermont
end of the bridge. It was a long tunnel, I remembered, and I walked
holding my mother's hand that was clammy with her own apprehension.
I could see nothing of the river below and she only thought of moving

quickly to reach the lighted land on the other side. I hollered when I realized I would not be allowed to see, and my father came back and lifted me on his shoulders and we strode through the remainder of the planked way, pausing at each opening so I could look first far down the river from where we had come, at the green, deep, swiftly flowing water between the acorn-brown fields overturned for planting, and I could look north to the straining water headed for the dark underside of the bridge and under me. That was my early sense of the river as something vast that could yet be crossed. Since that time I had never seen it again. I knew some of our relatives lived in Vermont, and I could imagine how they had gone. Even my sisters, Fanny first, and then Wealthy, had traveled over. When I said to Hiram that day, "We will move to Vermont," I knew quite firmly that it could be done by us.

He was not convinced. This was strange since he had made the same journey I had forwards and in reverse since his father had settled in Lunenburg when Hiram was a boy. Hiram should have known the power of a river crossing, but he did not. To him, having grown up so close to the river and to the bridge across to Lancaster, the proximity was nothing remarkable. His father had made a move as a family man, and Hiram had gone back and forth to see family (including me) and, when he was old enough, to work.

"What would that gain us?" he asked doubtfully.

"It will be more opportunity," I said. "People will know us because of your father and mother and sisters and brothers, and our rich uncle and aunt, but they will not know of our poverty and how we have been on the paupers' list."

He looked very unconvinced. "Everybody knows everything," he said. "The towns are just across the river from each other."

I was stubborn, setting my jaw in the way he had come to know well over the more than twenty years we had known each other.

Don't forget we were cousins, first cousins. Our fathers had grown up together with the same father and mother, and brothers and sisters. And even though he was much older than me, we had known each other from when we were children. We knew each other in the way that family knows each other. We had seen with our own eyes the disappointments, the tears, and the unexpected windfalls of our families.

"I have known you since you were a mewling baby," he liked to tell me, though this was not true.

"I have known you when you were still in short pants," I retorted, which was true and usually stopped the conversation.

"Why do you think it will be any better?" he asked me about Vermont.

"Can't your father help us find a farm we can rent? A better place than we have now. He would know who to ask. That is our trouble over here. We don't have anyone behind us."

"He wouldn't give us any money," he said.

"I know that. I don't mean that. But he knows our troubles, so wouldn't he want to help us get a new start? You're healthy now."

Hiram studied the kitchen floor, scuffing the toes of his boots.

"At least ask him."

When Hiram came back that evening from his job, he agreed that it would do no harm to ask his father. On Sunday afternoon, his only hours off from his work as a laborer just over the border in Bath, he stood over me as I wrote down his words in a letter to his father.

Hiram had never learned to write. He could read a little, but never learned his letters. This was not an uncommon condition among the people we knew. I was his scribe.

"Dear Father," he said, and I wrote, sometimes his words tumbling out too fast for me to write down and sometimes so slow I paused and twisted the pencil in my fingers. "I would like to make a new start in Lunenburg. I want to bring my wife, Emeline, and my boy, Charles. You know the neighbors, so I am writing to ask that you help me find a farm for us to rent. You know we have had hard times here. I believe Vermont would be kinder to us. Your son, Hiram."

I addressed the envelope, and sealed the piece of paper into it. The next day, Hiram stuffed it in his pants pocket and took it to the post office in Lyman to mail. Then we waited. No letter came. A week went by, and two and three. The waiting took on a shape of its own, and I began to despair.

It was a Monday, seven o'clock in the morning, and Hiram long gone to work, on a summer day so hot the little house held onto the heat. It was one of those rare days when you go to bed hot and try to sleep in a hot knot of stickiness, and wake up hot. Charles was getting on my nerves, running a stick up and down the gaping boards of the woodshed. The windows in the kitchen were all open, and I was making bread. It was too hot to make bread, but we did not have much left so there was nothing else for it but to soldier on, pounding and kneading the dough, the flour in soft clouds, while I sweated. I was just getting ready to put my head out the window and holler at him to stop what he was doing and do something useful, like water the garden before the full heat of the day, when I was distracted by a sound from the front road.

"Go and find out what is going on," I ordered Charles.

A matter of a few seconds later, he burst into the kitchen. "It's Grandpa."

"Oh, Lord," I sighed. And Hiram not home. I had no time to more than set the dough in the bowl under a towel, when I saw my uncle pass by the window.

"Emeline," he called. "Hello, are you home, Emeline?"

"I'm in here," I replied, meeting him in the passage to the kitchen door.

"Hot day," he said. "Already hot. I should be home haying. Those boys don't work as hard when I'm not there."

"Do you want… I have a jug of water cooling in the stream."

"No time, Emeline. Where is that boy of mine?"

"You should at least have a glass of water in this heat," I said. It was a strange feeling, playing hostess to my uncle. It made me feel like I was playing at being grown up. He had never been in any of my kitchens. This was a shabby one, with the floor soft in places from dry rot and tilting badly downwards from rotten sills. I remembered the time I had been in his wife's large, clean, organized kitchen with the windows looking out across her flower garden.

"Run and fetch the jug," I told Charles.

"It's hotter in here than outdoors," my uncle grumbled.

"I will take a chair and you can sit under the tree," I said.

He would have argued, but I pushed past him with one of the kitchen chairs. By the time he was seated, mopping his brow with his large white handkerchief, Charles had come with the jug and I sent him to the kitchen for a glass. Please let it be clean, I thought.

"Hiram is at work," I told him, pouring him a cool glass of water.

"No good," he said. "I can't wait. I have to get back to the haying. He never said in the letter he was working."

That was true, an oversight.

"He's in Bath at the Cone's farm. Everybody's haying."

"That doesn't do me any good at all. I came to tell him about the farm I have found for him to rent. There are two other people who will take it if he doesn't. I don't have time to wait. A wasted trip."

"Tell me," I said.

"What on earth good would that do?" he said.

"I can tell Hiram what you have to say about it."

"That would be useless," he said. "A report on the kitchen and the number of bedrooms in the house and the size of the parlor will do him no good at all."

I gazed at him in disgust. I bit back all I wanted to say, which would have come out rude however careful I was with my words. I took a deep breath to steady myself. We could not lose out on this chance.

"Tell me about it," I said. "Not the house, but how many acres and how many are already fields and is the land rocky and how will we get through the winter if we are so late in the season moving to this farm? And how much is the rent and where is it and why is it being put for rent in the summer?"

My uncle gaped at me, then his gaze grew sharp as he studied me.

"I should not forget who your father was," he said, the closest to a compliment he would ever give me.

"The man died," he explained. "It was sudden, an apoplectic stroke in the heat two weeks ago when he was out in the field. There is corn in, and grain, and a big garden of vegetables. There are fruit trees, and a good enough barn with one cow. There is a spring that is still flowing. The house is all right enough, too, solid and I would be no judge of the kitchen even if I had seen it, but the wife managed. He was not a young man and his wife has already gone to live with her daughter. The family wants someone who can farm to take it over now and finish out the season and they can stay the winter, too, all of the winter, while the kin figure out what to do with it. They might sell it or rent it, or maybe one of them will move to it. The rent is thirty dollars a year, and if I vouch for Hiram you will not have to pay any money up front. It's near the Guildhall border, up the hill from the Lunenburg-Guildhall road. It will do well enough for you, get you going again. I know it has not been easy." That last was said kindly, and he patted my knee. I was sitting by then in a chair Charles had brought me.

"We'll take it," I said.

He looked at me hard. Then he nodded and, handing me the empty glass, stood up, easing out his back with a long groan.

"I'll be back Wednesday with the wagon. You be packed up and ready." He waited, as if for my protest of not enough time.

"Alright," I said. "We will be ready."

And so we were. None of the furniture in the rented house except two chairs and the bed was ours. I packed up my kitchen tools, and my prized bowl, and our clothes and bed linens and towels, and my few personal items. When my uncle arrived Wednesday morning at six o'clock in the morning, everything going with us was in the side yard. In less than a half hour the wagon was loaded, and Hiram and Charles and I set off with his father for Lunenburg.

When we crossed the bridge, I walked alongside the wagon, though I could have ridden, and Charles raced ahead, going from side by side to look down into the river. I walked calmly, but my heart was racing and I made sure I, too, looked in both directions to see the waters of the big river slicing between the shores of New Hampshire and Vermont.

g̃

Chapter Fourteen

1860

THE FIRST LEG TO VICTORY

PICTURE US ON THE DAY EIGHT YEARS FROM OUR HUMBLE START ON THE RENTED FARM, WHEN WE WERE SETTLED, NOT ON THE FARM WHERE WE ORIGINALLY WENT — THAT HAD BEEN SOLD — BUT ON A NEAR-BY PIECE OF RENTED LAND CLOSER TO THE MAIN ROAD GOING BETWEEN THE TWO TOWNS, GUILDHALL AND LUNENBURG. Picture us after all of the hard times in New Hampshire, feeling like they were well behind us, and though we still had no farm of our own, we were at least not living on the edge of poverty. Of course, we had never had a carriage. And this was a fancy one, suited for a prosperous merchant or a doctor or the wealthy farmer who had wrecked it. It was painted black and very shiny from all of the polishing Hiram had set Charles to do. It was suited for our one horse, with a padded seat filled with horse hair that seated the three chil-dren comfortably. If I had wanted to sit there, to be driven by Hiram, one of the children would have had to be seated on my lap, but I had chosen to sit up with my husband on the high seat, while he handily guided the horse with his ever-sure touch and the firm, and sometimes gentle, tones of his voice that told Blackie to speed up when she lagged or to slow when she threatened to move too quickly.

The ride to town on that clear morning in May, just as the hint of summer was warming the hours from evening to before dawn, was one of the high points of my life. The rhythm of the horse's hooves on the dirt road and the pull of her strong body in the harness between the shafts made a combination of sound and movement that settled into me. We were five miles from the village, and so I settled in for the one-and-a-half hour trip.

As we rocked gently in the carriage we could see every detail at our leisure, as the horse went between a walk and sometimes a slow trot. We could see the individual leaves on the trees that bent low to the road, and we could see the sheep in a pasture chewing the grass with steady persistence. I could count the stones on the walls we passed if I so chose, and watch the heavy motion of the water we kept pace with by the river. I could see over to New Hampshire to the mountain ranges, looking the color of slate in the heat of the day. I could wave at the farm ladies and their daughters hanging out wash, and inspect their hens stalking bugs in the yards. The farmhouses along the river were surrounded by level fields, and in the distance, we could see a team of horses pulling a mower. Blackie whinnied loudly when she sighted them, and broke into a trot that Hiram pulled her back from after a short burst.

This carriage ride was so different from the wagon we always traveled in, that seemed so heavy and plodding. We were not going any faster, but it was so elegant I felt like I was. This was more like walking, unburdened, on a day with no cares except to pick a few field flowers for the glass jar on the kitchen table that once held pickles and would again before the end of the season.

We stopped in a meadow at the edge of an apple orchard for a picnic lunch of chicken, boiled eggs, and filled cookies with my blackberry jam – the last jar from last year. The river was in the distance, and we had spread a blanket in the shade. We didn't linger, eager to be in town.

I felt like I could have ridden forever that day. But all at once we were climbing the last hill before the village, and Blackie hit a quick trot to get her up there faster. I could see the top of the Congregational Church steeple and the backs of the houses, with the clutter of sheds trailing un-evenly into their back gardens of vegetables and henhouses and pig sties. I spotted the minister's black-spotted pigs, a pair snuffling in the dark ground in their enclosure.

"Here we are," Hiram announced. "I am going to take us around the green."

And so he did, turning neatly at the corner and climbing the slope past the Methodist Episcopal Church, on the east side of the green, up to the level street that he led us on so we could wave at the men seated on the steps of the hall and get a close view of the stained glass windows of the church. Another wide, easy turn and we were past the school and the cemetery and down the hill to turn right back onto the main road and hence to Cutting's store, a short way down the steep street that headed out of the village to Concord.

If ever there was a moment when the Presbrey family gloried, it was that day.

Hiram guided the horse to the front of the store and everyone in the store scrambled out to see us and greet us. Mr. Freeman, and Mary Phelps, and Augustus, and Norman Hicks, and even the younger Mr. Cutting and the boy who helped him in the store – all of them lined up across the porch to get a look.

There was a hubbub of excitement, and voices calling all at once. Hiram got down from the seat and passed the reins to Mr. Cutting who had come down off the porch first to inspect the horse. While he held the mare in place, Hiram helped me down, putting his square, rough hands around my small waist and swinging me gently until my feet were firmly on the ground. Charles was helping Fanny, taking her hand so she could step from the carriage, and then guiding down Biathy who fairly leaped out head first in his excitement.

Men tipped their hats to me, and Mary came to press my hand. I knew who she was, but had never spoken with her before. She was a Congregationalist and I was brought up Methodist Episcopalian, or we might have met.

In a moment, I was forgotten, except by her, and the men surrounded Hiram and the horse and carriage. Since that was why we had come, I did not mind, and we women and the young children (Charles had stayed close to his father) sat on the bench on the porch and watched for awhile. Other men seemed to come from nowhere, easing from the sawmill next door and the gristmill a little further down the hill. The blacksmith arrived, leaving his shop near the store, and men came from the starch factory. I saw the doctor hurry from his office entrance, trailed by a patient struggling to pull on his jacket.

"You have drawn quite a crowd," Mary said, smiling.

I nodded. "I did not know there were so many men about."

Of course I had known, as had Hiram, and we had carefully planned our moment of arrival for after the heavy midday meal when men were back at work, but more than ready for a diversion.

"It will be awhile before you will be able to do your shopping," she said.

That was true. Mr. Cutting and the shop boy were tightly packed in with the others.

"That's alright," I said. I wished Mary would be quiet. I wanted to soak in the conversation from the scene on the road.

She took my cue of short responses to her comments, thankfully, because I could not afford for her to think me rude. Mr. Phelps was a canny farmer and dealer in land. He could afford the horse and he had the land I coveted, up on the road to Victory.

Horses were very important to that Vermont world of 1860. A horse was used for everything: plowing, harvesting, haying, logging and transportation. A man without a horse, or at the least an ox, was no farmer. Men needed horses and consequently had a fierce interest in them, knowing every animal in the small town, who owned what, and the strengths and weaknesses of owners and beasts. Of Hiram, it could be said his strength was his skill in training and working and breeding horses, and his weakness that he could not afford good ones. Now the weakness had been erased, thanks to the black horse that was no ordinary horse. Hiram was at the center of things, and I was just outside that center, eagerly observing and as watchful from my place as he was from his. Together we could turn this miracle of a horse into something that would outlive it.

The scheming to trade the horse was mine. I had felt so proud of Hiram, seeing him standing there at his ease talking horse training and the merits of the black horse with what seemed like half of the village men.

When Mr. Cutting turned at last to re-enter the store, pulling his helper unwillingly along with him, I decided I could leave the men to the rest of their doings. He knew the excitement was dissolving and in ones and twos the workers would go back to the mills, and the doctor and his patient to resume the consultation, though I would expect the latter to have forgotten his ailments, at least temporarily.

This left me free to go into the cool, relative darkness of the store with the children. I waited patiently while Fanny and Biathy concentrated on the long row of candy jars and studied their contents before they made their choices. The store was peaceful after the dusty, hot mayhem outside.

"That is quite an animal your husband has, Miz Presbrey," Mr. Cutting told me.

I smiled widely, "Yes, he has done amazing things with her."

"It looks like you have hit good times," he added.

At this remark, I studied him as carefully as Fanny and Biathy did the candy jars. Was he being dryly caustic, knowing we were poor farmers on a rented place? Or did he know something I did not yet know about an offer for the horse?

I was shy of Hiram Cutting as were many people in town. He was an educated man, studying for many years in formal schools and on his own. This was well known in these parts for he was a rarity. Instead of doing other things, though, he had come to Lunenburg where he joined in with an uncle and ran the store. It was puzzling, because in some ways he was an ordinary merchant with no more schooling than eighth grade, but in other ways, in his bland, detached manner, he had no more connection to the place than a duck that lands on the river in autumn and is still there in the winter, hoping the water stays open. Mr. Cutting kept an observatory in his house near the store, and he was known to record weather, day after day, noting the ordinary and peculiar in the same fine hand. He had hundreds of books, it was said. His housekeeper, though no gossip, had been heard to describe the annual spring cleaning when she would take them from the shelves one by one under his supervision and dust and return each to its place. He was an important man in town: he, along with his father, had helped build the Congregational Church on its height of ground on the green, leaving the M.E. Church the less predominant place on the eastern side of the slope.

"I mean because of the fine character of that horse and all your husband has done to make her into what she has it in her to be," he continued, giving me to understand that he meant only good by his comment about our good times. As he spoke, he hemmed a little in his throat, and bobbed his head at me. I realized by this that I had been staring a beat or two too long, and that if he made me nervous, the same could be said of my effect on him.

"Mr. Presbrey is very skilled with horses, certainly," I agreed, smiling again and meaning it – a rare thing for me to give out two such smiles in one afternoon.

"Your husband gave us to understand the animal might just be for sale," he said, in his bland, indirect manner.

"We are entertaining offers," I replied.

"Hmm," he said.

"What do you think she is worth?" I asked abruptly.

Mary, at my elbow, who had been listening and watching, gave a little choke of astonishment at my boldness. Who asks a merchant the worth of something? My eyes did not leave Mr. Cutting.

He considered my question, arranging a display of boxed crackers unconsciously before he spoke.

"At least one hundred dollars," he delivered the verdict at last. "Your husband should not take less than that, and the carriage, if he sells that, should be extra." He paused, and smiled his own little smile at me. "But you did not hear this from me."

Mary's eyes were as round and astonished as if she had heard a cat had borne puppies instead of kittens. I put my finger up against my lips and mimed a "shhh" at her playfully so she knew the caution from him was meant for her, too.

"I am in need of tea," I told Mr. Cutting. "Please, three ounces of the Chinese black there. And three pounds of coffee."

Mary and I admired the selection of fabric, the bolts of cloth displayed on the shelves with an edging of each hanging down enough to show the richness and softness and colors. Checked patterns for dresses were all the rage, a change from plain colors. Mary wore a beautiful dress with a blue check design set off by a dark blue ribbon tie at the neckline that gently traced her collarbone. When there was money, I hoped, after the harvest, I would buy some cloth, enough for dresses for me and Fanny.

By the time Fanny had selected five pieces of candy for herself and a big lollipop for Biathy, Hiram had come in along with the regular crew of men who frequented the store. He came to my side, and put in his request to Mr. Cutting for tobacco, a small can of cut plug. When it was added to the small pile of my goods, he pulled out his leather purse and counted out the coins in payment.

"Come and see me," Mary said.

"I would like to," I told her. "But I don't know if I can."

"You could come up some day with the horse."

"If we still have her, I might do that."

We said our goodbyes and went outside where Fanny and Biathy and I sank tiredly into the back and I leaned contentedly against the seat. Charles climbed up front to ride home with his father, and even had the chance to take the reins on the long, flat run between the fields near the river just before the bridge across to Lancaster.

I was content to rest, feeling the cool breeze that came from the motion of the carriage, and half dozed to the rhythm of the horse's hooves clopping on the dirt as we headed home. There would be time enough for Hiram and me to talk later, at the day's end.

I studied the back of his head, his hair showing brown and shiny below his hat. I admired the way his shoulders moved under the fabric of his coat as he leaned into directing the horse. I was pleased, with life and him and the sight of our son, eager to be learning to drive and taut with the excitement of all he had seen and learned in the village.

There was a bustle once we got home. Hiram left us by the house, while he and Charles went to the barn, to do the careful disengagement of Blackie from harness and wipe her down and clean the leather, and wipe down the carriage, and see the horse was fed and watered. It is a lot of work to keep a horse. Hiram was sweating before he was done. After helping his father with the horse, Charles milked the cows, and saw that our other horse had feed and fresh hay.

I had supper to prepare, a simple meal of bread with milk poured over it, since we were all tired. I put Fanny and Biathy to bed, and Charles uncomplainingly went up the stairs, too.

That left Hiram and me in the kitchen. He waited while I washed the plates and cups, setting them to drain on the edge of the sink.

"Let's go sit outside," he said.

We went out to a bench he had made, near the kitchen windows, but far enough so we could talk quietly in the growing dark and not wake the children. There was the sound of birds out for the evening, distinct cheeping far apart and slow, not like the agitation of the day. A lone firefly flashed its green lantern near the lilac bush at the corner of the house. Hiram lit his pipe, and the smoke distinguished itself from the night, curling over our heads.

"What happened today?" I asked him.

"The men were all in astonishment over the horse," he said, and I could sense his smile in the dark from the slow way he spoke, slower than usual. "You would think she was the only horse of quality they had seen. Even the doctor was there, and the man who owns the gristmill. The word will go around everywhere after today."

"Did you get any other offers?"

"Oh, no, but I wouldn't there," he said. "People will come quietly to me."

"Mr. Cutting said the horse is worth one hundred dollars and we shouldn't take less," I told him.

He sucked in air loudly at that. "He told you that!"

"I asked him," I admitted.

"But he told you," Hiram said, admiringly.

"I was thinking," I said. "What if we were to trade the horse for that land your brother had, that belongs to Mr. Douglass? He acted real interested in getting Blackie. What do you think?"

There was a long silence while Hiram considered the enormity of what I proposed. It was enormous to him I could tell, as it had at first seemed to me. It looked impossible, until I had kept turning it this way and that in my mind so I was used to it. Like me, he had gotten so accustomed to us never owning land he had put it out of his head.

"We could try," he said after a pause so long that, if I had not known him so well, I would have thought he never intended to break it.

"Sleep on it," I said. "If we are going to do this, we will have to plan it out carefully."

The next morning, leaving the children with Charles, Hiram and I set off in the carriage to pay a visit to Ira G. Douglass in Guildhall.

Ira G. was the kind of man who keeps his cards close to his chest and with a face designed not to show much of what was going on in his head or heart. If he was surprised to see us when we appeared at his house in Guildhall, not far up the brook road that led after some miles to the corners where my niece, Myalina, would eventually live with her husband and in-laws, he did not give any sign of it. He was in a far field haying and Mrs. Douglass sent her young son, a spindly boy of not yet eleven who was struggling with a growth spurt. He trotted out of the yard like a colt, all legs, with his long arms crooked at the elbows, and appeared after a short wait with his father, the boy deliberately walking quite a few paces behind him.

Hiram and I had agreed that he would take the lead initially in the man-to-man greeting and then I would step in, since a woman's involvement would be a surprise and since I was the one who could read and write and who had seen my father do deals.

"Good morning," Hiram said. "We are sorry to draw you from your haying, but you asked for a promise from me to tell you before we sold the horse so I am doing that."

"You have had other offers," the man stated.

Hiram nodded.

"Mine stands at seventy-five dollars."

"The horse is worth more than that," Hiram said.

"You have had other offers," Mr. Douglass said.

Hiram was not a man to lie. He knew that Mr. Douglass meant had we had other offers of more than his seventy-five. I realized this was the time for me to speak.

"We would like to propose a trade," I said.

He turned his head a slight rotation, ten degrees or so, just enough so one eye saw me. Before that I had been invisible once he had told me good day. Having seen me with that slight movement, I became invisible again as he attended on Hiram, waiting for him to speak.

"This is what we would like to propose," I said, determined not to be intimidated by his attitude.

At this, Mr. Douglass again rotated his head and shoulders, an encouraging improvement, I decided. His look was cross, though, as if a fly had landed on his face and he, in flicking it away, had banged his nose.

"You own that land on the road up from the Guildhall line, near where we live, in fact. It is where Leroy Presbrey owned before his sudden death four years ago. We know that farm, and we would like to trade the black horse for the farm."

Mr. Douglass had gone as still as a boy hiding behind a bush waiting for a rabbit. Then he went into what, for him, was a scurry, looking back and forth between Hiram and me. Hiram was as calm as the pond at dawn, with the mist obscuring the surface. I, on the other hand, was bright-eyed and ready, like the red fox sitting in the high grass, listening and watching for the mole tunneling up.

"That piece of land has been vacant for two years, and is ripe for planting next season," he said at last. "It is thirty-eight acres. You know the house, and barn. There are woods, too, of maple and some beech. I would need more than the trade of the horse. That property is worth more than seventy-five dollars, more like one hundred and fifty dollars, double the horse."

I looked at him steadily. "The horse is worth more than seventy-five dollars," I said.

"I am not accustomed to dealing with women," he said coldly, to no one in particular it seemed.

"A trade is a trade," I said.

"The horse is worth more than seventy-five dollars. She is right," Hiram offered, and then was silent, as if to say that this comment would be all that Douglass would get from him now.

"Do you want the horse?" I asked. "Because we want the farm."

"One hundred twenty-five dollars," Mr. Douglass said. "That is my best offer. The land for the black horse and the carriage and twenty-five dollars."

"We are not selling the carriage," I said serenely, having suddenly decided that. Hiram looked surprised. We had planned to include the carriage as part of the deal, since it was a repaired vehicle and we had never had one before because it was a luxury item and a wagon was good enough. "We will trade you even: the horse for the land. It will all be spelled out in the deed fair and square."

Mr. Douglass did indeed want that black horse. I offered him the chance to own it while he unloaded a small farm he had no use for.

"You will have to pay the fee to the clerk," he said.

"We do not have any cash," I said.

"Then we will put the fee in the deed, and you can owe me that plus the hundred dollars or that plus the horse, and interest on what you owe."

He and Hiram shook hands while I looked on, gleeful at how I felt inside already at the knowledge that we, at last, would be landowners.

Hiram trotted the black horse more than his usual wont, all the way home.

"We did it!" I shouted to Charles, who had hurried in from the field where he was planting corn, a hard job when done with numbers and back-breaking when done alone, and more of a lark while watching tiny Fanny who he had put in the shade of the stone wall, but she and Biathy wandered the field attempting to help and keeping him from working much. He had her piggyback and was pulling Biathy along by the hand in order to reach us quickly.

He set Fanny down in the grass and picked me up and spun me around and kissed me loudly on my cheek, and shook his father's hand, grinning.

"When do we move?" he asked. "Tell me all about it."

"Not until after the harvest is done," Hiram said.

I told him all about it, every detail, every word, every expression.

The next morning, neglecting the farm the third day in a row, but for good cause, we travelled to Lunenburg village to the town hall where we met Ira G. Douglass, and I sat with my back straight and my chin high, watching while the clerk constructed the language of our agreement that deeded us the land for $100 or for the delivery within three weeks of the black horse owned by my husband, Hiram Presbrey, along with six dollars and interest. The deed was between me and Mr. Douglass, and I read it carefully word by word, not once, but twice, to be sure it stated what was intended by me and Hiram.

We did not wait anything like three weeks. The next week, a neighbor took the younger children so we could carry out our business. We rode in company the seven miles to Guildhall, first Hiram and me in the carriage pulled by the black horse, and Charles behind us, riding our chestnut mare. At the barn of Mr. Douglass, we made the trade official, Hiram slowly unhitching the harness, and handing her off to her new owner gravely, after a soft word near the animal's bent head and a pat on her muzzle. He and Mr. Douglass shook hands, and then the man disappeared into the barn with the fine black horse. Charles and Hiram hitched our chestnut horse to the carriage and we rode home. But we went past our house, and continued the mile uphill to our new farm, just to take a look that day, and walk the fields and woods and unlock the door of the house and go through every room. I stood in the center of the new kitchen, big and empty except for a cast iron range, and smelled the sweetness of what was mine. It was the Hiram and Emeline Lucy Presbrey Farm in Lunenburg in the County of Essex in the State of Vermont.

Part Two

§

Road From Victory

Chapter One

JUNE 1871

THE DAY THE SHERIFF CAME TO THE DOOR WAS A DARK DAY. The sun was shining – the pale sun of the winter long gone and replaced by the intensity of summer. So many months had gone by since the burning of Samuel Hannux's house that even I, who should have known better, had been lulled into imagining that my life, our life, would go on as it had before. But the consequences of the fire were not over. I should have known this would be so when Samuel did not go back across the river where he should have stayed.

That morning in June, the sheriff came to my kitchen door. He was apologetic at bothering me, he said, standing on the worn wooden steps turning his hat round and round in his hands. I knew him, Mr. Cossitt. It was clear he had waited until David had gone for the day.

He stood on my steps, saying, "I am sorry to bother you so early, Mrs. Beede," even though it was not early – I had been up since dawn as he well knew since I was not a lady of leisure with domestic help. Fanny moved behind me in the shadows of the kitchen and I could see his eyes following her.

"Could we go out to the garden?" he asked me, not meeting my eye.

"Alright," I said.

I untied my apron, and placed it folded on the top step.

"I'll be outside with Mr. Cossitt," I called over my shoulder to Fanny.

"I thought she would be in school," he said, chewing at his upper lip where the edge of his salt-and-pepper mustache curled.

"She is fourteen, Mr. Cossitt," I said, gently, as if my voice could tell him how shamed she was to know he was standing at my door at eight o'clock on a Tuesday morning on a beautiful morning in June.

We walked silently to the edge of the vegetable garden, my shoes getting wet in the dew, and the coolness of it pooling up around my stockings at my ankles.

"I am sorry," he said, "But I have to ask you some questions."

I looked surprised, raising my eyebrows.

"About the fire."

"The fire?" I said, with puzzlement in my tone. I would not make this easy for him, oh, no, that I would not do.

His pale face was slowly turning an unattractive tomato-red.

"This is not easy for me," he told me, so I almost felt sorry for him. But he had to do his job and so did I.

"You will have to tell me why you have come here," I said.

"It is about the fire at Samuel Hannux's house last winter," he said in a rush.

"What could that have to do with me?" my voice was sharp and I instantly regretted it.

He gave me a long speculative glance.

"If you will wait a moment, Mrs. Beede, I will tell you why I am here."

I took a deep breath. Who would not be edgy if the sheriff were standing without warning in the garden on a morning when the only plans had been to drag the wash tubs outdoors and do the weekly laundry with a daughter who was old enough now to really be a help?

"You must know about that fire," he said. "It destroyed the man's house and he lost everything, except his life. His children could have died."

"Yes, I heard about it," I said. "I did not know what fire you meant. There are always fires."

He nodded. "But this was especially bad."

"I thought it was caused by the pipe to the woodstove. Isn't that what the *Gazette* said?"

He ignored my comment and my question.

He asked his own question. "I need you to tell me where your husband was that night. It was March 27 – one of the coldest nights of the winter."

My heart was hammering so loud I could hear it in my ears. I wanted to gulp air to calm myself, but I could not let him see me show fright.

"Why do you ask me that?" I whispered. Surely any wife asked such a question would be afraid.

"I cannot tell you why," he said. "This is business of the law. But I need you to tell me where your husband was between the hours of midnight and four o' clock."

"Why, he was home with me," I lied to him, willing my sharp eyes flat and my voice low and shocked that he would wonder such a thing.

"He was seen in Lancaster that night, Mrs. Beede. He was seen in the tavern as late as 11:30. More than one person has told me this."

I knew and he knew that it took at least two hours to get to my house in Jefferson from the village of Lancaster, even for a man like David who never spared his horses. Four hours between midnight and four o' clock was a long time to be accounted for, and I had committed myself to a lie and could not save him.

I had hoped the fire was forgotten, let myself believe what I wanted to believe. But it was not over. I wished there was a chair I could sink down onto. I wished he would go so I could run into the barn and bury my face in my hands and cry.

But Mr. Cossitt was not done with me.

"I understand that your husband did not get along well with Mr. Hannux."

I knew then that our goose was cooked. Someone had told the law about the bad blood between my David and Samuel.

"Mrs. Beede, you understand the consequences of lying," Mr. Cossitt said to me.

But I knew a wife cannot be forced to speak against her husband in a court.

"I do not know about any issues between them," I said flatly. I would not help Sheriff Cossitt. If he succeeded in ruining us, David and our family, he would have to do it on his own.

With that, he started on a long litany of questions – when had we come to Jefferson, and why? Had we not lived in Lancaster first? Were we not neighbors in Lunenburg of David and Susan Kimball whose children had been living in the house with Samuel at the time of the fire? Was not David Beede badly injured in the war in an accident? I would not help him. I would only answer the facts of when we had moved to Jefferson – for a new farm. And that my sister and her husband had been neighbors of the Kimballs, not me and my David. I claimed to not know about my husband's war experiences.

Again, he asked, "Mrs. Beede, are you sure there was no bad blood you know of between those two men? It is a crime to lie."

But I lied, knowing it was no crime for a woman to protect her husband and keep her family intact.

"I do not know what you are talking about," I said.

At last, after what seemed like forever, Sheriff Cossitt gave up on me. He left me standing next to the vegetable garden, shaking and afraid, though I had not shown it. When he had come, there was friendliness between us, but when he left, we were sworn enemies, and he barely contained his anger, raising his hat to me and stalking across the still-wet lawn to his horse and wagon.

All that day I had stewed and fretted, waiting for David to come home. When I had gone back to the house after the sheriff left, Fanny was sitting in the rocker waiting for me.

When she saw me, something of my distress reached her, and she got up abruptly, leaving the rocker thumping back and forth on the wooden floor.

"I'll make tea," she said.

I sank into the still-moving rocker, and kept up the rhythm, a frenetic motion that did not soothe me.

"You could have stayed in the house," she said. "You could have invited him in. I am not a child. I know what he came about. They know, don't they?"

"How do you know?" I whispered, shocked at her matter-of-factness.

"Charles and I are not stupid," she said.

"So he knows, too."

"Of course we do. You don't hide things as well as you think, not from us."

"What about George?"

"Well, that's not the same, is it?"

George was different, not in the same way as Biathy, who would always be a child. George went to school, but he had a slow-witted manner, as if he, like his brothers and father, had been to war and come home shell-shocked.

"How much do they know?" she asked.

"A lot, I would say," I told her, taking the tea cup on its saucer from her. She had gotten out the good cups, as if to say, "we will be alright since we are still drinking out of the good cups."

I blew and sipped on the hot liquid, my agitation calming in the process of slowing my rocking to be able to drink my tea.

"Do you think they can prove it?"

"I don't know, Fanny. They have people saying he was at the tavern at 11:30 pm and the fire was just after midnight. It takes over two hours to get here from the town, so he had time. I told the sheriff he had been here all evening, but he knew I lied."

"Was he nice to you?"

"At first, but then he got angry when I would not say what he wanted me to. I had to lie."

She nodded.

"Didn't I?"

"Of course, you did, Ma. But what if it comes to court like the last time? You can't lie then."

"A wife does not have to testify against her husband. The law is very clear about that."

"I am glad I was sound asleep all that night," she said. "Are you angry, Ma?"

"Oh, Fanny," I tried to laugh, but it came out sounding bitter.

We sat in the kitchen silently awhile, glad George was working. At last, I said, "Today is wash day. I guess we could do the wash."

"We might as well," she agreed.

Together we went into the open shed off the barn, and dragged out the heavy tubs. Fanny began hauling water from the spring, and I set a fire to going with a pot for heating the water. It took a long time to get all the water we would need. While she did that, I went indoors and pulled sheets off the bed, and collected David's and George's shirts, and our aprons and personals. We were late getting started, and by the time we had scrubbed and rinsed and wrung, it was long after noon as we pinned the dripping clothes to the lines.

"I don't think they'll dry today," I said.

93

"There's nothing we can do about it."

"We can leave it out all night."

"It'll be so damp with dew, though."

"Maybe it will dry. There's light till almost nine."

The work had done me good. I was hot and damp with sweat.

"Let's hitch up the horse to the wagon and go see your aunt," I said.

Fanny stared at me. "Really?" she said.

"Yes."

"Do you know how to do it?"

"I have done it before, with your father. Well, I helped."

Harnessing the horse, and backing her between the shafts as she fidgeted took us over an hour. By then we were not just hot and sweaty, but dirty.

I looked at her and started laughing. "Look at you!" I exclaimed.

"You don't look no better!"

Our hair was coming loose and sticking to our faces, and dirt from the yard had clung to the wash water on our dresses. My right stocking – it was part of an old pair – hung down my calf in folds, and Fanny had smudges on her cheek from rubbing it with her dirty wrist.

"We could have got there faster walking," Fanny chortled.

"But we wouldn't have had half the fun," I replied.

I hitched the horse to the ring on the side of the barn, and we went into the house and overhauled our appearances. We put on our going-out dresses after scrubbing our faces and washing our hands and my putting on newer stockings. We polished our shoes with a damp rag, and took down and put back up our hair. We marched out to the barn, and I untied the horse and climbed up to the seat, steadying the horse while Fanny joined me. With that, we set off on a weekday, on a beautiful June day, on the ten-minute trip to see Wealthy.

To say Wealthy was surprised to see Fanny and me pull into her yard in the middle of a weekday afternoon, as if it were a Sunday and church day, was an understatement. Since she was a girl, whenever she was taken aback by something, she would stand with her hand on her hip, and her eyes would narrow in contemplation.

Ella had been outside taking down laundry (that household was way ahead of us that day) and when she saw us she shrieked so loudly with excitement that it brought her mother outside.

"Are you going to ask us in?" I said dryly, observing my sister while she stared at us.

"What are you two doing here? It's wash day, ain't it?"

"Our wash is done," I said grandly, "And we have come visiting. How about serving us tea?"

With that, we were out of the carriage, and surrounded by Ella and her younger brothers pulling at our skirts with what I supposed with a sigh were grubby fists, went into Wealthy's kitchen.

Once we were seated and tea was served, I got down to business. By now, the noisy boys had been sent outside by their mother, and it was quieter, even with us women talking at full pitch.

"The sheriff came this morning," I told my sister and Ella.

My sister went still, the way an animal, watched in the forest, will do at the hint of danger in the wind.

"Tell me," she said softly.

I did tell her, the whole story, leaving nothing out.

She muttered as I talked, another of her traits, but I paid no mind.

"What will you do?" she asked me, when I was done.

I shrugged. "What can I do?"

"What about him?" she asked, and I knew she meant my husband.

"I won't see him until later, whenever he comes home."

"Do you think he did it?" she said bluntly.

I shook my head, as if to say no, but she could read me, and knew I was not certain of his guilt or his innocence. She was worried. The wrinkles on her forehead looked like furrows in a just-plowed spring field.

"If things get rough, you had better send Fanny to me," she said.

⚹

Chapter Two

1868

H ER WORDS SET ME TO THINKING OF HOW DAVID HAD GOTTEN ROUGH WITH ME BEFORE, IN THE SPRING OF 1868, AND NEARLY KILLED ME. He had threatened to do so, and beat me, all over the fact I would not give him more money for his gambling and drinking. This was right after the day when he had gone after my son, Charles, and committed arson against him.

That was the reason that I had moved that fall of 1868 from the road to Victory in Vermont to a hamlet in the south of Jefferson, near Cherry Mountain, that was just on the border with Carroll. I had moved there because of David's trouble with the law in Vermont. You will hear all of the details about this soon enough. I had bought the property – acres to farm, and a house and barn – from Calvin Knight, who bought our property in Lunenburg at the same time. I favored this land because of two things: it was flat land and the soil was good, and we were assured of water because of the marsh extending to the back of the property. The house was on the Turnpike Road, and close to a store, a church, and a mill. My land was on the great plain of Jefferson that is surrounded by the distant mountains.

Whereas Lunenburg is hunched into the side of the mountain with its front facing the direction of the river, and houses are more often than not built on a hard-won scrap of level ground, Jefferson is out in the open. The mountains, which are the grandest in New Hampshire or Vermont, are close enough for the viewer to feel their awe, but far enough away that the town has plenty of room to spread out.

I had chosen Jefferson because it was some distance removed from Lunenburg and in another state, giving me distance from the shame of what David had done. It was also near my niece, Myalina, who was in Lancaster at the time and to my sister, Wealthy. My other sister, Fanny, was in Lisbon, a long ride away. My brother was dead by then, struck down even younger than our father.

The reason we moved was simple: it was because of the act committed by David in March 1868 in Lunenburg on the road to Victory. I had sat in the courthouse in Guildhall on the hottest day in September 1868 – or at least that is how it felt – with the flies having sprung out from the cracks in the wood and doing their slow buzz until falling onto the floor by the hundreds. This was not uncommon in barns and attics. The courthouse, built in 1830 so I was told, replaced the one on top of the ridge above the common where the cemetery is. Unlike the lordly aspect of Lunenburg, Guildhall, which is the shire town of Essex County, has a humbler appearance for all that it is on the river. The green is flat and quite small, surrounded by the court, the church, the town or Guild Hall that is a simple affair like the one in Lunenburg, houses, a hotel for all of the people in town for court business, and the store. At the north end of the town, near the wrought iron fountain, the road goes over the long bridge that crosses the rapid, rough water in that part of the Connecticut. It is a long, double-arched bridge and carries the message of being strongly built enough to convey in safety all who go to and fro between Guildhall and Northumberland, New Hampshire.

I had no real opinion of Guildhall, but after the court appearances I was happy to leave that place and never go back, though we had luck of a sort there.

I could have coached David in the time leading up to the court date to tame any cockiness he might feel creeping forward in himself. "Look humble but confident," I would have told him again that morning of the case, adjusting his thin black tie into a crisp bow and inspecting his white shirtfront one more time. It would do no hurt, I thought, that my David would stand before the court tall and straight, with his confident, handsome face and neat appearance.

He had been out on bail only because I had put up for collateral the land we owned. This was an unexpected benefit of having my own farm that I never could have foreseen. He spent one night in the jail in Guildhall, but by my mortgaging the farm for $200, a fraction of its value, he was out. That was a great amount of money, a sum we could never have come up with in cash. The farm allowed him to be free while he waited the long five months until the court date. Two hundred dollars was more than I had paid for Hiram's and my first farm. It was more than the value of the black horse. And the lawyer I hired had worked down that bail number from the five hundred demanded by his counterpart. They claimed David would run, that he would leave the state for New Hampshire as he had left New Hampshire once for Vermont right after the war ended. Our lawyer put the case that David was a different man now, a married man with a farm he owned and a family. Thus the judge set the bond at $200 and the bondsman Horace Stone – a tall, thin scarecrow with dark hair hard to tame rising in tufts – was there in Lunenburg to sign the paperwork that April day that gave him the farm if David did not appear in court September third, 1868, as mandated.

He did not appear, though, and so escaped the consequences of what I had wanted to believe at the time he did not do.

"He is a patriotic man who did his duty for four years, in service in the Great Army of the Republic," his lawyer would have told the court. "He was injured while raising works in South Carolina and he fought honorably in the battles with his company. Three of his sons served in that Great War and two of them died, two of his sons died in defense of the Union. And he is an upstanding member of his community of Lunenburg. He is a landowner, a farmer. He contributed his hard-earned money to the cause of the proposed railroad that will link our town of Lunenburg to the world of commerce. He goes to the Methodist Episcopal Church with his wife, who is Vermont-born, and their children. He is a hard worker who is part of the hard-working fabric of these towns along the river. Is this a man who would answer yes to these false charges put against him? I tell you, no, this man is not guilty."

But the lawyer never delivered those words because the day set for the court trial came and went. The lawyer, Briggs was his name, and I were there, and we waited in that hot anteroom in the building on the green in Guildhall but, as we both feared, David did not appear. Charles was there, with the prosecutor for the State for whom he was to stand witness, sitting a few chairs from me, and we did not speak or meet one another's eye that morning.

David had been gone for months by then, and the last day I had seen him had been the worst of my life and the worst of any scenes between us, because I feared for my life. When the court time came, my lawyer and I, and Charles with the prosecutor from the State, were called into the courtroom, and my lawyer had to tell the judge that his client had not appeared. And so I would lose the $200 and therefore my farm because I did not have the cash money.

I went back home to the farm on the high hill below Mount Tug on the road to Victory and had to face that we were marked. While I wanted to believe in his innocence, there were many who did not. It crept up on me, this awareness, in church, at the store, on the road to visit neighbors, and in certain homes where I had once felt welcome. I understood slowly that though he had escaped imprisonment because he had not come to trial, he had run and therefore was not only not a free man, but had showed himself guilty by his running. He had not really escaped and because he had not, I had not. I did not have a husband in jail, but I had the shame of people's gossip about not just him, but me, and I could see the reluctance in town to invite Fanny to parties. He had taken his son George, poor boy, with him.

My face burned, the heat of confusion and anger rising through me, at night when I lay awake thinking of slight after slight. That everyone in town knew our business, I could not pretend was not true. There were the marks on me, on my arms under the long sleeves of my dress, and the bruises on my face that had gone from livid red to mottled purple and were now yellow. And Charles was dark with rage. He and I had land dealings with one another, but he could not bear to look at me when we met. He lived on the next farm over with Amanda, and Fanny had gone to live with them that spring after she had seen what had happened between me and David. I could not find her after those events and had had to search for her for hours before she would come out of hiding in the woods beyond the apple orchard. She had seen what David did, first to the goods he had stolen at gunpoint from my son and then what he had done to me.

Amanda did not like me. She was a Presbrey, the daughter of my cousin, Hollis, who was Hiram's brother. She held herself cold and straight when Charles first brought her home to me, with the intent of marriage. He did not see it, but I did. I knew what went on behind that pasted-on smile, as if she were a paper doll with not only sets of clothes, but sets of expressions – paper lips that showed a pained smile at me. By that time,

I knew I would soon be married to David so I did not share my displeasure with my son. I knew she was of the mind that "her" Presbreys were superior to ours. Too bad for her she had fallen in love with her cousin, Charles, and so linked herself even tighter to us than she was already by the fact her grandfather and my father were brothers.

Because of all that had gone wrong because of my marriage to David she despised me more than ever. I am sure she was one of the people who called Hiram indolent, but without the kindness behind it showed me by James Smith. He was a kind man, married into the Presbrey family, and took in those women less fortunate among his wife's relations – the woman whose husband went to California for the gold rush and never was seen again, and that man's daughter. He held to the old value of family that did not let his judgments make him turn his back on any of us.

I do understand, though, how Amanda must have felt, trying to raise a family that already consisted of two boys – one from her first marriage – and surely another on the way soon. There I was like a burr under her saddle, and her household whined and groaned from the addition of Fanny. I would walk the quarter-mile to Charles' house to see Fanny since she would not come home for fear of David.

Amanda would nod at me, and soon enough find a reason to leave the room, carrying her boys with her as if being in the room with me would harm them.

It was worse after the day of the trial when David did not appear and Charles lost a day in the fields. He at least would get back his $50 that he had had to guarantee his appearance with as a witness for the prosecution. That he would never get back the cost to replace what David had destroyed was clear to him. If I could have then, I would have paid him, but I was barely managing, having mortgaged my farm and given up much of my savings to pay David's lawyer's fees. With all of that hanging in the air between Amanda and me, she did not even see a reason to be civil to me, and fairly ran past me from the kitchen to outdoors when I knocked lightly, brushing her shoulder against me with unnecessary force.

I did not think long about what to do after David did not appear for trial. I had had all spring and summer to think. I walked across the fields to Charles' house a week after that date and told Fanny that we would move to New Hampshire where my sisters were.

That is how we came, in late September of 1868, to go from the road to Victory down the long hill past Neal's Pond with our belongings to the village of Lunenburg and then to Guildhall and across the river to Lancaster, following the road to our new farm in the south of Jefferson. We still had the wagon, though David had taken the chestnut mare, and I drove the old horse I had bought cheap that spring from Mary Phelps so Biathy and I could do the plowing. I bought a second horse from Mary to have two animals to pull the wagon.

Charles did not stay in Lunenburg, either. He uprooted his family soon after I left and moved north three towns to Bloomfield, Vermont where some of his cousins lived.

8

Chapter Three

THE WAR

I TRIED TO MAKE EXCUSES FOR DAVID'S BEHAVIOR TO ME AND TO CHARLES. For one thing, David was one of the unfortunate fathers who had many sons of the age to go away to war and nothing to keep them from it. He, an old man of forty-four, stayed behind at first, in the early days, but his eldest sons, his namesake, David, and, William, a boy of seventeen, joined up that summer of 1861. The year before the war, David and his wife, Sabry, lived on a rented place in Hooksett, down in the southern part of New Hampshire, with seven children. The youngest, a girl by the name of Capatola, was a year old. He and William brought in the income, working as laborers for farmers. His eldest son, David, was living away by then, working where he boarded on a farm.

That year, 1860, David told me, had seemed like any other. It was a noisy household without many resources. They lived on the small earnings of him and William, and relied on a big vegetable garden, the milk and cheese from a cow kept in a shed, and eggs from a flock of chickens. He did send all of his children to school, even that year when William was sixteen. The only possession the family had of value was a clock belonging once to his wife's mother and guarded carefully by her on a high shelf where the confusion of nine people in a tiny house could not hurt it.

The war came and disrupted it all. In July 1863, his son Charles was old enough and went off to match the service of his brothers. There was no reason for David to have gone. In fact, there was every reason for him not to, considering his age and the family he should have stayed to support. He told me it had become clear it was his duty to go, following in the hot-blooded zeal of his youthful sons. I suspect he was fooling himself and wanted to go, to take leave of all of his tedious labor working for another man, and the responsibility of a large family. Whatever the case, he and Charles went off, both in the Fourth New Hampshire Infantry, leaving behind his wife who now had Willard, age thirteen, to depend on as man of the house. Like his father and brothers, Willard went out to work, doing labor on a nearby farm. So it was that Sabry had two sons at home, thirteen and eleven, with the prospect now of a long war and they were growing up fast. But she was spared the anguish of that, casting her own shadow over the family with her death of fever in the fall.

The war was close to its end, when Charles and William died within a day of one another in Wilmington, North Carolina, three weeks after the Fourth had captured that city.

When the two Davids came home, finally, in the summer of 1865, there was only a shell of a family left. The father had been with his two sons when they fought and then died in the south. But son David, in the 10th Infantry, had gotten the news late of the deaths and had never seen his brothers since the day he left for the war four years before.

The youngest child, Capatola, had also died during the war, of illness, leaving only George and Willard, under the care of their elder sister, Adaline. She was seventeen when her father and brother came back, but she looked years older.

As for what David felt, perhaps the feeling that would have rent him had he lost only one son had been slammed into the ground too deep for him to ever find it. But I did not know him before the war or immediately after so I cannot say what he was like. I have no scale to measure who he was and how he changed. When I knew him he seemed forever young somehow, a man with no cares who was handsome and knew it. He seemed reckless and free of care, a bachelor with only a teenage son, and no property. His daughter, Adaline, had her mother's clock. The tragedy of what happened during the war was one shared by many families. For months after my Charles came home, I breathed in deeply whenever I saw him, to know he was safe.

I don't know what effect all of this sorrow and all of the terrible things he had seen had on my David. I took him as he was at the end of it, and trusted he was as he appeared to me.

David was born in the inland Vermont town of Washington. It was a farming community like so many others. I never went there, but he described it to me with some fondness. It was the seat of his Beede ancestors – his father and grandfather. He pictured for me the protected, closed beauty of the place with a deep stream weaving like a ribbon loosely spread across the cleared pastures – sometimes the ribbon was moss green, and sometimes slate blue and sometimes gray with cold.

"There are only small hills," he told me. "It is nothing like this town set on the edge of the mountain." He was wistful sometimes, and that was when he would tell me again about the village of farms in the countryside that was as soft and without clear edge as the coat of a sheep or a down comforter spread across the bed. Four of his boys were born near his birthplace.

"We should have stayed there," he would say to me. "If we had stayed there, with all of my family, it would have been better."

There were still Beedes in that place, but he never went back.

I suggested it once.

"Do you want to go and visit? You have cousins, surely, and uncles and aunts. I will go, too, and we can take George to see his family."

He looked at me, shocked. "I would never go back there."

I dropped the subject quickly, loathe to stir anything in him. From that moment, I only listened quietly when he spoke of the towns where he and his sons were born. What had gone on there, I could only imagine and did not want to do so. This instinct of mine grew stronger after the incident in Lunenburg in the late winter of 1868. Both of his crimes took place at that time of year, when the winter is almost over, with only small piles and ridges of snow in shady, north-facing places, and spring is making itself felt with daffodils in bloom along the southern foundation of the house and the first robins have come back from their wintering. The coincidence of this fact of spring and his misdemeanors I could only observe and speculate about.

8

Chapter Four

WINTER 1866
HAPPY TIMES

I HAVE WRITTEN ABOUT THE FIRE, BUT NOT ABOUT WHAT PRECEDED IT IN VERMONT. What David did there was so serious. The two-hundred-dollar bail was sign enough of that, if the reality itself was not. I wanted to believe in his innocence because I had to – how else to regard the man you married in good faith, the man you love. I had stood by him before when he had stood accused of small misdemeanors – an assault in a tavern after he had been drinking; removal of chickens on the road that were not, of course, "wild" birds with no mistress; and a more serious assault after a disagreement with a man in Lancaster over a debt the man claimed he was owed – and I would stand by him this time, paying his bond and his lawyer's bills. But this time I could not believe what he said, where he placed the blame, because it involved my son, Charles.

David had told me about the injury he suffered in the army. It was the summer of 1863 when the Fourth New Hampshire was in Hilton Head, South Carolina.

"We were building a stockade," he said. "It was hot, always hot, and there were mosquitoes, big as horseflies I thought. We were always dirty. Many of the men got sick. There was malaria and fever and shit that never stopped running until some of them died. I didn't get sick. I had signed on as a carpenter. You know how handy I am with my tools. It has always come in handy, working on farms. Look at all of the things I have built you."

I nodded. He had done projects in the house and barn, from almost the day we really started courting. That first day in the winter when he had visited me, with his son, George, he had noticed a shelf tilted danger-ously in my kitchen, on the wall across from the woodstove that held the extra kerosene lamps.

The next time he came, for us to take a drive in the sled he had borrowed, he brought his hammer and a pocketful of nails.

"I'll just get that shelf when we come back," he told me casually, putting down the hammer and fishing out the nails he placed in a neat pile on the edge of the drying shelf by the sink. I liked that, that he had noticed it and taken action and that he did not put the tool and nails, which might be dirty (though they were not), on the table where we ate.

It was a grand ride, the horse pulling us quickly along the hard-packed snow from our house up the road past Phelps and on up and up along the road to Victory. We could see the white caps of the distant mountains, to the east across the cleared fields. We went faster than I was accustomed to, and what a thrill to feel the cold air freezing my cheeks and the tip of my pointed nose. How I laughed. I forgot for a little while how much I missed Hiram and how his long illness and hard death had taken its toll on me. That was what David did for me when I needed it – he made me laugh. He was not a funny man, but he did not have the burdens of life I had. By that I mean a house and farm, and concerns about what to do once the winter was over.

For weeks that winter, we hardly talked, but he would arrive and hitch the chestnut mare to the sled and we would go out. It was hard to talk when the horse was flying across the packed snow of the road, either down to Lunenburg or down from Mount Tug where he had taken us. And when the horse went uphill, there was the quiet between us as we sat back and watched the snowy fields, and the boughs of the spruce trees heavily laden with the last storm. The fields stretched like a billowy white shawl, broken only by the tops of the stonewalls that showed their gray spines in places where the snow had blown around them. When we got back to the house, I would go inside to warm myself and make us something to eat, while he unhitched the sled and rubbed down the horse, and settled her in a stall. He would bring a huge armload of wood for the box by the stove, tossing it down with a thunderous crash as it slammed into the sides of the box.

It seemed like we knew all about one another because of what other people had told us. I knew about the loss of his sons and wife, and how he had been an old man in the war. And he knew about Hiram's cancer that had killed him, and here I was alone with a young daughter and a boy who could not be normal, on a hill farm in the cold of January and February. He would chop kindling, and when he left, back for the village, he would check to be sure the fire in the range was going well.

He eased into our lives, so non-threatening, as if he were a neighbor we had heard of and seen so we felt we knew him before we met him and he was just as we expected.

It was not until the spring, that exact time of the daffodils in bloom from the bulbs I had planted the year Hiram and I bought the farm, that more of who he was showed. Unlike in the winter, when the cold of outside and the contrast of warmth indoors had lulled all of us, like cats under the stove, the spring seemed to catch him off guard. Suddenly, he could not sit still. He would jiggle his right leg rapidly, sitting in the kitchen or even in the carriage. Instead of a silence that seemed mutually agreeable, I began to feel there were things to be said. I wanted him to ask me about my life. I wanted to ask him. But since that is not how we had started out, I was unsure where to begin with my questions.

One day, we were sitting on a bench out by the orchard. It was an April day, early afternoon, and we had finished Sunday dinner and come outside while Fanny cleared up and George bounced a ball against a wall of the barn.

"I might as well tell you about the war," he said suddenly. He started, just like that, to tell me about what had happened to him.

He and his sons, William and Charles, were in the Fourth New Hampshire, all privates, though William would rise to corporal before he was wounded near Petersburg, Virginia and died of the injury.

"I was the biggest and strongest man in my unit," David told me. "Because of that I did the heavy work. We had dug ditches and were raising timber for a stockade, down where I told you about in Hilton Head. The sea was not far off." He paused, and I could see him thinking about the ocean's vastness unlike anything he had ever seen before and that I never would see. "I was standing over a ditch and straining to turn a big timber when my strength went out of me and I collapsed, unconscious with the pain. They carried me off on a stretcher after I failed to get up, and the doctor told me later when I had roused that I had injured my spine and was paralyzed. For two weeks I laid in bed in the hospital and could not move my legs, but slowly I recovered and went back to my duties. But I was weak, and did not recover my usual force of life for a long time. That was in January in 1864. I was discharged, later that year, and went home, but I signed up again not long after. I have never been quite the same," he concluded, staring off in such a manner I was not sure if he remembered I was there and he was telling his story aloud to me.

How hard David worked when we first met! It seemed he was everywhere at once, tending to the wood box that was Biathy's job, and making sure the barn and house were tight against winter winds. In the spring, he helped with the plowing and planting, and later with the harvest. He brought his son, George, too, and I began to give David a little money to offset the work they lost as laborers for other farmers. I had some savings, hard put by from the crops and grain Hiram and I had sold. My plan was to buy more and more land. I could see that without more we would stay poor, eking out a subsistence. I had watched and listened all of my life to men talking and knew that it was a resource, with possibilities for timber if the right choice were made. I knew a man named Joshua Silsby who lived in the village, and had heard him talking in Cutting's store about partnering with someone for timber rights. He would buy the rights along with a landowner and then harvest the lumber. This had stayed in my mind. When the time was right I would see him myself.

David's hard work astonished me because, to be truthful, Hiram had not been much of a worker. He did what absolutely needed to be done and no more. This was simply how he was and I never questioned it in any serious way. The reason is because I had always known him, and I knew his father and mother, and his brothers and sisters. He was as familiar to me as my own family – he was family. Horses were the one thing that he would exert himself for, just as for some men it was vices that called them – making hard cider or playing cards for money.

As a result of what happened between David and Charles, though, I would learn the extent to which other people viewed Hiram as not worth much. This stung me, I admit. It was in the affidavit that James Smith, the innkeeper and farmer, did to support my cause in September 1869 for getting back the bail and not losing my farm, that I read the words. He sang praises of me, of my industriousness and saving nature that got my family a small farm and then more land and larger farms. But he called

Hiram indolent – a harsh word – and feeble, and a poor manager. That all of this was true did not make me feel any better. My stomach clenched when I saw how other people had seen these things in him. I had tried to be sure that he remained the man of our house in charge of our destiny even though I knew he was not.

I knew then, at the time of James' words being told to the town clerk in Lancaster, that I was no judge of men at all. I had known it for a long time, but seeing the words about Hiram written out made my stomach knot.

There was no malice in Hiram, of that I was glad to remember.

James had said other words, too, in that document. But you will know soon enough about that.

I was lucky in the friends I had and the relations who stood by me in this hard time. How Mary and I cried when I left Lunenburg for Jefferson that day in September 1868. She hung onto me and I to her, as if we were in the water and hanging on to one another tightly enough to stay afloat. As if each of us were, for the other, the overturned rowboat or the drifting log to which we clung. Our lives were so different in so many ways, but we had been close, and adversity had made us closer after Hiram died and then her husband, Augustus, and then there were my troubles with David that led to the harsh winter of 1868 into 1869.

As I have told you, I was lucky in my purchase of Calvin Knight's property in Jefferson and in selling him mine on the road to Victory, but moving from Lunenburg did not prove an end to my troubles. In fact, there were many days that long winter, with David gone I knew not where, that I wished for the cherished land I had once owned on that road that led from Lunenburg up the long incline with the view of mountains, over Mount Tug. I longed for Mary, and for the neighbors I had been so willing to cast off in my move across the river where I was not known.

I am a small woman, but I have long fingers. If you look at my photo, the nice one of me looking pleased with life, when I was dressed in a frilly white blouse under a plaid gabardine jacket cropped at the hip, and fitted to show off my trim waist, the lace held in place by a pin at my throat, and my hair done prettily, you will see my hands casually posed. One is in my lap, folded fingers curled toward my skirt, and the other hangs easily from where my forearm rests on the edge of the table with its brocaded cloth. If you study my hands, you will see how fine-boned they are, the fingers lean and dexterous. They are a working woman's hands without looking rough and thick. My hands could sew the blouse I wore, making tiny, even stitches, and they could make the dozens of baskets that I sold the winter of 1868 into 1869 to keep us in food and necessities when David had gone off, having run from the law and his court date that September. I had escaped the bondsman by moving across the river.

Making baskets was something left for the poor to do, and I was in some bad straits at being forced into it that winter. The job was engaging at least, and I liked choosing the particular strip of cane and weaving it methodically through the main structure of the basket. It was soothing work, and I liked using my hands in this way to feed us. Fanny helped me, and bent her head industriously to the task, on the days when I took my supplies and walked the road to my sister Wealthy's house where Fanny lived. We would work together, mostly silently, in her kitchen.

With me there, on a winter's day, and all of us cooped up in her warm kitchen, and the materials for baskets taking up space, it was crowded. I was used to the calm of Fanny and me, with only Biathy in the background, but Wealthy's kitchen was never calm. She had boys in school, but she was baking or ironing or doing mending for five children still at home and sometimes for the boys out at work. Wealthy was a whirlwind, here and there and all over at once. My being there did not perturb her, and I needed Fanny's help with the baskets and Fanny would not come to our house for fear David would come home while she was there.

As for me, on the more frequent days when I was alone in my house, with the small solace of a pile of dried marsh grass, and the woodstove hot, I had the fear and the anticipation of his arriving. I would half listen to the sounds outside on the road. If he did come, pulling into the yard with a horse and wagon, and stabling the horse in the barn beside the horse Mary sold me cheap, I would have time to be ready for him. I would have time to fear his mood and to wonder if he would be antic with the cold and happy, or full of the darkness that made him a danger to me.

All that winter, that is what I did, anticipate and fear, but he did not come.

One day, though, I got a letter from him. In that way, I knew something of what he was doing and where he was. It was at this time, too, that Horace Stone was pressing for his bail money.

§

Chapter Five

MARCH 24, 1868
WHAT HAPPENED

A LL OF THIS GOES BACK TO THE MONTH OF MARCH 1868 HIGH ON THE HILL WHERE WE LIVED ON THE ROAD TO VICTORY. Telling it now, I know it was a lifetime ago, time enough for a child to go from baby to grown up. Much has happened since then. But it is all still clear to me.

The spring was reluctant that year. March had come in like another month of winter, not spring. Every week saw a storm, not a few inches to laugh about, but a quantity worthy of December or January. The first days were severely cold, and I eyed the woodpile anxiously, trying to calculate how much we had left. David had not been working consistently at all that past year, leaving the preparations for winter to Biathy who could do it, but not plan it. Mary had seen all of this, and would have sent one or two of her boys, but for knowing David would not have allowed it. I helped the best I could, stacking wood that Biathy chopped, waiting until night when David had gone off to wherever he went. By this time, he was not welcome in the tavern in Lunenburg village and had to seek his pleasures across the river in Lancaster. One night – a full moon in October – I worked until the moon had set and the sun was just below the horizon. It was a strange feeling, working silently and all alone once Fanny and Biathy had gone to bed and the lights in the house were all put out. I had never worked outdoors at night, never had to, but that job of the wood had to be done. I loaded the wheelbarrow, a rickety affair with a wobbly wheel that needed fixing and that, once, David would have fixed, and pushed it to the shed door where I stacked the wood, hearing the hollow chock of each chunk as it hit another. The moon had been huge when it came up that night in the cold chill of autumn, enormous as it ever gets and close to the earth – a soft yellow like a round of cheese at Cutting's store. There had been a brooding quiet in the kitchen when Fanny and I put dinner on the table, eying David as had become our custom. He did not talk much, grunting as he ate to get a bowl of potatoes or the milk jug pushed his way. When he was done, he pushed away from the table, gouging the soft floor with the force of his scraping the chair back. Then he was gone, and we heard the noises in the barn of the horse being hitched to the wagon and the metallic rattle of harness chains growing faint as he passed out of the yard and down the road to the village of Lunenburg and beyond.

"The wood has to be stacked tonight," I said matter of factly, pushing out of my chair. "If you can clean up alone in here I will get started."

Fanny nodded. "I will come and help you after the dishes are done," she said.

"But only for a little while," I told her. "It should be a quiet night and I want you to sleep. Biathy, too."

He started at his name, the way he was wont to do. I was often not sure what he was listening to, but he always understood what I was doing, appearing at my elbow like a shadow. It was no different that night. I went right out into the hour before dusk to the woodpile where he had worked all day, and together we loaded the wheelbarrow and he pushed it to the shed where we unloaded it. The moon rose in the hour when it just shone out against the darkening hills, and it seemed to have come up over a nearby ridge, nearer to my farm than was usual.

At ten o'clock, I sent Biathy to bed. Fanny, true to my word, had come out for only a few minutes to check on us after the dishes were done, before going back inside.

"You have cows to tend in the morning," I told him quietly, the sound of my voice strange in the moonlight since we had not been speaking at all. You did not converse with Biathy in words the way you did with just anyone. "And you can keep on with the chopping tomorrow. I was very glad of you tonight."

He did not hesitate, but eased toward the house with the side lope he had, as if one leg were shorter than the other, which it was not. I heard the inner door shut and stood watching the light from the kerosene lamp he carried as it moved like a firefly across the kitchen, disappeared, and popped up again in his bedroom. I watched to see it went out before turning to the task I was now doing solo.

We got through the winter on the little money still left in my savings, hidden in a hollow tree in the orchard. I had seen David searching in the house and barn on a day in late February when there was a melt, his mind working at whether I had more money he had not yet taken, but he would not find that. It was in a tobacco tin, the latch firmly fastened against mice. I had put it there months ago, when I first had an inkling of things not being what they should be.

In the winter, he had been calm. He was good company, and I felt myself relax, and Fanny relaxed – what else could we do? He did some repairs in the barn, and he even worked in the woods, helping Biathy and hauling logs on the sledge hitched to the chestnut horse. A cheerfulness came over the house, with Christmas greens in the parlor, and even a fire in the little stove there one mild day, when we laughed and shivered for an hour or two before leaving it to die down while we scurried to the warmth of the kitchen. He oiled tools, sharpening the sickle and scythe, and polishing them with a rag dipped in oil. We settled into a rhythm and one day he even took me out in the sleigh.

It was like old times and I began to hope.

But February's warm days stirred the itch in him. I saw it happen, a big melt and the sun higher and brighter.

"I need money," he told me one day, quite abruptly, when I was scooping the fat off the milk.

I was startled at his tone, one I had not heard from him for so long. A few months were enough for me to have almost forgotten.

That was the start of everything all over again.

"I don't have much," I said hesitantly. "There isn't much left from…"

He didn't let me finish.

"It is not your money," he said nastily, and suddenly had tight hold of my arm, in the soft place above my elbow, stilling the motion of the spoon.

"When will I get it through your head that it is not your money. That money is my money. You married me and since I am your husband, this is my farm and the money is mine. I let you manage it this winter, but I can see I was mistaken."

He slightly shoved me and the spoon clattered on the table and then went to the floor. I had gone still, and I was afraid. I could feel Fanny hardly breathing in the door to the pantry.

He went to the shelf where I kept the lard tin with all of our cash and he easily reached up and took it down and rummaged through it. He was impatient now, at what he perceived was my resistance, and dumped the contents out onto the counter, coins clinking across the surface, some dropping and rolling across the floor that tilted downwards in one corner. I did not turn to watch, but heard all of his fumbling and the sound of his banging out of the room and the usual sequence of a pause and then the horse and wagon leaving my farm. It was my farm, of that I had no doubt.

This was the way it went as the winter edged into March.

We did not have a sugaring operation. The sugar bush was on Charles' property. He owned half of the lot in our range, the easterly half, and the maple woods were on it. In the good days, that first spring of 1867 when David and I were a few months married, he had gone to work with Charles, as had Biathy. Charles at that time saw no harm in David. He knew that I needed a man to work my farm, and had accepted him well enough. David was a big man and very strong; in fact, that strength had been the cause of his injury in the war. He had lost some of it, and was not a young man by any means at over fifty, but he was good help, and handy besides. That year he had gone over in the middle of February to help Charles with the sugaring.

That David was a help that year cannot be denied. In the jumble of sugaring equipment were dozens of wooden sap buckets. They took a beating each season, from hanging in all kinds of weather from the maple trees, collecting the sap. He and Charles spent days repairing the buckets, organizing the equipment and cleaning out mouse nests and droppings from the long months the building was abandoned. The sap can flow in late February, sometimes not until March and in a bad year, in April. The farmers looked for the warm days and cold nights that made the sap run. The buckets had to be placed on the trees, the men tramping some years through the deep snow on snowshoes to put them out and then collect them, using a yoke from which they could suspend two buckets. All of the sap was brought to the kettles over the fire where it was boiled down into maple sugar. It was a good year for sugaring – 1867 – and the rewards to David and to us had been pounds of it, enough for me to use in cooking and some left over for us to sell.

The late winter of 1868, as I have said, was not giving many signs of spring. The severe cold at the start of March gave way to a northeast storm that covered the ground with more than two feet of snow. It was a widespread storm, cancelling a lecture at the town hall because of the bad travel. Unlike a warm spring, there was no weather right after to settle the snow and melt it so we started March as if it were dead winter still. This weather put a craziness in David. He had been caught away from home the night of the storm – a blessing for us – but came home in a rage. We did everything he seemed to want and never crossed him, and he paced the kitchen. I sent Fanny on errands to Mary, glad he didn't seem to notice she was gone or home.

"Go and stay the day with Mary," I told Fanny every morning, and even in the cold, she walked the twenty minutes, sometimes lucky enough to get a ride from a passing sleigh.

People joked that there would be six weeks more of sleighing before there was spring.

By the middle of the month, the weather broke and the long-awaited spring thaw set in. It was then that David, in a frenzy at how little money there was, took himself off to Charles.

"Charles owes me for all the help I gave him last year," David said out of the blue one morning.

I said nothing.

"He got all of the reward from my work. That is how it always is with people like him. They use my labor and pay me pittance and keep the hog's share of it. I am going over there and getting back some of what he should have given me. I let it go because he is your son, but he is just like you and thinks because his name is on something it is his."

This was a long speech for David and I knew it had been growing in his mind all the time he had been feeling cooped up like a rooster in a box.

What he said was not true. He had been paid well in sugar by Charles – an arrangement Charles had made with me for Biathy – and then, with David in the picture, had extended to him because he was such good help. Charles had a mortgage on that property – as David well knew, though David did not know the details of it nor would he ever be told that I had given Charles the money. I had a plan for the land that included Charles, and he and I were in on these dealings, entwined together like fir boughs into the metal circle that makes them a wreath.

David had been paid very well, and we had gotten good value from the maple sugar we sold. He had been satisfied, very satisfied. Suddenly, he was a man with his name on a farm and with money saved. But that was then, and now he had spent all of the money on drinking and gambling, not only that money, but the money from the crops and produce we had sold, so there was little more than a crumple of paper money and some coins in the lard tin.

It was with the motive of getting money that he set off that day, the snow melting on the edges of the road, and draining into the road so the mud would soon be thick.

It would have been better if I had not been home when he returned. I knew this, but I could not think what to do.

To say the demands he made on Charles were not received well is to so far understate the case that it is like comparing a butternut to its tree. I heard all about it from both of the parties. I think David could have run faster than he even drove the horse, such was his rage at getting home to me after getting nowhere at all with Charles.

"You talk to your son," he ordered me, standing over me and fairly screaming. "You go over there and tell him he is a crook and a cheat and I want my fair share." He grabbed me by the shoulders and lifted me like a doll and shook me.

There was nothing I could say to him, nothing at all. He set me down roughly and pushed his unshaven face with his hot, unpleasant-smelling breath in my face and hissed at me, "I need money. You had better get me money."

And so, against my will, I set off on the road to Charles' house, on foot, hopeful that when I returned, David would have taken the horse and wagon off to Lancaster. There wasn't much in the lard tin, but he could take it and then there would be nothing. I knew that he knew this – the specter of almost nothing becoming nothing with no prospect of cash until the harvest, except of course for Charles and his maple sugaring business. Fanny was with me, and we held hands, hurrying up the muddy road.

When we turned in at Charles' farm, I could see the white face of Amanda at the kitchen window. She was gone as quickly as I noticed so I could almost fancy I imagined her.

"Amanda won't be glad to see us," Fanny whispered.

I sighed. "She will be glad enough to see you. It's me she has no welcome for, and I guess today I can't blame her. You run ahead and ask her where Charles is. Then you come back and tell me and you go sit with Amanda and the boys. She won't mind you."

Fanny scurried across the muddy yard, holding her skirts bunched in both hands as she ran. I saw the door open and she spoke with Amanda who gazed over the girl's head at me with an appraising look. Then Fanny was back by my side.

"He is in the lean-to," she whispered.

"Alright," I said. "You go back now to Amanda."

It was my turn to clutch my skirts out of the dirt, trying to stick to patches of snow as I made my way to the lean-to built off the back of the barn. There was no sign of him, just the faint whine of a drill in hard wood.

"Charles!" I called out, not wanting to surprise him. "Charles!"

I stood a moment, to see if he heard me. There was a silence.

I called again, closer this time.

He appeared in the doorway, hard to see with the darkness behind him.

"What are you doing here?" he said gruffly.

I didn't know what to say.

"Can I come talk to you?"

"You're here, ain't you?" he said, his words coming poorly in his agitation.

I bit my lower lip. I moved toward him.

"You just stay where you are," he said.

"Charles, I'm your mother, please," I said.

Then he was silent and we faced one another down, he in the dark of the building where I could not see his face. He had the advantage, with me in the bright sunlight, surrounded by piles of snow.

"Alright," he said finally, and disappeared from my view.

I followed him into the shed and went to where he was standing in

the light from the one small window where he was working on his buckets. They surrounded a rough looking bench where he had been sitting to
examine each one to be sure it was in good repair and mending the ones
that were not.

He stood and I sat. For awhile, we did not speak.

At last, I broke the silence. "He made me come," I said.

"I know it," he told me.

"He is desperate," I said.

"Why don't you just give him more money," he asked.

"I don't have any more."

He looked at me, a long evaluative stare, and I dropped my eyes.

"You always have some more tucked away, Mama," he said.

"He doesn't know it."

"I think he does know it. That's why he's so mad."

"I can't give it all to him."

"Why not?"

"Because I have plans for that money. You know I do, plans that will
make life better for all of us."

"But he don't see it that way. Maybe things are just too far gone for
those plans."

"Never!"

"Amanda is so mad I'll be surprised if she lets me back in the house."

"She's not mad at you; she's mad at me."

"But you're my mother."

We were quiet.

"Do you know what he said to me?" Charles' voice grated.

"I have a pretty good idea."

"He called me names I wouldn't even repeat to you and he threatened
me. That's a first. Here I am on my own property and he comes and
swears at me, and then he threatens me. I've a mind to go to the sheriff."
The last he said defiantly.

I drew in my breath sharply.

"You wouldn't," I whispered.

"I just might. I have had enough of him. He's your husband and I
won't insult you by saying what he is. He's putting all of us in danger
– and now my wife and children, too. Look at all I put into this place and

how I still struggle, how I had to take another mortgage. Then he comes in here, a man who hardly works, and accuses me of being a thief who stole from him. Stole from him! And he can't even drink in town anymore because of how he behaved. Everybody is talking about it – feeling sorry for us."

"I don't know what to do! What would you have me do?" I cried out.

"I don't know," he said. "I have tried to puzzle it out, but I can't."

He bade me come in the house for a hot cup of tea and a plate of stew.

"I'm not welcome," I said.

"It's my house, too, not just hers, and she will have to put up with it while you get warmed up and fed."

"I hope he won't be there when I get back," I said. "But I can't be gone too long."

"This won't take long," he said.

I was right that I was not welcome in that warm kitchen with the rich smell of stew and warm bread. Charles had gone ahead and said something to her, so when I came in she was not in the room. He dished me up a plate, and Fanny poured me tea from the pot Amanda had made for her.

None of us talked much about anything except the break in the cold and the longed-for spring. We would have talked about when the sap would run, but that was not a subject for light conversation anymore.

Before Fanny and I headed back home, he drew me aside and said in a low voice, "I've hit on a plan. You give him a little from the money you've held back and say it is from me. That way it will look like you did what you were told and I gave in, but only a little, and you won't have to let him know about the other money."

That is what I did. When I got home, David was gone as I had hoped. I set Fanny to fixing supper for Biathy and I went out to the hollow tree in the orchard, careful not to leave tracks and grateful the trees were on a sunny patch so most of the snow was melted. I reached deep into the back of the hole, and pulled out the tobacco tin. I considered as I held the money in my hand, and pulled a few bills from under the string that held it all in a band. I had $600.

When David came home early in the morning, he stumbled against the stairwell, dragging his feet as he came upstairs, mumbling loudly, and sometimes cursing as he crashed down once on his knees. He fell fully clothed across the comforter and was asleep, snoring loudly.

In the morning, when he came downstairs, his beard very thick and dark now from two days of not shaving, I handed him the bills without a word.

"That's alright then," he gloated, counting his bounty. "I knew he would not play the fool with you."

The problem was that the money, as much as it seemed to him when he had it in his hand, did not seem like much once he set to spending it on drink and in a matter of days, with the spring madness in him, it was gone.

It was then, after the night of March 23, when he had spent the last of it, and no doubt lost badly at cards, that the trouble began.

§

Chapter Six

MARCH 24, 1868

I KNEW THERE WAS TROUBLE BREWING WHEN I AWOKE AND HE WAS NOT IN BED BESIDE ME WHERE HE HAD COLLAPSED IN THE EARLY MORNING HOURS. I crept down the stairs, listening cautiously to the silence of the house for any sound that might show me where he was and what he was up to. There was nothing much, only a whisper of something from the kitchen, like paper against paper. I stopped, though, hardly breathing. I had avoided the spots on the treads that made the most noise, but I knew my descent had been far from soundless. If he were in the kitchen, he had already heard me. Indeed, I expected he had been waiting for me and if I did not come in now he would come in search of me and that would be worse. I only wished I had warned Fanny to stay in her room until she knew it was safe to come down.

He was sitting at the table, ramrod straight and facing the door from which he knew I would enter. The stairs went up from the front door, and at their base was also the door to the parlor and a narrow passageway, too narrow to be called a hall, that led to the kitchen. When I went in, my hands knotted at my sides, there he was in the dim light of pre-dawn. I could see the shadowy lines of his face, and his dark eyes like smudges of soot with no reflection of light. In his fingers was a slip of paper and it was that I had heard as he had twisted it in his agitation so it rubbed against itself with a rustling sound like a mouse in the wall.

As soon as I was in the room, he began to speak, his voice low and full of menace.

"This is what it has come to. I am the man of this house and I sit alone in my kitchen with no one tending me or even pretending to care. I am wearing the same clothes I had on last night and no one even helped me out of them. Where is my wife? Have you seen her? Because I have no wife here. A wife would have waited up for me and helped me out of my clothes whatever hour or condition I came home. Here I am sitting here.

Is there any hot water for me to wash my face or shave? Is there any coffee made? Is there even the beginnings of breakfast before I start my day?" He paused to gulp air.

"Do you see what I have in my hand?" he snarled at me.

He thrust out the paper at me, but I stayed put, my mind racing at how I might escape.

"This is a note, Missus Businesswoman. Do you know what that means? I am in debt, this time to that fat bastard over in Lancaster who owns the gristmill. And how am I to pay it? You tell me there is no money. I own this farm and have a wife, but how am I to pay this debt?"

He stood up sharply and I cringed, but he was only reaching for the lard tin on the high shelf which he took down and shook hard, but there was no sound and he tipped it upside down and jerked it a few times, but nothing fell out. Then he flung the tin with all his might, hard against the floor so it bounced and the metal rang and the sound echoed in my ears. If I had been a mouse, I could have run now for the hole in the baseboard and disappeared to shiver in the darkness and hear him rant. But I was no mouse, though I felt small enough, shrunk down in the spot from where I had first seen him at the table.

He sat back down hard in the chair. He was silent awhile, turning the piece of paper in his hands.

I knew now where he had been, and that he had been playing cards for money though he had none. And he was sitting here now like a judge over hell because he had not had money enough to get really drunk, just enough to take out the meanness, but it was back now because the liquor had worn off soon.

I heard the two cows lowing in the field. It was time for milking. Even as I thought this, I heard the loud creak of the stairs like the shot of a gun in the strained silence of the house. It was Biathy, who passed out the front door, opening and closing it almost as softly as the rustle of the note.

It was as if the coming and going of Biathy had wakened David from a bad dream, and he sat breathing heavily in the kitchen that was growing into lightness with the rising of the sun. He pushed back the chair with such force it toppled back and hit the floor with a sharp crack. He went out of the door to the shed, not bothering to shut it, and crashed through the shed, kicking a basket of kindling so I heard the cane buckle under his boot. I did not move, but stood where I was, as if made of ice; I was cold enough and the stove had gone out in the night. I did not move until I heard the horse neigh and the rumble of the wagon on the frozen ruts of the yard. I ran as fast as I could to the window in the parlor. From there, I could see the road and I saw that he turned the wagon up the road in the direction of Charles' house and Victory.

Back in the kitchen, I saw that he had left the note and I picked it up to read that he owed the owner of the gristmill ten dollars. It could have been worse, much worse. I sighed, wiping my eyes, and tucked the paper in the pocket of my apron. I heard sounds upstairs as I thought what to do next. By the time I came back with a handful of kindling from the broken basket in the shed, Fanny was getting out the jar of flour. She looked up at me carefully to be sure that I was alright. Reassured, she set about making muffins for our breakfast. They would be plain this time of year, but we had jars of blackberry preserve left and that would taste good spread with butter on the hot muffins.

Of course, I could not eat. But the making of the muffins marked the time and I forced myself to concentrate on Fanny's movements, slow and deliberate and as familiar as time, measuring out the flour and two tablespoons of sugar and a half-cup of milk. Making muffins from the old receipt that my mother and probably my grandmother used is simple, and a soothing process, if I had not been so agitated, my pulse hammering and my hands ice cold. She greased the old battered tins with butter and divided out the batter and soon the muffins were baking. I did not trust myself to cook the hash brown potatoes without burning them, but I shakily prepared last night's potatoes anyway, set aside in a bowl from supper for this purpose. I cut them into small, precise pieces, my hands trembling so I had to steady them consciously before each chop.

It was just before the muffins were to have come out that we heard the horse and wagon tear into the yard, David's shouts at the mare ringing clear in the room. I ran outside into the cold morning, a clear morning with the intent of the sun to make the day warm. I was just in time to see the wild-eyed horse, her mouth foamy, come to a sharp stop that set the wagon bed shuddering. To my horror, I could see it was piled high with sap buckets and, as I watched, the top buckets on one tipsy stack tumbled onto the ground with the abrupt stop of the wagon.

"Get out here," he was shouting. "I want all of you out here. Go get that daughter of yours and get her out here. I want you all to see what happens when I am crossed."

I spun back into the kitchen. Fanny, silent and white-faced, was pulling out the tin of muffins.

"Forget those," I hissed.

"They will be burned," she said calmly, and continued with what she was doing, placing them on the stove top, closing the oven door and even pulling the skillet of potatoes to the cool edge.

"Get out here," he kept shouting and we were there, even Biathy who had come out from the barn to see what was happening.

David leapt onto the back of the wagon and began handing down buckets; there were dozens of them, beautiful buckets all repaired and cleaned for the sugaring season. Of course, I knew whose they were.

"Take them, hurry up," he shouted. "There's no time to lose."

He was fairly throwing the heavy objects at us. Biathy was best able to handle this, though he staggered under the weight of a big, unsteady load. Fanny and I fared less well, and our hands were scraped up, knuckles raw and nails chipped from the rapid, hard tosses of David to us. At last they were unloaded, in a huge pile in the frozen ruts of the yard. I was shaking so inside I kept hiccupping though no one could hear because of his shouts and the crash of buckets as they hit the pile, cracking and settling. In the midst of all of this, I saw a wagon go past the house fast, on the road from Victory in the direction of Lunenburg. It was not Charles, but his neighbor, Darius Phelps, and the horse was moving at a fast clip.

Then it was that David sent Biathy to the barn for a tin of kerosene and when it was brought, he poured the liquid over the buckets. He pulled a crumpled handkerchief from his pocket, one of the big white ones I had washed and ironed that week, and set it on fire with a match and tossed it onto the assemblage. There was a pop and then a roar as we all leapt back at the explosion of fire.

We stood, in a row, the heat of that fire turning our sweaty faces orange from the glow. The burning appeased him for some moments, but then he went back to the wagon and pulled off the kettles used for boiling the sap and the sap holder that was really a big wooden vat used to collect all of the sap from the buckets. He spread them out on the ground, and he took a sledgehammer from the wagon – not ours – and he methodically began to attack them, his great strength evident in every blow he struck, smashing the kettles beyond recognition as anything that could ever hold anything, and demolishing the sap holder in two swift blows.

When all of that was done, and the fire was still burning, it was my turn and I knew it.

He dragged me by the wrist to the house and I was screaming. He flung me around that kitchen like I was a pile of those buckets and it was only that I was made of blood and bones that he did not burn me up.

"You see now!" he hollered, when I was huddled in a corner of the room. He left the the kitchen in ruins, chairs broken, the muffins strewn across the floor and mashed into the boards, dishes broken, and the silverware drawer pulled out and dumped onto the floor. If it had not been for all of those things, it would have gone worse for me so I did not mind their destruction as much as I might have. Somehow my pottery bowl, the prize of my house, had escaped, being on a cupboard shelf. It was what he had said to me as he hurt me that did not leave me, that I could not stop remembering.

"I will kill you," he had screamed at me, punching me in the face, and I knew he could do it.

Suddenly, it was all over. I was alive and he was gone from the house.

I did not see that the sheriff and Darius Phelps, Mary's son, and three men from the village were there to meet him. Before he could turn the wagon, they had come into the yard and were upon him, subduing him. Darius stayed behind, coming to me where I was still hunched in the kitchen, but the rest took David to Guildhall where he was locked up in the jail.

Darius helped me up, and he fetched warm water from the kettle on the stove and filled the metal basin.

"Are you alright?" he kept asking. "Should I fetch the doctor? Is anything broken? Oh, I wish my mother was here."

I guess I was in some kind of shock because though I could hear him I could not answer, as if he were a long way away. My ears rang and I mopped the blood from my cut lip with my handkerchief, fumbled from my pocket. I washed my face, and longed for something cold on my smashed cheekbone and a piece of fresh beef to take the heat from my eye. He vanished, and Biathy was there instead, patting my hand and making me sit in the rocker. Darius had gone for his mother, and by the time he returned with her I was more in myself.

"Oh, God, Lucy," she breathed when she saw me. Then she was all business and shooed Biathy and Darius from the room, telling them to not let anyone in if someone should come by. She helped me out of my blood-stained apron and dress, and she helped me wash up. She sent Darius home for a piece of beef for my eye and she cleaned my cheekbone and my cut lip and commiserated over how my tooth had been chipped, but was at least still there.

Then it was that I said, as if sitting upright in bed after a bad dream, "Where is Fanny?"

No one knew. I insisted on getting dressed and putting on my boots, and we all went in search of her – me and Biathy and Mary and Darius.

It was hours before she would come out of the woods where she had hidden herself, not until the sun had set and the chill of the approaching night drove her to us. Biathy and Darius hauled bucket after bucket of water and Mary heated it on the stove and filled the tin bathtub with steaming water for Fanny to bathe. I had been holding her in my lap all that time, rocking us both and comforting us both. She could not stop shivering, from the fright and from the cold she had endured all day in the woods. Tenderly, I undressed her and guided her into the soothing heat of the tub where she got warm at last.

Since no words of mine could assure her that David would not come back, and indeed I did not have that assurance, we bundled her in blankets and she went back to Mary's house with Darius and Mary. I would not go. My place was there at my farm, and I would not leave it.

Biathy sat with me in the warm kitchen. He went to bed and still I sat, rocking, my hands not busy with knitting or anything at all for once.

In the night, at what time I am not sure, I stoked the fire and put in extra wood to hold till morning and I went to bed, hugging a brick warmed on the stove and wrapped in a towel. I shoved it deep under the covers and undressed and got into my nightgown and crawled in to curl my cold feet around the warmth. Biathy's calico cat was on the top of the pile of quilts, but I did not move her. She purred and stretched, and went back to sleep. I slept, too, and missed the dawn and the sound of the cows. I awoke at first confused as to what had happened, but knowing I was stiff and ached all over like I had the flu. Slowly it all came to me, the events of the day before, and I did not want to get up. Nothing this bad had ever happened under David's hand, but I was familiar with the routine of the court. I would have to go in search of the lawyer. David had been in jail more than once. If he was just drunk, he would be out, but it was more than that this time, and I guessed they would know that at the court, but I was not sure. I did not even know what had happened at Charles' house the previous morning.

I got up as carefully as I could, my head pounding and my left eye swollen shut. My right arm was stiff as a sheet hung on the line in January. My cheekbone ached where he had hit me. I felt the chipped edge of my side tooth and touched my lip that was cracked and swollen. It took me a long time to get dressed, but I managed it, and it took me a long time to get down the stairs, holding onto the side of the wall, feeling dizzy and a little nauseous. There was a fire in the stove; I was glad of that. I sank into the first chair I came to and tried to be still and sit straight so my head would stop spinning. I was not sure what time it was. Hiram's watch had been sold long ago when David needed money. I thought, by the sun's angle in the east window, that it was about eight o'clock.

I sat, trying to think of what to do, but not able to come up with a plan because of my aching head and all of the other places – my hands raw from the buckets and my ribs sore. Really, I could not find a place that was free from injury. When Biathy came quietly into the kitchen, that is where I still was. I could not seem to move, not for tea water that should be on the stove, or a pot of coffee for Biathy, or muffins if I could find the tin. The kitchen still bore much of the signs of disaster, though Mary had done a lot to set it to rights the day before.

Biathy studied me in that slow way of his, his eyes looking at me a very long time, waiting for me to speak to him.

"I am not feeling…" I started to say and trailed off as I realized how talking pulled at the jagged edges of my cut lip.

He frowned, and spoke some sort of words himself in his own language that was a series of mutters and grunts in a variety of pitches.

Then he got the kettle and filled it with water and set it on the stove. He found two cups that were whole and set them on the table and measured out tea into the little strainer. The teapot was smashed. He found the pieces where Mary had left them by the sink, and showed me, mimicking putting them together, and set them on the table. He made tea for the first time in his life, and luckily I had sat in a chair within reach of the cup he filled with hot water. He brought sugar from the can on the pantry shelf since the sugar dish was not to be found, and he brought a cup of milk, fresh from the pail he had brought from the cow. He poured in some sugar, a lot of sugar, and milk, and stirred it briskly so that the tea splashed onto the table.

The tea was very hot, and my hand trembled as I brought the cup to my mouth, trying to blow on it with my sore lip, thirsty for the hot liquid the way a morning tea drinker gets. It was as I sipped and blew, and blew and sipped, my brain starting to clear with the ingestion of the strong, heavily sugared tea, that I heard a wagon come into the yard and I went rigid. Biathy loped to the window with a view in that direction and turned back to me, bobbing his head with what I took to be approval. I relaxed. That was not how he behaved with David. David never bothered him, not considering him worth it, but when David was around, Biathy became invisible in the way he could. He let himself be claimed by the shadows of wherever he was,

It was Mary, with Darius and two of her other sons.

"I left Fanny home," she told me right off. "I wasn't sure whether…" and she shrugged.

"You did right," I whispered, thinking if I spoke carefully and quietly, I would not hurt as much.

The men shuffled their feet and stared at me, their hats in their hands, as if they were at a funeral. I saw from them how bad I looked.

"Now you boys go on outside," Mary scolded. "If you must stay, you just don't bother us in here."

"I'd like to get my hands on him," I heard one of them mutter, as they turned and filed out through the shed. I knew they would not let their mother be here without protection.

Mary went about fixing breakfast for Biathy and me. She found eggs that he had collected that morning, and she found butter and made us muffins and eggs, and percolated coffee for Biathy. She gave me another cup of tea, just as hot as Biathy had fixed, but without as much sugar.

"Do you know what happened?" I asked. "I don't know what happened at Charles' house. Have you seen him? Is he alright?"

"Charles is alright," Mary said. "The boys saw him in town. I am not sure what happened up there. What went on here? I see there was a fire in the yard."

"He burned up sap buckets," I told her. "I think, all of them. He came back here with them. The wagon was full of them."

"Oh," Mary said, and looked sober. We both knew what that meant: Charles would miss the sugaring season unless he could replace the buckets. And he had lost kettles and his sap holder.

"It was worse this time," I said.

"I know," she said, appraising my injuries.

"Not me," I said. "That, too, but what he did was worse. He has never done anything on so big a scale."

"What will you do?"

"What is there to do? I will have to find the lawyer and see about getting him out of jail."

As it turned out, I did not need to get David out of jail. Mary and the boys were still with me when he walked into the yard. I heard the men talking and heard David's voice. It did not surprise me, but it pained me that he was back already. I had hoped for a day. With one day I had thought I could get back on an even keel again.

He came right into the kitchen as if nothing had passed between us. Mary's boys came with him and the room seemed small with all of them standing.

"They had nothing on me," he boasted. "It was all Charles' word against mine. That little bastard thought he had me, but he don't. So, Mary, what's for breakfast?"

There was a stillness in the room when he stopped speaking, with so many words unsaid, and only the heavy sound of the men breathing and a piece of wood that popped loudly in the stove.

That was how he was, acting as if not a thing had happened, and the men hated him for it and Mary would have had him a bug on the floor that she could have crushed him under the heel of her boot.

In that silence, he turned at last to me, and I saw in his eyes, because he was looking at me alone, that he knew what he had done. There was a flicker in them of defiance, anger and something else, a shudder, if eyes can be said to show a shudder, like a wavering shadow in the woods at night when you are wise to be afraid. That was all. What we would have to say to one another would have to wait until we were alone. I was not afraid anymore, now that I had seen that look in him. He would behave for now.

§

Chapter Seven

MARCH INTO APRIL 1868
TRUCE

IT WAS THE WEAKNESS IN DAVID THAT I USED. He was a big man, as I have said, 6' 1", and he used his size to intimidate. He was big and when he was frustrated and did not know how to get what he wanted, he tred on people. But he was weak. If his character were a wagon wheel, made of wood with a metal rim, there were spokes missing and so the wheel was not strong. I was a small woman, barely five feet tall. It had never mattered before since my character was strong. While he intimidated me physically and therefore forced me to do things as his wife that I did not want to do, but felt it my obligation to him, he did not control my heart, which stayed firm. He had made a mistake when he chose me. He saw my land, and that I was a helpless widow and in good condition to work, but he misread my interior condition. He would come up against my strength over and over, and though he would threaten to kill me, it was only my physical being he threatened because my will was indomitable.

There was a silence for the next days. The worst of it was that I did not see Charles. I could not go to him and I knew he would not come to my farm because of David. Mary did not come either, because of him. Her men would not allow it and they did not want to come themselves.

Between him and me, there was a truce. He had a sly way about him, and now crept about the place doing some work, which he always thought was the way to placate me. He had played not just a card with the destruction of Charles' property, but a whole hand, and thrown in the deck, too, for good measure.

He was up before I was, and came in for meals and stayed out the whole day. He jollied Fanny, who could barely conceal her terror of him. I could smell her fear. She gave off a cold, rank odor. Her eyes had a blank, dull look, and she was jumpy.

He praised her cooking – the sweetness of the dried apple pie she made, the creaminess of the butter she churned, the lightness of her doughnuts. Slowly, I saw her unwind and though she was watchful, she stopped sweating in the cold mornings before the kitchen was warm. She smelled sweet again, and I had given her my last bar of fancy soap that had been a long-ago luxury. Her own girlishness melded with the sweet soap and I felt relieved in being with her.

It would be a late season sugaring. The weather that spring was like winter, with a succession of storms dropping heavy, wet snow that made the roads impassable, first with the snow and then churned up with mud that set into frozen ruts in a cycle that kept repeating itself.

Perhaps that is what delayed the consequences of what he had done. Anyway, it was early in April, a clear day, when the sheriff arrived with the notice for David to appear at a court of inquiry held in Lunenburg by the justice of the peace, William Chandler, on April 16.

"I am looking for your husband, Mrs. Beede," the sheriff told me when I went to the door at his knock. He had come on horseback and I could see the mare's legs and underbelly and rump were mud-spattered. It was early. He had hoped to avoid the melt from the sun, but here on the high ground the sun was already at work.

"He is in the barn," I said. "Can you tell me why you have come?"

The sheriff studied me, marking the yellowed bruises on my face, I knew. He hesitated. He had known me a long time, and Hiram and our families, and he had had acquaintance with David on more than one occasion.

"I should not," he said. "I am only sent to deliver this." He did not tell me, but he held up the paper he carried long enough for me to read that it was from the state and then he unfolded it and held it so I could read the summons.

"Thank you," I told him.

"Can you get him there?" the sheriff asked. "He needs to be there."

"I will do what I can," I said.

I went back to the kitchen.

"Go upstairs," I told Fanny sharply.

She started and in looking at me, her face went white.

"It was the sheriff and he has brought a summons for your stepfather to go to court in a week's time. It is a court of inquiry, but serious."

She ran from the room and I heard the hard echo on the stairs of her heavy gait.

Barely had the sheriff ridden off the property when David erupted into the house.

"What the hell is going on?" he shouted, flinging the paper onto the table. His eyes were almost bugging out of his head and the vein on his forehead bulged.

My heart was beating fast, but I showed none of my agitation as I picked up the paper and pretended I was reading it for the first time.

"It is that goddamn son of yours! I have come into a nest of vipers. You put him up to it. You put this idea of charging me into his head. When did you run to him? I will have all of you for this."

"I did not go to him," I said. "You have cut me off from my son. Do you think I would go to him or he come to me?" I spoke very deliberately and worked to look him in the eye. "Sit down and I will make you some coffee and we will figure out how to handle this. I am on your side. We will work this out."

To my relief, he did sit down. I poured him coffee and added the sugar and milk the way he liked and put it in front of him and sat down across the table. I saw his hand was shaking as he lifted the cup. He did look at me, and I saw that he was afraid.

I took a deep breath.

"We will take care of this together," I said again.

"I was pushed into doing it," he said. "You know I was. I never would have done it if Charles hadn't provoked me. We're all in this together. Why would he accuse me? We have helped him out. He wouldn't have his farm or his sugaring or anything if it weren't for us. Doesn't he know that?"

"We'll fix it," I said.

"Everybody is against me," he said. "They want to send me up. Why is everybody against me? I don't stand a chance, you know. Even you, my wife, even you are against me."

"I am not against you," I soothed him. "If I had more to give you I would," I lied. "You know I would."

"That's why I hurt you," he said. "Because you were against me. That's why I went after Charles. He would be nothing if we hadn't helped him. He wouldn't even have a sugaring operation if I hadn't gotten him going last year. Why is everyone against me?" He had a whiny tone rippling through his protests. It was always this way when the law finally caught up with him, or some authority like the owner of a tavern who cast him out or a man in town who would not buy our produce because of his behavior.

"We'll fix it like we have before," I assured him again. "We'll get a lawyer if we need one and it will all be fixed."

Why would he not believe me? That was how it had happened before, over and over, in the year and a half of our marriage. He had been fined for disorderly conduct at the hotel in the village. He had been named in another incident at the tavern. He had been accused of setting fire to a box of wood in a shed of a dealer who would not take our grain, but nothing had stuck. In all of these cases, I had paid the fines and hired an attorney to set things right for us. I had scrimped and saved only to see the money go to settle the results of his activities. Why should this be any different?

But it was different. I am not sure why. But the men who had come for him that day in March had tromped through our yard and seen the smoldering fire in the middle of the driveway. The sheriff had been there and he had seen it. And then Charles had gone to the law. He had filed a complaint and agreed to stand as State's witness.

The day we went to the court of inquiry in Lunenburg, the county clerk was in attendance, and the State's attorney, by the name of D.S. Storrs, and we stood before the justice of the peace, William Chandler, who ruled that the injury of the destruction of property of Charles Presbrey was an act against the laws of the state. He agreed to the value of $25 for eighty-two sap buckets, and the value of ten dollars for the two kettles and another ten dollars for the sap holders, and David was charged to appear for trial at Guildhall at the court, the third Tuesday of September in that year 1868.

Horace Stone was there, and he stood as bondsman for David. Two hundred dollars – more than I had paid for my first farms. There was nothing to do but mortgage the farm to Horace Stone.

I stood rigid, with a heart as heavy as the stone that is bounced along the bottom of the river in the flood.

It was said that David was a risk to run. I said that I would guarantee he would appear, but that was not enough.

Justice Chandler was kind enough to me, but he fixed a stern eye on David, instructing him that if he did not appear for the trial to face the charge of larceny, the bail would be forfeited. And so I feared we would lose the farm.

David and I and our attorney went to the clerk's office in the town of Lunenburg and we signed away our right and title to my farm for $200.

But I did not really think David would leave, even then, in the quiet of the clerk's office as the clerk slowly and beautifully penned the mortgage that kept David out of jail and guaranteed his appearance in court.

We rode home in a terrible silence. On the public road, he held in his rage, but when we were safe at home, he pitched into me, and it was the day of the firing of Charles' buckets all over again when David took out his rage on me and did everything but burn me. He beat me and again threatened to kill me. In his mind, I had betrayed him. I had lied to him and fixed nothing because I was his enemy and favored my son over him and was in league with my son against him as I had been from the beginning of our marriage.

That night, he left and I would not see him again for a very long time. Fanny ran all the way, the long mile, to Mary Phelps, and Mary and her sons came for me and she took me home to nurse me. Biathy went back and forth to the farm for the next weeks, riding the horse Mary had given me.

§

Chapter Eight

1859-60

H OW WE ALL CAME TO BE ON THE ROAD TO VICTORY IS WORTH TELL-
ING. If you can picture how this happened, move by move like the
checkers on the board the men gather around at Cutting's store, it helps
understand the bigger picture.

Really it was the land dealings that drove me. Without that instinct
to trade land which I had inherited from my father and which Charles inherited from me, our lives would have looked very different. Without the
land, we would have remained poor, struggling to subsist. In that way the
land was good. Without the land, David Beede would never have been
attracted to my siren call. In that way the land was bad.

What started out as a simple, creative step was my finagling the purchase of the land on the Guildhall border using Hiram's black horse.
There we were, at last, on our own land. It was small, though, a parcel
of thirty-eight acres, more or less, as the deeds are wont to say. This was
where his brother, Leroy, had started to farm and died doing it, just shy
of his thirtieth birthday. He had got the land because of his father. Unlike
Hiram and me, Leroy had stayed near his father and mother, and never
married. He was a hard worker, but had not long come to that farm when
he succumbed to illness and sold it to move back home with his father
where he would die.

It was not much, that first place of mine. James S. Smith, who was my
cousin by marriage to a cousin, and who would support me later in my
trials after David's final arson, in New Hampshire, would tell the judge it
was "a small farm." He gave me full credit for finding the means to obtain
it, and that praise from him – a man of substance, a businessman – I held
dear.

I knew that piece of land and though it was broken up from when
Leroy had owned it, having come down to thirty-eight acres from sev-
enty-six on parts of two lots on the Guildhall border, still it seemed a good

place to start. There was a house and a small barn, and a small sugar bush of maples, and some pasture and enough acreage to put under the plow for some crops. I kept hens and we had a pig each year.

That purchase filled Hiram with uncertainty. Never one to make a quick decision and often not making one at all, to our continued detriment, he faced the fact of our own farm with little enthusiasm. But he was not one to buck me because he did not have the energy for it. He had let himself be swept along by my planning, thanks to the accident of acquiring the black horse. If it had not been for that, we would not have gotten a farm so soon since I had been saving for a place, as James S. knew, but was not within reach of my goal yet.

I had started saving after our move to Lunenburg, with the shame of the paupers' list fresh in my memory. It had taken me ten years to put aside an amount even close to the price of a small farm. Hiram did not know of my saving, not because he would have tried to stop me or take the money, but because I did not want him to worry about this event so far in the future that it might never take place at all. The ambition was mine and I kept it close.

That first farm, the twenty-six and one-half acres on the east side of Lot Twenty-two in the fourth division and twelve acres on adjacent Lot Twenty-four, was located as far from the river as any settled lots went. It was a hill farm, perched on the side of the hill and with long views to the mountains of New Hampshire. Though the land was hard to farm, with fields of rocks that seemed to grow through the winter and pop up on the surface like mushrooms in the spring, the views were solace to me. The simple fact that I had achieved what I set out to do was heady, the way the fragrance of apple blossoms fills the spring air and you can breathe the sweetness deep into your lungs.

To be in that clerk's office on the third of May in 1860, with the winter long over, and the summer still to come; to see the clerk, Stephen Howe, pen out in his flowing letters the deed from Ira G. to me, Emeline Presbrey, thrilled me. Hiram was there, and his name was listed as the owner of the black horse, but it was my name put down in the black ink as the buyer. I was an owner at last.

That could have been enough. If it had been, I would never have lived on the road to Victory, and I would have seen my husband buried in the burying ground that was on Lot Twenty-four even when Leroy bought the land. I would never have met David Beede, never been forced to cross back over the river to New Hampshire. Those are the what-ifs.

Of course, like my father before me, I could not be satisfied.

The border of Guildhall was appealing for one reason: it put me closer to my sister, Wealthy. Our land was geographically even with where they lived in the hills of the other town – the shire town where the courthouse was, and the bridge to Northumberland across the big river. It was there that Myalina met George Washington Gage, her husband, and where my Charles met her sister, Malinda, that caused him so much heartache even as the war went on and on. How easily we all traveled back and forth, between my mountain road and hers. It was there, too, in that enclave of houses where many of George's mother's sisters lived with their husbands on land owned by her father, that I came to know Samuel Hannux. And it was on the mountain road where Wealthy lived that Hiram and I came to know David and Susan Kimball and their children, them being neighbors of my sister. Their two children, Cornelia and Alfred, ended up living with Samuel after their father died suddenly of pneumonia, and their mother was taken ill, too, and so close to death, she was taken in by a sister who nursed her back to health. Eventually, she would marry Samuel and the family would be reunited.

We were all there, on those farms in the hills, getting to know one another without ever thinking of how this would matter in our futures.

As I said, if I had been satisfied with the one transaction, my life would have looked very different. But I wanted more. I could see that the small farm of thirty-eight acres was not enough. I could see that we would subsist – there was enough for us to live on frugally – but not enough to prosper. It niggled at me that some of the parcel owned originally by Leroy had been split off to a man named Daniel Kimball, an uncle of David Kimball. Knowing what the property once was, I fixed in my mind to bring it all back together under my name. With good years of crops, and Hiram working hard under my guidance, I saved enough to do it. In January of 1863, I would become the owner of one hundred acres, paying Daniel Kimball for twenty-five more acres in neighboring Lot Twenty, and for seventy-five acres in the third division, a distance from the other land, which meant I was spreading out.

To do this transaction, I used $50 I had set aside, and from James S., I borrowed the rest. Hiram and I signed to a mortgage of $175. I shivered with excitement, standing in the clerk's office for the second time as a landowner in my own right. At that time, James S. owned an inn on the common in Lunenburg. He was prosperous and his standing by me gave me the opportunity I needed.

We developed this new land in concert with what we had. I admit I drove Hiram. The mortgage ate at him, and I ate at him, pushing us to pay it off quickly with bigger crops. It was in the next year that his sickness began to show. Surely, I did not cause it, but I could not help but continue to push him because of the loan. We paid off the $175 at the end of two seasons, in late August 1864.

I could not rest. The same day we paid off the money, we sold all of the one hundred and thirty-eight acres to a woman named Abby Lewis for the grand sum of $650. Humble me, who had started with a farm worth the value of the black horse, now was commanding over six times that for what Hiram and Charles and I had built, even with our son gone to the war and injured. This time, I held the mortgage, for $150, for the Lewis couple.

Two days later, I bought the land on the road to Victory, up the road past Neal's Pond. For $500 from a couple by the name of Azro and Adelphia Goss, I bought eighty-four acres on that road, and half of another lot and all of a third. The latter two parcels of land had what I hoped was good timber to be sold later to the mill.

It was a great day, the culmination of careful planning with the advice of James S. who knew what I wanted and knew the lay of the lands in the town.

It was on that day, August 31, 1864, that I became Lucy E. Presbrey, re-creating myself in prosperity. It was also the day that Charles F., my son, first came to the clerk's office and stood as a witness to what I did.

&

Chapter Nine

1860

IN ALL OF THE TIME WE LIVED ON THE GUILDHALL BORDER, I FELT CLOSE TO MY SISTER. We had been apart for many years following our marriages, starting with hers to Lucius Larrabee. He was a stocky man of average height with heavy, beetle brows of heavy hair. His hair on the top of his head was thinning, even when I met him for the first time, and he wore the balance of it long around his ears. He had eyes that formed into long, narrow slits under the hoods of his brow. The bones over his eyes protruded markedly. He was not a pleasant man to look at by the time he reached his mid-thirties, and the wrinkles of outdoor work for years on his farms had turned his face into a craggy, ledge-like structure. He had a gruff voice, and a deep, hoarse cough. He was always blowing his nose loudly into his big white handkerchiefs, which he kept about his person, not one like most men, but several. And he was a cold man in his physical being, always dressed in a dusty-looking coat, even in the fields and barn, except on the hottest days of summer. All of that would not have mattered if his temperament had been better. He was a cross, easily stirred-up man with never a good word to say about anyone, including his sons, though it must be said he had a soft spot for his daughters that came out in dry teasing. He ran a tight household. He ordered how everyone dressed, and when purchases were made, and what food was put before him at the mealtimes he determined. It is no wonder that his daughters fled the constrictions early into marriage, and also left behind the tight circumstances of a family of fifteen.

"What did you ever see in him?" I wanted to ask my sister. But I held my tongue. The fact was I did not want it thrown in my face that while Hiram might be (slightly) better to look at, Lucius was a worker and always had been. The discussion that would follow would be rancorous and I was not eager to have it.

She could, however, bring up the subject of his faults as long as I was careful to only nod in sympathy and never say a word myself against him. If I did, she was quick to defend him.

"Our situation is at his door," she would say to me. "You know he gave up the land he owned, a gift from his father, the year after we married. He could not stand to think of being held to the terms of caring for his poor, mentally incapacitated brother and his stepmother. She was remarried within the year of his father's death, anyway, and Hinney, the brother, was out to work and living with his sister, Sylvia, so what would we have had to lose by staying put on that farm?"

I was not expected to answer that question.

"We have never saved a penny since, not with moving every few years to one rented, worn-out farm after another," she said.

I did not mention that having a child every two years was part of the equation of their limited circumstances, as she called them. I would not bring that up since I was thin-skinned about that subject of her having babies easily and my struggling to do so. I did not want her to answer back to my comment about her excessive childbearing with a remark about my inability. I did not think she would, but she could be sharp-tongued, fixing me with those dark, glittering eyes of hers that missed nothing. She could make a person cry, knowing what arrow would hurt the worst when it struck its mark.

We had the conversation many times about our husbands' virtues and lack thereof, but that day I remember particularly. It was the spring of 1860 and I had come with Fanny and Charles and Biathy to tell her the news of my farm. I had not said a word of it before because I did not want to scotch the deal with the horse and Ira with my loose talk. But two days after signing the papers, I had Hiram hitch the chestnut mare to the wagon and went to see my sister. The next day we would be moving to the new house.

"I want to tell her before she hears it," I told Hiram. "News travels fast."

He nodded.

"Charles can stay with me," he said.

Charles' face fell. I knew why. I knew he had his eye on my niece, Malinda, pretty as a garden rose, not a rose by the side of the road with its petals waving in any breeze, but a fancy garden rose of palest pink with a slight flush of peach. She was thirteen and just come into her beauty.

"Hmm," I said, torn between wanting Charles to be pleased and my instinct against his relating to his cousin. But I knew I could never stop that if he chose it and fighting him would only make things worse.

"I was thinking maybe we could all take a little holiday," I said cautiously to Hiram. "After today it will be all work, what with moving and then pitching into what needs doing."

"Alright," he said quickly, as I had guessed he would. "I'll go fishing. Don't you want to fish with me, Charles?"

Charles scuffed the toe of his boot in the dirt, and looked down.

"Come into the house with me a minute," I said to Hiram.

He shrugged and we went into the kitchen.

"What?" he asked, impatient at my secretive manner.

"He wants to see his cousin," I said in a low voice.

"What?"

"His cousin, Malinda. She is quite pretty, now, you know. Beautiful," I explained. "He is very taken with her."

"Oh," his face lightened with understanding. "Good heavens. Well, alright."

Charles took the reins and we followed the road out of Lunenburg from our farm into Guildhall and up the road by Cat's Paw Brook toward Cow Mountain where my sister lived. It was a warm day for early May. It seemed every bird was in the meadows chirruping, and the grass was a pale, yellow-green full of promise. Everywhere we saw sheep grazing, and men out working in the fields plowing and planting.

The road climbed up and up, and we did not take any turns, but went along the main route that went into the hills that sloped below the mountaintop until we came to the small, weathered house and equally weathered big barn. Lucius was out in the fields that spread around the buildings, and I could see his two eldest sons were with him. The elder was Lucius, his namesake, a small-boned boy of eleven, with light, wavy hair and the fine features of his mother, and the younger was Charles, a nine-year-old replica of his brother. Lucius and Charles were handsome in the way of their beautiful sisters, while their younger brother, George, even at age five, always looked startled because of his big eyes. All of the boys would be hard workers, raised that way by their father who set the standard high for them, and they were needed to help feed the big family.

At that time, 1860, my sister had seven children, with another on the way, due that summer. Myalina, the eldest, was fifteen, and the rest went in two-year steps from there down to baby Ella who was three. When her mother went into labor, she would be sent to family friends down the road – the Webbs – who would care for her until her mother got back into a routine with the new baby she would name Thomas. Of course, the girls, Myalina and Malinda, were a big help to their mother, looking after Josiah and George, and shepherding even the older boys.

Many of their neighbors were daughters of Aaron Rowell, who had owned a great amount of land in Guildhall and in neighboring Maidstone. But one of their neighbors was a man by the name of Samuel Hannux, who lived on a small farm with his mother, Polly, an elderly woman, proud of her one son who was only twenty-five when I first met him. He had brought his mother that day, to leave her with Wealthy, for company. The women would sew all day, working on quilts, while he went back to the farm to work. It happened that my visit that day coincided with his dropping off his mother.

I have to say he struck me right off as a little odd, the way men who live too long with their mothers get. His father was long dead, and he had no siblings, so the two stayed on together on the farm.

"Emeline," my sister said. "I would like you to meet my neighbor, Polly Hannux, and this is her son, Samuel."

We women smiled and nodded at one another. She was originally a tall, lean lady, but time and hard work had hunched her over slightly and turned her length to lankiness. Her gray hair was roughly pulled into a bun, as if her sore joints had kept her from placing the hairpins properly so strands escaped and hung at odd angles from her head. She seemed pleasant enough, hanging on her son's arm for balance, until he eased her into a chair.

He shared his mother's long, lean look, but he was young so his hair was red, and his face unlined. He was so fair that he wore a wide-brimmed hat against the sun. Even so, I could see pink spots here and there on his face and neck from working in the spring sun, and he was freckled. What was disconcerting was an almost wolfish look to his teeth, which were enormous and when he, well, it seemed, instead of smiling, he leered at me, and he looked at me just a little too long without dropping his gaze at the appropriate social time. It was those teeth, the incisors hanging disturbingly from his upper gum and his green eyes staring a little too long, that made me think he was not altogether acclimated to living among people.

In the sunny front room of her house, Wealthy got Polly and Fanny, who could sew a fine stitch like me, started on the quilt. Then she went to the kitchen to check on Myalina and the younger ones, with Samuel trailing along behind us.

"It's a fine day, ma'am," he said to me.

"Yes, yes, it is," I said politely.

"You must have had a fine ride this morning," he continued. "Where is it you come from?"

"Lunenburg," I told him, trying to be polite and wishing he would go back to his farm. I could feel his eyes on me, just those two or three beats too long that made me uncomfortable.

"That's quite a long drive," he said. "Where exactly do you live?"

At that moment, Wealthy unwittingly created a diversion.

"Where is Malinda?" she asked her other daughter. "She can go in with Fanny and Mrs. Hannux to work on the sewing."

Myalina blushed, and didn't meet her mother's eye.

"I asked you a question," her mother said.

"I bet she's off with Charles," I said.

Myalina started, and darted me a glance that said, "How did you know that, Aunt?"

Wealthy shook her head and pursed her thin lips.

"So that's how it is," she exclaimed.

I shrugged. "He passed up a day of fishing with his father."

She spun around and headed back into the front room, followed by me who was followed by Samuel.

"How did I miss that?" Wealthy said to me over her shoulder, as we walked down the narrow hallway past the stairs.

"I guess boys don't keep their counsel as well as girls," I said. "She's beautiful, you know. Both of your girls are."

All at once, her sharp gaze fixed on Samuel.

"Shouldn't you be getting back to the farm?" she said pointedly to him, never one to mince words.

He dropped his gaze and muttered something I couldn't hear.

"Well, alright then," Wealthy said, opening the front door and giving him no choice but to go. "You come back for your mother about four o'clock. Don't be late."

He left immediately, to my relief, and I took a moment before we joined his mother and Fanny to whisper to my sister, "I have something to tell you."

Wealthy (who went by her first name Roena then), found an excuse to draw me from the house on the pretext of looking at a chicken with a crooked leg.

"Excuse us a minute, Polly. I have to show Emeline that hen of mine with the leg so crooked I wonder if she will survive."

When we were in the safety of the barn, she giggled and said in a loud whisper, "Somebody has an admirer!"

I knew, of course, what she meant and slapped her hand from where it poked my arm.

"Well, you do," she said, giggling more. "He likes you! Too bad you're taken."

"Oh, be quiet," I said, feeling my face redden.

"He's quite a catch, you know. A younger man."

"God," I said. "He gives me the shivers."

"He's a mama's boy," Wealthy said. "What he needs is a wife to set him straight."

"What about one of your girls," I said, meanly.

"Hah," she laughed. "He has an eye for the older women," she said, nudging and winking at me. "He never gives my girls a second look."

"I'll just have to break his heart," I said, struggling to be cold and not giggle myself, "Since I have a husband already."

"So what do you have to tell me," she asked, sobering up. "We can't stay out here long. I wish today wasn't the day I had invited her to sew."

"I bought a farm," I blurted out.

She stared at me, her dark eyes looking bottomless.

"How?" she said.

"I traded Hiram's black horse to Ira Douglass. It was worth a good sum of money. We bought Leroy Presbrey's old land, up on the hill road just across the border. It's not much. The land got split up from when he owned it, but we've got thirty-eight acres, and the house is small and there's a barn. It'll get us started. We're moving tomorrow. That's why I came over today."

I could not read Wealthy's expression. It was as if she had swept a shade across her features.

"We'll be closer, a little closer to each other," I said, wishing she would say something.

"That's good," she said in a small voice. "I mean, about your getting a place. I know it is what you have wanted."

I nodded.

She took hold of my hand and squeezed it.

"I'm happy for you," she said.

"I had begun to think it would never happen."

"I know."

She had a distant look, and though we were standing together and she was holding my hand – we both had small, cold hands with long fingers – she was removed from me. I knew she was thinking of her own situation. With her free hand, she rubbed her belly, and I knew she was thinking of the birth of an eighth child and how she had no hope of ever being more than a renter on a series of farms as she and Lucius moved every few years. I was patient with her as she was with me in those moments. I knew what it cost her to not be sharp with me in her jealousy of what I had now and she did not. I waited until she mastered herself.

"Tell me how it all happened," she said.

We sat on a mound of hay and I told her everything. We had both forgotten about Polly Hannux and the sewing. When I was done, she said,

"Hiram is a lucky man."

"I don't know that he thinks so," I said. "He is not ambitious, never has been. I pushed him into this."

"If Lucius comes in, don't tell him," she said abruptly, as if reminded of her husband when I spoke of mine.

"Alright," I agreed.

"I will have to think how to do it," she said, and once again she was far from me, thinking this time of how displeased he would be to hear the news of her sister's new prosperity which was a small thing, yet, even so, was not news he would like to hear.

"He'll find out anyway from someone," I said at last.

"I know." She was silent. "Would you mind terribly if I tell him that it was all Hiram's doing and leave you out of it? That would sit easier with him, even if he doesn't believe it and even when he hears different in town."

"That's alright with me," I said, feeling I could afford to be generous in my new ownership. I had told her the farm was in my name.

"How did you get to be the way you are?" she blurted out.

"I am like our father," I said.

She did not disagree with that.

We went back to the house in silence, but it did not last long because even before we entered the kitchen we could hear the shrieks of small boys. Josiah, age seven, was chasing five-year-old George around the room. Those two were close from boyhood. Myalina was in the midst of kneading dough for bread, her arms white with flour up to her elbows, with a white mark on her cheek from rubbing it with the back of her wrist.

Three-year-old Ella was on a blanket on the floor, and she smiled her sweet smile at me as I bent to scoop her up.

"Stay with me, Aunt, and I'll make us some tea," Myalina said.

Her mother had gone in to her visitor and Fanny.

I was easily persuaded and sat in the rocker with Ella, a pudgy little thing, on my lap.

"I just have to finish the kneading and I'll put it aside for the rise," Myalina said, giving the big lump of dough a few more skillful punches before rounding it out and putting it in the big bowl. Covering it with a dish towel, she put it on the side of the stove. She moved the kettle to a spot more directly above the heat and set out cups for us and got out the tea pot and tin of loose black tea. I admired her competence. As the eldest, she had a calm responsible nature, and at fifteen would be thinking hard of her own future.

"Come and sit," I said. "You have flour on your cheek."

She ran to the little square of looking glass above the shelf near the door to the hall and rubbed at her cheek with an edge of her apron.

"Oh, it's made it worse," she exclaimed. She wet a cloth at the sink and cleaned her face properly before coming over to sit by me.

"Let me look at you," I said.

She sat obediently still and straight. Her dark hair fell to her waist, and it was pulled back in two graceful sweeps from her face and was held in place by a ribbon. She had high cheekbones and dark eyes most often serious and accented with long, full lashes. She was done growing, but she was taller than her mother, very slender, and moved with long-limbed ease.

I nodded my approval. I didn't have to say anything. She could tell by my expression and my small smile that I approved mightily. She knew she was beautiful, even from seeing herself in small sections in the hall mirror.

"You're all grown up," I said.

She smiled then, and her face lit up with it.

"You'll be thinking of marrying," I said.

At this, a wash of pink stained her cheeks, and she dropped her eyes, but I saw the secret curl to her lips.

"Who is he?" I asked. "Tell me about him."

"Oh, Aunt, he is wonderful," she said, raising her head to look at me, and seeming much younger as she did so.

"Boys, be a little more quiet," she scolded her brothers, and got up to pour boiling water into the tea pot and put some ginger cookies on a plate.

"Be polite," she said to George and Josiah sharply as small hands reached out for cookies. Josiah and George had the wide Larrabee head and broad features.

"They should have been in school today," she said with disgust. "But the older boys stayed home to help their father so the other two stayed home to make mischief and drive me to distraction. Tomorrow I will walk them to school myself."

"Tell me," I said. "I want to hear about this boy of yours."

"He's no boy," she said proudly. "He's twenty-eight this week."

"What's his name?"

"George, George Gage. He lives just up the road with his parents still, but not for long. He is handsome, aunt, so handsome. He is tall and has dark hair, almost black, and very dark eyes, and very light skin, white skin, not like me." She stretched out a hand to show me the olive tones of her complexion. "It is from the French blood of my father's family," she informed me. "Not French Canadian," she added with scorn, "but France."

"I thought your father was from northern Vermont," I said.

"Oh, well, that's where he was born and my grandfather was from Massachusetts, but I am talking about way back, centuries ago," she said grandly. "That is when his people came to this country from France."

She paused to let me properly absorb this information before continuing. "George's father and mother have a farm, and he and his brother work on it. He has a sister, too, younger than him. He will have his own farm soon, he says. He is very grown up, and he has a serious nature, and plans. They are a close family. He has aunts and uncles all living in the neighborhood. His mother's sisters all settled up there. His mother is very nice to me."

"It sounds serious," I said.

"Oh, it is," she told me earnestly.

"You're just fifteen," I said.

"Mother wants me to wait until I am sixteen," she said soberly. "She needs my help here, you know. She wants me to wait at least until the baby is born."

"How much longer till the baby?" I asked.

At that moment, the kitchen door opened and in walked Malinda with my Charles right behind her. The two boys rushed at him, tackling him with enthusiasm.

"Can we go out?" Josiah asked him. "Take us outside."

"Ask your sister," Charles said.

"Please, go," she laughed, and he herded the younger ones outside.

It was very quiet then. Ella had fallen asleep in my lap, warm and solid against me.

I had not missed the proprietary way Charles had guided Malinda into the room and the soft way she accepted it.

"Good Lord," I thought, "She is only thirteen."

Fanny had come unnoticed into the kitchen, and I looked up when I felt a hand settle on the back of the rocker.

149

"Fanny," I said. "Done sewing?"

She nodded, her gaze not on me, but shyly focused on her cousins.

"We have to go home soon," I said. "There's a lot of work to do." I bit my tongue before I mentioned the move. Wealthy would do the telling later after she had told Lucius.

"Charles tells me you're moving, Aunt," Malinda said quietly.

"What?" Myalina said, glaring at me. "You never said a word."

"Your mother wants to tell your father first," I said. "She made me promise not to say a word."

Myalina and Malinda flashed looks that said they understood about the caution needed about their father.

"Where are you moving?" Myalina asked.

"Just up the road from where we are now, to what was your Uncle Leroy's place. But we'll be closer to you. It's right on the border," I said.

"She bought it," Malinda said admiringly.

"You did, Aunt?" Myalina said.

"Your father is not to know this," I said sternly. "Your mother will tell him what she thinks appropriate, and she wants to leave me out of this and let him think it was my husband's doing."

"But it wasn't," Malinda assured her sister. "Charles told me all about it. Aunt traded Uncle's black horse, you know, the really fine one, for the farm that used to belong to our Uncle Leroy before he died."

Charles had been thorough. I sighed. I would have to speak to him about passing on family business, but I guessed my cautions would be fruitless where this rosy-cheeked cousin of his was concerned. And of course, she would tell her sister and her mother, too.

"You and Charles had quite a talk," I said.

She had the grace to blush.

Myalina giggled.

I shook my head in pretend disgust.

"Young ladies in love," I said.

"Oh, Aunt," they chorused.

"It's time we set off for home," I said, handing off Ella to Malinda and getting up. We went to the front room to say our goodbyes and Wealthy walked us out to the wagon. We headed back at a fast clip to finish packing up and loading the wagon for the next day's move to my new farm.

g

Chapter Ten

SUMMER 1860

A T THE SAME TIME OF THIS VICTORY OF MINE IN SECURING OUR FUTURE, OTHER DEVELOPMENTS AROSE TO CAUSE ME PAIN. Not long after we had moved, after the planting, in early June, Charles went off on his own. He went to a job as a farm laborer for a stranger, a man named Wheeler who lived in Littleton, across the river south of us in New Hampshire. He was eighteen, more than old enough to do as he wished and to get a job, but we needed him with us on the farm.

It was because of his father that he left. The discontent had been brewing. Charles, unlike Hiram, had a deep-rooted energy and a vision to plan ahead. He was a hard worker. He wanted to push hard and, like me, wanted to add more land.

"We can't do anything with this little bit of land," he said.

I begged him to be patient.

"I'm eighteen, Ma. I can't wait," he said. "You know he will never move faster than he does."

"Don't speak badly of him," I said, though I knew he spoke the truth.

He scowled at me. "You see him for what he is, Ma," he snapped. "It's me you're talking to."

"He's your father," I said, always loyal.

"I know who he is and what he is," he retorted. "You heard Mr. Smith the other day."

I cringed. I had not wanted Charles to hear what James had said about Hiram. We had been in the orchard – really just a few trees – when James had made his comments. Hiram was in the barn. It was late morning and he had not yet gone out to the fields.

"He holds you back, Emeline," James said. He was looking at the few trees for fungus that should be treated, showing Charles and me what to look for, and explaining the treatment if we found the disease. He was showing us about pruning for the best results, and encouraging us to plant more trees so we would have a good apple crop and could make cider to sell or at least have extra apples to sell.

His comments came as we stood under the heavy branches laden with blossoms.

"It should be a good season unless we get a late frost," he said.

We could see the barn clearly from where we stood. We could hear the rustle of the harness chain.

"Has he been out yet today?" he asked me.

"No, not yet. He did the chores," I said.

"It's late in the morning," he observed.

"I know."

"Is it like this every day?"

"Pretty much. He just moves slow. He gets work done, but he moves slow."

"He'll never get the crops in in time for a long season."

Then James turned to Charles who was listening, his hands deep in his pockets and his head down.

"Why aren't you down there helping him?"

Charles' face reddened, and his head jerked up. I held my breath, but he held his tongue. He did not altogether refrain from a remark though, because his eyes, in a squint, gave James a fierce, unfriendly look that shocked me. It happened so quickly, and he set off down the hill away from us, but not before he heard James say,

"He'll hold you back."

He meant Hiram, and it was a conversation he and I had had before privately, but Charles took him to mean himself.

"You shouldn't have said that to him," I said quietly to James.

"He should be down there with his father," James said defensively.

"He tries his best, you know, to help, but he is just a boy and his father is his father so his word goes. He wants to do more and has ideas, but even I can only push Hiram so far and he is certainly not going to listen to a boy. Hiram wants a son he can fish with and hunt with and enjoy being a man with. Charles is too much like me and they don't get along."

"I'll go and apologize to him," James said stiffly.

"It's too late for that," I gestured to where Hiram and Charles were leading the horse to the plow in the field in back of the barn.

"You tell him for me then," he said.

I sighed. "Alright." The last thing I needed was this new trouble.

"He is talking about going out to work," I said. "He says he is tired of getting nowhere here."

"But you have just started!" James said. "Doesn't he see that?"

"He thinks it will all come to nothing. He blames his father."

"You can't manage without him."

"I hope it won't come to that, but I'll manage somehow. I'll have to."

That night, after Hiram had gone up to bed, I told Charles what James had said.

"He asked me to apologize to you," I said. "He was sorry after for what he said implying you weren't doing your work."

"What do I care what he said," Charles grunted.

"He's trying to help us," I said.

"He should mind his own business. Doesn't he have enough of it with that inn of his without nosing into our business?"

"Charles, he's a relative. He wants to be helpful. He has given us good advice."

"I don't care what he is. I don't like him hanging around here. This is our place."

I sighed.

"What would you have me do?" I said. "Kick him off?"

"You don't have to be so friendly, that's all."

I shook my head. "We need all the help we can get if we're going to make our farm work."

"It's not my farm. Pa don't listen to a word I say and I work twice, three times as hard as he does. He can't plan and he…"

"Not another word about your father," I cut him off.

"You can stand around with a stranger and criticize him, but I can't say a word even if it's true and even if I'm the one doing more than half of the work."

"Mr. Smith is not a stranger. He has advice to give and we may need him some day for a loan. He's family."

"You shouldn't be talking about our business with him," Charles persisted.

"We're just talking in a circle," I said. "I'm trying to do the best I can to improve our lot."

"I know that, but maybe it's just not enough."

I was stung, badly stung, by his words. I got up and turned away so he wouldn't see the tears in my eyes.

I felt his hand lightly on my shoulder, and then it was gone so fast I almost thought I imagined it.

"I'm sorry, Ma," he said. "I didn't mean that."

"Wait a little, please, Charles. Give us time to make this work. It will all be yours some day," I said.

In his contrition at hurting my feelings, Charles made a show of doing all he could to help his father. But only a few weeks passed when, after a Sunday when he had gone off, to see Malinda, I thought, he came in from the morning barn chores early to tell me his news.

"I've got a job, Ma," he said tightly, without expression, as if I were the stranger. "I'm going to work for a man named Wheeler over in Littleton. He has a big farm, and only two young children so he needs a man."

I didn't cry then, but I cried that afternoon when I went to put butter in the springhouse. I cried until my face was hot and wet, and I made no sound so no one would hear me. That is a hard way to cry. It strains the throat and makes the chest tight and the face hurt. When I was done, I washed my face over and over in the cold water of the spring, splashing my neck and my wrists. I patted myself dry with my apron and went back to the house to make supper.

That is what the young men did, at fourteen, fifteen, sixteen, seventeen, sometimes even thirteen, go out to work on the more prosperous farms as laborers. It was a simple matter of the need of these farmers who had hundreds of acres cleared and whose property bore a high yield or who wanted more land cleared to improve the yield they had. My father's brother, Elisha, is a good one to remark. He had over one hundred acres cleared out of the two hundred he owned, and on that farm kept twelve milch cows and eighteen sheep. He profited from hundreds of pounds of butter and cheese, and from wool, and sales of his excess grains such as buckwheat. His farm in cash money was valued at way over $3000. He had hired men, he had to, especially with few children. I was shrewd enough from studying the farms in Lunenburg to know what it took to achieve that level of land wealth and prosperity. To say I coveted it for myself is not to stretch the truth, though I also knew that with Hiram it would not be possible. I had placed my hopes on Charles, believing him and me capable of creating a dynasty – that is too grand a word, but it conveys the spirit of my desires. If he would work, I would manage and strategize and soon he would take on the reins of management from me. He cast that aside, unwilling to be patient.

To be truthful, I have not given a fair picture of Lucius Larrabee. I have said he cast away his opportunity to own land, but he had structured his life with a big family without elder boys to help him by renting better farms than he could ever have owned. Sour he was, but he was a canny manager of whatever he took on. The farm in the hills of Guildhall where he was neighbor of the Gages had a value close to $1000, and the reason was seventy acres of cleared land, about half of the lot he rented. On this he kept nine milch cows. This was what he made his money on – selling the milk. He kept no other animals except one sheep and one sow. He hayed and he sowed a field with buckwheat and raised some potatoes, but the milch cows were what he kept going with, paying his rent and feeding his family with some left over. When he needed to plow, he bartered a horse or ox from his neighbors, Samuel Hannux or the Gages, in exchange for milk. He worked a large sugar bush, yielding hundreds of pounds of maple sugar that he sold. For all of Wealthy's longings for her husband to buy a farm, he kept them well with his good management and his working with the main asset they had which was his labor that was unceasing.

I would not have wanted to live with him, and be set aside in the kitchen and vegetable garden with my woman's work of tending house and children to the exclusion of the use of my fertile brain of schemes. But Wealthy, who could not read and write, and who was fertile in other ways than her brain (though she, like all of the Presbreys, well, at least many of them, could not be slighted on her ability to think) could not complain of how her husband provided for her. There were no frills, but she dressed nicely and kept a good house with a large, well-appointed kitchen.

I had plenty of time to think of all of this after Charles went off to the

Wheeler farm across the river, a long day's ride.

"Learn all you can," I instructed him the morning he set out with another boy from the village who had a job on another farm in Littleton. "If it is as big and well-laid out a place as you say then you will be able to learn a lot by being around the man and by doing work as he sets it out for you."

Charles had nodded impatiently, and I knew he had not heard a word of what I said, eager as he was to be off on his adventure.

In another way, I had no time to think because I became more than ever the driver of what went on on our farm. It was the season for our first harvest before I knew it. There was not a lot to pull from our thirty-eight acres, but there were apples, and extra grain and corn and Irish potatoes. Hiram found a tree in the woods with wild honey that he harvested with admirable persistence, coming home with few stings thanks to the make-shift netting I had constructed for him to wear under his straw hat that I had also made. We let a neighbor who kept bees put some of his hives in our orchard and we were paid in some honeycomb that I sold. I arranged the sale of the extra grain and even sold some of the extra root vegetables I grew – kohlrabi, beets, turnips and carrots. Without Charles to feed and with Hiram working harder than he ever had, and with even six-year-old Fanny helping weed the garden – so sweet and painstakingly careful to pull weeds and not plants, crouched in her little sun hat by my side, along with Biathy whose earnest face gave no clue to what he lacked – we paid on our mortgage as I had planned and there was a little extra I squirreled away in the tobacco tin that even then I did not keep in the house, but hid.

That year, 1860, and the year after were years when we focused on thriving.

In December, a few days before Christmas, Charles came home to stay. He had not been back since the June day when he rode off in the wagon with his friend. He had written me two short, unsatisfactory letters, with what looked like the fat stub of a pencil better intended for a carpenter's marking tool on wood than a writing instrument. But they reassured me he was at least where he had said he would be, and I was not much better about writing him, though I used proper paper and a good pen, since I had barely a moment for something as frivolous as letter writing, rising before it was light to get household chores done so I could work in my large garden all day, and falling into bed exhausted when the kitchen was put to rights.

Charles appeared without warning, at the start of a snowstorm. I heard nothing of his approach late that day, in the dark, when he walked up the hill from where his ride with a trader had ended. He had walked the two miles up the long hill, and when he reached us, he was like a snowman, his hat piled high with snow and the shoulders of his coat crowned with wedges of white.

We were at supper when we heard the stomping of his boots on the side porch.

"Who could that be in this weather?" I said.

Biathy scampered from his chair to open the door just as the knob was turned from the outside and Charles stood there, his cheeks red as apples and his eyebrows crusted with frozen snow.

Biathy gave a crow of what I knew was his sound of delight and Charles scooped him up and spun him around. Then it was Fanny's turn with snow flying everywhere and his boots leaving a trail of snow that puddled in the warm kitchen.

I was scolding everyone. "Leave off that! Oh, you're making a mess!"

But I didn't mean anyone to take me seriously and they didn't even hear me. Finally, it was my turn and I didn't care about my son's coat wetting the front of me and the back of me as he held me close and lifted me off my feet in his exuberant greeting.

There was a great fuss of getting off his coat and boots, and unwrapping his layers. He had a pack made out of a blanket that I had sewed him when he went away, and when Fanny noticed it, she exclaimed, "Did you bring us a present?"

From his expression, she could tell that he had.

"Let him have some hot food first," I scolded. "Oh, Charles, what a long way you walked in the snow."

He didn't pay me mind, much to Fanny's satisfaction, and rummaged in his bag for what turned out to be two tiny wooden tops, a red one for Fanny and a blue one for Biathy. They settled at once to these treats, and left Charles to me and his father at the table.

"Tell me all about it, Charles," I said. "I want to know every detail."

"I'm home to stay, if you'll have me," he said.

"Oh, Charles," I sighed, and my eyes teared up, just a little.

"We could use you here," Hiram assented.

With that settled, Charles told us about the big farm, and the family with the two little girls, and the constant work of tending animals and fields, and the work he had done even after the snow fell, of working in the barn and in the wood shop where he learned to repair tools and other implements of the farm.

He had matured. His voice had added depth, and he had filled out some, though he still had the leanness of youth.

"Have you seen my aunt?" he asked.

I grinned. "And Malinda, too. She is fine, but I think she misses you."

"I wrote her a couple of times, but she never wrote back."

"I'm not sure she can," I said quietly.

He looked startled.

"Then she never even could have read what I wrote her."

"What did you write?" I asked, suddenly concerned. It was Lucius who collected the mail from town.

His face, red from the cold and then the heat of the house, darkened with embarrassment.

"I wrote her a very proper letter," he said stiffly.

I did not say any more, thinking of his letters read first in silence by Lucius and then, since they were open, looked over by Wealthy who regretted then that she could not read for herself, before being passed along to Malinda who naively suspected nothing, and mistook the tobacco scent left by Lucius' rough hands to be from Charles, her beloved, and passed it to her sister to read aloud to her in the secret quiet of their bedroom shared with baby Ella.

⅘

Chapter Eleven

1861

THE YEAR 1861 WAS TUMULTUOUS, BOTH PERSONALLY AND FOR THE NATION BECAUSE OF THE WAR. We were as far removed from all of the unrest of the rebellion of states seceding and of the first battle in that April in a southern state we were scarcely aware of except in the news that came to us in the few pages of the weeklies we had access to, often read days after the event. President Lincoln declared hostilities officially on April 15, three days after the aggressor rebel states had struck and what had been brewing for months, even years, could not be denied. Charles was still eighteen when the call came for volunteers. As any mother would feel, I worried about him, fearing his enlistment as the young men and not so young men he knew took the step and soon were gone from our midst. I was glad he was home with us, at least, and busy with the work of the farm as he and I focused on our goal of paying off the mortgage and expanding the cleared land so we could raise more crops to sell and buy more land.

Malinda remained his sweetheart, and grew more and more lovely, gaining her height of a woman and some of the shape, which was slender and on the tall side for a woman, coming almost up to Charles so eyes met eyes directly level. She was fourteen, fully versed in the work of the house and caring for children.

"Promise you'll wait until she's fifteen," I said to him. I would prefer him to wait until she was sixteen, but I knew if things continued as they were, this would not be practical.

In the meantime, Myalina and George were very serious. I knew Malinda was observing her elder sister and mimicking her. George was twenty-nine in May, and his brother, Horace, would be twenty-six soon. That George was serious in his ways was obvious from my few meetings with him. He was well-mannered and soft-spoken, with never a lot to say. He seemed a hard worker. But I had questions. I wondered about this man, almost thirty, still at home as was his brother. He never went out to labor on other farms, and I thought some of this came from his mother's upbringing, with her Rowell blood and her sister, Ruth, who had married James Follansbee, a smart, ambitious man of good family who schemed with his father-in-law to increase the holdings of farm land, even on the river, in Guildhall and Maidstone. Of course, the land that had gone to all of the daughters of Rowell was hill land. He had died in the late 1840s. Harmon and Betsey owned the lot they farmed, but the gossip in the town was that she had a guardian in this ownership that kept her husband from selling it or mortgaging it, in fact, from doing anything on it but farming and living there without the permission of his wife and her guardian.

Like Lucius, Harmon was a crusty, weathered man and he was old, in his sixties, when the war started. He was not much of a worker, and liked the tavern, but this guardianship hung over him and kept his behavior regulated.

Betsey was a lovely woman in her gentle manner. She was very religious, attending the Methodist Episcopal Church in Guildhall most Sundays unless the weather prevented her. She and Harmon kept a horse, for the purpose Myalina said, of her traveling to church each week. She was tall, like Myalina, and she encouraged the relationship of this girl and her son, inviting her to church where they sat together, with the men of her family on the end of the pew. She saw to it that her prospective daughter-in-law had a Bible, and was encouraging of her continued schooling, reading with her when Myalina came to visit.

Myalina was my favorite niece. She was such a strong woman, even at sixteen, and so striking in her beauty, and she was intelligent. She was not a woman to laugh much, and her life had not encouraged laughter though she was good with her brothers and sisters, and willing to coddle and scold lightly, so they adored her. She would play, too, sometimes, but there was not much time for that with all of the chores.

The year before, Wealthy had borne Thomas in the late summer. At thirty-two, she was now the mother of eight and while other births had gone easily, this one had not. Lucius had come for me, after he had gone for the doctor. When I arrived, the baby was just arrived, and he was very small and sickly. Despite all odds against it, he survived the day and was named Thomas. But Wealthy did not get up quickly from this birthing, and laid in bed for weeks through the hot summer. Little Ella was sent to the family friends, the Webbs, who added her easily to their brood and she was happy enough, Myalina told me. This left the full burden of duties on Myalina, with some help from Malinda who was less constant in her work.

It was now going on a year later, and her mother had been up and around since the winter, gaining strength. Ella came back, and life for the Larrabee household had settled down to normal.

It was then that Myalina determined to be married, perhaps driven by the recollection of her mother's long recovery and the fact that she herself was of childbearing age and still caring for her mother's babies. She must, too, have realized that her mother would soon be pregnant again as was her pattern.

Myalina told me and her mother first. I was visiting my sister in the middle of the month, a short visit because I had so much to do at home, but the harvest was mostly in, and we had had the first frost and I would be digging up the remainder of the carrots, some for the root cellar and some to sell.

I looked Wealthy over critically.

"You look almost back to health," I said.

"I am glad to hear it," she said dryly.

"I mean it as a compliment," I said.

"I am sure you do. What happened to, 'Oh, you look so good,'" she said.

"You would not believe me if I fibbed," I scoffed.

"I might just," she said. "Do you remember when we looked like them?" She jerked her chin (her hands were full, holding Thomas) at her girls.

"We were never that beautiful," I said.

That made her smile. "But we were that young," she said.

"Hear you talking like you were an old lady."

"I sure have felt old," she said.

"You're coming back though," I assured her. "You look almost like your old self."

"Old," she said. "There's that word."

"You have a handsome baby boy," I said. "Look at it that way."

She was quiet, and looked sad, rocking him in her arms.

"I almost lost him," she said.

That had not happened to her before. I knew well enough how that felt – to lose a baby, during pregnancy and then, worst of all, when he was stillborn.

I was quiet then, and we were in communion, thinking of her near loss and of my losses that trailed behind in my past like moving shadows of leaves when the wind rustles the tree branches in the full moonlight.

Myalina walked in on us.

"Are you doing alright, Mother?" she asked. "Hello, Aunt," she said, and kissed my cheek. Her lips were cool from being outside.

She had a basket on her arm, filled with eggs, smooth and brown and speckled, warm from the hens. Trailing behind her was Ella, carrying a tiny basket with two eggs tucked into a scrap of cloth. She solemnly came to me and thrust out the treasure for my inspection.

"They are beautiful eggs, dear," I praised.

"I found them myself," she said.

The basket deposited with me, she ran back out to join her brothers in the yard. I could hear their whooping and shouts of play.

Myalina put down her own basket. She took Thomas from her mother and laid him in the crate that was a make-shift crib, arranging the coverlets carefully around him before going to make us tea.

"I have news," she said, smoothing her skirt from her thigh down as far as she could reach below her knee. "I may as well tell you both at once."

She had our full attention. Wealthy had a wary look, and I wondered if Myalina were taking a misstep in telling us this news together and not her mother first.

"George and I are to be married," she said.

It was expected. I wanted to ask dozens of questions and issue cautions, but all I did was hug her in turn after her mother.

"Are you sure?" I asked.

Wealthy looked grateful.

"I'm sure," she said quietly. "We have been courting a long time. He is twenty-nine now, and impatient. I am sixteen and old for my age. I am sorry, mother, to leave you, but I am ready for my own family."

With her steady words, how could I have said all of my reservations about George still at home and the poor example of his father? I could not. It would only have angered her and strained our relationship to no purpose. I did remember my own staunchness of purpose when I married Hiram, though I had no father, and my mother, remarried, was busy with her own affairs and had washed her hands of me when I refused to move with her into a new household, preferring to stay with my brother and his wife in our father's house.

"When?" Wealthy asked. She looked very tired all of a sudden, and had a gray cast to her face I had not seen when I came.

We held our breath at the answer.

"Next month. In a few weeks, in October. Once George talks with my father, he will ask the preacher. We will be married by the Methodist Episcopal priest here in town."

Later, I walked with Myalina out to the springhouse to get butter.

"I am worried about the war, Aunt," she told me.

"Is he going?"

"I don't know. I have tried to get him to promise he will not. But his brother has gone."

I knew that. One by one the men signed up. George's brother, Horace, had mustered in in late July. He was twenty-six, not young, only nine years younger than me. And George was almost my age. Horace was God only knew where, in some place we did not yet know.

"He is marrying you. He won't want to head off soon," I tried to reassure her.

"Or he is eager to marry before he goes so I will be his wife."

I did not have any placating words on this subject. What she said could be true. There were many last-minute marriages.

"You don't have to marry," I blurted out.

She turned on me sharply. "What do you mean by that? Of course, I don't have to, if that is what you are implying, but I love him and I want to marry him."

"Don't be silly," I said. "I wasn't implying anything like that. I know you love him and he loves you. I just meant you could wait."

"Well, I'm not going to. I want my own house and my own babies."

I soothed her, and soon we were walking arm in arm, but my uneasiness about him remained.

The marriage came off as planned, on October 10, a bright, sunny morning when the brilliance of the fall colors – reds and oranges and yellows – made the day even more filled with light.

For the short number of weeks before the wedding, I had gone as often as I could to help Wealthy and Myalina sew a special dress. It had a rich burgundy skirt with a loose-sleeved white blouse with the fashionable dropped shoulders. We sat in the front room and sewed and talked. The day before the ceremony, I gave my niece a special present, a small gold-colored pin the shape of a rectangle with a design etched in black.

She and her family, and George and his family, met in the parlor of the minister, Mr. Adams, in Guildhall. Hiram and I rode down, with our three. It was a crowded room, but the words of the marriage rite were few, and quickly, so quickly, my beautiful niece was Mrs. George Gage. She looked very pale with nerves, but once the words were said, she composed herself and laughed at everyone's congratulations.

We all went to the former home of the bride where Wealthy and Malinda had prepared a lunch. Lucius and the older boys had set up sawhorses with a board across for a table, and it was covered with a cloth and they had brought out all of the chairs from the house and a bench from the barn. There was all manner of food – roasted chicken, pickles and relish, dishes of beets and potatoes, large slices of bread, biscuits, apple pies, and even a cake, in several layers, in honor of the day.

All too soon, we had eaten and then it was time for us to see Myalina and George into the wagon he had borrowed from his father. They were going for one night across the river to a hotel in Lancaster, quite a luxury, and after that would be living with Betsey and Harmon. It would be just the five of them, with Horace off to the war and the younger sister, Lauraette, married. Only Charles Gage, the consumptive, remained at home still with his parents.

Hiram and I went home with our brood, and life went back to the usual events of post-harvest. There was always work to do on the farm, though we were coming to the calm of winter when the ground was frozen solid and then the snow would come, though not always in that order.

I had no idea of what was to come, falling into a complacency out of seeing my niece married and believing that the late autumn and winter would bring peace.

§

Chapter Twelve

LATE OCTOBER 1861

T HE SHOCK CAME ONLY A FEW WEEKS AFTER THAT WEDDING. The autumn had continued mild, with a string of sunny days. We had done well that season, better than I had expected.

Charles and Hiram and I discussed this one day, a week or so after the wedding, sitting at the table with the money gained from sales of crops on the table.

"So what is the verdict, wife?" Hiram said jovially, both hands firmly holding the edge of the table in expectation.

Charles was relaxed, one cheek pushed into his elbow planted firmly as he slouched forward.

Neither of them knew, though Charles may have suspected, that I had already removed a sum from the accumulated cash, and stashed it away for safekeeping in the tobacco tin.

I told them the sum of what laid on the table.

Hiram nodded, a surprised look on his visage.

"That is good," he said.

"It will easily cover our mortgage payment," Charles said.

The two men waited for me.

"I think we should pay a little extra, as a hedge against next year," I told them.

They nodded.

"And Hiram, since there is extra, and Charles gave up his job to help us, perhaps we could give him something, kind of as wages?"

Hiram considered this, rubbing his chin with his fingertips slowly.

"That seems fair," he finally agreed.

Charles was like a coiled spring. He said nothing, but I could feel his eagerness. I knew he had saved most of his money from his wages and that he expected to someday put it into land.

I had already decided a sum that was appropriate, if Hiram agreed as I expected he would, and so I counted it out and passed it to Charles.

"Thank you, Ma, Pa," he said gravely, and carefully, so as not to appear greedy, took up the bills and folded them into his wallet for safekeeping. I knew he would store the money away, and use it wisely.

We sat then, and talked about the season just passed.

"It was the weather," Hiram said. "We were lucky in that."

"And we had more land cleared," Charles put in.

"The two of you worked well together," I added, causing pleased looks to pass over the faces of the men.

There was no talk of war, or going to it, and I collected the remaining cash and stored it in the lard tin kept high on a shelf in the pantry where it looked like a rusty lard tin and no more. Hiram took money when he wished, always mentioning it to me when he did. He and I were like that, letting each other know what we spent. He depended mostly on me to provide what was needed, but he liked tobacco (he had his own tin of tobacco for his pipe) and he liked the occasional visit to the tavern in the village where he saw his friends. He was a quiet man, and liked the solitary pleasures of fishing and hunting, though he would always take Charles if his son wanted to accompany him. I depended on his luck in the streams and on the deer and partridge he hunted in the fields and woods. I had loved my husband for a very long time by then, since I was a girl, so it seemed even a longer time because everyone knows that time moves slower when you are young and speeds up until in middle age it is fleet of foot and you lose sight of it if you do not mark it with care. In old age, it slows again, as the infirmities of the body with the aches and pains make the days drag.

Hiram was out most days now, hunting partridge. I laughed to see him one morning, from the kitchen window, trudging across the stubble of the corn field with three partridges held by their feet. I knew we would have partridge pie for our big midday meal. It was a dark, gamey bird with so much flavor. I knew just how to cook it to keep the flavor and remove the unpleasant game taste. Fanny was old enough this year to learn.

I remember that day especially, October 31, because Charles could not be found.

"Where's Charles?" I asked Hiram when he brought in the birds and I had finished extolling their virtues. "Was he out with you?

He shook his head. "I haven't seen him since chores this morning."

"Did he say anything of his plans?

"No, I told him I was going hunting, but he didn't want to come. That's not unusual." He shrugged. "He'll be in for food. Maybe he's up in the sugar bush, seeing what needs to be done. One of the big trees fell, you know, and he was talking about cutting it up for firewood."

But though I went out and stood in the yard, I could not hear the sound of an axe. I don't know why I felt anxious. Usually the men went about their business all day and I only saw them for meals. I attributed my unease to the change in seasons, when the rhythm of the farm changed from the work of the harvest, and began its turn toward winter.

I forgot about him in the flurry of preparing the birds. Fanny knew how to pluck a chicken and this wasn't much different. We made short work of that, setting aside the prettiest feathers for decoration for some project or other. I showed her how to handle the sharpest kitchen knife, a tool she had been warned against since she was old enough to help me and had never handled. She was alert and proud at being allowed to do more than watch me on the second bird, as I guided her through the process of taking the meat off the bones without waste. Her light little fingers held the knife with confidence and she did the third bird all by herself.

Together we worked. She made the pie crust, rolling out the dough, while I cut up carrots and potatoes, and cooked the partridge into a stew thickened with flour. I poured the mixture into Fanny's pie crust and soon there were two pies in the oven and the smell, such a delicious smell, wafted through the house.

Hiram arrived early, drawn in by the aroma that reached him where he was chopping wood.

"When do we eat?" he demanded.

I laughed. "Same time as we have for the last nineteen years!"

Fanny laid the table, and soon the pies were out and cooling. We had bread and pickles I had made from the cucumbers in the garden. There was rhubarb preserve with its tart sweetness.

But there was no Charles.

"He's alright," Hiram said off-handedly, concentrating on his big slab of partridge pie surrounded by condiments and two slices of bread.

I bit my lip. It was not like Charles to not be there for a meal unless he told me. I tried to calm myself, to think about the success of the pie, how Fanny's buttery crust melted in my mouth and how the partridge was rich and tender. My mouth was dry, though, and I could hardly swallow. I pretended to eat, and neither my husband nor Fanny noticed because of their own busy shoveling of the excellent meal into their hungry mouths. Biathy noticed, eating busily, but sparing me glances. When they were sated with the main course, I brought out apple buckle, the fruit baked with a maple sugar and flour mixture on top that melted into the apples and formed a sweet, crunchy topping. I refilled glasses of milk, and only when Hiram pushed back his chair did I speak of what was in my mind.

"He has gone to enlist," I said.

"What?" Hiram looked startled. "What do you mean? Did he tell you?"

I shook my head. My hands felt ice cold.

"Where else could he be?"

We stared at one another. Hiram said no more and I knew he knew I had hit on the truth. He went slowly back outdoors, Biathy trailing behind him.

"Would he do that, Ma?" Fanny said in a small, scared voice.

I had forgotten her.

I bent down and put my arm around her small shoulders, hugging her to me.

"I think he would, dear," I said. "You know there is a war and the men are patriotic. He is doing what he feels is his duty and we have to be brave and let him know he is in the right and we are proud of him."

"I can do that," she said. "But he'll be going, won't he? Will he come home first to say goodbye?"

"Of course," I said quickly, hoping I was right, thinking I must be. He would enlist first and then there would be time for him to come home and tell us and collect his things.

But that was not the way events played out that day, the day of the partridge pies, that has stuck in my mind like a wedge in a piece of wood on the chopping block. It was not long after we had finished eating, and the table was cleared, the dishes washed and dried and put away, and Fanny and I sat in the yard in the fall sun sewing and repairing holes in socks, that we saw the wagon on the road. It was a strange wagon and a strange horse, but it was Charles at the reins and beside him sat my niece, Malinda, a bright rose shawl over her shoulders, her hair swept up on her head. It was then that it came to me, the truth of that day: Charles had gone off to marry his cousin.

"Look, Ma, Charles has brought Malinda to visit," Fanny said excitedly. She was in awe of her older girl cousins.

I sighed and wrapped my shawl tightly around my shoulders and followed her to greet what I knew were more than visitors. When Charles did not meet my eye, I had no more doubts about my guesswork – as finely drawn as needlework.

Malinda focused on Fanny, hugging her and kissing her, with warmth that she had never shown before. How grown up she was trying to be.

Charles caught my hand, pulling me from looking at his new bride and my daughter toward the house. I let myself be led, knowing what he had to tell me, and deciding to not make it hard for him, harder than I imagined it already was.

He stopped in the hall, where the door was open, and we could see Fanny and Malinda in animated talk. Her delicate features, with the pale rose complexion, were animated, and how happy Fanny was to have the full attention of her cousin.

"Ma," he said, keeping hold of my hand.

"I was worried about you, Charles," I said, unable to stop myself from getting in the first word. "It's not like you to be so thoughtless. Your father brought in partridge and we waited on you for the midday meal." The last was not true, but he was not to know that.

I had stopped him in mid-track. He had to gather his thoughts and prepare himself once more to tell me. I realized I did not want to make it easy for him. I was angry, at how he had deceived me, at his childishness, at his bringing me this child for his bride.

"Today is not a Sunday when we have the leisure for visitors," I said, more sharply than I intended.

"Ma," he started again. "I have something to tell you, something important." Finally, he looked me in the eye, and seeing my expression, he dropped my hand, and his arms fell limply to his sides. He slumped, and was defeated. "Oh," he said flatly. "You have guessed."

"Of course I have guessed," I hissed, keeping my voice low so the girls did not hear me. "You have been gone since early morning and missed your meal, and your father and I were at a loss to know where you were. Now you blaze in here in the afternoon in the middle of the week with Malinda who is dressed like it was Sunday. Of course, I guessed."

"Can't you be a little glad?" he asked.

"Oh, Charles," I said, my voice trailing off. "I am disappointed. She is barely fourteen, just a child really. And what about all of your plans? our plans? Where do you plan to live and how will you support her? And what if she has a baby?"

Out in the yard, we could hear the laughter. How animated Fanny was, rare for her, in this spotlight of good grace from Malinda.

"I had hoped," he gulped, and stopped.

I fixed my eyes on him, pointed my hawk-like nose like a bird of prey would do.

"You hoped you could bring her here to live," I said, in what I hoped was a sinister tone.

He gulped again, and nodded.

"Does your aunt know about this? And what about your uncle? Did you ask for her hand?"

His eyes were wide now, with the realization of facts set before him.

I shook my head in disgust.

"You're going to have to," I said. "Today. You're going to have to turn that wagon around, and whose wagon is that, anyway? And you're going to go to visit your aunt and uncle. You might as well start with him and if you're still alive after that, your aunt's reaction will be like a balmy summer day. And you can stay here, but you'd better go and break the news to your father and ask him. He'll be glad to have you, no doubt, and Fanny and Malinda are gossiping merrily already. I'll put her to work," I said darkly.

"Aren't you even a little glad for me, Ma?" he asked timidly.

"Off with you now," I directed him, not deigning to even notice what he asked. I was not glad, not even any tiny bone in my tiniest toe was glad. But it was done now and so I would make the best of it.

He tore off to the barn, like a not-too-friendly dog was chasing him. I picked up my shawl that had fallen to the floor in my distress, and adjusted it around my shoulders once again before going out to the girls, both of whom now belonged to me.

When Malinda saw me coming, she stopped talking to Fanny and turned to give me her full attention. I had always suspected Malinda was a little afraid of me, and I could see now it was true. The pink had faded and she looked white with trepidation. I kept on walking and I did not smile.

Fanny was oblivious to any undercurrents, and took hold of her cousin's hand.

"Is it true Malinda is going to be staying with us? That will be such fun," she said.

At these words, Malinda looked like she was going to be sick and I took pity on her.

"Yes," I said. "It's true, since your brother, Charles, and your cousin were married this morning." I even managed a smile that I felt was watery, but would have to do.

Malinda appeared grateful for even that small concession.

"Why didn't you tell us?" Fanny said. "I would have liked to have gone to another wedding. Myalina's wedding and the party were very, very nice."

"Will you go indoors and start fixing your cousin and me some tea?" I asked Fanny. "And put out a plate of the ginger cookies you made yesterday."

Without another word, my daughter raced for the house, puffed with pride at being asked to entertain Malinda.

I took Malinda's hands that were very cold and squeezed them and kissed her cheeks that were cold.

"Welcome, dear," I said. "We've got to get you indoors where it's warm."

We were just inside the doorway when Charles rushed out of the yard in the wagon.

"Where is he going?" she cried.

"He is going to tell your father and mother," I had the satisfaction of saying.

With those words, we proceeded to the kitchen, where Fanny plied her with tea and cookies. Malinda sat at the table in her wedding finery, drinking her tea in small sips, but refusing the cookies. She looked ashen, and on the verge of tears, and I could not be mean or cross any longer, not with her. She was a child. Charles, on the other hand, was a man. He would feel my anger for awhile longer.

"It will be alright," I said. "Charles has to do what is right and tell your parents. Your mother will not be surprised, I think?"

She perked up a little at my words. "No, no, I don't think she will be," she said.

I did not say a word about her father, for which I thought she would be grateful. I hoped he would be harsh on my son. I really hoped he would make him feel the weight of what he had gone ahead and done.

Since Charles had not returned, Fanny and Malinda happily set to making supper, Malinda's finery wrapped against spills in one of my biggest aprons. Charles still had her small bag in the wagon. Hiram had been in to greet his new daughter-in-law warmly, and then he had gone back out. It was warm in the kitchen and I could not help smiling at the sound of the girls' chatter.

The only catch was that Charles did not return soon and when he did, he was not alone. Supper came and went, with Malinda sitting stiffly, trying to eat the leftover partridge pie and the beets and biscuits she and Fanny had prepared when she was still happy and awaiting her groom. But he had not come. It was long past the early dark of late October. The dishes were washed, and the kitchen ready for morning. I did not like to see this girl so pale and her cheeks and lips pinched tight in what I knew was an effort not to cry. It was getting on for bedtime. We all were in the kitchen – Hiram, Biathy, Fanny, Malinda and me – not the way this romantic child would have imagined her wedding night.

"It's alright, dear," I told her more than once. "He'll be here soon. Maybe he had to return the wagon and walk. That would take time."

"It was loaned to him until tomorrow," she said in a small voice.

How young she was, I thought again. It was her older sister, Myalina, who had the maturity and clarity of purpose and Malinda who had done as she was asked, but without much self-direction. She did not have to be self-directed because her mother and sister took charge. She could be the flighty, pretty, cheery girl. It would have been a better match if Charles and Myalina had taken a fancy to one another. Together they could have done anything they set their minds to do.

I had my own worries, but one of them was not where Charles was or what was delaying him. I knew he would be home soon enough for his bride, and I did not waste time inventing scenarios of what held him up because I suspected it was due to Lucius. That Lucius would be displeased was no leap of imagination. He would be angry for several reasons, at the top of his list the fact that Charles and his daughter had circumvented his authority and married on their own. She was so under his control that he would have been beset by shock, quickly indistinguishable from fury. It would not help that Charles' mother was his wife's sister and he would suspect collusion against him, which he would root to the bottom of with Wealthy. A second cause of rage would be the fact that now his wife had lost both of her helpers. On the one hand, he now had two less mouths to feed, but on the other, the big household now had just Ella, only four, as the only girl to help his wife.

My own immediate concern was where to put the newlyweds, at least for one night. Our house was very small and the upstairs consisted of three rooms – the largest where Hiram and I slept – and two small ones carved out of a room the size of the big one. The upstairs of this little, roughly made cape was hardly more than the size of an attic in a larger house.

I had gone out to the barn to talk with Hiram while he had finished up chores before supper, with Biathy's help.

"It was all well and good to agree they could stay, but what are we to do with them?" I said. "Where are they to sleep?"

He looked at me blankly. I could tell he wondered why I was asking him. The house was my purview.

"If they weren't married, I would put her in with Fanny, and Charles could sleep in the barn or in with Biathy. But I can't do that tonight. Certainly not tonight."

He continued to pitch hay to the cows.

"I was thinking that tonight, just for this one night," I stressed, "That they could take our room. I could go in with Fanny and you could go in with Biathy. Then I'll have to figure out something else."

He shrugged. "I don't mind." He grinned, then, "If the bridegroom ever gets back, that is. He said you sent him over to tell her old man. That should break him in fast as a husband."

I smiled back at him.

"You won't mind having help in the house," he said.

"I won't and Fanny is quite smitten with her already."

"It'll keep Charles around," he said. "Maybe it will turn his head away from the war."

I grew somber at this thought.

"I hope so," I said.

When Charles did arrive, some hours later, luckily, I was in the front room, sitting idly because it was too dark to sew, and saw them arrive. A lantern wobbled in the darkness, from the motion of the wagon. It could only be him. I decided the best course of action would be to go out and meet him to hear his story first.

I hurried out into the dark, cold air of fall with only my light wrap, but I did not want to delay to get a cloak. When I came close into the circle of light, I saw the borrowed wagon had been returned to its owner, and he was riding with his new father-in-law.

"Good evening," I said to Lucius as he got heavily down from the seat. "Thank you for bringing my boy home."

Charles had leapt down from the other side and he scuttled away into the dark as fast as he could go. I was left with Lucius, who hauled down his daughter's bags and set them near my feet in a series of thuds.

"I suppose you knew about all of these shenanigans," he grunted.

"Hardly," I said coldly. "Do you think I would encourage my son to marry a girl who is barely fourteen?"

"Your boy acted fool-headed," he said. "He should be off to war like the rest of the able-bodied men his age."

"Easy for you to say with boys young enough to be safe at home with you."

"They would do their duty," he said.

"I have no doubt," I said tightly, trying to contain my anger. "Now you've had your say and kept him away well into the evening, what do you propose to do? Have you come to fetch her home? I have no doubt she would go with you, whatever it cost her."

"Home? Home?" he said roughly. "She is home. She's your problem now. She made her bed and now she can lay in it."

"Do you want to see her?" I asked.

My answer was his climbing back into his wagon, and stirring up the horses.

I stomped back to the house, in a rage myself now, at that man's rudeness and callousness and his insults. It was very dark, but I followed the light in the window and made my way inside.

In the kitchen, there was gloom. Malinda looked scared, her eyes big and round, and her hands curled into fists in her lap. Hiram and Biathy had gone to bed earlier, and I had tucked Fanny in, with the help of Malinda, with promises of joining her soon. She was delighted that I would be sharing her room, though she had hoped it was to be Malinda, and drooped a little when I explained that it was Malinda's wedding night and she would be sharing a room with her husband from now on.

It was the three of us in the kitchen – Charles, Malinda and me. He was angrier than I had ever seen him, his face and neck a dark, mottled color. I could see his jacket over the back of a chair and there was straw in his hair, and his pants, stuffed into dusty boots, were covered with dirt.

"He made me help him with his chores," he said in a strange, high-pitched voice. "He humiliated me. He made me wait until he was done with chores and had his supper, with my wife waiting back here. And then he made me take the wagon back. It was loaned to me until tomorrow morning."

I sighed.

"That is over now," I said. "You did as he asked and it is over."

"It ain't over," he proclaimed, clenching and unclenching his fists. "He won't treat me like that."

"It is over," I said firmly. "You need to put it aside now. You're scaring her."

At that, he started, and turned to his wife, all of the anger going out of him.

"You're to have your father's and my room tonight," I said. "The room is all ready, and I have put her things there. You bring in her other bags from the yard and take them up."

"Thanks, Ma," he said, and his voice sounded normal.

He was holding hands with Malinda, having drawn her up from her chair so her fists uncurled. He dropped her hand and put his arm very tenderly around her waist, and bent to kiss her cheek.

"You go on up with Ma and get settled and I'll come right up with your bags," he directed her.

Happily, she skipped ahead of me down the hall and up the stairs to what was her room for the night. I knew Charles would bring in the bags and then want to wash his hands and face.

"There's hot water still on the stove," I told him.

"Thanks, Ma," he said.

That was all settled for this one night. How I would manage after this, I did not yet know.

g

Chapter Thirteen

WINTER 1861-1862

T HE FACT IS WE DID NOT MANAGE WELL. There was only so much space and it had barely worked before with Charles in with Biathy, and Fanny in her own tiny room. Now it simply did not work at all. If it had just been me, I might have given up the big room to my son and his bride and gone in with Fanny. But it was not just me and I could not rearrange the sleeping to accommodate Charles and Malinda. Hiram, who had an easygoing nature and a soft heart, urged me to let them stay in our room for an extra night, and so it was done, but then it was the morning after that second night.

I went out to the barn to talk to Charles on my own, on the pretext of going to the springhouse. When he saw me, he dropped the shovelful of manure and came to me. We sat on the rough wooden bench. He knew what I had come about, of course.

"I have been racking my brain, Charles," I started off the conversation. "I can't figure out what to do about a bedroom for you and Malinda."

"Couldn't Fanny go in with you and Pa?" he asked.

I snorted. "Hardly," I said. "She's seven, too old to be in with us."

"Couldn't Biathy sleep out here?"

"In the barn?" I exclaimed.

He nodded.

"Use your head," I said. "He's eight years old."

"He'd like it," Charles said stubbornly.

"Like it, not like it, my eight-year-old is not sleeping in the barn."

Now he got around to what he had been hatching up all along.

"We could sleep in the front room," he said.

"No," I said, right off, without thinking. I liked that room. The kitchen was very dark, with only one window since the shed went across the back. I used the front room to sew and sit, and I liked all of the windows that faced across the yard and the road and some meadows to a view of mountains.

"What else is there?" he asked crossly.

"You should have thought of that before you got married," I said.

He looked sulky, though he had the sense to drop his eyes.

"You're a man," I said softly. "Since almost three years ago."

He knew what I meant. It had been the start of 1859, when Charles was only sixteen, that his father had posted the notice in the newspaper that his son, a minor, was free to act and trade on his own without his father claiming his earnings or his debts. He had asked his father for that with his plans to work out that summer for money. He had worked for his father for no pay and for a neighbor for cash money, setting aside his wages.

"Please, Ma," he said. "What else is there to do?"

I considered, thinking hard of my front room.

"You don't use it in the coldest months," he said. "And it's November."

"You could bunk in with Biathy and Malinda could go in with Fanny."

Even to my ears this did not sound reasonable. My son got a pinched look around his mouth and the tips of his ears reddened. I did not want to give up my front room. I had planned to put a woodstove in that room for the winter.

"Alright," I gave in crossly. "But you will each keep your things upstairs. Malinda's with Fanny and yours with Biathy. You can buy a bed and move it into the front room, but all you will do is sleep there. In the daytime, it will not be a bedroom even though it has a bed. You can dress upstairs. And I am putting a woodstove in and I will be using that room for my sewing during the day."

He knew that was the best he was going to do.

"Thank you, Ma," he said.

That was the arrangement we made and kept. He went off that afternoon with the wagon and returned with a bed, bought secondhand from the same friend who loaned him the wagon and I knew he had that bed in his sights long before his wedding day.

I snorted when he and his father unloaded it, peering out from the front room windows. Malinda and Fanny and I had spent the afternoon rearranging the chairs and the small table in a tight cluster against the windows. It made the room very crowded, what with the space left against the kitchen wall for a stove, and the bed and the front room furnishings. It made me cross and I admit I was not good company that day, short-tempered and giving orders in an unfriendly manner.

It had not helped that I had overheard a conversation that morning between Charles and Malinda who had spoken in whispers in the hall that nonetheless carried up to where I was changing the sheets on my bed.

"Why can't we have the room to ourselves?" she had asked in a plaintive voice. "You can't mean it is to stay a room that everyone will still use."

"That is just what I mean," he answered tightly.

"I want our own room," she said.

"You have as much as you'll get in this house," he said.

"Why is your mother being so unreasonable?" she asked.

There was a silence in which I fumed and listened.

"She is being generous," I heard him mumble.

"You're on her side!" she said, outraged.

"Oh, come on, Malinda," he reasoned. "It's her house."

"We should be in our own house," she said. "You promised we would have our own place. Even at home, Myalina and Ella and I had our own room."

"You could have your own room here, with Fanny," he said shortly.

At this point, she burst into tears, and I decided it was time I went downstairs, which I proceeded to do, shutting my bedroom door with a sharp thud as I came into the small space near the stairs and headed down. By the time I reached the bottom, there was no sign in the house of Charles and Malinda. I looked out each window and saw them at last under the big maple, where he had his arm around her and she was rubbing at her face with a handkerchief – one of her tiny squares, embroidered with white flowers and trimmed with lace. I could see he was talking earnestly to her.

From this point forward, from day three, of Malinda's living with us, she and I were not on the best of terms. I could not forget what she had said about me, and truth be told, she was never my favorite though I had always strived to be fair in my treatment of her compared to Myalina.

There was a strain in the house, with Charles walking a fine line between his wife and me, his mother. Hiram did not notice. Fanny noticed, but did not understand the cause. How could I put it into words for a seven-year-old – that a new bride and her mother-in-law were in an ages-old contest of wills? But it was my house. Whenever I felt qualms about my behavior over the front room that is what I told myself. Fanny and I sat in the front room every afternoon sewing, with the comforting warmth from the woodstove Hiram and Charles had hauled in and set on a makeshift hearth. We sat facing the view and I tried to forget that behind me the room was crowded with a bed and nightstand that did not belong to me. Malinda did not sit with us, but pretended to work in the kitchen. I will not belabor the point that it was my kitchen, too.

Thus it was that we passed through November and December and into January. It was that month, on January 21, that Charles joined his cousin, Hollis, and signed up to be a soldier in the Eighth Vermont Volunteer Infantry. A day later, he was off to southern Vermont for training and two months after that, in March, he was gone, headed to what we later learned was the state called Louisiana, leaving behind what he had started – a young wife who had gone to live even before that with her sister.

From the beginning, the marriage of the cousins was a mistake. He thought, because they were family, that he knew her and he was swept away by her loveliness, but what he thought was easy was hard. Because of a combination of her youth and her lack of maturity, she was not a good girl to have in my house. What had seemed small, but workable with the five us, became constricted and untenable with her among us.

"She thought you were her path out of her family situation," I told Charles about a month after his wedding.

"But it takes time," he said. "Why doesn't she see that?"

I bit my tongue, knowing that to lay on him all of my observations of the young woman would only anger him.

"It is not what she dreamed of," I said. "She's young."

"But Myalina is young. You were young when you married," he protested.

"Women are all different," I said. "Myalina and her mother and I are one way and Malinda is another. That's all. She is not patient. She heard your promises of a house of her own and expected you meant right away, that you would take money and buy a farm and you would be set up just like that."

I knew what was bothering him, though I would not bring it up if he did not. And he did not. Malinda was sleeping with Fanny. A few days before, I had heard footsteps on the stairs clearly striving to be quiet. It was after even I was in bed, and I am a light sleeper, always have been, and awoke to this burglar tread on the steps, from someone who did not know to avoid certain spots on certain stairs. I eased out of bed (no fear of waking Hiram who slept the sleep of the just, as the saying goes) and went to the door that was open a few inches. It was Malinda, I could see even in the dark, by the pale floating of her white nightdress, topped by a jacket draped across her shoulders. She pushed open Fanny's door that was ajar slightly. I went back to bed and did not hear her come out. From then on, for a few nights, I awoke to the same muffled steps and knew she was sleeping in Fanny's room.

Fanny said not one word to me, and I acted like I didn't know what was going on. In fact, I didn't know what was the cause, but I could tell Charles was edgy and unhappy.

"It will be a few years before I can buy a farm," he admitted to me glumly.

I sighed. I knew all about how long it took to save money.

"She wants other things, too," he added.

I waited.

"She wants clothing, a new dress and some boots she saw in Cutting's store. And she thinks I should be paid for working here since I am a man."

He paused, and I could see his mind working.

"She's sleeping with Fanny!" he finally said, the words coming out in a torrent. He studied me. "But you know that. You always know everything," he said, with wonder. "She swore Fanny to secrecy, but you must have wormed it out of her."

"You know I'm a light sleeper," I said. "Fanny never said a word, but I have heard Malinda every night come up the stairs. No wonder she looks so tired."

"She's very angry," Charles said.

He was angry, too, and humiliated, that she had left his bed and that he could not provide what she expected even though he knew she was not reasonable.

I decided to intervene. One morning when Fanny went out to collect eggs, I had Malinda to myself.

"I have something to say to you," I told her. We had not been speaking for weeks, except to exchange the basic communication of whatever work was going on that day.

She looked up from her work of jabbing a needle and thread in and out of the heel of one of her husband's socks.

"I know you have been sleeping in Fanny's room," I said, putting up my hand when she began to speak. "Let me finish. Fanny didn't tell me. I have heard you every night, going up the stairs and into her room and not coming back down until morning. I have given you time to work out whatever is going on between you and my son, but enough time has passed. I don't want you sleeping in with my daughter anymore. You have a place with your husband. You are young, and I try to be understanding, but you are a married woman and you belong with the man you married. Do you understand me?"

She glared at me, her lovely features contorted, and I knew she wanted to hiss at me that she hated me and wished me dead. I had been a daughter, too, facing authority I did not wish to follow.

"Do you understand me?" I repeated.

"Yes," she said sullenly. She returned to jabbing the needle in and out of the wool sock and I knew I would have to find it later and take out the stitching and repair it properly or Charles would get a blister. She had a fierce look, a sullen, dark look on her features, and she did not look pretty. She had no allies in this house, except her seven-year-old cousin, and must have felt a prisoner.

I decided the best thing would be a visit to her sister who I hoped would talk some sense into her. The next morning, I said, "Would you like to go with me to visit Myalina?"

I was relieved to see her brighten, and forget herself in her excitement.

"Yes!" she exclaimed, not hiding her pleasure even from me.

"Can I go?" Fanny asked.

"Of course," I said.

The three of us bundled into the wagon on the cold, but sunny day in early December and set off on the road that would take us into Guildhall to Myalina.

Myalina and George were living with her in-laws. Horace, gone to war for months now, left her and her husband to keep the old people company and the farm going. She was happy enough. Her mother lived right down the road, and she could visit her and help her some days, with the blessing of Mrs. Gage. The house, though not her own, was a tidy, tightly built place. She and George had one of the big bedrooms upstairs, and her in-laws had moved down to a spare room off the kitchen that was warmer in the winter. The son, Charles, who was consumptive even at the start of the war, had a tiny bedroom upstairs and often was not seen, keeping to his bed, where his mother or Myalina brought him food and cared for him. On his good days, he would sit close to the fire in the rocking chair or, if the weather was especially warm, outdoors in the sunshine.

Harmon was severely arthritic, his fingers twisted and swollen, and the cold bothered him badly. He depended on George to manage the small farm that had a simple prosperity, enough to keep all of them well enough.

It had been willed to Betsey, and by extension to him, after her father died in the late 1840s. With the help of the two sons, fifteen acres had been improved and there were another eighty acres in woodland, including a sugar bush where they tapped trees and made maple sugar each spring. They kept two cows, and made a few hundred pounds of butter from the milk. They raised wheat and Indian corn, Irish potatoes and barley, tending the fields with a pair of oxen. They kept eight or so sheep and sheared the wool. It was a nicely tended property, each of the men bringing a skill to bear.

Betsey lent a calmness to the house that transferred to the outdoors in the demeanor of her menfolk. That Myalina was fond of her and vice versa was apparent. The two women were alike, one in her sixties and the other not yet twenty – determined, quiet, hardworking, religious. To see them together was to feel they had been working in the same house for all of Myalina's life, and to forget how young she was.

Into that household, I brought Malinda with my hopes for a miracle.

"What a nice surprise!" Betsey exclaimed when we arrived. She and Myalina hustled us inside to the warm parlor where the woodstove popped, and soon we were out of all our heavy garments, sitting in comfortable chairs with cups of tea and a plate of apple cake. Talk was light, of the gossip of the neighbors, and the weather. When Betsey went to replenish the tea pot, I followed her.

"It is so good of you to come all this way over," she told me again. "It is a bright spot for Myalina."

"She looks well," I said.

"Oh, she is," Betsey assured me. "I am so lucky to have her with me. She is like a daughter and we are friends, too."

"I wonder if I can ask you something," I said.

"Of course, dear," she said.

"It's about Malinda," I said.

She set down the kettle and gave me her full attention.

"Oh, is everything alright?"

"No," I said, surprised at how forthright I was. "We are crowded," I said. "It is not easy and she is so young. She thought, well, she thought she would be in her own house by now. I thought maybe, if she had some time to talk with her sister, it would help. Her sister is so mature, so steady."

"We'll finish up our tea and then I'll send the two of them upstairs to see Myalina's room and then you and Fanny and I will be in the kitchen when they come back down so they can have plenty of time to get caught up."

That was a good plan, I thought.

It did not help, though. That Myalina counseled patience, I did not doubt. She came to find me after some time had passed, leaving Malinda in the parlor, and Betsey took Fanny with her to find the cat. That left my niece and me to talk.

"You look so well," I told Myalina. She did; her dark hair fell like folds of satin from a bolt of cloth, and she had just a hint of rose blush on her high cheekbones.

She smiled, and thanked me for the compliment.

Then we were serious, and bent to the work at hand.

"It is not so good with my sister," she said.

"That is why I have come."

"She and Charles acted rashly," she said.

I nodded.

"I don't know. She had big dreams. She saw me married and was eager for the same thing herself. Charles should not have listened to her," Myalina said.

"Does she want to go home?"

"Not that! Our father would never allow it," she said fiercely.

I was not surprised at this.

"She does love Charles, you know," she said. "She loves him quite ferociously," she added and blushed, thinking she had said too much.

"We don't get along," I said. "I am not patient with her and we don't have enough room. She had taken to sleeping with Fanny and I forbid it. I am at a loss."

"I have encouraged her to be patient. Spring will come and she won't be so cooped up. I told her to focus on her love of him and be patient for the future. But she is not patient, and even spring seems like an eternity away to her," Myalina sighed.

We went back home, and I hoped Myalina's counsel would have calmed her sister even temporarily. I was prepared to make these visits every couple of weeks if need be. But the upshot was that that girl, that foolish young girl, went to live with her sister the week after Christmas, where she had a small room of her own.

The same day Charles enlisted, in January 1862, he paid for a notice to be posted in *The Caledonian* newspaper advising the public that his wife had left his bed and board, and forbidding all persons from trusting or harboring her on his account in that he would pay none of her debts.

It was with that sourness curdling his stomach, and the shame of a runaway wife, that he left Lunenburg on January 22 for what would be one year of service in the war, and would result in his being wounded in a skirmish on the rail line in a place between Algiers and Bayou des Allemands in Louisiana.

I went to the village that cold, blustery January morning to see him off. Despite the extreme chill, there were dozens of people gathered to give a rousing farewell to these men, going in wagons to meet the recruits from other towns and begin the journey to Camp Holbrook in Brattleboro – a town on the Connecticut River just at the border with Massachusetts. We all knew this Eighth Infantry was formed for special duty in the far south, but that was all the information given out.

I watched Charles, standing wrapped in an overcoat, light flakes of snow falling onto his cap and shoulders. The early morning light turned the white world a pale, luminous pink. I could see him searching the crowd, his gaze passing from group to group and back over us all again. I knew he was looking for Malinda. He started when he recognized Myalina, there with George and his parents. He must have wondered if Malinda was with them, perhaps hidden from his view behind her sister. But she was not there. I had been looking for her, too, willing her to have come to see him off and put a good face on what pained them. He had given me the money to post the notice, and I would do it today, sending the cash enclosed in an envelope with a note of what was required. He could not afford to risk taking on her debt with her beyond his house with her sister.

The snow suddenly intensified, surging in with a blast of air, and the visibility dropped. He was turning away when all at once Malinda was there, like a vision coming out of the squall that lifted as quickly as it started. I saw her, too, and watched as she gravely pushed her way past people and came to stand in front of him.

I never knew what was said between them, and they did not have long before the men hove off from Lunenburg green, but I saw her cast herself into his arms, and I saw how he clung onto her and she him. She stood, her neat figure garmented in a long, gray wool skirt, and a heavy cloak, with a scarf twisted around her head and neck. She was straight in her stance and did not waver until the men had disappeared from view down the long hill toward St. Johnsbury where they would take the train. It was a two-day journey, following the river south to Brattleboro. The shouts of the crowd overtook the music of the small band playing marches, our cheers echoing and echoing in the cold air.

Hiram had his arm around me, and I was grateful to know that if I faltered he would keep me steady on my feet.

I watched that girl as she made her way back to her sister.

"Will you post the notice?" Hiram, who had missed nothing, asked me.

I nodded. "I have to," I said, following her with my eyes as she left with the Gages. "How will he pay her debts now she is not living with us?"

g

Chapter Fourteen

WINTER 1862

IT WAS A WINTER OF BITTER COLD AND UNUSUAL SEVERITY. Storm followed storm, and the temperatures dropped below zero. I had two letters from Charles, the first telling me, of course, how well he was, and the
excitement of the life of camp amidst the thousand comrades. He told,
too, of the harsh cold and the storms, and that there were many cases of
mumps and measles, but the men were comfortable and well cared for,
and he was not ill. Since I had nursed him through those two diseases, I
could be glad of his health.

"You can share my letter," he wrote. I knew he meant with Malinda.

I stewed on this matter for two days, staying awake at night in the
frigid temperatures of the bedroom when sleep at least made one forget
the cold for awhile, before I decided to take the letter to the Gage household.

"You wait for a warmer day," Hiram told me. "It is too bitter for a trip
over to Guildhall."

Since he almost never directed me in any way, I took his advice.

"She won't know the letter has come," he pointed out mildly.

"Alright," I said. "It's just I have agonized for two days about whether
to go at all and finally have got up my courage. Maybe this cold is a sign
I should keep this letter to myself."

He studied me mildly. "You know Charles wants you to take it to
her."

Almost a week passed before Hiram determined it was safe for me to
make the trip to the Gages. I wanted to stop and see my sister, too. The
sun was out, and the eaves were dripping at ten o'clock. That was how he
decided it would be a good day for me to go. He insisted on driving me.
We took the wagon fitted with runners, and he packed me and Fanny and
Biathy in with blankets and a bearskin throw (many years ago, he had
taken a bear and had this throw made). Then he climbed up, and wrapped

himself in a quilt and off we went. I admit I was excited to be going some-where after weeks stuck indoors. The sun felt cheerful, and though the wind caught the sled in bursts, we went at a steady pace down the hill to the Guildhall road and up into the hills to my niece and sister.

Myalina ran outside when we were scarcely stopped in the yard. She shouted with delight.

"Hello! Hello! What has brought you? I am so happy to see you."

She helped Fanny and Biathy down, after we had untangled from the coverings, while Hiram lifted me to the snowy ground.

"Bring in all of those blankets," she told Hiram. "We want to get them warm for the trip back."

She was all business and bustle, her cheeks and nose red in the cold, and shepherded us into the comfort of the kitchen where Betsey greeted us warmly. She rubbed my cold hands, and pushed a chair close to the stove for me. Malinda was there, too, and she took charge of Fanny. Biathy helped his father get the horse to the barn, and they brought in the wraps from the wagon to put them in a heap under the range.

Once we were warm again, the mid-day meal was served – a pork roast surrounded by potatoes and turnips and carrots, and plates of fresh-baked bread, and a bowl of thick gravy to pour over everything, and applesauce, and pickles. I had come with a jar of honey, wrapped in a scrap of cloth and kept under my coat on the drive over so it would stay unfrozen. We were wordless while eating, the loud sound of nine sets of cutlery clanging against the china. We filled the kitchen, crowded around the table, shoulder to shoulder, George and Harmon just in from the barn with Hiram and Biathy, bringing in the cold in their heavy clothing, and Malinda and Myalina, and Betsey and Fanny and me, and even the wraith-like consumptive, Charles.

Once the eating slowed, the real visiting began, and Myalina rose to bring the apple pies.

"What has brought you out in the cold?" Betsey asked, her hostess duties giving way to her curiosity.

"We waited for the warmest day," I said. "I have a letter from Charles. He asked me share it. Go and fetch my bag, Fanny."

I had kept my eyes especially on Malinda when I spoke of the letter and was gratified to see her blush deeply.

With the letter crackling in my hand, I had everyone's full attention. In the quiet of the large room, with no one even breathing loudly, I read Charles' letter to them.

"He sounds well," Betsey ventured.

"Very well, aunt," Myalina said.

"It sounds like a great adventure," Betsey said.

At these words of his mother's, George became agitated. He got up quickly, and mumbling an excuse, grabbed his coat and hat and left the room.

Myalina stood when he did, and made as if to go after him, but instead, sank back into her chair and looked troubled.

"We have not heard from Horace in awhile," his mother said.

"It must take a long time for letters," I ventured, wanting to reassure her, but not knowing how. Horace Gage was with the Third, and by now had been in service for more than eighteen months. News filtered back, weeks after events, in the newspapers, and she did not know where he was. That regiment had seen all of the worst of the fighting – we did know that. In fact, he was encamped that winter in Virginia and safe enough, but in May would come the battle at Chancellorville.

We were quiet, all thinking of Horace, as brash and loquacious as his brother was silent and slow-acting.

"Let's go into the other room," Betsey said. "We can clean up later. I imagine you will be stopping to pay a visit to your sister?"

"Yes, I want to see her. We can't stay long. Hiram is worried about the weather," I said.

I watched in what I hoped was an unobtrusive manner, and seeing that Malinda hovered by the stove, I hung back and let the others go past me into the other room. It was then that I pulled from my sleeve a small folded piece of paper that I had showed no one. It had slipped out of the letter from Charles, a small, almost unnoticeable piece of paper that bore on it the penciled legend, "Malinda." I had told no one. It was that which had kept me awake two nights, thinking whether or not I should give it to her.

I pressed it into her startled hand, and went without a word to join the others.

The year 1862 was bad for many reasons, beginning with Charles' rift with Malinda and his going to war – the two events entwined inextricably for me. I arrived that day at my sister's to find a severe lack of welcome. Myalina had come, too, and we would leave her back home on our way home.

Wealthy lived not even a mile from the Gages, and it was almost not worth the effort of us all getting into the sled and riding there when we could just have well of walked. But Hiram was not a walker to no purpose. He walked his fields with a plow and he walked to hunt or to his fishing spots, but if he could use a wagon or a sled, he did so.

Fanny had stayed behind with Malinda and Mrs. Gage. She had fallen in love with her cousin during Malinda's stay with 's and had been confused and unhappy when she left us. It was a treat f r her to be cosseted by the two of them. Betsey had promised to show her a new embroidery stitch, and she always had the best materials, which added to the treat for my daughter.

I walked happily into my sister's kitchen, only to have her spin on me with wrath.

"You!" she spit out the word. "You! showing your face here. I would not think you would have the gall to come to my house with your false smile in the middle of a cold winter's day."

She stomped across to the open cupboard and retrieved a newspaper that looked like a rat had been gnawing and worrying it. It was folded into a small segment and she shoved that paper at me, poking me in the chest brusquely.

"You are behind this," she snapped. "And yet you dare walk into my house as saucy as a cat finished with a bowl of milk."

She stood, stiff with anger, and we faced off – two women built the same, standing at the same height, my back up at her attack and meeting her outrage with my own.

I snatched the paper from her and peered at the words in the small folded square. My heart sank as I read. It was the notice from Charles.

"Oh," I said, deflated.

Myalina took the news from me and studied the item.

"Oh, Aunt," she said when she was done.

I sat down hard in a straight-backed chair. Around us were my many nephews and nieces, all silent in the midst of their mother's outburst. Little Ella came to put her tiny hand on my knee, looking shyly into my face with her lovely brown eyes with hints of hazel, but her mother grabbed her back from me and waited with her daughter backed up against her knees.

"You don't have a word to say," she remarked. "Why would you do such a thing? You have shamed your family. You have announced to the world that my daughter has left Charles. You have made her look bad, very bad. You have ruined her reputation."

I admit I had not thought this through. I stared at my black boots, the tiny buttons that had to be affixed with a metal hook made for that job. In my anger at Malinda's treatment of my son and her lack of maturity, and my grief and fear at his enlistment, which I partly blamed on her, I had only thought to be sure she did no further damage to him.

"It is a formality," I said weakly.

"A formality!" she repeated, her voice ugly.

In her tone, I could hear the lameness of what I had said.

"I'm sorry," I said finally. "It was not me. It was Charles. He was hurt and angry that she had left. And he can't assume her debts when he has no control over them. You must see that now he is gone for a year and she is not under his care that he cannot take her debts. What would he do if she spent money he does not have?"

"That has hurt all of us," she said. "It has cast a bad light on all of Malinda's family and you are one of us. It says January 23. Charles left the day before that. How did he get it to the newspaper when he was not even here?"

"He gave it to me to do," I admitted, figuring being honest was all I could do now. "He gave me the money and the note of his intent and entrusted me to mail it."

"But why would you do that?" she wailed. "Aren't they going to reconcile? That is what my daughter has told me."

I blushed at my ignorance. "I don't know," I said. "How would I know? My son marched off to war that day. What would you know about that? Your daughter is no confidant of mine. She publicly kissed my son who she had spurned and then went back to her new home without so much as a glance at me."

"Your son, your son who made promises to my daughter he could not keep. Your son who lured a young girl, a child really, from her mother. And how welcoming were you to her? Did you take her under your roof like a beloved niece and a daughter? That is not what I have heard."

"Mother, Aunt," Myalina interjected herself between us. "Stop before you both say more that only hurts us all."

We stared at her, deciding if we should listen to her.

"You know, Aunt, you must have known how this would be hurtful," she raised her hand to shush me. "Let me finish, both of you. There it is in print for all to see, and you never even gave us warning. I felt shame when I read that, for my sister and for my cousin, that all of their business is published fact. But, you, Mother, must understand why he did it. You know how Malinda can be. She is still a girl, Mother. We are lucky Mr. and Mrs. Gage were willing to take her in or she would be back with you, or who knows where. You can't expect Charles to take on unknown expenses she might incur. The Gages took her in because she is my sister and certainly Charles will do the right thing by them when he comes home."

Wealthy and I considered this long speech. There was gristle in it for both of us to chew and swallow. We both swallowed. I saw Wealthy's Adam's apple bob slightly and I felt my own do the same. I was itching to retort back to my sister's comments about me and my son, but I bit it all back. We eyed one another darkly, like two marsh hawks over one patch of meadow.

"You two kiss and be friends again," this peacemaker Myalina told us.

We did as she directed. In a chilly, begrudging way, we kissed one another.

"I think we should go now," Myalina said. "I'm sorry not to have had a longer, pleasant visit, but at least I have seen you are well, Mother. I think I should take this newspaper to show the Gages. They have a right to know of it."

"Will you show Malinda?" I asked. My sister and I awaited her thoughtful reply.

"We'll see," she said. "Mrs. Gage will know what is the right thing to do."

That shut up any argument I could make, and my sister narrowed her eyes, her small bright eyes, but said nothing.

She and her daughter hugged, and Myalina bent to kiss Ella and scooped her up when she began to cry.

"I'll come again very soon," she assured the little girl. "I promise." She handed off her sister to her mother. "I'll ask George to bring me one day this week."

Hiram was still in the barn, when Myalina and I walked outside. We walked to the outbuilding where we found the men. Lucius eyed me with such unfriendliness that my gut knotted.

"Hello, Father," Myalina said. "We are going now." She guided me straight up into the wagon.

Hiram looked startled, but he didn't waste any time. He and Biathy climbed onto the driver's seat and we were gone, leaving Lucius glaring balefully after us.

That was not a day I would care to relive.

Affairs did not improve that year. News from Charles was sporadic. As far as I could tell from his letters, his lot was not a bad one with the Eighth. They had traveled by train in March down the Connecticut Valley, feted and cheered at the big cities along the way. Patriotic spirits ran high, and women served refreshments to the troops along the way, and bands played and crowds turned out and politicians gave fervid speeches. Upon reaching the city of New Haven, with over one thousand men, they boarded the steamer Granite State, and arrived on the East River where they docked in the great city of New York. His letter read like a travelogue, and his excitement at the journey and the patriotic fervor was plain in his descriptions. There had been no fighting, unless he concealed it which he might have done though I would find out when he returned that they had no engagement with the enemy troops until shortly before the incident in which he was shot in the shoulder.

From New York, the soldiers engaged in a three-week long voyage in ships down the coast of the United States to reach a place called Ship Island. Charles could not get over the tropical atmosphere, the white sand of the beaches and the fierce ocean storms that threatened to over-sweep the island where over 14,000 men were encamped.

"We were all seasick," he wrote in one letter. "The ships were huge and packed with all of us. But what sights I have seen. The ocean is vast. It is not a sight that can be described so you would understand what it is really like."

One day in April, I walked to the schoolhouse, just up the road from us. It was the end of the school day, as I had planned, and the students were all gone when I arrived. The teacher was picking up her papers and writing the next day's quotation on the blackboard. It was Abraham Lincoln she quoted.

"Mrs. Presbrey," she said in surprise. "What can I do for you?"

"I wonder if I might look at your map of the United States," I asked. "You see, my son, Charles, is in Louisiana and I would like to see exactly where that is."

"Why, of course," she exclaimed and walked to the big parchment-looking wall map with the states all appearing in different pale colors. Vermont was a shade of green. It was a big map, much taller than me. I stood and marked Vermont with my eyes and traced the journey Charles had made by train down the Connecticut Valley through Springfield and New Haven and into New York, and then, the states now in my reach, lightly traced with my index finger the coast from New York down to the mouth of the Mississippi at the State of Louisiana. It was unimaginably far. Louisiana was pink, trying to be red, but faded.

"There are rice plantations all along the river," he had written. "The river is brown and deep and as wide as half a dozen of the Connecticut."

"He's a soldier?" the teacher asked.

I nodded. "With the Eighth. They are on special duty in the south. He writes, but I wanted to see for myself on the map where exactly he has been and where he is now. He's in New Orleans. They're the police in that city now, taking the place of the enemy."

"My fiancé is with the Third," she said. Miss Pinkham, I recalled her name was.

"My niece's brother-in-law is with the Third," I said. "Horace Gage."

"He was wounded, but now he is back with his company," she said, as if I had not spoken. She was looking out the window at the snow that was giving way to spring, the fields with patches bare of snow. "They are seeing all the worst of it."

"I hope he comes home safe, Miss Pinkham," I said.

Hearing her name brought her back to me.

"Thank you, ma'am. I hope the best for your son, too."

I took my time walking home, thinking of the succession of pink and green and yellow and blue and green states interlocked like pieces of a jigsaw puzzle. That was what the war was about – the interlocking of the different states, north and south, and whether slavery could pull them apart.

Sugaring season came, with the warm days and cold nights, and Hiram tapped the trees with Biathy's and even my and Fanny's help. I helped gather the sap buckets, too, for Hiram to pour into the vat mounted on the wagon with its runners. There was still a packed road of snow into the sugar bush. Hiram had erected two posts from tree trunks stripped of bark, and attached a heavy pole between them from which he suspended his kettles over a fire and boiled off his sap. It was a good year for that; we made over one hundred pounds of maple sugar, enough to use in our kitchen and enough extra to sell.

From there, the planting season followed with no lapse, and Hiram was busy following the plan I had helped him come up with. I worked out in the fields helping, too, pushing him to finish the plowing and the planting, coming into the barn with him after breakfast and leaving Fanny to clear up and start the midday meal. If I did not guide him, he quickly lost interest and I would come to him late in the morning and find him still pondering the work of hitching the horse to the plow. He was not one to proceed from one task to another without a long pause that often resulted in the next job never getting started. He was like a waterwheel in the dry season that barely turns and waits for a rainstorm to send down more force from the stream. I was the rainstorm, a series of them that summer, with the farm now in its second season and Charles far away.

The heat of June and July drove on into August and the harvest began. I was out with Hiram many days, helping him determine what the goal would be and working by his side to take in the corn, loading the wagon for the gristmill. It was a day late in that month, and we were haying. I was out in the field on the far side of the orchard with a long rake, when I saw motion and stopped my task. I peered into the bright light, and finally made out it was Myalina running toward me, her hands gathering up the sides of her skirt and her long hair flying behind her, dark and glossy in the sun like the feathers of a crow. I dropped the rake and hurried to meet her, fear making me gasp for breath.

Her face streamed tears and when we were close, she flung herself at me and I caught onto her waist and she wrapped her arms tightly around my shoulders and sobbed so hard I was even more afraid.

"There, there," I soothed. "There, there. What has happened? Myalina, what is wrong?" When she did not stop crying, her frame racked with her weeping, I gently, but firmly unfolded her arms from me and placed my hands on either side of her face to calm her and get her to talk.

"You have to tell me," I said. "I can't help if I don't know."

My heart was hammering; was it her mother, Malinda, one of the children, Horace...Charles?

"It's George!" she got out the words at last. "It's George! He's gone and enlisted. For three years. He's gone and enlisted in the Third to be with his brother. He's leaving in a few days. Oh, my God, what am I to do?"

A hundred thoughts flared through my mind. Not Charles, no one dead, my sister safe, but Myalina was losing George, her husband whom she loved, to the war.

I took her back in my arms, and she continued to cry, though with less heat, and I rocked her like I would a baby. Hiram had come to stand close by and he watched us silently.

"It's George," I told him, over her shoulder. "He has enlisted."

He shook his head and looked mournful. One after another, all of the men were going. Now both of the able Gage sons would be at war, leaving only the consumptive son who moved like a shadow around the house and only went outside to sit on warm days in the sunshine.

But the hardships were not over with this news of George. It was hardly a week later when Wealthy's baby, Thomas, died. He was barely two years old, taken quickly by a fever, that, in his weakness, perhaps of his heart, he did not survive.

Lucius came with the news. For once, he did not exchange any unpleasant words with me. He knocked on the door that day of September third, and Fanny sent him out to find me digging potatoes alongside Hiram and Biathy, the bushel baskets filling up with the hardy Irish potatoes.

He was a silent man, Lucius, and I jumped out of my skin when I heard his gruff voice calling to me out of the air behind me.

I pulled myself stiffly up and, wiping my dirty hands on my work pinafore that kept my dress clean, I went to him.

"The baby has died," he said abruptly. "An hour ago. I have come to fetch you."

I ran ahead of him to the house, my face wet with tears now, to change my dress and go with him to try and comfort my sister.

Lucius and I never said one word the entire drive between the houses. With all of the silence around me, I built up a vast store of words and feelings. He lifted me down in his dooryard and I ran to the house and found Wealthy and we held one another, crying. I was crying for Thomas, a sickly little boy whose course had run out, and for all of my lost babies. She had brought him down from upstairs where he had died in her bed, and washed him with the help of her daughters, Myalina and Malinda, who had come to her before me. He was laid out in the front room of her house, on a couch until Lucius could build the coffin. He was such a pretty little boy, with the curly hair and wide forehead common to the boys in that family.

More and more people arrived from the neighborhood. Mrs. Gage was there, and her sisters, Sally and Margaret, and a woman named Stone who lived next door. Mrs. Hannux was there, too, brought by Samuel. People had brought food, and there was a murmur of voices throughout the house as it filled.

"It happened so sudden," Wealthy whispered. "He was just alive and laughing with Ella and the next minute he was hot and flushed and crying. I could not quiet him. Lucius went for the doctor, but it was too late when he came."

She had never lost a child, and how hard it went with her. I knew how it felt, to see a child laid out. I knew how quickly life went from a body, the breath going without a whisper and the child you loved, whether for an hour or a day or a week or two years, dead.

She was pregnant, and as she spoke and cried and listened to words of comfort from the women who had come, she absently rubbed her belly, concealed in the heavy folds of her dress.

In two days, Thomas was laid to rest in a grave in the cemetery called Nellie Sweet. My sister's friend, Mr. Keith, had given the space next to his wife, Ruth, dead fifteen years, and their son who had died at age twenty-nine three decades before. The grass would grow quickly over the disturbed ground. Thomas would be joined one day not long in the future by this elderly man, befriended by Wealthy and so generous to her in her grief. And when Lucius and Wealthy moved from Guildhall, they would not be leaving their boy alone.

This trauma of losing Thomas started Wealthy into labor early, and, four days after her little boy's death, she gave birth to Horace. It was a terrible time at that house, with grief and birth all tangled together.

That is not all. Another date in that month and year, September fourth, 1862, is embossed on my memory for another reason, very close to my heart. In one of those unpredictable coincidences, that day following the death of Thomas and two days before the birth of Horace was the day that Charles could have died. I did not know of his injury for many weeks, and I never really understood what happened until a few years ago when I read an account of the incident in a history of the Eighth in a book about Vermont in the Civil War.

"I was wounded while protecting a rail line," he wrote me from a hospital in Louisiana. "I am healing fine. Don't worry about me."

My hands started shaking as I read of his injury, and my heart was racing. I had been reading the letter aloud to Hiram, who had brought it just moments ago from the village post office, and Fanny and Biathy were listening to me, too. I had no warning; the words leapt into my mouth and I spoke them, and the shaking started.

We were outdoors, clustered by the wagon. I had wasted not a second in slicing open the letter with Hiram's pocketknife. We had not heard from Charles in months. It was November, the fields cleared and the house banked with leaves raked from under the maples around the house. The woodshed was full of wood, chopped and split for winter, the nights already dropping down way below freezing, and the meadows rich with frost every morning. Winter was coming. We had had flurries, and one day an inch of snow covered the roofs and the fence posts and everything else from leafless tree branches to the stiff bristles of sheared corn stalks. The pig had been slaughtered, and the tons of hay long stowed in the barn.

I steadied myself against the side of the wagon, and forced myself to read aloud the rest of the letter. The words meant little to me, and rereading them later, I saw that they told me nothing I wanted to know. Two months had passed since he was hurt, and six weeks since the letter. I was left with an image of him in the hospital and there was nothing I could do. Was he really better? Was he still there or was he out? And which was worse, recovering still or exposed again to injury and worse?

I carried the letter around in the pocket of my dress for days, reassured and agitated all at once every time I brushed against it and heard the crackle of the thin paper.

When Charles came home, three months later, he would not say any more than he had said in his letter. He would talk about other things from that time – the enemy men, women and children dispossessed of all of their belongings and their homes, so they wandered in the city streets of New Orleans; the mobs of angry men stirred to riot by the Confederate effort, setting fire to buildings unscathed by fighting; the hundreds of slaves encamped in a wide, scattered band around the Union troops. On and on, he would tell details of the consequence of the war, but he never said what had really happened that day of September fourth.

In the book written only a few years before the present day, I found an account of how my son, Charles, was part of a small group of sixty men acting as a train guard under Captain Clark of Company K – the Lunenburg man who had recruited him to enlist and who would die as a soldier. They rode on platform cars, on the train running from Bayou des Allemands to Algiers. Some of the men operated the twelve-pound howitzer on a forward car. When the train entered the point of the enemy troops' ambush, every one of the artillerists, and some others, were killed or wounded when the Confederates fired upon them. Luckily, the engineer was able to keep the train moving, as the remaining men with Captain Clark, including my son, returned fire. The train thus escaped capture and proceeded on to Algiers, but out of those sixty men, thirty-five were killed or wounded, some mortally, and several were taken captive, including Hosea Aldrich who would later marry Mrs. Gage's nephew's widow, Martha Gray Hutchins.

Charles' shoulder healed, but it would ache the rest of his life, and I would see him unconsciously kneading it with the palm of his hand to ease the discomfort on a damp day or after a hard day of work on the farm. His hand that had nerve damage never recovered fully.

"I have seen a great many things, Ma," he told me. "It is a big world out there. I had no idea."

Back home, Charles wasted little time in seeking out his wife, Malinda. He did not speak of his decision to me, but told me of his plans a week after his return.

"I have found a place for Malinda and me," he said. "The Johnson house is empty. Her sons are in the war and she has gone to be with her daughter. She is happy to have someone in it, and for not much money every month it is a good place for us."

I clenched my teeth hard. The Johnson farm was just down the hill from me. That was good, but I was dismayed that he had taken Malinda back.

"I can work here this summer some, if you want, and do some of my own farming," he said.

"Alright," I said.

"I don't expect you to be glad about this, Ma," he said.

I dropped my chin to my chest. There was no use in pretending. I was not glad.

That spring and summer passed in a blur. I did not have to visit Malinda and I did not. She stayed in her house, too, and any visiting she did was confined to her family and friends in Guildhall. Her mother had another baby, and she went home to help for a week, leaving Charles to fend for himself, though since he was working with his father many days, he ate with us.

Of import was my acquisition of more land that year. Indeed, it was my big news for Charles.

"We have bought one hundred acres," I had told him, the day he returned home.

His eyebrows jumped in surprise.

"One hundred acres," he echoed.

"Lot twenty-two," I said. "All adjoining these thirty-eight. It is the land Daniel Kimball had from Leroy's property. Now it is all back together."

"How much did it cost?" he asked.

"Two hundred and twenty-five dollars," I said.

"Whew!" he whistled. "You had that much and have been paying off the mortgage on the other?"

"I borrowed some," I said. "James Smith lent us one hundred and seventy-five dollars."

He considered this. "Was that wise?"

"Very wise," I said. "We can pay off our debt faster with more land. This thirty-eight acres is not enough for us to keep growing the way I have in mind."

"What about Pa?" he said. "That is a lot for him."

"You're home," I said. "I hoped you would be helping."

I had not said one word about Malinda and neither had he that day as he agreed that I could count on him.

He had found a house for her, and I hoped she would be happy and would make him happy at last.

That was not to be, but other thoughts preceded any of this because less than a month after Charles came back from the war, Myalina's first child was born on March seventeenth.

It was a happy day and a sad day all at once. Happy because she bore a healthy boy and named him Simon. Her sister had gone to be with her, and Wealthy was there. Charles took me over as soon as we got word. But it was sad because George was gone, seven months gone, and she had known of the baby before he left.

"If only I had told him, maybe he would still be here," she told me, cradling the baby and looking into his tiny red face. She was in the downstairs bedroom that belonged to Betsey and Harmon. It was warm, with the kitchen door left open and a fire in the fireplace.

I did not know the answer to that "what if" of hers. Like all of my "what ifs," it was only real to the person who thought of it. For the rest of us, what had happened had happened.

"You are in good company in this house," I told her.

She brightened. "I know." She was treated like a true daughter of the Gage household. Betsey's daughters lived in distant towns across the river and here she had her husband's wife and child right in the same house with her.

"He'll be grown by the time his father sees him," Myalina said, somber again.

"Fathers never have anything to do with babies," I chuckled. "He'll be just the age when George would start to notice him. 'Look at his strong legs and steady gaze,' he'll mumble proudly," I imitated George. "Simon will be a big strong boy and a source of pride to his father. You could have his picture taken. That is just the thing. Once he is older, on a warm day in April or May, you can take him to Lancaster to have your picture taken and send it to George."

"Really, aunt?" she asked, her mind racing at the possibility of this, and I could see a glimpse of her youth – she would soon be eighteen.

"Really," I said. "You ask Mrs. Gage. She will arrange it."

I looked up to see Malinda hovering in the doorway. She seemed to get prettier every time I saw her. She was growing up, and at sixteen, appeared more self-assured. Perhaps being mistress of her own house had done it.

"Come in," I beckoned. "No need to stand out there in the hall."

She came into the room.

"Can I hold him?" she asked her sister.

Standing with the baby carefully supported by her small hands, I could see that Malinda wanted a baby very badly. I wondered if maybe it would happen.

g&

Chapter Fifteen

1863-64

O N THE FARM, WE DID NOT MARK THE YEARS SO MUCH JANUARY THROUGH DECEMBER AS WE DID SEASONALLY FROM MARCH OR APRIL WHEN WE SUGARED THROUGH THE GROWING SEASON AND HARVEST, ENDING IN THE DREGS OF WINTER IN FEBRUARY.

The 1863 to 1864 period was no different in how we paged through the days. With Charles home, and the new hundred acres to consider, our work for the growing season and even for sugaring was laid out plainly for us. Daniel Kimball was like us, about the same age, with a small family, though his children were younger. His property, by virtue of its size, was valued at more than ours, but it was of a piece with what we had, by which I mean that it added some cleared fields and some woodland to ours. This allowed us to sugar more, increasing our yield by about fifty pounds, and it allowed us to plant more grains, mow more fields for hay, and plant more potatoes. There was more room to graze sheep, and we added three sheep to bring our small flock to five.

Through that summer all we did was work, the time passing in a blur where I hardly knew one day from the next, marking the hours as one piece of sun or rain or wind or darkness when we mostly slept, though on some moonlit nights we would be weeding the garden or pulling in crops. The weather cooperated in our goal to pay off the mortgage the next year, in 1864, with hot days sweetened with rain so what we planted grew and the animals thrived.

Charles and I had determined on this goal, and as its fruition edged closer, we were more and more excited. With Charles home working, Hiram did less, but we did not care, my son and I, convinced that the two of us yoked to the proverbial plow could accomplish all we set out to do.

The other thing driving Charles to work and work more was Malinda.

He told me what was going on, at the end of one long, blistering hot day, when he had worked with a hard, unceasing energy, as if he were a top spun into sharp circles by a fierce outside force. He was short with his father and me, snapping out directives to us whatever our tasks. It was late June, the month just ready to turn into true summer of July. The months have a way of doing that – in June there are already harbingers of summer heat, just as in February there are preludes to the spring, and a day in October can remind one of the long, bleak days of November.

Finally, after he had yelled at me for missing a row of weeds, I had had enough of whatever was ailing him.

"Enough!" I shouted back.

He glared at me.

"You heard me," I said. "Enough. And enough of that face of yours. If you want to tell me what is going on, tell me. Otherwise, start to behave like a civil person to your father and me."

He and I were alone in the potato field. He shoved his hoe, handle first into the soft dirt.

"You want to know, I'll tell you," he said stiffly.

"I'm listening," I said.

"All of this," he swept his arm around him, turning in a circle so he covered three hundred and sixty degrees. "All of this is yours."

I nodded, and waited.

"None of it is mine even though I am here all day, every day, sometimes past dark. You say it will all be mine some day, and I believe you. I am the eldest son and the only child likely in line for it. But you are not that old and Pa is older, but he's not standing with a foot in the grave. Sometimes I don't know what I'm working for," he finished.

"You can see why we can't put your name on it," I said weakly.

"I see alright," he said. "You've got two other children, both of them young, and one a girl and one, well, you know about Biathy. I just don't know about waiting, you see. I have some money saved, but it's going fast, paying for another place where I rent. I haven't had time to do more there than plow a garden for Malinda. She's been by herself all summer."

At the mention of her name, I started to perk up for what he would say.

"She's over with her sister or her mother," he said, "More than she's home. I go home and I never know if she'll be there or not. I go home and there's no sign of her, some days, and no supper. The house is quiet and just empty. I went to see Myalina, late one day, and she told me Malinda is lonely. She wants her own house and me in it, our own farm and us working together. But I can't give it to her. I don't have it. She wants a baby, too, and that don't happen either."

He was silent, and so was I, thinking about what he had said. None of it sounded unreasonable, prepared as I was to think ill of her.

"You see," he said. "It's not my mortgage. However I try to explain to her what our goal is, she only sees that this is not my place, not her place, and that I am not working for her and me, but for you."

"She can move back here," I said.

He shook his head. "She would never do that."

"You could make her," I said without much conviction. "She would have company if she was here with us. I'll give up the front room for a bedroom, like Betsey did for George."

He looked glum.

"I don't suppose you could loan me money to buy a little place of my own," he said.

"Oh, Charles! How could I do that? I owe, we owe on a mortgage now," I said.

"You always have something stashed away," he said, wistfully. "Maybe with that and what I have..."

"The plan is to build on this," it was my turn to sweep my arm around. "We can't add to what we have unless we work together."

"Maybe James Smith would loan me money!" he burst out.

I rubbed my chin, and felt some of the drying dirt on my hand move to my face.

"Maybe," I said. I did not add any "but" because I could see he did not believe James Smith would loan him any money.

"How much do you have?" I asked.

"Fifty dollars," he said. "Almost fifty. Forty-three."

The upshot of this discussion was that, at the end of the summer of 1863, once the few vegetables were harvested, he brought the milch cow from his rented place to us, and the horse and wagon, and gave up the rented farm. Malinda went back and forth between her sister and Charles. I gave up the front room and it became their bedroom with no other use.

She was moody, some days bright and eager to please, and other days in a dark humor, talking to no one. They had been married two years, and she was sixteen, more beautiful than when he had first noticed her, and torn between the life of a wife, though yet with no baby, and the life of a single girl who could flirt and be noticed for her loveliness. When she was with her sister or her mother, she felt all sorts of possibility, but when she was with us, she felt like her fate was sealed forever.

I know this because Myalina told me when I sought her council.

On through that winter of 1863-1864, we trudged. I did not know which was worse: to have her with us and moping, or to have her with her sister and Charles be despondent. I took, with some guilt, to doing my sewing in the front room on the days when she was not with us. All the time I sat, in the pleasant chair near the windows with the view to the mountains, I was at least a little aware that Malinda might appear suddenly as she was wont to do, without warning. I was prepared at all times to fly up from the chair, gathering all of my sewing and rushing from the room to look innocent in the kitchen – dark and tiresome as it was in the winter with bad light. At the end of my sewing in the illicit pleasure of the front room, I picked up every scrap of cloth and piece of thread, scanning the floor and table to be sure I left no sign. Of course, though, one day, I missed a tiny scrap of wool I had been using to mend a pair of Hiram's pants.

Malinda had come back early the next morning from her sister's, rushing past me into "her" room. Within minutes, she was back, the scrap of rogue cloth dangling accusingly from her fingers.

"I knew it," she said. "You have been using my bedroom! You promised it was mine, and you would stay away, but you have been in there all of the time!"

What could I say?

Fanny was horrified that I had been caught. She had predicted it, and now her foresight had come true.

Malinda burst into tears and went back into the bedroom and closed the door, even though it was daytime and we had agreed that the door would stay open during the cold winter days so some of the heat from the stove would heat the rest of the house.

Malinda did not go often to her sister's in those coldest months of winter. George's consumptive brother, Charles, was very ill, and Myalina and Betsey took turns nursing him, between caring for the baby. In February, Betsey got word that her nephew, Robert Hutchins, had died of pneumonia in a hospital near Washington, D.C. Only a few days after this news, her son died, on February twenty-fourth. He was only twenty-three, taken down at last by consumption.

The house went into mourning. Myalina looked drawn and pale, and Mrs. Gage had aged suddenly, her lined face gray and sad.

I wondered if even the return of spring, with the few last heavy snows that didn't last and gave way to birds singing and the sun warming the ground, would cheer her.

⚹

Chapter Sixteen

SUMMER 1864

WHAT A SUMMER THAT WAS IN 1864! I knew as I marked the days that the harvest would be good, prayed that all that was making it so would continue.

We worked as we had never worked before. Hiram was showing signs of what we would later know was his cancer, but at that time we attributed it to hard work and he took long breaks as he seemed to need them, even staying some days in his bed with Fanny to care for him.

It was in the summer that Charles gave up for good on Malinda.

All through the spring, she had been staying with us regularly. After she caught me in her bedroom, she had determined to stay and stake her rights in person. With her scrupulously around, I stayed clear of her bedroom. I only minded for a few weeks, though, and then it was warm enough to work outside and I left the house to her and Fanny. I would come in to supervise the two of them, but until we were gathering enough vegetables and Fanny was picking wild berries in earnest for preserving, I did not hardly show my face.

There was one day, though, when Charles and I brought in Hiram from the field, supporting him between us, and his face the color of days-old ashes in the grate, that I stayed. Fanny and I did our best to make him comfortable in Charles and Malinda's bed because he could not go upstairs.

The doctor came. It was the middle of July. Malinda stood in the yard staring into nowhere, staying out of the house while the doctor was there. How she hated to be around illness.

I went and found her when the doctor left, after issuing dictums and potions, but with no clear idea of what was wrong.

"Maybe heatstroke," he said.

"Could it be his heart?" I asked.

"Too soon to tell," he said. "Keep him quiet and keep him inside."

I stood beside Malinda, trying to see what she was looking at so intently, but I saw nothing and, perhaps, neither did she.

"The doctor thinks maybe it is heatstroke," I said, though she had not asked. "He has to stay quiet for some days, and he can't go upstairs. You and Charles will have to take our room."

She set her lips, and swung away from me, like a sheet hit by a gust of wind, and went into the house without a word.

The next morning, she was sitting by the road with a small bag and a bundle, stiffly waiting. Charles had left the house very early, way before light. I had heard his footsteps on the stairs, quiet enough so as not to disturb his father, and listened as he fumbled in the kitchen that was just on the other side of the head of the bed. He must have grabbed some bread, and maybe drunk a mug of cold coffee. I blamed myself later for not getting up, but I was concerned to wake Hiram.

I decided, in the absence of Charles, that I should go out to Malinda.

She did not even glance my way when I approached her, sitting on the edge of the stonewall that fronted the property.

"Where are you going?" I asked.

"I am going back to my sister's," she said.

"Because of that bedroom?" I snapped. "Surely you can see your uncle is ill."

She did not answer me.

"Answer me," I ordered.

She did not say one word, only tightened her thin, pink lips even tighter.

"Does Charles know?" I asked.

"Oh, Charles knows," she said, in such a tone that I believe I shivered in the heat that was building even so early in the day.

"And who do you think is going to ferry you wherever it is you have in mind – your sister's, you say?"

"Someone will be by soon enough," she said. "I will wait until they do."

I spun on my heels and walked away from her. I wanted to shake the silly girl, with no thought in her head for anyone but herself.

In fact, we were rid of her. I kept checking on the pose of that foolish girl, from where I was tending Hiram, trying to be subtle so he did not notice. I need not have worried; he was groggy and stayed that way, sleeping and on the edge of it, all day, with the help of the medicine the doctor had left.

That girl sat out on the wall for two hours. At last, Mr. Stone came by and she leapt up to wave at him. In an instant, he was lifting her up and tossing in her bundle and bag and I was watching her stiff little back disappear. I had no doubt he would see the pretty miss all of the way to Myalina's.

We were rid of her.

Charles certainly did know. When I finally left Hiram in Fanny's care to go help Charles and Biathy, I was glad that my daughter was so occupied with her father that she did not have time to brood over her cousin.

"She has gone to Myalina's," Fanny told me in a confidential tone that made her seem forty years old instead of ten.

"Yes," I sighed.

"I don't believe she will be back," Fanny continued in the same adult vein.

I looked at her sharply.

"I know all about it," she said airily.

"And how do you know, might I ask?" I said.

"I heard last night. They were not so quiet as they thought," she said smugly.

"Do you want to tell me?" I asked, trying to act casual and not too interested.

"I don't think I should repeat it all," she said thoughtfully.

"I'm your mother. It would be alright to do so."

"I don't think so," she said apologetically. "It is a conversation better forgotten."

"Can you do that? Forget it?" I queried.

"I can," she said. "But you never would."

That shut me up. I considered this young daughter of mine seriously. She surprised me sometimes. I would get my information from Charles.

But Charles was no more forthcoming than his sister.

"I do not want to talk about it," he said, clipping off his words like pieces of Christmas candy cut by the kitchen shears, and dropping with a surprisingly loud sound into a bowl.

I had come up behind him where he was throwing hay into the wagon.

"Charles," I said, so he would not be startled, but he started anyway. I saw him jerk, but he didn't stop his work.

"Charles," I said. "Malinda has gone with Mr. Stone."

I could see his shoulders tighten and he paused a moment, with the pitchfork level with his waist, but then he kept on with a swiftness that pained me to see it.

That was when he said, "I don't want to talk about it."

I set in to help him. It was only when he paused to move the horse and wagon along that I really saw his face. It was in the shadow of his wide-brimmed straw hat, but I saw, lining the ruddiness of his sweaty, grimy face, the marks I felt sure were made by tears.

My heart clenched in me at that sight. I had never thought to see my son cry, since he was a small boy and cut his hand on the blade of his father's axe.

"How's Pa," he said at last, hours later, when we were back at the barn with the wagon loaded with hay.

"He's been sleeping," I said. "Fanny is taking good care of him."

He looked at me thoughtfully.

"You could have stayed with him," he said.

"I know, but I was better useful with you and Biathy. Don't you think?"

He nodded.

"I couldn't keep her, Ma," he said then.

I couldn't think of a word to say.

He tried one more time, taking a hard-won, inconvenient day from the necessary time we needed to do our farm work. I could not hold him back from that. But it was to no purpose. He paid to put a second notice in the newspaper. This time he spelled out her maiden name, as if to emphasize the finality, and notified all readers that his wife Malinda Presbrey, once Malinda Larrabee, had left his bed and board and should not be trusted on his account because he would pay none of her debts. That was toward the end of July.

He worked mindlessly, and if it was work he sought to forget his troubles, there was plenty of that. His father came and went from the fields. On some days, Hiram seemed like his usual self – slow and steady, with a dry wit. But on other days, he seemed to not be fully present.

"Are you in pain?" I asked him, on one of the days when he was not good.

He shook his head. "But I don't quite feel up to it today," he told me.

Fanny and I bundled him back into bed, where he stayed until he felt good enough to get back to work.

The business with Malinda had one more unpleasant chapter in store for me. This time it was with her mother. I guess I cannot blame her for being angry with someone. This was her daughter, after all, for whom life had not so far dealt a handy card. The fact that the fault might be with the girl I did not expect my sister to see. Who was I to expect that when I doted on Charles? And my own comeuppance for that would come, soon enough, when all of my plans that linked my son and me like daisies in a chain would come apart.

Wealthy came to see me two days after Malinda had left us for good. She had come in the wagon, with her second-eldest son driving her. She stormed into my kitchen like a swarm of bees stirred rudely from the honey tree. She was not just one bee, but the many.

"You're telling me you didn't read that letter he sent Malinda back when he had just gone off to war? Do you take me for a fool?" she lit right into me. "You can read and don't I know you wouldn't miss a chance to know their business. It was a love letter, and you read it before my daughter had a chance to hear it."

It took me a minute to realize she was referring to that letter from two years before when Charles was in the army.

"I never read it!" I hissed. "You have no good opinion of me at all if you think that. I could have. Yes, I could have. It was just folded up in his letter to me, but I did not. Perhaps I should have. Perhaps I should have read it and thrown it into the fire, but I did not."

"You have never wanted my daughter here," she went on as if I had not spoken. "You have ruined her marriage and you have ruined her life. What is left for her now? You're my sister and look how you have treated my girl!"

We could have talked a hundred years and never come to any resolution on this matter. She knew it, too, and left as fast as she had come, never one to linger anyway. She had told me off, placing the blame the only place she could stand to see it go.

Indeed, it was many years before she would see that daughter of hers settled. But that day, Wealthy left me stirred up, and I admit to reviewing over and over the years of my son's marriage, wondering if I had some responsibility.

PART THREE

§

Burning Down the House

Chapter One

1864-65

FARM LIFE TOOK A HEAVY TOLL ON US WOMEN. It was easier, maybe, on women like my sister and me. Small as we were and roughly built, we simply toughened with work, our bodies growing harder and leaner as hard times and hard work seasoned us like chunks of wood left outdoors for the heating season.

Looking back, sitting in the dark room of my daughter's in November of 1895, with the rain pouring down on the road just outside the window, I can see we were like pieces of paper blown about every which way by the winds that came and went without any doings of ours.

I look at my daughter, Fanny, with three children, and how she went from being a child, fresh-faced with a rosy complexion beneath her dark hair, to a matron, her face round and her eyes with most of the brightness spent. She is my link to the past now, and I am in what is her house, and her husband's, my days of machinations long over. I am in the room I specified for myself for my last days in a deed, the last I will ever see my name laid to. I try to be matter of fact, but I am dying. Fanny tells me, "No, no, Ma. I will nurse you and you will get well," but I know the way my body is coming out from under me.

It is not that Fanny was second best to me, but that as a girl she could never give me the leg up I always sought. Charles was to be my salvation. With his sharp brain and how he could make a plan, how he and I could have made an empire – a small one, perhaps, but still, a property I could have been proud of and see as the fruit of my aspirations born when I was a young girl watching my father. Instead, all of my plans with Charles came unraveled because of David Beede. It is Charles who made the profitable farm, in a railroad town, where the products of his labor had a ready route to a market. He moved away from me, north to Bloomfield, with his new wife, and left me to muddle through the rest of my life. How I grieved him, as if he had been laid in a grave as surely as Hiram.

That is why I at last turned to Fanny, my remaining child. She and her husband came to live with me in Riverton, on the land I coveted on the Israel River and of which not much ever came. By then, the markets had changed so much, the prosperity of the war years so quickly past, and the struggle to farm going on and on. I had coveted the land for the flat ground and the access to the river. But we never had enough land, and even with the husbands I had after David, nothing much ever was built. In the end, Fanny sold that house, with my permission as the deed specified, and we moved not far north to an even smaller piece of land, and her husband went out to work.

This is where I am now, with them, and I know I will be buried here.

It is hard for me to believe that the incredible brightness of those years of the 1860s was the quickly spent star of my life. With the criminality of David draining us, and forcing me to move, and losing me my son, my life wandered from there like the meanderings of a sick animal. Through three more husbands, two of whom I buried and one a scoundrel, I tried to make a go of that piece of land.

And I have not yet told the worst, of how my husband David burned my house. Whether or not he burned the house of Samuel Hannux, I will never know for sure, though I have always believed it. But that he burned my house in Jefferson, there is no doubt.

You know how I came to Jefferson in September 1868, down by the crossroads near the border with Carroll. I left the road to Victory with my daughter, Fanny, and my son, Biathy. Charles had gone away before me. He had sold his place almost before the stink of the ashes from his sap buckets burned on the fire had passed off. He moved north, where he bought land in the town of Bloomfield, with his wife Amanda and the two children. He did not tell me he was going or where. I heard the report many times removed, as gossip when I was in the village store in Lunenburg.

"How is your son doing?" Mrs. West said archly, daring me to answer.

When I did not, she continued, knowing, I am sure, that she hurt me with every word, "We hear he has a farm in Bloomfield."

I had not known. I sucked in my breath, and turned toward the display of crackers, as if my life depended on my selection of the right box. I had always made my own crackers. Boxed ones were a luxury I had never afforded, but that day I bought them. How dry and dusty they would taste, with the soup Fanny made. She and Biathy were delighted, and astonished that I said nothing as they ate the whole box in one sitting.

"It's a treat," I said, and ate one myself, fearing I would choke on the dryness of the crumbs in my dry mouth.

Let us look back to the unraveling between by son and me. It was 1866 when Charles and I both remarried. I married David Beede in the fall, after harvest in September, and Charles was not long behind me, marrying his cousin, Amanda, in November. With us both established as couples again, he and I had set about building our empire.

What I sold Calvin Knight was the fruit of all of the hard work of my son and me, close to one hundred acres improved. The road to Victory was kind to me. The land was open and stretched on friendly land across the top of the hill. There was ample sun, and always the view of the mountains. This was in contrast to the first land I owned, with Hiram, where the mountains and the river valley across to New Hampshire were only visible when we rode closer to the village of Lunenburg. The land on the road to Victory was quality. It responded to the hard work we put into it, and there was more than enough of a living for two families.

My mind plays tricks on me. I see now that I was like a horse set to plow a long row with the master and his whip behind me. That was how I handled the terrible things that happened one after the other in those days.

You know I loved him, that David Beede, so what he did to me, to us, was all the more horrible.

This is how it all went. Hiram and I moved to the road to Victory with our son, Charles, and Fanny and Biathy. It was August 31, 1864 when we closed our deal. We sold all of the one hundred and thirty-eight acres acquired since 1860 on the Guildhall border to Abby and Alfred Lewis who lived in Guildhall. It was the same time that I bought the land, the amazing land, on the road to Victory from a couple by the name of Goss, and we were all moved into the house by early September.

I still shake inside when I picture that day. I felt as coltish as any family loading up all their goods and going west to the land promoted so heartily in the newspapers as Paradise. My sister, Fanny, had done that, gone west in the years just before 1850, to New York only, but still taking advantage of the promised opportunity of unsettled land. We were traveling only about five miles, but I felt I was riding so high on that wagon, with a mountain of our household furniture and everything from pots and pans to a bag with my hairbrushes and hairpins. It would take more than one trip, but I only made the first, leaving the boys to bring the rest.

I danced around that empty house on the road to Victory, cleaning every surface with broom and pan after pan of soapy water and wet rags. Even now, over thirty years later, I can perfectly recall the emotions of that day. Fanny and I cleaned the windows, the many windows even in the kitchen, and I could see the mountains to the west. When the house was ready for the furniture that was piled waiting in the yard, the boys had not yet returned and Fanny and I walked all over this new place. We held hands, and swung our arms, linked together like schoolgirls on a fine afternoon at the start of the school year. We walked through the small apple orchard, and ran across a stubbled field where corn had just been cut. We were tired when we reached the woods, and slowly made our way from maple to maple, me thinking of how beautiful each tree was and how much maple sugar could be made in the season a short six months ahead. We went from there to the barn, the soft light of September coming through the cracks between a few wide, gray boards, illuminating the piles of hay left by Azro Goss. We sat together on a small pile of hay, our hips and shoulders touching, swinging our feet so our booted heels rubbed the hay, and surveying stalls for a horse and milch cow and ox, and looking up to the loft, dark in the shadows. There was a room with a stone foundation off the barn to make butter, and a lean-to on the other side for a pig and a shelter in a far field for sheep. There was a fine spring on the property, and a small, neat house covering it from the elements, and making a pool where I could store butter and milk in the heat of the summer.

That was the highlight of my life, I think, like the way I felt holding my baby, Charles, when he was newborn, and later Fanny and Biathy.

In a year, though, Hiram was dead, that year of 1864 into 1865 marred by the growing certainty of his illness that could not be cured. The war ended, that was good, but bad, too, economically, because the prices propped up by the needs of the armies did not stay high.

It was 1865 when my sister and Lucius took their family, grown to nine children, (leaving the tenth child, poor boy, Thomas, in his grave), across the bridge in Guildhall to Northumberland where they had at last bought a small farm. It was too far to see her, but I was so occupied with the farm and Hiram, I did not think so much of that loss of her closer company.

There was still a strain because of Malinda and Charles. We were not in dispute, my sister and me, but we had not regained our automatic intimacy we had had since childhood. Malinda was still with her sister, having shown no sign of leaving that Gage household. There was Horace back by now, thin as a fence rail chopped by hand from a fallen tree. George returned that summer of 1865, silent, his face hidden behind a thick, bushy beard, like his father-in-law's, only dark with a few threads of silver. I saw him the once at the welcoming party in Lunenburg, and was shocked to see those great, unruly whiskers with his dark eyes soberly looking out between them and the low cap he wore. A letter some weeks later from Myalina assured me the facial hair was gone.

"Don't fret, Aunt," she wrote. "His whiskers are shaved off. How I laughed to see your eyes grow as big as the cat's milk dish when you laid eyes on him. His face is so pale now, out from under that covering of hair, and will not gain any color for months. But he is clean shaven and I am glad of it."

Then it was September, and Hiram passed, with the long winter ahead of me. The men were busier in winter than us women. They chopped wood for the stoves, and kept the spring chopped open for water, and hauled buckets in the worst weather, and got wood out for the sugaring that was to come. By that time, David was visiting often. He and Charles got along. I look back on that and remember. I had forgotten. They worked side by side in the woodlot, assisted by Biathy. How much work those two grown men could accomplish!

They got along all through the next spring and summer and fall, working side by side every day once David was working with us constantly, having given up his laboring job for another farmer.

Fanny and I had big meals fixed for their big appetites, pie and bread and fried potatoes and eggs, and whatever else we added for meat. The farm, that wonderful farm on the road to Victory, bloomed before my eyes. The men cleared land, more and more land, and planted oats and buckwheat and hill upon hill of Irish potatoes. We had sheep, too, five sheep. Fanny and I made butter to sell, working in the tiny outbuilding with its back against the barn. The work was hard, every day, from the earliest rise before dawn to the long hours later when it was too dark to see outside. If I was born to a life, that was it. I did not mind the labor unceasing, as long as I could see the fields of crops, and sheep, and the orchard with apples red as those in a fairy tale, and two hundred pounds of maple sugar to sell, and wool sheared for the market, and bushel upon bushel of Irish potatoes taken to the market.

Only one disquieting event occurred in this time and I did not give it enough notice. It was midmorning in the late summer, and the men long gone from the house. I was indoors, turning summer squash into pickles. I was a mess, but not minding it, with my hair tight in a bun and the sweat from the hot kitchen dampening my face and neck and torso. Fanny was helping me, and we were, of all things, singing some church hymn, loudly and off key. Such was our joy that morning at the accomplishment of our harvest's turning into food for the winter and the fact that Charles and David and George were hard at work as they should be.

Suddenly, there came a thundering knock on the side door frame – the door was open to let out the heat of our cooking – and our singing and merriment stopped still and we turned as one to see who was there.

My jaw dropped at the sight of Samuel Hannux, of all men alive, standing straight in what were clearly not his work clothes, but a Sunday suit and highly polished boots.

"Madame," he said gravely. "Good morning. And good morning to you, Miss," he addressed Fanny. "I have come on business," he added.

"The men are in the field," I said, but he was looking straight at me, with a keen, expectant look.

Revealing his wolfish teeth from under his pink lips, he said, "It is you that I would like to speak with. Will you come outside with me?"

"I cannot imagine…" I started to say, but he had turned his back and gone down the steps. "What on earth?" I sputtered to Fanny, but, wiping my hands on my apron and then lifting the apron skirt up to mop my face, I followed him.

He was standing under the maple tree just beyond the kitchen door, and his green eyes followed my every step with what I was puzzled to see was admiration. When I was close enough to him to hear his soft voice, I stopped.

"I am sorry to hear of your widowhood," he said.

I dropped my head in acknowledgement.

"I am alone, too," he said. "My mother is dead and I have the farm. It is a good farm and I am a hard worker."

He paused, and his eyes that looked quite unpleasantly moist up close were fixed on me, and I squirmed. My head was still in the pickle-making process and stupidly, I could not see what he was driveling on about.

"I am sorry about your mother," I said, for something to say, and because he was making me so uncomfortable.

"Don't be," he said. "It was long past her time."

Then he went on with what he had come to say.

"You are a woman with property and I am a man with property. Since you are a widow lady you will have no one to take care of it for you. I am asking you to be my wife, and so what we have will be joined, and you will have no cares."

I simply stared, and felt heat of a different kind than that caused by my labors in the kitchen, racing through my chest and up into my face. Unfortunately, he continued to stare at me, and apparently misinterpreted my lack of speech and my stare to mean I matched whatever sentiments he had, because he leaned forward and grasped my forearms firmly and kissed me, as if to seal an agreement.

I jerked back in horrified astonishment.

"Mr. Hannux!" I squealed, and scrubbed furiously at my mouth that was wet from his lips.

He would have said more, but at that moment, to my increasing horror, David came across the shaggy grass at full tilt, roaring.

"You cur," he shouted, his face the color of raw meat, from sun and rage. He gave Samuel a great shove that almost knocked the smaller man over. "Get out of here before I kill you! She is mine! You get out!" He went to strike a blow, but Samuel was too quick for him, and dodged, and I heard his fist hit home on David's ribs. The fight was on, and though David outweighed Samuel by at least two stone, Samuel was younger and more agile. David kept hollering threats as he fought, which did not help him, and Samuel fought silently, landing precise punches. All of the while the fight was edging in the direction of Samuel's horse and wagon, and suddenly, with a burst of speed, Samuel leapt away and was up in his wagon. He fended David off with the whip that laid open his cheekbone, and Samuel was turning the horse and wagon, and careering out of the yard and down the road with great purpose.

It took me an hour to calm David, taking care of the gash on his face, and listening to his raving about that man who had come to steal his woman. I was relieved to learn that he had not seen the kiss, but only my horror at the man's impertinence. David felt like he was my hero, and that saved us all for the moment, but maybe, in the long term of events, it would have been better if his rage had turned against me then, before I had made him my husband.

I said enough derisive comments about my unwanted suitor, though, to keep David on my side. Within a month we were married, and I thought Samuel Hannux was gone from my life for good. We were happy as we had been all of that spring and summer, a happiness that seemed would carry me on its broad back the rest of my life.

All of it came apart just as fast as it had gone together. Before it did, though, I had moved fast with no inkling of the disaster to come.

First off, I made sure that Charles had land of his own, adjacent to mine. I knew by that spring of 1866 that he would make a match with Amanda. She was more mature by then, with already one husband to her credit, and a small son by the last husband. I knew her, since she was a child of a brother of Hiram, but not well. I had made up my mind to learn from the mistakes I might have made with Malinda and consequently set out to help Charles become a landowner with a house to bring his bride into when the time came. Maybe my love for David had softened me. I was giddy with my own loving, and thus appreciated Charles' growing happiness with Amanda.

I was forty that year, but I didn't feel old. I knew that was not young, but I had started fresh on the road to Victory, and even with Hiram's death, continued in my re-creation of myself as Lucy E. The Emeline (or Emerline as some records falsely say, the clerk's spelling by ear misleading him) of my insolvent youth was put behind the newness of Lucy E. How well I liked any excuse to write out my signature with a flourish. It was as if by changing my name, I had given myself a whole reinvented life.

Darkly, I admit I considered the first letter I received from my sister in that same year, signed Wealthy R. Following my lead, as younger sisters will, she had decided without consulting me to become new herself. She was Wealthy R., dropping Roena that she had been all of her life and assuming her middle name that came from our mother's mother. It was with a mix of feeling irritated and flattered that I considered this mimicking act of my sister.

In the end, I decided to let flattery rule the day. If we could both achieve better times with our new names then who was I to feel irritation? And imitation, as the saying goes, is the sincerest form of flattery.

There we were, Lucy E. and Wealthy R., set to take on the world. Soon I would not even be Presbrey anymore, the only last name I had ever borne, and would be Lucy E. Beede.

I had not even a year of bliss in my new name, though. In considering those years from my marriage to David into and through 1867 up to when David committed his crime against Charles, I can see the frenetic agitation of how I lived, but at the time all of what Charles and I did seemed full of purpose. In that purpose, certainly David felt an outsider. I knew that because he told me, but I ignored it, so consumed with my goal of empire that I willfully left him outside. Should I blame myself for all that came after?

"I am a hired hand," he told me tightly. It was early summer of 1867, after a successful sugaring season, with planting begun. "That is how you treat me."

David had come in before Charles that day. I was frying potatoes for supper and at first did not turn to him.

"Listen to me," he said sharply. At that, I did turn, slowly, with an unease in me.

"What?" I said.

"You and Charles treat me like your hired hand," he repeated. "You think I don't see all of your planning and plotting, a purchase here, sale there, a new mortgage, the acquiring of timber land. I am not dumb. I read and I write and I see what you are doing. Oh, you tell me what you do, and I know my name is on the odd deed. But there are two of you, acting like you own the world up here. You're my wife, though, see. I have a say. You had better start treating me like that."

"I'm sorry, David," I said. "We don't mean... I don't..."

"No, maybe you don't, maybe you do. But I am telling you you had better stop." He spun away from me, and slammed out the side door.

My mind raced with confusion, trying to sort out what had brought this on. Charles came in soon after.

"What is going on with David?" I asked.

"You noticed, too?" he said.

"He came in here angry a little while ago and told me you and I treat him like a hired hand. Where is that coming from? Did you quarrel?"

He shook his head. "He has been like this with me since yesterday when he came back from town."

"He went to town?" I asked, incredulous. "When?"

"You were at Mary's with Fanny, remember? Not long after you walked up the road, he mumbled to me he had errands in the village and left me clearing the upper field. He was back before you were. He never said what he was doing?"

"He never said he went at all," I said.

My son stared at me, unwilling to say what we both knew. David had gone to town to the tavern.

Charles went home to his wife and family while I remained in the household increasingly traumatized by my husband.

Let me tell you all we had done, Charles and I, that spring and into the summer. You be the judge of whether it should have impacted David as it did. I say this, but I am not being honest myself.

One of the reasons why my son and I had done what we had done was because of David. While the day in the spring of 1868 was his first open aggression against us, we knew that he had been drifting away from our work on the farm. It had begun to happen once the maple sugar had been sold and there was ready money. First, he was oily as grease on the bacon pan, casually going off in the middle of the day for errands, he said. The first couple of times I did not think much of it. Why would I? But he was gone more and more often, leaving Charles and Biathy in the middle of the work of the day, with no explanation at all.

Charles kept it from me at first, but I would hear and see the horse and wagon go. He was always back by supper or before the dark set in. He wore a strong scent sometimes, I would notice, cheap and pungent. I did not like it, but there the bottle stood on the top of the dresser in our bedroom – men's hair treatment.

Long ago as it was, I carry the exact procession of events between Charles and me, as money slipped from our accounts, first like a pinhole leak in a pot – unexplainable – and then enlarging to where the vessel hardly held water.

I was in thrall to him.

"He is my husband," I wailed to Charles. "What am I to do?"

"He is ruining us," he said, his voice flat, his eyes unwilling to meet mine.

I had first transacted to buy part or all of Lots Seventy-one and Sixty-seven and Thirty-five that August of 1864 when Hiram was still alive. In January of 1866, I added the south portion on the westerly side of Lot Thirty-five, twelve glorious acres that were prime homestead land and adjoined my other piece of land. I owned almost one hundred acres and felt a peace within myself that came from security.

What if I had stopped there? What if I had stayed as I was – a widow lady with many years left to her? What if I had not been charmed by David, his handsomeness, his force of personality, his intensity of ability to work? What if I had let Charles be enough for me, and let our plan unfold with the sense of purpose we shared?

It would be Charles who would carry out the plans we had. He would choose a town where the railroad passed through. That was a big piece of his success. What if I had been free to go with him, sold my land on the road to Victory and gone north a few towns with him to invest in another farm? It is idle to speculate like this, but my mind drifts with the what ifs, and I see myself near him even now, instead of having the bitter taste of our separate lives even now in my mouth, like the pasty, useless medicine Fanny gets for me from the pharmacy.

The railroad was critical to the last decades of the century for farmers. Lunenburg had been passed by. In 1865, the year the war ended, with so many men back in the community and our resources stretched thin from it, one of the influential citizens got up a petition for a rail line to be laid. Many of the men, including David and Harmon and Horace Gage, put up money for the show of investors, but it came to naught. Lunenburg, our beautiful town, was caught in the wasteland between the line that went all along the Connecticut River and then jogged straight north from St. Johnsbury, bypassing us, and the later line that connected Portland, Maine to Canada. Bloomfield was seated on the latter route. Charles, with his ready business acumen, bypassed the villages with no rails. How often he and I had talked about the importance of the railroad to get our goods to market! To hear that day in the village store from that lady that he had gone and carried out the plans we could have shared pierced my heart, and the bile rose from my stomach into my throat.

I would visit his farm one day in 1872, when David was locked up and could not harm me or Charles. It was a bittersweet day, my son and I walking like strangers, his touring me around his lands and answering my questions politely about his yields and acres and livestock as though I were a visitor from a foreign land interested in agriculture. Like our other farms, first on the Guildhall border and then on the road to Victory, his was in the hill country, located near the end of a road with the impassable mountains at his back. But he worked with single-minded purpose on developing what he owned, and neither Amanda nor his children nor his mother were any distraction to him.

He had moved into the neighborhood of his father-in-law. Amanda was happy to be near her mother, and there was instant support from an experienced farmer who had cleared more than half of his land. Charles started out small, with only fifteen acres cleared, but he owned one hundred acres in a town that was still growing in the late 1860s. By 1880, he owned over two hundred acres, almost half of them cleared with the rest forest and woodland. He was worth $1500, and raising Irish potatoes, among other products.

Before that day in 1872, my son and I had not conversed with any sympathy since before David Beede had burned and destroyed the sugaring equipment. Amanda stiffly served me tea that day. Fanny was married, and I had come alone.

"This is it, Ma," Charles told me, showing off all he was achieving, and I wanted to weep to hear my son call me "Ma" with his old warmth.

§

Chapter Two

LAND POETRY

———————————

THIS IS HOW IT ALL WENT. It is like a lullaby, if you listen right. I put myself to sleep some nights with my recitation. Azro Goss and wife, Adelphia, sold to Lucy E. Presbrey, Lots Sixty-seven and Seventy-one and part of Thirty-five in August of 1864. Henry Harris sold to Lucy E. Lot Thirty-seven, the south half, in January 1866. Lucy E. borrowed $200 from Mary Phelps, toward the purchase of Lot Thirty-seven. Lucy E. sold to Charles F. Lot Seventy-one and all of Sixty-seven in the third range on the east side of the road that passes through the lots, totaling one hundred and ten acres. Charles F. mortgaged some of the price that January 1866 to his mother. Less than a year later, Charles F. sold all of the above to Joshua Silsby, the lumber mill man, while still owing money to his mother. In March 1867, Joshua Silsby sold to Lucy E. Lot Seventy-one, east side of the road, one hundred and ten acres. In May of 1867, Lucy E. and David Beede sold to Charles F. the homestead on Lot Thirty-seven, on the west side of the road to Victory. In June 1867, Charles W. King sold to Charles F. Lot Thirty-seven, south half, east side of the road to Victory, thirty-eight acres. Lucy E. and David sold to Charles F. in November that year Lots Seventy-one and Sixty-seven and Thirty-five, including the premises where Lucy E. and David lived and excepting 8,700 feet of spruce lumber to be cut by Joshua Silsby off the Howard Lot, and Lucy E. still with $200 owed on a mortgage to John Hartshorn, and $200 to Mary, and Charles now owing $425 to his mother. Charles F. sold the homestead to Lucy E., the part on the east side of the road.

On April 6, 1868, Lucy E. and David took a mortgage on the homestead for $200 for his bail. Charles F. sold to Charles W. King Lots Seventy-one and Sixty-seven and Thirty-five, the west side (the Howard Lot), being the one hundred and fifty acres where he lived. And Charles F. sold to Joshua Silsby Lot Thirty-five, being seventy-five acres.

On September 30, 1868, Lucy E. sold to Calvin Knight Lot Thirty-seven, the south half, on the east side of the road to Victory, with the homestead, a total of fifty acres.

To make sense of all of that is not easy, and I lived it. Looking back, I see it was as much about money, juggling it like an actor with bright-colored balls at a fair, standing on a rough-made stage. The bottom line is that Charles and I struggled because of David. With his draining money from our enterprises, it is a wonder we stayed afloat at all. That we did is the result of us juggling together, handing off one piece or another, to keep every piece in play. We moved around, back and forth between the road to Victory and the house on another road on the lots where the timber was the resource. At one time, we were living in one another's pockets and nothing good came of it.

One way or another, Charles and I both ended up with enough money from selling out of Lunenburg in 1868 – he had $700 and I had $1,000 (putting aside the question of the mortgages) – to set up in other towns. He chose the railroad town in the north and I chose to go across the river into a new state, hoping to leave behind the courts and the charges in Vermont. As you saw, I did avoid the loss of my farm and livelihood, thanks to a kind judge in Guildhall who, in 1869, forgave David's bail jump. That decision on the part of the judge was a way of Vermont's saying good riddance to David Beede. That he was gone and that his reason for coming back to Vermont – me – was gone were a positive for that state. That is what the lawyer and James S. told me bluntly, the lawyer doing the talking and James S. nodding emphatically at the end of every sentence.

"The state will be glad to be shot of him, and sadly, of you, too, since they believe he will come back to you at some point. He is not worth pursuing from their viewpoint since the quarrel was with you and your son. You are now in New Hampshire, and he will be its problem."

I put my head down, and let the shame wash over me, but if I could keep my property, I would let that fact wash away the shame of what my reputation now was, and the sorrow at leaving Lunenburg where I had spent the best years of my life, other than the early time of my childhood in Shrewsbury.

I did have one letter from David, written in pencil. It was three pages long, and it was a love letter, in great part, professing his sorrow at his treatment of me and telling me of my great qualities of forgiveness and compassion and strength.

"A strong woman like you may find it hard to forgive the weakness in me, but I am begging you to." That is one of the lines he wrote.

He did not say where he was, but the postmark was in the south of New Hampshire, near where he had been living before the war with his wife and children.

I could not have written back even if I had wanted to, and I was glad not to have to make that decision. But, still, I wrote a hundred letters in my head to him, ranging from angry to sorrowful to loving and forgiving. When you love someone like I loved him (had loved him, did love him, I was not sure which), it is not easy to believe in his badness, not in a badness that goes deep to the bone.

Fanny and I settled into our new life in Jefferson, New Hampshire. By that time, Wealthy and Lucius had given up the farm in Northumberland and were living in Lancaster, sharing a farm with Myalina and George. It was a property with a huge farmhouse, not a little cape-style huddled near the ground, but a full two-story house with an attic and a series of outbuildings listing off the back end. There were so many of them all in together that I had to think about how many, counting on my fingers as I recited the names in my head. Myalina and George and baby Simon – that was easy – but there were Malinda and her baby – father unknown – at least to me. That was why George and Myalina had left his parents, one of the reasons – Malinda's pregnancy out of wedlock, though I suspected she was still married to Charles even though he was married again.

"Technically, I guess she is married," Myalina admitted to me shortly when I brought up the subject. "But no one has the money for lawyers so it stands as it does. The baby is certainly not Charles' baby, if that is what you are wondering."

I had not thought that. Charles was too far away, and he was busy enough, I thought. But of course, I did not really know. Anyway, Myalina had claimed the baby as hers when the move was made and all of them were known as Gages.

What they did was their business. She was a cute baby girl, and none of what went on was her doing. I stuck my nose in because of her relationship to my son, but as Myalina pointed out (she was in quite a temper that day), I had no reason to pry.

"It is really none of your business, Aunt."

"I suppose it is not," I snapped back.

"Only if you choose to make it so," she retorted.

We sat in sour silence, me tapping my shoe on the floor of my kitchen.

"Will you stop that tapping!" she exclaimed, and burst into tears.

Myalina was not having an easy time, living in proximity with so much chaos. Some of her brothers were working out, but the house was full of children and the confusion of multiple households.

"I miss Mrs. Gage," she sobbed, as I patted her knee and handed her a handkerchief.

I sighed. I could well imagine she did miss the calm of that household. Mrs. Gage had other people living with her, though. Her nephew Robert's widow, remarried to a veteran named Hosea Aldrich, was living with her and Harmon, helping run the farm because Harmon was elderly and failing and Horace was ill with consumption. He no doubt had a predilection for the disease, as had his brother, Charles, who died of it, and the hard life of the war had weakened his health.

Wealthy's household always had a manic agitation. It was like a millwheel in a stream where the flow of water comes in great bursts and then for periods of time, there is none at all. She was almost my age, and had another baby, Frederic. Like Thomas, he was fair with a high forehead and clear, soft brown eyes and a wavy, flourishing head of hair. Like Thomas, he would not live long, and my sister would feel sorrow added onto sorrow. She was pregnant again and would bear her last child, Willie, in December 1869. The state of the combined household was that potentially eighteen people had rights of space, though only about fifteen availed themselves of it. On top of that, there were girlfriends of the older boys and boys from neighboring families courting Malinda.

"You can come over here whenever you can get away," I told Myalina, shuddering to think of having to live the way she did now.

I was not discontented, all events considered, for the fall and winter of 1868 when I was glad to be in a home that I could call my own and relieved to have David not appear, though I confess I expected him and some days looked for him. A sound of a branch scraping the side of the house at night would bring me to a startled expectation that it was him at the door, letting himself in. I would hear a wagon or sled on the road that seemed to interrupt its steady pace and I would rush to a window to see if it was him. It never was, and by January, I had decided he did not know where I was and I was free of him.

Fanny was courting. She would be fifteen that year, and had caught the eye of a boy from the town, a nice, steady boy, I thought, of a good, steady family. She looked prettier each day, from happiness. I encouraged her to take her time, and when I said that, she looked at me with a pitying gaze.

"Of course, I will take my time," she said. "There is no hurry. He is in no hurry and his parents expect him to use good judgment."

"Of course they do," I muttered to myself.

"What?" she asked me.

"Nothing," I said. "I coughed."

She studied me suspiciously.

"Don't you like him?"

"Of course, I like him," I said. "Who could not like him? He is a very nice young man."

Satisfied, she turned back to her work, thumping the iron across a shirtwaist. It was ironing day. The irons weighed what seemed like a ton. The heavy metal detached from the wooden handle and had to be heated on the stove top. Ironing was a solitary job, the thumps of the iron and the hiss of water sprinkled on the surface of sheets and shirts blocking out conversation.

But Fanny kept on thinking as she ironed. When she paused to change her iron for a hotter one, she explained to me seriously,

"You see, Ma, I learned from my cousins. I would not want to end up like Malinda. She married too young."

I was pleased to see her seriousness. I smiled at her.

"You are a good girl, Fanny," I told her.

The way she beamed back at me, I realized I needed to tell her that more often. Soon she would be a married woman, and I would be alone.

⅍

Chapter Three

NOVEMBER 1869

DAVID CAME BACK TO ME JUST BEFORE THE WINTER OF 1869. It was after the trauma of the fear that I would lose my property to Horace Stone and had made my case to the judge in September. I had been safely back home from all of that distress for more than two months. That sequence of events – the call to court and the threat of losing my home – had reopened the wounds around David that I had suffered, not physically, but in my heart. Once again I found myself listening for him, and once or twice when I was in the town of Lancaster, I had a bad start when I thought I saw him.

"He doesn't know where we are," Fanny soothed me, and herself as well.

She had been my rock in this time. For the first time in my life, I had confided in her, fraught enough as I was in the days before the court appearance to risk causing her pain.

"Our cousin, James, will be your salvation," she had assured me when I was doubting everything and only saw us as paupers once again as we had been in 1850, before she was born.

She was pale as mist rising off the fields in the autumn morning. Her hands were icy, and we lay side by side in my big bed. She had crawled in with me, trembling, in the middle of the night. I was cold, too, despite the extra quilts piled over me. I was reminded of when she was a girl and had a bad dream, and crept from her room to comfort herself snuggled between her father and me.

"Did you have a bad dream?" I asked her, because I was awake when she quietly slipped under the covers and I could feel her trembling and took her cold hand in mine.

"You did," she said softly. "I heard you cry out. I couldn't sleep."

I had been startled awake by my dream, though I didn't know I cried aloud. I had been in the wagon, and it was slipping backwards down the road to Victory and I could not stop it.

"I was dreaming about our house on the road to Victory," I said. I thought about that house so often and the farm up there, and it was often in my dreams.

"You miss it, don't you?" Fanny said.

"Very much," I sighed, trying not to cry.

"I think of it, too," she told me. "I miss my father. It is like a big hole in my heart, where he is gone."

"I think of him, too," I shared. "And Charles. I miss Charles."

"Do you think of David?" she asked.

I froze inside at hearing her question. What a question for my daughter to ask me! I did not have to answer her.

"Yes," I whispered. "I do."

That is when she soothed me, "Our cousin James will be your salvation."

We slept fitfully that night, turning and tossing, but after our talk, at least I stopped dreaming of the wagon I was not strong enough to keep from sliding backwards down the hill road.

When David returned, it was a week past Thanksgiving. The remnants of the big meal were long gone. We had gone to be with my sister and her great, extended brood. There were thirty of us. Fanny and I had cooked to what seemed like excess in the days before and contributed pies and a cake and all manner of rolls and three jars of preserves. We had not returned empty-handed, either, with Wealthy supplying us with enough leftovers to feed us a couple of days.

The day he came back, Fanny was sorting a pile of men's socks – remnants of our menfolk's belongings stuffed into bureau drawers.

"I can salvage some of these for Biathy," she told me.

I was ironing. Two women like us did not have much laundry and consequently even less ironing. Biathy was not living at home; he was working out with a man named Eastman back in Lunenburg.

It was a rainy morning, and dark in the house the way rainy days in the dark days of November are.

"I hate this darkness," I grumbled. "We might as well be working at night."

"There's nothing else to do to pass the day," she said, wistfully. I knew she was thinking of her beau, and wondering what he would be doing on his father's farm with the hard rain making outdoor work unlikely.

When the knocks came on the door – slow, steady, almost hesitant knocks – the sound about scared my wits from me.

"It's him!" Fanny trilled, as if her thoughts had brought her young man to her just like that, magically.

But when she opened the side door of the kitchen, I saw her fall back from it as if she had been struck. She backed away slowly and purposely, leaving the two figures in the open doorway in plain sight for me to gaze on.

What I felt then is hard to explain. First, a starburst with a meteor falling fast, but not hitting the ground. That is the image that comes to mind. Glad with an old dizziness, that made me gulp for air. Then a heaviness, and helplessness and dismay – the way I had felt when I was in the wagon slipping down the hill in the slippery mud.

"David," I found the breath to say.

"Can we come in?" he asked. That was the way with him – how he stood humbly on the stone step of the side door, uncovered by any roof, in the streaming rain of late November. The rain poured from the lip of his broad hat, and dripped visibly from the soaked coat he wore. Just behind him, I could see his son, George, his head drooping miserably in such a way I knew water was going down the back of his neck. But David's head was not drooped. He looked straight in at me, with his eyes plaintive and asking for me to forgive him.

"You can come in," I said.

What if I had rushed across the room and slammed the door and shoved the bolt into place and leaned my back against it with all of my weight, digging my heels into the rough floor? Would he have quietly gone away? Could I have gotten there fast enough that he would not have seen my intent and shoved his leg into the opening so I could never have closed the heavy door against him? And if I had been fast enough, would he have disappeared and never returned? Or would he have come again and again, penitent, until I could not refuse his request for shelter? What if it had not been raining? What if Fanny and I had not been home?

There was no talking at first, while I adjusted to the idea of him again in a house of mine, and he and his son disengaged themselves from layers of wet garments after they had set down what I saw were bundles of their belongings.

"Put your wet clothes in the shed," I directed. I was all business. "Fanny, please go and find some dry clothes for them upstairs."

I had kept all of his clothes when he had gone. What was I to do with them? They were packed in a trunk in the upstairs hallway where they would have gathered a damp, closed-up smell, but they would have to do.

I would not let him upstairs. He and George could change in the shed where they would not leave damp garments staining my floors or chairs.

It was when he was still wet, standing in my kitchen with his son just behind him, that he moved slowly, reassuringly until he was standing behind me at the sink filling the kettle. He put his hand ever so lightly on the back of my neck and when I did not flinch or move away, caressed the place where my spine began and his hands, unexpectedly, were not cold and wet, but warm, oh how warm.

Thus it was, he pulled me back to him. I let him back into my house, and I let myself believe that he was reformed.

He did seem to be a new man. He was like he was when we courted, gallant and kind. I was cautious, like a woman looking for holes in the fabric of a beautiful dress found on the porch steps one morning. It was a gift, or so it appeared, but why?

"You didn't think I'd go for good," he said. "I was waiting for everything to blow over."

I stiffened at the introduction of this line of conversation and he, ever a master of manipulation (there, I've said it), easily turned the talk to the potential of this new farm.

"There's some work needing doing in the barn," he assessed. "George and I can use some of the scrap lumber stacked in the loft to repair the roof."

For all of that winter, David was amenable to living quietly with Fanny and me.

"Where is Biathy?" he had asked me that first day he was back.

"He is working out," I said. "He is old enough and it is good for him."

The fact was Biathy was more than I could handle as he approached manhood. He would no longer take direction from me, and I had decided he needed to be with a man who could control him. Moses Eastman agreed to take him on. He was cheap labor, being termed idiotic, and since he worked hard for room and board and only a few dollars, his service was a bargain.

That left David and George, and Fanny and me. Fanny was half-way gone by then, dreamy-eyed with her future marriage.

"What is going on with your daughter?" David asked me in puzzlement. "She seems like she is somewhere else in her thoughts."

I laughed a little. "Oh, she is somewhere else alright," I said. "She is courting and will be married once she is old enough."

"When will that be?" he asked.

"A year or two," I said.

"Will she wait that long?" he was skeptical.

"She'll wait."

She had her own questions for me in the days of David's return.

"Do you think this is wise, Ma?" she asked.

"What else am I to do?" I snapped, more harshly that I should have. "He's my husband."

"You don't have to have him back after what he did," she said.

"Oh, I don't? Is that so? And who says so?" I was angry. Before she could answer, I said, "Is that what people are saying? That I don't have to have him back?"

She turned white, and was silent.

"You may as well say it," I said. "What is it you are hearing?"

Unlike me, Fanny got out into society, going to parties and visiting her future in-laws. I saw my sister and niece and their families and that was about all.

"I don't like to say," she said.

"What do people know about it anyway?" I said roughly. "All of that is behind us, what happened in Vermont."

She looked at me pityingly.

This made me even madder, that my own daughter seemed to feel sorry for me.

"It is not, Ma." That is what she said.

"What do you mean? Of course it is."

She shook her head.

"The sheriff knows what he did and knows why you came to live here. Vermont doesn't want him. That's why they don't come for him."

I gaped at her. It all sounded so terrible coming from the bow-shaped mouth of my girl, always so steady and patient. I thought I would cry. I turned away from her, and tried to concentrate on the basin of butternuts. They were shaped like footballs, their weathered, wrinkled dark skins the color of mud. They held onto the nutmeats fiercely, and could only be split open by the use of a grip and hammer. But the meat was sweet and a lovely honey color and made a tasty cake. The nuts seemed to swim in front of me, as my eyes teared.

"You shouldn't have let him come back, Ma," she said.

At that, I spun on her, the sides of the bowl held tightly in my grip that pulled it painfully against my ribcage.

"That is not for you to say," I shouted. "You are just a girl. You think you know everything. Well, let me tell you, you don't. This is my house and I have done as I see fit."

I was satisfied to see her shrink back from me, her eyes huge, and her skin pale.

"I never want to hear you say that again," I said.

I will not lie and tell you that the household was peaceful. Fanny was remote from me. George was at school some days. And David, I admit I kept an eye on him. I had hidden my tin of money the day after he arrived, taking it from behind the loose board in my bedroom and concealing it in my favorite hiding place of a hollow in an apple tree.

Whether or not what Fanny had said about people talking was true, I did not know. I thought about it, and held my head high on the rare times I was in town.

Spring came, and I could not help but be glad to have the work of two men – David and his son – clearing trees off another section of land just up from the stream, and hauling rocks that had come up in the ground's shrinking and expanding in the big field. They planted Irish potatoes, buckwheat, rye, and Indian corn and helped me set in a big garden of

241

peas and beans. I buried myself in work, the way I was wont to do, and felt a content growing to see the season progress into summer and the crops grow tall.

"We'll start again," David had told me, his voice assuring and soft with feeling.

I very much wanted to believe him.

g

Chapter Four

FALL 1868

―――――――――――――――――――

As I have related, the first land I had bought in Jefferson was in the southern part of the town. It was Lot Nineteen, Range Six, in the vicinity of Cherry Mountain. It was so far from Lunenburg geographically, at least I thought so on my way there, guiding the horse across the open plain. Whereas in Lunenburg, the great mountains of New Hampshire were a distant view, and the hillsides around me seemed intimate, in Jefferson we were in the mountains. We were closer to what I had been looking at on the road to Victory, and viewing on the trip down to the village of Lunenburg, much closer. This land was, truth to tell, not much. It was forty-three acres, and managed well enough by Calvin Knight, but I knew quickly why he had wanted to leave. They were not lands to make my heart beat faster. But I had bought them after one visit by stage, and would have to make the best of what I had for the time being. The growing season started a little earlier than on my hill farm in Lunenburg, and it ended a little later. I was not isolated, with neighbors I knew, and I did not have to be unsure of whether they would be welcoming because they knew who I was and what I had fled from. The land was flat – an advantage I am hard put to describe, but to us small folks farming, it meant the work was less back-breaking. This wide area of open land went on for miles and the mountains surrounded it like the edges of a rough bowl. It allowed for a small settlement, a gathering of public buildings – a store, two churches, a school, a lumber operation, and a gristmill – and houses of my neighbors. I was relieved to have houses within view, believing these close by neighbors would afford me protection should David appear.

The trip had taken Fanny and Biathy and me two long days. I had bought a second horse so I had a team to pull all of our household goods and us the journey of almost, I calculated, twenty miles. The first day we went as far as the village of Lancaster. That meant the last slow walk of the horses down the hill on the road to Victory, with the gradual approach to the town, with the back of the town hall and the spire of the Methodist Episcopal Church at last in view. It was late September and the leaves were turning color – the brilliant orange and yellow of the sugar maple, and the glow of beech, illuminating the landscape all around us.

"Do you feel a little sad, Ma?" Fanny asked me quietly, as we looked at the scenery and the few passing houses on what would be my last ride down that hill from the land I loved.

I almost snapped at her. How close I came to retorting, "Don't be silly, girl," but I caught the words back in time.

"A little," I admitted, and then had hard work holding back the tears. I did not want my eyes to blur for this last ride. I felt I was leaving all of my hopes behind me.

How fast it went, and we were on the road out of the village, moving toward the river. I did not see too much else of that day. Oh, I saw, enough to guide the team surely and steadily toward our new home, but I didn't see to recollect it in any detail. The journey took us more than half of the day. It was, luckily, a dry day and our goods stayed nice, but the dust rose around the wheels and by the time we reached the end of the nine-mile jaunt into Lancaster town, I was feeling travel-worn and glad to stop.

We spent the night at the inn that James S. owned, right in the center of the commerce. It had been arranged by him that he would put us up since we were his wife's kin. We stopped nearby, and I sent Fanny to find him. He came right out and greeted us with a bustle and good cheer that made me feel better than I had all day. He helped me down from the wagon, and directed a boy to take the horses and wagon to the stables behind his inn where they would be safe for the night.

"I'll take you right up to your rooms," he said. "Did you make the journey well? You look well. My wife is not here. Her mother is ill, but my daughter, and my wife's relatives living with us, will all join us for dinner in the dining room tonight."

I was quite breathless with astonishment at all of this treatment. He had given Fanny and me a spacious room looking right down on the wide main street and we could sit by the window and look at all of the people doing trade in the many stores. (Biathy had his own small room across the hall.) This was the central town for the entire region, across the river and right around here, even from Jefferson. There was a big mercantile, a photography studio, a milliner's, and more than one inn, a funeral parlor, lawyers' offices, and the big brick courthouse that I gawped at on the way by without any foreboding that it would play a part in my life not many years hence. There was a bank, and taverns. Looking at all of this activity, I felt, not for the first time, how isolated we always were on the farms where we strove to make our livelihood. At the same time, I felt how closed in this town was, with views of only itself and no wider extension out to the mountains. I was glad I was not a domestic in one of those large houses I had seen or a worker in one of the factories.

I had never stayed at an inn, or hardly set foot in one. Only once when I was a girl, I went with my father into the lobby of the hotel in Bath where he met a man selling farm implements.

I am afraid I gaped like the schoolgirl I was, and did not blame Fanny and Biathy for staring around them all of those years later in Lunenburg. Indeed, I could hardly stop myself from staring, sitting at a table in the dining room of the inn of my cousin. I had never eaten out like this, and we were a gay party, all of us cousins together, laughing and glad of the luxury in which we found ourselves thanks to James.

Fanny and I giggled as we got ready for bed, settling in with our nightclothes in the large bed filled with down comforters and a featherbed. We lay on our backs and marveled at the sounds from the street, voices and an occasional burst of laughter, even though it was dark. Of course, it was not completely dark, because of the lights from the street and the windows of houses and from above the stores where people lived.

"I will never get to sleep," I said to Fanny. But I was tired enough from the journey and the continuing strangeness of the day that I slept deeply until about five. I woke up abruptly, and felt I had been having a dream and Hiram was beside me. It was in our first house near the Guildhall border and our last night there. In the morning, we would be going together to the farm on the road to Victory. When I realized where I was, with Fanny's soft, even breathing in my ear, I knew the truth of the day and that I had left that place in the hills above the village of Lunenburg forever. I cried. I could not help myself. I cried in great silent distress, for Hiram, and my lost children, for the land on that hillside across the river, for Charles, for my father dead when I was still a girl, and for my mother lost to me another way. My tears included David, I cannot say they did not.

I had been looking for him in Lancaster, thinking perhaps he would be there. I wondered if I would elude him with this move or if he would find me.

The next morning, early, standing by the wagon in the cool, just-awake dimness, James asked me, his voice low, "Have you had any word of him?"

My heart leapt and it must have shown in my face when I jerked my eyes up to look at my cousin.

"I have not either," he said. "If I do, I will get word to you."

With that, I had to be satisfied, and started out again – a woman alone with her children – for a farm she had seen but once.

We followed the Turnpike Road once we were in Jefferson, beginning in Riverton, the hamlet where I would end up living out my final days, though I, of course, had no foresight of that. It was also where the train would run, that conduit of prosperity, and where the Israel River flowed widely. It was on this road that my breath caught at the sight of the highest mountains, snow-capped from high-elevation storms. I felt I was driving into their embrace, and quickened the horses' pace, but I soon saw the way the mountains tantalized me, staying far away even as I went closer and closer. After some miles, I turned just enough west to move even further from them. But the landscape absorbed me on that road, opening up around me like a double fan.

We stopped when we were hungry to eat the lunch James S. had sent with us – pieces of roast chicken, slabs of bread and butter, and a jug of buttermilk. I spread the horse blanket on the edge of the road, and we sat in the sun of September, eating and then drowsing until I forced myself up and back in the wagon.

We drove on and on, the nearly ten miles from Lancaster village, and were always accompanied by some distant arrangement of mountains like silhouette cut-outs against the pale blue sky. We passed through a swampy region that seemed to not end, and then came out to make the last few miles to our house. We passed the churches, and the huge store owned by the lumber company, and a smaller store, and the school, and mill.

"We're almost there!" I exclaimed in relief.

Fanny was slumped against me in her fatigue at all of the events of the two days. Biathy was perky though, chirruping with excitement.

"Will Aunt Wealthy be there?" Fanny roused herself to ask.

"She'd better be," I muttered. One of the things that had kept me going was the thought of my sister awaiting me, with a hot meal ready, and energy enough to help make up beds once her sons had helped us bring the furniture off the wagon.

Sure enough, I soon made out her tiny, straight-backed form amidst what looked like a schoolhouse's worth of children standing on the grass at the side of my house. The young people were waving like a parade was coming. She wasted no such energy, but waited until I turned into the drive to gravely lift her hand in greeting.

Soon we were in each other's arms, and taking comfort from that closeness that had been absent for so many years I would have to stop and think to count them up. We were surrounded by her children, some of whom seemed unfamiliar, and there was great confusion.

"You are dusty," she pronounced, looking me over critically when the hugging and greeting were concluded."

I rubbed unthinkingly at my cheek.

"Oh, sister, don't do that," she scolded. "You come inside and get washed. I have a meal ready." She hustled Fanny and me indoors where her boys had set up a makeshift table of planks on sawhorses. It smelled good in that well-scrubbed kitchen – with a crock of beans on the stovetop, and bowls of potato salad, and condiments, and a plate of bread on the table.

"You bring in chairs first," she hollered out the open door to the boys.

"Who are all of those boys?" I asked. "They aren't all yours!"

"Mine, and some neighbors. Lucius kept our two eldest at home working with him. They were some disappointed to miss the excitement," she said. " Ella, come," she motioned to a shy girl trying to be invisible. She stepped toward me at her mother's bidding, and I saw another beauty. My sister's girls were lovely.

Ella, the youngest, was twelve, and carried the same soft blush complexion of her sister, Malinda, but her eyes had a darker flash to them, and her hair was very dark and full of waves. It was pulled back from her face and set with a bow on top, while the curls flowed down her back.

I smiled at her, and kissed her cheek, warm from the stove and the work of helping her mother cook.

"You are prettier every time I see you," I said, and saw the paleness turn deep rose in the wave of pleasure of a modest girl at my compliment.

"You show them where to wash up," her mother directed.

After that, we females took a turn through all of the rooms, leaving the kitchen for sight of the small pantry, the front room, the parlor, and we even climbed the narrow stairs where there were three bedrooms. I was glad the space up there was divided into rooms. Fanny chose hers and soon we were all superintending the placement of furnishings carried by the boys.

"She left the house spotless," Wealthy said approvingly, referring to Mrs. Knight. "I came over the day they left. I think she hated to leave this place after all of those years here."

It was near dusk when Lucius arrived with his eldest sons: Lucius the elder, and Charles. There were not enough chairs for all of us, but some of the neighbor boys went home and there was a rough bench brought in from the barn for the rest.

I was tired enough that I felt like a sleepwalker. After the dishes were washed and put away, and the frenzied confusion of leave-taking ended, Fanny and Biathy and I went directly to our beds. I was comforted by the familiarity of the old, soft sheets and the wool blanket and quilt that made up my bed. I surprised myself by sleeping almost instantly. No thoughts were strong enough to break through the tiredness of that long day.

⚓

Chapter Five

FALL 1868-SPRING 1871

A T THAT TIME, MY SISTER, WEALTHY, DID NOT LIVE IN THE HOUSE NEXT DOOR, CLOSER TO THE INTERSECTION WITH THE CHERRY MOUNTAIN ROAD. That would come more than a decade later when she would be alone with her two youngest boys, and I would be in the hamlet of Riverton on the other end of town. In that fall of 1868, she and Lucius farmed a place up the Cherry Mountain Road, a mile or so from where I had come to farm. To think she was in the hills is misleading. The mountain did not start its climb for a ways from her, and like me, the land around her was quite flat. She and Lucius owned their farm. Their family was diminished with Myalina, of course, married, and Malinda living with her and George, in Lancaster. Like me on my farm, Lucius had forty-three acres to work with, and most of it – thirty-three acres – was improved. He had two milch cows, and that fall harvested Indian corn and four hundred pounds of Irish potatoes. He had a horse, a pair of oxen, twelve sheep and a pig, and Wealthy made about one hundred pounds of butter. Although he had a small operation, he did well, working from before sun up to dark, and sometimes into the dark on clear nights.

Before the end of that year, I bought more land, and could boast of eighty acres, though only thirty were cleared. With the work of David and George, in the growing season of 1870, we raised Indian corn and oats, a little buckwheat and enough Irish potatoes to sell. We had one cow. We showed very little profit, though, because by the end of that harvest, David was long into his familiar habits. The horses were gone, sold to pay his debts, and there was only the ability of our legs to take us to the store or church or visiting if we had the mind to go. He took the stage when he was fixed on gambling and drinking, riding to Lancaster or in to Whitefield. The relief was he would be gone for days at a time; the weight was knowing he would return.

Fanny longed to be married, and turned fifteen and then sixteen. I sensed no unwillingness on the part of her beau, but suspected his parents did not favor the marriage now they had seen and continued to hear about the escapades of my husband.

How we would get through that season of 1870, I did not know. I managed to rent horses from a neighbor for plowing, though, and David, in one of his unpredictable turns, calmed down in time to be of use. I had determined to hire a man to do the plowing, if need be. George was a help – a quiet boy cowed by his father – and who had, I had begun to see, a slowness of wit. I was always kind to him, and he repaid that with hard work. He looked to his father with a stupor of longing for affection and attention, which was rarely paid him, but he never gave up on his desire for it.

As for David and me, it can only be said that I wished I had never let him back into my house that day of rain. It was only my sense of wifely duty, believing I had married him in good faith and must honor that commitment regardless of his behavior, that kept me going on the track on which I had started.

Moving from Vermont had changed nothing, if anything it had made things worse. If only I had stayed on the road to Victory, I sometimes thought, where the law would have been seeking David and kept him away from me.

All of this wore on and on, like a poor mule pulling a too-heavy load, but too stubborn to ever stop, until the late spring of 1871.

§

Chapter Six

EARLY MARCH 1871

IT WAS EARLY MARCH OF THAT YEAR. David returned from one of his days-long excursions. But unlike his usual results, he had been lucky beyond all imaginings. When I saw him pull up by the house, with a carriage finer than I had ever owned, pulled by two bay geldings, and saw him step down wearing a handsome suit of clothes, I felt a chill run down me. I hurried to meet him, and hear what he would say.

"Lucy!" he exclaimed. "I hit the luck. I am a rich man."

Before I could back up, he had his big hands around my waist and lifted me into the carriage. Spryly, he leaned into the back and soon plied me with packages that filled up the front seat. There were bolts of cloth suitable for a dozen dresses, and packets of lace, and a pair of shiny new boots in my size, and a Merino shawl, and a beautiful cloak lined with soft wool.

I couldn't think of one thing to say. Or, rather I thought of so many things, I could not get out a word of them. I simply stared at him. Full of himself, and out of his senses with his good fortune, he took my silence as august approval.

"I'll get all of these presents inside for you," he said. "You get into your best dress and we will go for a ride in our new carriage. Fanny can come, too," he added grandly, seeing her standing on the back steps.

I did not argue, but rushed into the house, once he had deftly scooped me up and put me on the ground. I pushed Fanny along with me, through the kitchen and upstairs.

"What is going on?" she said sharply.

"You just do as you're told," I snapped.

"I don't want to go out," she said stubbornly.

"You just do it," I said. "Get on your good dress and take a shawl."

"What is all that?" she protested. "What has he been up to?"

"We'll find out soon enough," I said. "Please, Fanny, will you cooperate?"

My mind was flying like a shuttle across a loom. I did not like to think what David had been doing to come home acting the banker or lawyer. I expected the sheriff and his deputy to chase us as we trotted briskly and smoothly with the suspension of the lavish carriage cushioning us from bumps in the road.

The road unwound quickly, and he drove like we were on a golden carpet set out for royalty. He took me on my favorite route that I had only walked for the past year, up through the bowl of the mountains, crossing the shining waters of the river over bridges as it curved and curved.

"Everything is different now!" he talked as he drove. "I have hit my lucky streak. We have money now, no more farming, no more grinding labor for you and me."

Slowly, the story came out – him tantalizing me with the details of the hotel in Littleton where he had gone to gamble and the men who fell before him at cards, as he raked in the money of their bets with hand after hand in every configuration of good fortune. It was all solid, what he told me, with some embellishments, of course, but none that changed the true fact that he could pull from the pants' pocket of his new suit a roll of bills that made me gasp, and even startled Fanny from her coldness.

David had won big.

David winning big was a new creature. He walked with more than his usual swagger, and he found any occasion the right time to pull that increasingly smaller roll of bills from his pocket. He took me to the hotels in Lancaster and Littleton to eat, and he took Fanny and me to have our photos taken in our new clothes that we had spent days making, at his insistence. It was coming on for spring, and the planting, though weeks off, began to occupy my mind, and I itched to be in my garden, poking into the soil as I planned, and thought of the days to come when I would be watching to see when the first sprouts of peas rose up and began to climb the trellises.

"I won't hear of you out there," he ordered, the first and only morning he came down early to see me in my dusty work dress, with dirt on my hands. "You have a new life now, like I always promised."

What I wanted was to get my hands on some, just some, of that money and salt it away for harder times and I wanted to take some and buy more land. I wanted hundreds of acres, some with timber, which I knew the lumber company would buy once the railroad was here, and I wanted some with acres of cleared fields, and a big barn for my many animals. With even a small part of that bankroll of his, I could have made us a future that would have been passed down to our children and them to theirs.

How fast that month of March passed, and we were the talk of the neighborhood and the town, and I was sure the surrounding towns, even across the river to my old home. He spent and spent, bringing home another horse, and a new-fangled washing machine, and had delivered a new set of kitchen furniture with a shiny table for eight and eight stalwart new chairs, and my old table, worn and full of character, he had hauled to the barn. He took me shopping and insisted I buy new china, fancy with dozens of little painted flowers, and tablecloths, and new plated silverware with a matching teapot.

My horror at all of this grew, but I dared say nothing. He was a man possessed, and I watched with fascination at how his roll of bills shrank in a matter of weeks and he did not seem to notice. But by the last week of the month, even he could see what his problem was – that the money he had won would not last forever.

He came charging into the house, and he had the small roll clutched in his hand, and made me hold out mine for it.

"See what has happened," he accused. "Heft that! Don't you see what has happened!"

His face was red through his olive skin and his eyes pierced into me, demanding an explanation.

I had thought about this moment that I knew would come and I had an answer for him, ready made.

"You must take what you have left and do what you did again," I said calmly. I opened the roll and counted out the bills slowly, as if I had not done it before. He did not always have that money in his pocket. It sat on the bureau at night when he was fast asleep. What he had started with, I did not know, but I had the proof in my hands that the many hundreds of dollars, enough for us to have been prosperous farmers, were down to a few hundred.

He stared at me, his dark eyes glittering with this plan I put to him.

"You think I could do it again," he said, some hope in his voice.

"I know you could," I told him. This was no lie. What he had done once was possible again. Perhaps luck would run for him once more, and he would be called unstoppable and the men around would not want to gamble with him anymore. But this time, they would be eager to get their money back, and he could play as much as he wanted.

"Don't do it all at once," I cautioned. "Take out a little at a time. Test your luck, like a fisherman throwing a line into the water."

"I know what to do," he snapped back. "You don't."

"Of course you do," I soothed. "I was just imagining how skilled you will be again."

He looked at me suspiciously to see if I was poking fun at him and was satisfied I was not.

That night, I would find, did not go well for him. He did not take my advice, and most everything he had left he lost, quickly and like in a dream. That was the night he burned down Samuel Hannux' house on the north side of Lancaster, and came home to me silently, with the stench of smoke in his hair and on his clothes and under his fingernails that I attributed to the smoke-filled tavern where I guessed he had been.

Now we flash forward to the place in time where the sheriff came, weeks into May, to my door and I lied for my husband.

"He was here with me," I told the law officer.

It was the aftermath of that encounter, leaving me cold and shaking all day, that led me to do what I did that night.

"Fanny, go to my sister's," I told her that afternoon, after having thought of what I must do.

"Why, Ma?" she asked.

"I don't want you here when David comes home," I said.

She burst into tears, the tension of the day coming out in her at last.

"You aren't going to do anything foolish?" she wailed.

"Perhaps I am," I said, my face under control. "That is why you are going to your aunt's. I'll help you hitch up the mare to the wagon and you go on, now."

Nothing she said changed my mind, and soon I watched her guiding the wagon onto the road and turning right in the direction of Cherry Mountain Road and my sister.

With her gone, I settled to wait for David to return.

"So you burned down his house," I said to him the moment he walked into my kitchen.

"What?"

"I know what you did," I said calmly, my heart pounding. I was determined not to lose my nerve. "It could have been murder," I added softly. "That boy and girl."

"Have you been drinking?" he said roughly. "What are you talking about?"

"The sheriff was here today, sniffing around. He thinks you burned down Samuel Hannux' house and I think he is right. But I lied for you, and now I want you to get out. I want you to take your clothes and go out of my house."

I had barely finished those words when he struck me, a blow across my face that sent a stream of blood out from my nose and made my ears ring. But I was ready for him. I had hidden a metal pole under the table and I got to it and I raised it and swung it with all of the fury I felt and caught him on his kneecap. He screamed with pain and without pause grabbed me and flung me across the kitchen so I was airborne and crashed down on my back, my head banging the door to the hallway. I was dazed and the blood was in my mouth from my nose and the pain in the back of my head made me dizzy and blurred my vision.

He stood a few feet from me – the kitchen was small – and I could see he would come for me again and I could do nothing.

It was then I heard a voice, a piercing, strong voice.

"If you do not back away from her, I will shoot you," it said.

David started and spun toward it, with the energy of an angry bull.

I tried to see, but my vision whirled the room around me.

"You," he snarled, and gave a snort meant to be a laugh and made to come back my way.

"I will just as soon shoot you in the back," the voice continued.

He turned again, and I tried to prop myself forward to see under the table and between the chair legs.

It was my sister. My sister. Wealthy stood in the open side door and she was holding a pistol. I was dreaming. She was erect and there was coldness in her eyes I had never seen before and would not ever see again. Her hair was tightly back in a bun, with not one stray piece, and her waist looked so tiny and she stood so small compared to David's six feet, but she had taken charge, and the pistol did not tremble in her hands that held the barrel in his direction.

Then I saw he was a coward.

"You get out now," she said.

And to my amazement, he turned and walked toward the door that led through the woodshed.

Suddenly, he spun, and shouted, "I'll be back! I'll be back and I'll burn this house down!" And he vanished into the dark hole of the shed.

I was on my feet by then, and I heard a roar of sound from the yard and went to the door next to the pantry and saw there was a crowd of people on my property, standing in loose, random groups and singly like cows in a pasture. I watched, my hand shaking as I tried to push back the hair that was all around my face, sticky with blood from my nose, and I saw David walking through that crowd, as their voices buzzed, but no one seemed to see him, though I know that was all they saw, except for the few who had turned to notice my beat-up figure in the doorway.

I watched him walk catty corner across my grassy yard and onto the road. He had nothing with him but whatever was in his pockets, and he was very dark in the late rays of sun. I followed him with my eyes until I could follow him no more.

When I turned back into the kitchen to escape the stares now coming my way, I saw that the pistol was gone, and Wealthy was pouring water into a basin.

"Come," she said.

⚔

Chapter Seven

MAY 1871

T HEN THE WAITING BEGAN.

He had always come back, and there was no reason to think this time would be different. His threat hung in the air like a great celestial clock, with every turn of the minute hand bringing his arrival closer.

The first night, Wealthy stayed, unrelenting in the face of her husband's demands that she come home with him when he arrived with the wagon soon after all of the hullabaloo was done.

I could see he was unmoved by my appearance. Indeed, he hardly glanced at me.

"You belong home," he said gruffly to his wife.

She tipped her head down in a way I had seen her do since we were children that meant she would not budge. He had seen it, too, and muttered, "Have it your way then," and left us.

They had an entire argument she won without saying a word.

At least Fanny had been spared what happened that day. Obeying her aunt's orders, she stayed with Ella, and did not come near me.

That night, Wealthy got me into bed, and a kind neighbor lady stayed with me. My sister wanted to send for the doctor, but I refused. What ailed me would only heal with time and no doctor yet had invented a way to speed up the clock.

She sat all night downstairs, with her pistol handy. That is what she told me she would do, her right fist on her hip in an attitude of defiance. There were men around, too. My next-door neighbor, by the name of Zed, did the milking, and the lights in his house never went out that night.

The hours passed, and I slept some with the medicine Wealthy sent a boy to her house to collect from Ella. I was glad of it, wanting the pain to be gone and knowing there would be time enough for fitful sleep and bad dreams.

The next morning dawned, and I insisted on dressing and coming downstairs.

"I'll only stiffen up," I said when Wealthy protested.

Wealthy went home.

"I have to," she said, red spots forming on the tips of her cheekbones. "You come home with me."

I shook my head, and winced at the pain I caused.

"You must be reasonable," she said.

"I can't leave my house," I said, speaking softly and feeling like my sore mouth was full of jagged marbles.

"I don't want you to risk it," she blurted. Her eye that drooped sagged more than usual in her anxiety.

"If I lose my house, I have nothing," I said.

She was quiet. She did not throw in my face that I could rent and survive as her family once did.

"Breakfast is there for you, on the stove," she said, putting on her bonnet and tying it firmly under her small pointed chin.

"Thank you, sister, for everything," I said.

"Bah," she said dismissively. "I will ask John Duggan to come and stay in your barn."

She raised her hand at my inclination to protest. John Duggan was a step above a tramp. He was a raggedy, slovenly character who roamed the town, and stayed here and there. He was not dangerous, but his mind seemed not quite in balance. His graying hair always stood in tufts around the edges of his hat, and his clothes were old and dirty, and his boots scuffed from years of being worn by someone else.

"He'll do it for food, and he won't bother you, but he will be some protection," she said.

How he would protect me I could not say, but he would be a man on the property, in the outbuilding, and maybe some deterrence.

"Try and keep Fanny with you," I said.

"I'll try," she said. "But I don't know if I can. I don't think she'll be kept from you."

Wealthy set off up the road home, walking with small, quick strides. I had tried to get her to ask Zed for a ride home, but she would not bother him at his work.

She must have passed Fanny on her way because not a half hour passed before my daughter was in the kitchen, untying her bonnet and hanging up her cloak, and muttering to herself at my appearance. Whatever she felt at seeing me, she did not show, but immediately began bustling about the room, straightening furniture out of place, shoving chairs under the table, and finding ingredients to make biscuits.

"You should be in bed," she told me sternly.

"No," I said. "Don't you start."

I sat in the rocker, with a cushion she placed to buffer my sore back, and watched her work as I sipped my tea gingerly, the edge of the cup hard on my sore mouth. She kept refilling my cup, and she gave me some medicine she said Wealthy told her would ease the pain.

"You're all grown up," I said suddenly, as if talking to myself because my words came out so low.

"What?" she turned from her flour-and-butter mixing.

I tried to smile, but couldn't. "You're all grown up," I said again, trying to articulate my words better.

She did smile, a small one, but it made it all the way into her eyes.

By late afternoon, John Duggan arrived, in time for supper. I had forgotten he was supposed to come and Fanny tried to be rid of him, and send him next door.

"My mother is ill," I heard her say.

"Miz Larrabee sent me," he said stubbornly, easing himself into the doorway to peer around Fanny at me. I was up, trying not to get stiff, and making milk gravy in the big skillet.

"He's right, Fanny," I said. "He's sleeping the night in the barn. Let him in for supper."

He hustled right in at this approval and stood in the middle of the room, considering me with black, button-like eyes.

"You're some banged up, ma'am," he said. "Begging your pardon."

That was pretty much all he said, except for "please" when asked if he wanted more salt pork and gravy, and "thank you," once he had it. He sat in the warm kitchen until the evening wore into darkness and accepted the blankets from Fanny before heading out to the barn. Zed's son had milked the cows, and the barn was quiet.

Fanny stayed behind me as I climbed the stairs whose steep rise seemed like the road to hell itself with the pain in my back and other places. Climbing made me dizzy, and I paused, reaching up to the bruised egg-sized bump on the back of my head.

"Just go slow, Ma, but don't stop," Fanny encouraged. "I can't really catch you."

We left lights on in my room and she stayed with me, and she left a lamp burning in her room and one in the kitchen and locked the doors, and I heard furniture scraping on the floor and knew she was wedging chairs under the knobs.

I refused a sleeping draught in order to stay alert in case of being awakened by danger and, of course, hardly slept, nor did Fanny, until almost dawn. The sound of the cows mooing awakened us, and she flew out of bed and down the stairs with only her wrap around her to reassure us that the sound of footsteps outside was our neighbor's son.

She wanted to get her beau to come and stay with us, to protect us, but I was cold to that idea.

"His parents will never agree and it would not be appropriate to have him here," I said.

He did come by to visit, and was horrified at my appearance. I thought he would faint, but Fanny shoved him into a chair and pushed a mug of strong tea into his hands that shook visibly. He could not meet my eye, and finally, I went into the front room, wishing I could have moved faster. I could feel he was watching my slow progress with anguish.

I stayed in the front room until Fanny came to tell me he was gone. She could not meet my eye either when she told me it was fine to come back to the kitchen, and flushed when she said it.

The days passed that week in this way, with John in the barn, and visits from her beau, and James S. came one day, and the neighbor's son milked, and James sent a hired boy to see to the work in the fields, and Fanny gardened with my direction.

We were waiting, and it was almost exactly a week when our waiting was ended.

⅋

Chapter Eight

JUNE 3, 1871

IT WAS JUNE THIRD, 1871. A Saturday. After the long days of waiting, beset by the anxiety of wondering if David would come and with the enduring of the pain in my body and mind he had caused, when Zed's wife asked Fanny and me to come for supper to their house next door, I said yes with relief.

"We can see your house from here," she reassured me when I hesitated. "Nothing will go on there without our knowing it. We'll eat in the kitchen and there is a window toward your place."

Supper was late, because it was a fine day, and the men worked longer in the fields, but Fanny and I went over early to help prepare the meal, and for the companionship of the woman of the house and her two daughters. It was a lively household, with a baby, and two young boys too little to help their father, and reminded me of a calmer version of my sister's domestic arrangement.

I felt freed of the watch at my house. I can only think of describing the feeling by asking you to imagine a sharp stone in your shoe that pricks at you all of the time and when it is gone, you can only wonder that you stood the discomfort so long. I forgot all about my house. We all did. The men and older boys came in, at last, in the early dusk of the long June day, to wash up, and we all gathered at the table. John Duggan arrived for his plate of food, and then went back to my barn – a tiny reminder of the worries of the past week.

It was all too soon that we women were washing up, a merry bunch of five of us chattering, and then it was time for Fanny and me to go home.

My house was very quiet, and, still sleeping together in the big bed in my room, my daughter and I drifted into sleep easily in our relaxed state.

Somehow I awoke abruptly with my heart hammering badly, like a saw blade at the mill out of control. It took me a second or two to know that it was the sound of window glass shattering that had brought me from my sleep. I shook Fanny awake.

"The window," I whispered fiercely. "I heard the glass break."

I was out of bed even as I had been nudging her awake and I could smell the smoke – an acrid odor as out of place as the shatter of glass on a quiet June night.

She was crying from fear, and we ran into the hall where there was already smoke. I ran back into the bedroom and grabbed up our shawls and pressed hers into her hands.

"Wrap it around your face and run," I told her, beginning to cough.

We rushed down the narrow stairs and shoved out the front door, and onto the grass near the road, gasping for breath.

By now, I could hear a voice I recognized as John Duggan's shouting, "Fire! Fire!" and saw him running toward our neighbor's house.

I did not wait, but headed at a trot, my nightclothes dragging, toward the back of the house where I saw smoke. It was pouring out of the room that was my pantry, and I saw what had awakened me – the top pane of glass was shattered, and bore a jagged hole where some object had passed through it.

Zed and his hired man and older sons and John came on the scene, bearing shovels and hoes and Zed smashed out the rest of the glass and the wooden frame, and yelled at the men to shovel dirt onto the smoldering mass inside. How he knew what to do, I don't know, and when I asked him later he had no answer but a shrug. The vegetable garden was right there, coming out from the corner of the pantry and shed that trapped the heat of the sun all summer. Their boots trampled all of my peas and beans and the squash plants and the tender tops of carrots and parsnips. They used the soft dirt from my garden to put out the fire that was a smudge eating into the wood floor of the pantry.

A crowd gathered quickly, and we all stood back staring at the smashed window and the smashed wood where Zed had used an axe to open up the pantry to the shovelfuls of dirt.

I did not see David, hovering at the edge of the far field where the row of scrub trees marked the boundary line, but other people did.

"He was right there, hovering like a shadow, but easy to see in the moonlight," one man would testify at the trial.

Of course, he was there, unable to leave the scene of the fire without seeing his handiwork. I thought to wonder, in the hours when I had fortitude and wit to consider what had happened, if he would have watched the house burn down and never raised a cry.

I was lucky.

"You are lucky, ma'am," Zed told me. "The house is saved. It is all in the backend. He must have thrown in a lit rag soaked in kerosene, but the floor back there has only a crawl space and it must have been damp. There's some smoke damage, though, and the wall to the kitchen is burnt."

While they had been busy fighting the fire, other people in the neighborhood had rushed into my house, and hauled out every stick of furniture they could carry and it was heaped in a pile in my front yard. Later, I would find that some of these possessions, including the fancy table David had bought me, were smashed, and I went back to using some of what I had stored in the barn during his spending spree. I had only $200 in fire insurance and would learn that there was $800 in damage. It was worse than Zed had thought, with the whole back of the house destroyed.

I wish I could have blotted that night from my mind, the way a man hit in the head loses consciousness and never remembers the blow, but that was not given to me.

The sheriff came, and questioned me and Fanny. Wealthy had come by then, fetched with Lucius by Zed's sons.

"He threatened to come back and burn down her house," Wealthy told the law officer.

"He was right there in the back of the field," a man added.

"The glass shattered," I said numbly. "I woke up when I heard the glass break."

"The house was full of smoke," Fanny said. "When we went into the hall, we didn't know if we would get out because of the smoke and we didn't know where it was coming from."

"We'll get him," the sheriff said.

By the small hours of that night, they did get David, and on Monday, he appeared before the justice and the bail was set at $1,000. I was not there, at the court in Lancaster, but word was sent to me that my husband needed $1,000 of bail money to set him free. But I did not come up with one penny of that, and left him to his fate. I will not say I did not lay awake night after night, wondering if I was doing the right thing to harden my heart against him, but every morning, when I could have changed my mind and dug out the tin from the apple tree and sold the horses and carriage and mortgaged my farm, I did not make a move.

That was June third, and into June fourth and fifth, and my husband was lodged in the Lancaster jail. I felt a relief come over me, that he could no longer have the means to hurt me. I held my head high, and did not consider leaving my farm. I had done that once, and look what had come to me.

I spent some weeks with Wealthy, Fanny and me squeezed into a room with Ella, who was delighted to have us.

The summer was hot and long, good for raising crops and there was an abundance of grazing for my two cows and the horses. I spent every day at my farm, and had used some of the money from my tin and work moved quickly on repairing my house. I walked back and forth between Wealthy's and my place.

By the end of June, Fanny had got married. She had not waited more than a few weeks after the incident at my house before running off with her beau. She lived some miles from me, and immediately took to visiting me, and we would sit in the yard under the maple tree of an afternoon, sewing, on rare quiet days. We fell into the habit of going back and forth to work together on whatever chores there were to do at our farms, ironing or washing or making butter.

"It's very peaceful," she said emphatically one day in mid-July, in between the thud of the irons on the two boards her husband had rigged up for us. We were in her kitchen that day, and she felt free to speak. I knew what she meant: that with David safely locked up there was a peace settled in our lives.

"His trial is not long off," I said, thinking aloud.

It was set for the court session of November in the Lancaster courthouse, a big pile of dark, heavy stone with a bell tower that loomed over the main street of that town like a message saying the law was always on duty. I would be testifying, as would Wealthy, and neighbor Zed, and heaven help us, John Duggan, who was staying in my barn until the cold drove him out late in the fall. I could not help but be grateful to him for his part in saving my house. I dreaded the day of that trial, the way anyone would dread standing as witness, and could only pray to God to keep my head and tell the story in the way the jury would believe.

The newspaper account had not bolstered my confidence. It had reinforced whatever guilt lingered like mist over the river about what had happened and my ensuing failure to give him bail money.

The newspaper said that he had tried to burn his wife's house, "with whom he had recently had some difficulty." The words implicated me in his crime, the way a troublesome mare would cause the upset of the cart and end with the driver on his head in a ditch. How this description of events stung me, maybe you can appreciate. If that wife had been a better wife, she would not have driven her husband to burn her house. When I would feel too guilty to bear it, I would walk around to the back of my house and see where the entire back of the house, my kitchen and pantry, had been replaced at considerable cost to me, though I had used the money wisely and the carpenter and his man had done the work at a reasonable price, far less than the grim $800 forecast of damage by the man from the insurance company. If I ever did get the $200 from them, I would be glad of it, but I had no high hopes since it was arson and insurance men used any excuse not to pay a claim.

More commonly though, guilt hit me when I was in my bed with the night dark and there were hours till morning, and I would sniff deeply and catch the still rank scent of smoke that lingered from what he had done to me, and I would pinch myself and tell myself to be glad I was alive.

"I have a letter from Charles," I said to Fanny that morning we were ironing, patting my apron pocket that held the crackly envelope and paper.

"Ma, why didn't you tell me first thing?" Fanny said, her face lighting up.

I shrugged.

"It is not a pleasant letter to read," I said.

"Oh?" she looked at me.

I sighed and got it out, and pulled the page from the envelope and unfolded it and smoothed it with both hands on my knees.

I read it to her, his words of recrimination about, "that man," and "It is long overdue for him to be where he is now."

She sighed, hearing what he had written. It sounded worse aloud than it had when I had read and reread it in my head.

"The important thing is you and Fanny are safe." I skipped one line, to spare her, about how he was surprised his sister would desert me in this time. By that he, of course, referred to Fanny's marriage.

"You left something out," she accused.

"I did not," I said, too quickly.

"You did," she said. "It's something he said about me, isn't it?"

"No, it's nothing," I said.

"Did he congratulate me on my marriage?" she asked, with dry wit.

I didn't answer fast enough.

"Did he?" she said triumphantly.

"Not exactly," I said weakly.

"Read me what he said," she ordered.

"He implied it would have been better if you had waited. That's all," I said. I would not read her that hurtful sentence, "I am sorry to hear my sister so quickly found it in her heart to desert you at this time when you need her."

"Alright," she said. "If that's all, what's the big deal?"

I sighed with relief.

"It's easy for him to make pronouncements from far away," she said with satisfaction.

g

Chapter Nine

July 1871

Escape

I DID NOT SEE FANNY EVERY DAY, OF COURSE, WHAT WITH HER NEW HOUSEHOLD, AND WE BOTH HAD NEVER-ENDING WORK, MUCH OF IT THAT HAD TO BE DONE IN OUR OWN HOMES. That was why I was surprised to see her appear the next day, banging into the kitchen in a manner quite unlike her usual calm demeanor.

"Fanny! Is something wrong?" I asked.

I was up to my elbows making raspberry preserves, my fingers dyed the color of the berry juice.

"He has escaped!" she exclaimed, finding it hard to catch her breath. "Oh, Ma, he has escaped!"

"What?" I gawped at her, my heart starting to hammer. "He couldn't have."

"He has, with two other men," she told me. "Someone snuck to the jail and passed in a wrench and they busted the lock and broke out. One of them was caught right off, but the other two, and one of them is David, escaped across the river into Vermont. That's what the sheriff is saying. My friend, Beanie, brought me the news after her husband got back from Lancaster early this morning."

"What if he comes here?" I whispered. "Oh, Fanny, what am I to do?"

"He won't come in the daylight," she said. "Maybe he'll be caught soon."

"Vermont is a long ways from here," I said, finding comfort in that. "If that's where they went."

"They'd stand a chance of escaping for good," she said.

I sat down on a kitchen chair, my sticky, bright pink hands limply in my lap.

"How could he have escaped from the jail?" I said, angry all at once. Getting up my dander tamped down my fear. "What is the use of a jail if people can get in and help people get out?"

"That's what everyone's saying," she told me. "How can we feel safe with a jail like that?"

"The sheriff will come here, sure as anything," I said gloomily.

I was right. It was not the sheriff himself, who was busy tracking my husband and the other man – a forger or liquor offender, I was not sure which – in Vermont, but one of his deputies.

"We are sure sorry to bother you, Miz Beede, but your husband has escaped the jail, along with another man, and we wonder if you have seen him."

I glared at him. "No, I have not seen him and I don't want to see him. How could this have happened?"

He looked sheepish, and scuffed his boot in the bare patch by the bottom step at the side door.

"You need to keep your eyes open for him," he told me. "Do you think he might come here? I need to take a look around."

I had to let him come into my house and walk through every room, up and down, and take a lantern into the root cellar under the kitchen, and peer into the crawl space under the roofline in the bedrooms. Finding nothing, he trekked out to the barn and looked in each stall, and climbed the ladder to the loft where we kept hay. He quizzed John Duggan who was sitting in the sun, his back against the warm wood of the barn, and he hiked out to the fields to find the man I had working for me and ask him if he had seen David Beede.

"I'm sorry to bother you, ma'am," the deputy told me. I had not left his side, but followed him everywhere he had been on my farm. He did not look sorry to be snooping around and he was certainly red in the face and sweating from the exertion of his day, and maybe from my persistence in sticking by him however many times he told me I could go back to the house.

From my house, he headed in the direction of my sister's farm. I looked after him in disgust.

"He's wasting his time," I said.

"What do you mean?" Fanny asked. "He's doing his job. Don't you want them to find the escaped men and lock them back up?"

I muttered to myself. I could have told that deputy that if my sister had seen David Beede she would have shot him down and they would be coming for him, dead or alive. I had not spoken of that day in my kitchen when my sister had drawn a gun on my husband, not to Fanny, not to the law, not to anyone.

In two days, word came that he and his fellow inmate had been caught and were back behind bars. The newspaper joked about how it was easy to get in and get out of that jail, and recommended a fence. That was the last of the excitement for that summer. Soon enough it was November, and my day had come to testify against him.

g

Chapter Ten

NOVEMBER 13, 1871

I WENT UP ON THE STAGE THE DAY BEFORE THE TRIAL TO STAY WITH MY
COUSIN, JAMES S., AND HIS FAMILY, OR, TO BE MORE PRECISE, HE PRO-
VIDED ME A ROOM IN HIS HOTEL AS HE HAD DONE BEFORE WHEN I MOVED
TO JEFFERSON THREE YEARS BEFORE.

He was very kind to me and met the stage that ferried me and my
sister, for she was called upon also to testify, from our homes in the south
of Jefferson to Lancaster.

It was a lowery day, the kind of day typical of November in the north
when the landscape is awash with grays and browns, and you count yourself lucky if there is sun. We left early, just after dawn, because we had
to meet one more time with the counsel for the State that was bringing
the case against David. The stagecoach was empty that morning, and we
moved quickly north, my sister looking out one side and me the other.
There had been a hard frost the night before, and the fields were white and
gauzy curtains of condensation rose from the twisting river and coated the
trees with ice that glinted in the morning sun. The peaks of the distant
mountains were iced white like a sweet glaze with the first snows of the
year that would not melt until the spring. Up we went on the Turnpike
Road and at stop after stop, the crossroads, and even in the small hamlet
of Riverton where I would one day live, there were no passengers.

I knew why. Every rumor monger and curiosity seeker in the county
would be saving up to go tomorrow to Lancaster for the trial.

Wealthy and I had little to say to one another for most of the ride. We
concentrated on watching the land go by, and the only sounds were the
heavy breath of the horses and their hoofbeats, and the directives to them
by the driver and his occasional bursts of song that were like the grating
of metal on metal.

She had left Lucius in what I knew was a dark mood because she had
told me he had tried to forbid her to go and the State counsel got involved

and explained by letter that she did not have a choice unless she wished to be considered in contempt of the law and subject to punishment.

Lucius would not be in the court the next day, but I thought and hoped at least one of her sons who worked out at Lancaster farms would come and sit in the room where we would be able to see him when we were sitting in the witness box.

Charles would be there, I knew, because, like Wealthy and me, he would be testifying against David.

"Sister," Wealthy said to me all at once, when we were on the outskirts of the town of Lancaster, and seeing the clusters of houses, "What do you suppose it will be like?"

"I don't know," I said. "I have only been in court the one time when he never came and we waited and waited. But that was just the small court in Guildhall. I guess we will be alright with the lawyers with us."

"What if the other side brings up the pistol?" she said.

"They won't," I said, more confidently than I felt. "It would mean bringing up other things that happened that day and why you had come."

"What if they do?"

"It will be a surprise to one of us first, but if it's you, I can prepare to tell whatever story you tell and if it's me, then you can tell the same story."

"We're under oath," she said timidly.

"We don't have to lie," I said.

"Maybe we should tell the counsel ahead of time," she said, not for the first time.

"I don't think we should. That is not a good thing in the law, to have a woman draw a gun on a man. It won't look good for us."

"But the lawyer will be on our side," she countered.

"I guess he is," I agreed. "But what if it gets all twisted around into a problem for you? Look at what the newspaper said, that David had had a problem with me, as if I am the guilty one. A lot of men think like that. And if the jury knows you ordered him out of my house, which they might see as his house under the law, then who's to know what will happen?"

The press had not been kind. Several reports left me out altogether, reporting David had burned his own house. And one that did include me, referred to the house as his, but said he had gotten into a "fracas with Mrs. B," and compared him as a poor imitation of the David who had slain Goliath, cattily implying he was no match for his wife. How this all rankled with me. It was my house, in spite of his having his name on the deed.

Wealthy sighed.

"We'll be alright together," I said.

"But what if his lawyer gets us rattled?"

"His lawyer is a kind man. I know him. I have been to him before. He takes pity on all of the weak and poor."

"But he's not our lawyer," Wealthy argued.

William Heywood, David's lawyer, was a legend on both sides of the river. He was a large, grandly mustachioed man with a strong voice and wit, and a direct approach to whatever he took on – in this case, the cause to defend a man abandoned to jail by his wife, and charged with arson, alone in the world, who could afford no counsel. On the other hand, our side, if that is what it could be called, was paid for by the State, from the firm of Crawford and Drew. It was all business for them. I was a poor woman and I was not sure they cared so much about me as they did about putting a danger to society in the form of an arsonist and jail escapee behind bars for as long as possible.

Wealthy and I met with them for one last conference that afternoon, our early arrival at my cousin's giving us time to refresh ourselves and drink hot tea and pretend to eat a generous lunch while James coached us.

"You will be fine, you two," he told us, in jovial tones mustered for us. "You have good counsel from the State and you are not alone in this now."

He did not let us be alone. He shepherded us briskly, waving off the editor of the newspaper who would have detained us, and he was a stalwart barrier between us and any of the curious public. He walked quickly from the hotel to the office of the attorneys, and we, with our short legs, fairly trotted to stay within his protection.

Charles was waiting when we arrived. He looked stiff and uncomfortable in his suit.

"Ma, Aunt," he said, kissing our cheeks, and he shook hands with James S., irritated as always by what he saw as the interference of that man in our affairs. We sat in the waiting room, the four of us in a row, silent, grim-faced and looking like we were at a wake for someone we were expected to mourn, but did not. Charles, by then, had his own problems, but at least I did not have the anxiety of knowing that yet. I would soon enough, when he could not meet his living expenses because of his gambling habit and juggled money, his livestock and land like a mad circus actor.

First, we all met together in the inner chamber of the lawyers, and then we met one by one, and then Wealthy and I were called in together. James would, of course, speak on my behalf.

I could not help thinking of those two lawyers as weasels, even though I knew they were on our side. It was the coldness of their manner, that I likened to the coldness of the sleek, well-groomed weasel seeking out the hapless frog edging into the embankment shadows to conceal itself from harm.

"Have you told us everything?" Mr. Crawford said, eying us each sternly in turn. "You know that cases are lost because the client leaves out the one detail that matters and sends everything over the edge."

He had asked us this before, taking turns with his partner.

"Your husband's counsel will press you hard. He won't be the kindly old man you think you know," he warned us.

I looked at Wealthy and she looked at me. Should we tell him or shouldn't we? He was a master at ferreting out truth from small gestures or looks.

"There is something," he said in a low growl. "You are not telling me everything, are you?"

༄

Chapter Eleven

NOVEMBER 14, 1871

T HEY BROUGHT DAVID INTO THE COURTROOM IN CHAINS. I should not have been startled. James had warned me.

"You may be set back to see him," he told me that morning of the trial.

I stared at him questioningly.

He hesitated. "He has been in the jail a long time and he escaped," he said. "It is likely he will be in chains."

I swallowed hard, and willed myself to feel nothing.

Here he was now, his feet dragging the heavy metal that hitched his legs together, and his hands hung in front of him with the chains around his wrists. He hunched with what I imagined was the weight, and his coat was dusty and ragged at the sleeves. I knew he had spent a night in the woods after his escape and had heard he had run and run through puckerbrush and brambles. His hair looked dark and heavy with grease from being unwashed, and he had about him an ill-used look, like a tramp long on the road after days of ungenerous householders.

All at once his head lifted and he found me immediately with his eyes, like a compass to north, and they bore a strangely empty look, as if the very hounds of hell had chased him and even they had found him wanting.

I dropped my head fast, and sat with my chin almost touching my chest. My hands were cold and clammy, and my heart beating fast. I could not help but think that, even as he had been my undoing, I had been his.

I was dressed in what had once been my second-best dress, but more recently I had used for housework. It was not exactly shabby, but worn, with cuffs that had been turned so the fabric was brighter than the rest of the dress and showed how faded it was. I had worn my scuffed boots, polished up to show I cared about how I looked, but polish could not hide the fact they were old and well-worn.

I was dressed to play the part of the industrious, poorly used wife who had nearly been robbed of the house she had struggled to get and keep by a husband who had gone bad.

James was called first, and the lawyer, Crawford – on my side – quickly guided this well-spoken, well-known member of the community through his paces that painted a picture of me matching his affidavit in 1869 that had helped save my house for me.

The opposing lawyer, the Honorable William Heywood, was a decent man, and still he attempted to gently discredit my cousin in such a manner that it might be supposed James was acting improperly in my affairs. But James asserted that his wife had many relatives, and it was the duty of him and his wife to offer the women abandoned, or in hard straits for any reason, the protection of their hotel or home.

It was common knowledge that he took care to see that his wife's family had in hand what they needed during their hard times.

From there, the questioning moved to my son, Charles. He sat upright – a small, bony-looking man with dark hair that swooped across the top of his high forehead.

He recounted the facts of David's destruction of his sugaring equipment, including the burning of all of his eighty-two sap buckets.

The words maliciously and destructively and wantonly were used by him and by the attorney for the State. The picture of David was again drawn as a violent man, incapable of self-control, who directed his anger even into the destruction of another man's property.

It was after this that William Heywood painted his own picture, fixing his benevolent, yet powerful gaze on my son.

He asked a question that stirred the room into a buzz, and that hit me like I had run my forehead up against the heavy metal shovel hanging on the barn door.

"Is it true that the reason for your quarrel with the defendant, Mr. Beede, was precipitated over a gambling loss to him?"

Charles' cheeks suffused with blood, turning his skin blotchy. His dark eyes caught the light from the big windows just so and I could see his anger and dismay.

"Please answer my question, Mr. Presbrey," Heywood said calmly. "Is it true you quarreled with David Beede over a gambling loss to him?"

"Yes," Charles mumbled. But his yes was audible throughout the silence of the court.

I prayed Charles would keep his temper in check. My heart was pounding and I felt a shame and dismay at hearing of this. My son had been gambling with David? How could that have gone on, and I had never known?

Beside me, my lawyer twitched with displeasure.

"Objection," he roared. "This has nothing to do with the case at hand."

"Objection sustained," the judge ruled.

"No further questions," Heywood said, sitting down with satisfaction at having introduced this stain against my son's character.

David, during this sequence of events, kept his eyes on Charles, watching him with the cold dispassion of a cat in the bushes eyeing a bird in the yard.

The passage of people called to testify continued: the jailer who testified to the escape by David and the two other men – a forger and liquor law violator – and to the destruction of county property when the break was made; and the sheriff who testified to the long pursuit of the fugitives, particularly David, and his capture.

There was a break for lunch, and I had to watch him led from the courtroom in his chains. Wealthy and I were quickly guided to a chamber downstairs where there were sandwiches and hot tea.

"What is this about your son's gambling," Crawford snapped at me.

"I didn't know," I snapped back, determined to not let this awful news distract me.

He studied me and clearly believed me because he let the subject drop.

"That won't hurt us," he said. "The facts of the burning of the sap buckets are court record."

During the morning the sun had vanished. When we climbed the long flight of polished oak stairs to the courtroom again, the room was still light because of all of the high windows arranged like those in a church, but it was the colder light of a cloudy November afternoon.

☙

Chapter Twelve

NOVEMBER 14, 1871

AFTERNOON

I T WAS MY TURN SOON ENOUGH. I told the facts, coached along by Drew, who had taken over from Crawford. I knew him less well. I had rarely seen him, and this was just as well, and part, no doubt, of the strategy of the counsel. I had more confidence in him because I had less chance to be irritated with him over the weeks of preparation for the key moment when I was in the witness box.

I laid my hand on the cold leather of the Bible, and gave my oath to tell the truth. Other than the tiny fact of the pistol held in my sister's hand that day in June, I would tell what I was asked.

Like a small, fierce terrier, I took the stand, and willed myself to look humble and keep my anger checked.

"Some tears are expected," Crawford had stressed to me. "But don't over-do it."

The facts stacked up of the years of David's misuse of me and of how I had stood by him in his brushes with the law for his gambling excesses and the drinking that made him violent. Then we were at the days leading up to the fire, and I told of his beating me and threatening my life and of how I would perhaps have died if my sister had not come, and how he had gone, but with the threat he would return to burn my house, and how that was what he had done.

"My daughter was upstairs with me that night," I said. "We both could have died in the fire if I had not been awakened by the sound of breaking glass."

I had a rapt audience. The courtroom was full to overflow – this trial was the entertainment of the fall session – and I was aware of the attention riveted on my words and my every gesture and my demeanor.

I had cried a little, enough to dampen my handkerchief – a big, freshly laundered and pressed square of pure white lawn that showed my simplicity and pride in small things even though I looked poor and shabby. I had cried in telling of his beating me, when I had lain with my back against the doorframe and felt the blood coming from my nose and lip, and listened as my sister stood up against him. These tears felt as if they came from someone else telling a sad story. But the tears I shed when telling of the destruction of my house, and the fear up in that bedroom that Fanny and I would die, were all of my own, and I had to take some deep breaths to calm myself, feeling all of that fear again.

But it was now the turn of the defendant's counsel, Honorable William Heywood, to question me. He wasted no time, but went directly to the soft spots in my story.

"You say your sister faced down the defendant and he left. She is a small woman. Look at her," he gestured so all of the room saw the tiny figure of my sister. "She is hardly bigger than a child of ten. She is smaller than you are. How did she succeed in convincing a man you have said is violent and who is clearly a big man by any standards?"

This was the moment I had dreaded. I had practiced and practiced what I would say and how I would say it, and yet when the time was at hand, he had framed the question in an indirect way that I had never imagined. Wealthy had been right, I knew in that instant, we should have told Crawford and Drew every last detail.

How I sweated. It was a cold day, typical of November, but the courtroom was sweltering with the big wood furnace running hot, and all of the people crowded into what had once seemed like a big space. How small it seemed now, and how the faces of those people blurred and refocused into an enormous, curiously fixed menace in the silence waiting for me to answer the question posed to me.

"She is a very strong woman," I said, calmly, getting hold of myself. "I know she is very small, but she has a strong disposition. I have seen her face down a bull, and you know how temperamental those animals can be."

"You are saying your husband is a bull," the counsel said gravely, and the crowd erupted in laughter, a wave of pitched sound that rushed around the room and up to the ceiling high above, until the judge thundered his gavel and shouted for silence or the room would be cleared.

"No, I am not saying he is a bull," I said when I could be heard again. "I am saying he is big in the way a bull is big and my sister is not afraid of a bull." It sounded weak to me and there was a lie at the heart of it – not the gun, but the fact that the day she had faced down the bull she was eight and I was nine and there was a fence between us and the bull. Still, she had done it, and the bull, unable to stand her gaze, had first backed up and then turned from us. It was an especially ill-tempered bull, which was why my father had bought it cheap. It had gored a man, not fatally, but he had been too ill to work again for many months and was never the same again, it was said.

"There must be something else," he persisted. "I am not convinced such a small woman would be any threat to a man like that," and he gestured to David. I looked at my husband then, his dark brown eyes were on me with a strange glitter like one gets in illness. His shoulders were straight, not hunched as they had been when he had first come back in after the recess, and I had not cast my eyes on him since that time.

He was daring me, I thought, the same way he had always pushed me to go at him. He was like a bull, I thought, with a handsome physique, but a temperament that could go either way, toward extreme malice or charm.

"She had a gun," I said, and had the satisfaction of the air leaving the room like a balloon suddenly popped with a pin. Such was the power of my words.

"She had a gun," I said. "My daughter, Fanny, was scared because he had come back and was in our house and he had threatened to kill me. She ran to my sister, on my order, as she had done on occasions before. But this time my sister came back. My little sister, you can see how small she is, it has been pointed out by this lawyer even, and you can see my husband sitting there in all of his great size. She knew as well as every eye here how big he is and how small she is and how small I am. And she knew that he had threatened to kill me several times before, and that he had beaten me almost to my grave. That is why she took her husband's pistol from the drawer in the kitchen. She ran all of the way to my house, almost a mile, you can ask her and she will tell you, and she was afraid for my life. She had reason to be. When she came into that kitchen, I lay in my own blood, my back bruised and my face bloody, and he was standing over me waiting for me to move enough so he could grab me again. You asked, and that is how a small woman like my sister saved me from death – with her husband's pistol. That is why he left, and that is why I am still here today."

Everything from there became a blur. I fainted. I had got out this part of the story we had never told anyone, and I felt the black space below my feet rise up to me and I lost consciousness.

When I awoke, I was on a cool-feeling comforter, and there was a cool cloth on my head, and the room around me was in shadows with the curtains drawn.

"It's Rebecca," she said, and the woman sitting on the edge of the bed I recognized as James' wife. "You're alright," she said quietly. "You fainted."

When I was sitting up against many pillows in a room in her house, and sipping the tea from the cup she held for me, all of the details of the day returned to me, except how I had gotten to this house.

Rebecca must have seen my confusion.

"It is all continuing," she said. "You were out so cold, even the doctor could not rouse you right there and you were carried into a carriage and brought here by James. He went right back. I gather you caused quite a stir," and she smiled a little at me.

She was used to all of the troubles of her female relatives, it occurred to me, and while only her husband had given me his advice in my troubles of law and property, I realized she had been the comfort and caregiver for many of the women in our family.

I smiled a little back at her, a rare thing for me, and she flushed.

I told her then what had happened, every detail, because she had not been at court, staying home instead with her children. Her eyes were wide like a child hearing a drama. She went out once to bring back more tea, and her small daughter followed her in with sandwiches and cookies, but was not allowed to stay.

When I was done, and the sandwiches were gone and most of the cookies and tea, we sat for a time in silence. I was calm. I had done what I had done and would have to face the consequences.

Into that quiet, we heard a door bang shut and before Rebecca was down the hall to see who it was, James had met her, and then he was in the room with us.

His beefy face was reddened with wind from the walk home, and he fairly shouted, the result of being in with so many people all day in a big space.

"It is all settled," he said in a jovial manner. "All settled. You did just the right thing, springing that on us, though Drew and Crawford had some harsh words for me," he chuckled. "I'm glad I knew nothing about any of it. They cross-examined me after the court ended. That is for sure what it was. But they are very confident now. It will all be settled tomorrow. You made quite a stir, little cousin, and your sister will do us all proud tomorrow."

I stared at me. I would have to go back there again.

"James! You have upset her. Oh, dear!" Rebecca exclaimed. "See how white she is again, and her color was coming back."

"It's alright," I said, my voice sounding shaky in my own ears. "You have to tell me exactly what happened, James."

What had happened was that after I fainted, and could not be revived and was carried out, the judge had ended the trial for the day and everyone had poured out into the late afternoon chill like water from a tipped jug.

We would begin where we had left off, the next day. The reason James had been so long was because he and Wealthy had been run across hot coals for several hours by the enraged team of Crawford and Drew. Wealthy was in the kitchen, having some supper, which she badly needed, and he had come straight to me.

"The attorneys feel confident," he said. "They were very, very angry at you, and your sister, for withholding information, but since you fainted, that gave them time to regroup and act like they knew all along and had planned the coup in court, and you performed better than they could have asked. You were convincing, very convincing. We could all see the whole series of events, just as if we had been there. Very good work, cousin."

That was how it was left and Wealthy rushed in to me then, and fell into my lap crying from all of the pent-up feeling of the day.

§

Chapter Thirteen

November 15, 1871

T HE NEXT DAY I WOKE FROM WHAT SEEMED LIKE A LONG DREAM, WITH
WEALTHY PRESSED INTO MY BACK, CURVED INTO IT IN THE WAY OF A
SLEEPING DOG OR A SMALL CHILD.

"I'm sorry," I had told her the evening before, patting her back as she
cried. "I just didn't know what else to do. You were right we should have
told our lawyers about the gun."

When she could stop crying and had finished with long blows into
a handkerchief, she coughed and told me, "I don't blame you. I would
have done the same. But how hard it was. You were out cold and I was
so scared and unable to go to you. They wouldn't let me. Then you were
literally carried out by the sheriff, and there was such a hullabaloo around
us." She sighed deeply and gave a great gulp that made me think she
would cry again, but she didn't.

"We'll get through," I said.

"How those lawyers scolded," she sighed. "You were lucky you were
out." She looked at me through her swollen, reddened eyes. "And you really were out," she said in amazement. "I thought after the first minutes
you were either dead or playing at it."

"Wealthy!" I exclaimed. "Well, I never." I was quite put out that she
would imagine me playing at that game of possum in a courtroom with
so much at stake. I said as much.

"Hmph!" was her reply. "You would do what you needed to, no question of that."

We were on the edge of a quarrel, but Rebecca entered the bed chamber, and we were silent. She stared at the two of us, and laughed.

"I believe you two have been quarrelling."

"Not yet," Wealthy snapped.

Now it was morning, and Rebecca was back in the room, tugging
open the curtains to reveal only darkness. She held a small lamp, and it

lightened her chin and the sharp edges of her cheeks. She set it on the side table by the bed, and lit the big lamp there with matches from her apron pocket.

"It's time for you to get up," she said.

So the long day began, before light, with washing up and dressing again in the same clothes from the day before. Rebecca had touched them up in the places that needed it, with an iron, and given us fresh handkerchiefs and had one of her boys polish our shoes.

"We're a lot of work for you," I told her. "We're grateful to you."

She was pleased with my comments, I could see.

After breakfast of muffins, oatmeal and sausage, we went off with James S. again, feeling like we had been run over the river falls in a barrel.

Our first stop, just as light was coming across the sky over the town of Lancaster was the chambers of Drew and Crawford.

I didn't realize how tight-lipped I was with tension and determination until James poked my shoulder with a long finger. "You'll manage fine," he said.

That snapped me out of my inward stupor, and unfroze me for what was ahead.

"You," Drew pointed his own finger at me, waving it around in front of me, "played a dangerous game," he said harshly.

I stared at him, my mouth clamped shut. I narrowed my eyes, and he dropped his and turned abruptly from me. I had enough to contend with that day facing whatever I would be asked by the opposing side, without putting up with this man's nonsense. He had had his way yesterday, scolding my sister to tears and he would not do it to me.

After that it was business, with his coaching us and laying out his plan, as best as it could be laid.

We took a carriage the short distance along the main street to the courthouse, and too quickly were back inside, and the minister was saying the prayer to start the session and the trial recommenced. Once again, I had watched as my husband was led in in chains, dressed in the same shabby coat and ragged, dingy white shirt.

First, Wealthy took the stand.

"Do you swear to tell the truth, the whole truth?" the clerk asked her, and her small hand with its long bony fingers sat on the top of the big Bible like a feather on a block of wood.

He seemed to doubt the weight of her hand and her words, the way he emphasized his own speech, and the way he held the Bible as if it weighed one hundred pounds.

Wealthy told the same story I had told the day before, with more details because while I had been half-dead on the kitchen floor, she had been standing, shaking inside maybe, but standing and facing David Beede with her husband's pistol pointed at him.

"Did your husband know you had taken his gun?" the attorney for the defense asked her.

"No, he did not," she said.

"Is your husband in this court today?"

"No."

"Did he disapprove of what you did?" She hesitated.

"Did he? Yes or no?"

"Yes," she said softly.

"Speak up."

"Yes."

"Did you know when you took the gun that he would not approve?"

"Yes," she had to say.

"But you did it anyway?"

"Yes."

"Did you promise to love, honor and obey your husband?" he asked.

She looked white as the lawyers' papers on the table in front of me. I held my breath.

"Yes," she said.

"Would you have shot this man, David Beede?"

"Objection!" roared Crawford. "Irrelevant."

"Sustained," the judge said.

"No further questions," Heywood said.

It was my turn.

"Did you include the fact of the gun in your affidavit?" Heywood asked me.

"No," I said.

"Why not?"

"Because it was not relevant," I said.

"Not relevant," he said. "A gun in a charge of criminal intent against your husband is not relevant?"

"Not in this case," I said.

"Why is that?" he said.

"Because he left and the gun was not used."

"But did or did not your sister threaten him with the gun?"

"She had it in her hand and she told him to leave me alone. If he felt that was a threat that was his interpretation. You said yourself she is a very small woman and he is a very big man. She had the gun with her, but she did not use it."

"What do you mean by, not use it? She threatened him with it."

"But she did not fire it, and he left on his own accord, unharmed, while I was the one on the floor beaten bloody."

I had thought he would continue, but he did not. I could see in his face a kind of hesitation, and his intent to pursue this matter suddenly dissolved in him.

"Nothing further," he said.

I had been spared the questions and commentary about a woman's duty to her husband, to a man who now sat in chains in court accused of burning his wife's house while she was in it.

David never spoke. Maybe it was just me, because he was my husband, that I felt that his silent presence in the room said all there was he could ever say.

The summations of the attorneys to the jury went on for a very long time. Crawford painted a lavish picture of hardworking Lucy E. Beede, who had by this hard work of her own hands attained a farm, and how she had worked making baskets and working like an ox harnessed to a plow to keep her land and pay her taxes, while her husband, David Beede, spent the money from her work and from selling the crops and the animals, on gambling and drink, and how she had stuck by him, paying his court fees and lawyers' fees, and how she had taken him back after she had started a new life in Jefferson and that he had threatened her with death and beaten her many times, and threatened to burn her house and had at last burned it at night when she and her daughter were asleep upstairs and they could have been consumed, and there was no doubt the accused was guilty of arson.

Heywood's turn came and he painted a picture of a basically good man who had served his country in the War of the Rebellion, along with three of his sons, two of whom had been killed, and that he served honorably even after he had been injured in the construction of defenses, and that he had married Lucy E. and made her farm profitable with his hard work and that of his son, and she kept money from him, and denied him the rights he had as a husband, and he had tried and tried to get from her the obedience due him as a husband. He had weaknesses, true, but they had come from the war and his hardships and the court should show leniency on him.

§

Chapter Fourteen

NOVEMBER 1871/NOVEMBER 1895

J AMES S. TOOK US HOME TO JEFFERSON. He was elated at the verdict and
the sentence, and did not try to mask his feelings. Why should he have?
He told us stories and laughed loudly at his own jokes. But my sister and
I, though I think we smiled in all of the right places and even laughed a
little (his high spirits could not be denied that), were thinking our own
thoughts.

For her, there was the reality of facing Lucius at home, in all of his
displeasure at what she had done in defiance of him. The news would
be all over the newspapers, neat rows of black type giving out the great
drama through the words they conveyed for all of the world to read. It
was a sensation, and little Wealthy and me were at the heart of it. He
would learn of how she had taken his gun without his knowledge and
involved his good name (for that is what he would say) in this dirty
business.

For me, there was the relief of it all being over. I knew the notoriety
would be brief, and soon it would be remembered only by the worst of
the gossips how I had defied my husband and how my sister had held a
gun to him, and he had burned my house and beat me, and I had let him
go to prison. In time, the ten years of his sentence at the state prison in
Concord, New Hampshire would pass, and David would be an old man.
I had the farm to run, and I would not be this tired by the morrow.

James left me off first.

"It is best that way," Wealthy said, as she let go of my hand she had
been holding all of the way toward home.

I let myself into my house, and cut and ate a slice of the fresh bread
Fanny had left on the table for me. I ate it laden with the sweet, fresh butter she had churned that day, and was grateful for the heat of the range I
knew she had stoked the last minute before she went to her own house.

I climbed the stairs and undressed and pulled on a nightgown that smelled faintly of wood smoke from drying near the stove, and I climbed into the big bed and nested into the featherbed below me and the quilts above me.

It had started to rain, and that both kept me awake and lulled me, the way it had a habit of doing with the rhythmic, muffled tapping on the shingles of the roof.

I must have dozed because I woke as if from a bad dream and my face was wet with tears or maybe it was sweat from my illness. Fanny was bending over me and she had lightly wrapped me with her warm arms against the front of her dress.

"Oh, Ma, I'm sorry," she said. "I meant to check on you before, but I fell asleep hard because of the rain and I just woke up."

I let her cradle me in the rocker where I was sitting because it was not November of 1871, the night after the trial of my husband, David Beede, but November of 1895. She crooned to me and lifted me in her arms the way I had seen her lift and carry her small daughter many years ago when the little girl was ill or over-tired.

When she had laid me in the soft bed and arranged the pillows behind me so I was sitting up the way I liked to ease the pain of the cancer in my belly, and the counterpane was lightly over me, she sat beside me, holding my hand, trying not to hold it too tightly in her anxiety for me that it hurt me.

"I can send for the doctor, Ma," she said.

"It's not that kind of pain," I said.

At this, she looked puzzled, and I began to tell the story of my life all over again, or least that is what I did in my own mind.

8

Addendum

FOR THOSE OF YOU CURIOUS ABOUT THE TWENTY-FIVE INTERVENING YEARS BETWEEN NOVEMBER 1871 and the time of the story's telling at the end of my days in November 1895, I will frame up a simple version of some of the events of that time.

The most sensational is the fact that I would marry three more times. These other three were all Civil War veterans like David, and wounded or troubled or both, in some or several ways.

First, I took up with a man who was a relation of some distance to Fanny's husband. His name was George Ingerson, and he had been so badly wounded, it was amazing only that he still lived. Really he was a shadow in my house, and in 1874 when I sold the land and the house David had set afire, I gave this man one acre of land for his own devices and comforts, and moved to the northern part of town, Riverton, where I would live the rest of my life. I had kept, of course, the value of the property and was able to buy a better place for farming. The land I bought in Riverton was shaped like a long piece of pie, with the Israel River on one long side and the road between Jefferson and Lancaster on the other. The wedge at the top where the crust edge would be nudged up against the bridge that crossed the river. I was close to the railroad, and with the river land and the transport nearby, and the proximity to Lancaster, felt I had the best of the bargain at last.

That was the same summer my son, Charles, had some trouble of his own. I had learned of his gambling the first day of the trial when the defense attorney sought to discredit him, and it ate at me, but I was determined to stay out of his problems even if he would have my help. But in June, he went across the river into North Stratford where he lost a considerable amount of money. In his panic at the loss of the huge amount of $110, he took the stage the next day to Colebrook, the town just north, and crept into the room at the Monadnock House where his gambling partner slept and he stole back the money he had lost, finding it in the pants pocket of the sleeper and making away with it.

That was on a Sunday morning and by Monday, the sheriff caught up with him and arrested him, and by Tuesday he was brought before a justice for examination, but the details of the case, including his arrest, being muddled, he was let go for a continuation on another occasion. This gave him the opportunity to take the stage to me and I returned with Charles, and with my new husband of the time, a man named Robinson, and gave the $110 into the hands of Charles' wife.

This was by no means the end of Charles' troubles. I was newly married, and my intent was on making the new farm in Riverton a success with the help of my husband. Allen, or E.A. as he was called, had his own troubles, though, as I soon found out. He meant well, that at least can be said, but he was sickly. He had been wounded in the war at the Battle of Cedar Creek, and some months after that, deserted. With the desertion hanging over his head, he acted the part of a fugitive even when the war ended and he, along with many other deserters, was pardoned. He did work on my farm as much as he could, but he was a consumptive, and died of that disease, suffering badly at the end, in the house near the river, in the summer of 1882.

It was on account of my marriage to him that my farm became known as the Robinson Farm, confusing to people who were misled into thinking it had been his and not mine.

In the midst of all this sickness of Allen, I, and even Fanny and her husband, did what we could to straighten out the affairs of Charles. What we did was buy his property in Bloomfield and hold it for him, out of reach of his mortgaging or outright selling it to meet his gambling urges. For some months, Fanny and her husband and children lived on the farm with him and his wife and their many children, with the property under Fanny's name, but that arrangement soon crumbled and she was back in Riverton.

It was also in this time, in 1880, that David Beede was released from prison, his ten years being up. He wrote to me, after all of those years, from where he was living with his elder daughter in southern New Hampshire. My horror and shock at the letter left me shaking and I took to my bed for an afternoon with a headache that threatened to lift off the top of my head and I would willingly have unscrewed that part where the pain lay and tossed it aside.

I did not respond, and within a year, in 1881, he was dead, in the soldier's home on the coast of Maine, and buried in the nearby national cemetery as a soldier. I got the news because he had listed me as his wife. Later, I would apply for his pension, as his widow, and, in the files I read about his account of his paralysis while building the stockade. It had been true, I guessed, what he had told me of his life during the war and how he had suffered.

I waited six months after the death of Allen before I made the last, and it must be said unfortunate, marriage. This time, my choice was a much younger man, fifteen years my junior, thinking he would be strong and live a long life, and he was an owner of property in his own right and could read and write. His name was Patrick Gleason, and he turned out to be the most ornery and mean fellow. He had been shot in the head in battle, and though he had recovered, he was completely deaf, and I guess that and the lingering effects of the head injury left his disposition poor. We did keep the farm going, but by 1887, I was on my own, though Fanny and her husband and children had been living next door to me for almost ten years and so I had their help with my farm.

The map of Jefferson, drawn in 1892, refers to me as Mrs. Presbrey, showing the small square that was my house in the corner of land abutted by the Israel River and the road between Lancaster and Jefferson. This designation was a misnomer, surely, and gave me some cause for merriment. I was an old woman transported back to my long-distant girlhood when Mrs. Presbrey was my mother and I was Miss, and even after that, when I had cause to wed my cousin, Hiram, and become Mrs. Presbrey myself. That was how the mapmaker recalled me, as did some of my neighbors, and so it was I reverted back to Mrs. Lucy Presbrey.

I say this because the map has given me a place in history – one tiny black square on a map of Jefferson with my name next to it. In 1892, I was 66 years old, and felt my age, and looked it, and sold my farm to my daughter for $500 at the end of December with the understanding she would care for me and not sell the place without my say so.

That house my daughter sold in June 1893, with my permission as specified by the deed to it, and I moved with her and her husband and children to another place a few miles down the road, further toward the village of Jefferson, but still within view of my mountains.

She and her husband bought a small farm, with a barn and some hillside fields north of where my farm was. True to her promise, spelled out word by word in a legal document at the town clerk's office, she gave me this north room, and access to the horse and carriage when I wanted to go to town or make visits, and I had all of the milk and cheese and butter I wanted from the cow.

That spelled the end of my property dealings, after thirty years of farming and making a living at it the best I could.

It was in that north room that my days were ending. I had held for myself the promise of the mountains as my comfort, and I was not disappointed. On a clear day, I could see the White Mountains, the highest peaks covered with the first snows of the winter. I was a survivor, and my life in that imperfect sense was still on the road to Victory.

g̃

ACKNOWLEDGEMENTS

T<small>HIS NOVEL IS BASED ON A TRUE STORY</small> I <small>UNCOVERED WHILE DOING FAMILY RESEARCH.</small> The drama at the heart of the book is true: Lucy E. (my great great grandmother Wealthy's sister) had five husbands, the second of whom was a Civil War veteran who was arrested for arson and convicted of burning his wife's house in 1871. To get to the facts, I spent hours pouring over documents from the 1860s and 1870s.

The first clue I had to David Beede's crime was in the book of Dalton, New Hampshire genealogy. It explained he served ten years for arson in the Concord, New Hampshire prison, as reported in the book, *Hard Time in Concord, New Hampshire,* a compilation by Milli Kenney-Knudsen of New Hampshire crimes. She reported news items from the *Northern Sentinel,* of Colebrook, that recounted Beede's escape from jail in Lancaster before his trial. Sadly, the court records of the trial were destroyed in a fire at the Lancaster courthouse in 1886. Many New Hampshire newspapers from 1871, however, reported on the man who had burned his wife's house.

The other clue to Beede's criminal tendencies I found in a land record in Lunenburg, Vermont that spelled out the mortgaging of the farm for bond for him, and noting that he would be in court in Guildhall in September 1868. The court records included affidavits from Lucy and from her cousin's husband, James Smith, from 1869, in which the sad story of Beede's abuse of his wife and his failure to appear in court were reported in detail. The records also included the description of his destruction of the sugaring equipment of Lucy's son, Charles.

I had great fun reading the old newspapers, including the *Lancaster Gazette, Northern Sentinel, The Caledonian,* and many newspapers from Concord and Manchester, New Hampshire. *The Gazette* first gave me the huge piece of information that David Beede had burned his wife's house.

I was also fortunate to track down the Civil War pension files for David Beede, Charles Presbrey, and Horace Gage. They gave me wonderful details about injuries, places of war service, and even information such as height and eye color, and the marriage date of Lucy and David.

Around this framework of facts, I let my imagination fly to create the world of these gritty country people.

This book would not have been possible without the support and help of a myriad of people, from friends and relations to kindly strangers, over the course of my five or six years of research.

I send out a big thank you to the town clerks in the Vermont towns of Bloomfield, Guildhall, Hartford, Lunenburg, Mount Holly, Shrewsbury, Washington and Woodstock; and in the New Hampshire towns of Jefferson, Lancaster, Lisbon, and Lyman.

I am very grateful for the wonderful reference librarians, Kathy Beaird and Jan Weiner, at Norman Williams Public Library in Woodstock, Vermont who catered to my ongoing requests for interlibrary loans of books and of microfilms of old newspapers and agricultural censuses. Thank you to the reference librarians and staff at Baker-Berry Library at Dartmouth College in Hanover, New Hampshire who also aided me with good cheer in perusing New Hampshire newspapers and agricultural censuses. Thank you to the librarian at the Vermont Law School library in South Royalton.

Barbara Robarts at the Weeks Memorial Library in Lancaster, New Hampshire was an ongoing and valuable resource. I also appreciated the help of the librarian at the Littleton Public Library in Littleton, New Hampshire.

A big round of applause is due Angelina Desilets and Juanita Merrill of the Vermont Superior Court, Essex County Criminal Court, in Guildhall, Vermont, for finding the 1868-69 court documents for the David Beede case.

Thank you to Mr. Marshall of the Jefferson Historical Society, and to Carol Wenmark of the Lunenburg Historical Society.

I am also thankful to the staff at the Vermont State Archives & Records Division in Middlesex, Vermont; the Coos County Registry of Deeds in Lancaster, New Hampshire; and the Grafton County Registry of Deeds in North Haverhill.

Thanks abound for the spontaneous generosity of Al McVetty of Guildhall who took my husband and me on an unforgettable ATV ride on the ancient roads that led to the area where my great great grandparents, Harmon and Betsey Gage, and Wealthy and Lucius Larrabee, lived on hill farms.

Thanks, also, to Penny Murray, a "distant" cousin, for sharing many of her research findings.

Thank you to Susan Orzell-Rantanen for her painstaking and loving editorial eye as she proofed every word, and pondered the meanings and nuances. I am particularly grateful for her knowledge of horses, Vermont farm life and animals, and her roots in the rural life and legacy of women like Lucy E.

This book took its shape in print thanks to the keen eye and the design skills of Jenny Buono, who is an artist and a fountain of knowledge and who came along at just the right time to bring this book into the world.

Of enduring importance to this book and to the quality of my life are my husband, Tim Sink, and my cousin, Diane Hutchinson. Diane started me on the family research quest that led to Lucy E. and David Beede. Tim is a storehouse of support for me and my writing and my search to understand my roots. He has even been known to do a moon dance of delight at finds he has made!

Lastly, but certainly huge in importance, is the memory of my mother, Aubigne "Doodie" Horner, who always nurtured my "authorial" inclinations and who, as the family archivist, preserved dozens of old photos, including the ones of Lucy E.

☙

CASSIE HORNER has written for a number of publications in Central Vermont and is co-publisher of *Rutland Magazine* with her husband, Tim Sink. She holds a Bachelor of Arts Degree from Vermont College. Cassie is a lifelong Vermonter. *Lucy E. — Road to Victory* is based on years of research. This is her first published novel.